ONLY A
BAD BOY
CAN *Love* HER

A NOVEL BY

PORSCHA STERLING

This PORSCHA STERLING, INC. book is being published by

Royalty Publishing House, LLC.

P.O. Box 924043

Norcross, GA 30010

ISBN: 978-1-63718-179-9

ISBN: (eBook) 978-1-63718-172-0

Cover Designer: Marion Designs

Format: Nina Simmons Designs, Inc.

Don't miss out on your chance to discuss the book LIVE with Porscha Sterling and the REAL Outlaw! Join Porscha's mailing list for announcements so you don't miss it!

AN EXCLUSIVE INTERVIEW

PORSCHA & OUTLAW

ARE GOING LIVE!

IN PORSCHA STERLING'S VIP READERS GROUP

ACKNOWLEDGMENTS

I can't imagine being a creator of book worlds without paying respect to the **Creator of all things**. No one and nothing would exist without the initial statement of "I am", followed by the question of "What else can I be?". The divine beginning of all of our stories. Imagination, creativity and expression is everything. I'm infinitely thankful to have been blessed with even a little, tiny drop. 🙏

Leo, Al and King-King. It's love *always.* 🤍 For your tremendous sacrifices in dealing with the real life issues that come with doing life with a writer—someone who prefers solitude but doesn't want to be alone, wants to be invited everywhere but doesn't want to go, wants to be loved but doesn't want to be bothered, wants to make plans but wants to stay home. Someone who spends 75% of each day having internal conversations with characters and the other 75% of each day with her head so far in the clouds that she doesn't even realize that those two numbers don't even equal out to 100—just thank you for allowing me to be free. Free to be. Free to exist. Free to be me.

Huge thanks to **Tara** for putting up with me ignoring emails, dodging meetings and forgetting things that "I thought, I said, you said, we said—wait, who said that and when? Was it me who promised that? When did I say I'd do it? Okay, I'll get it to you yesterday." Yes—thanks for putting up with me asking/saying things like that, which make absolutely no sense, because I've been writing and my brain doesn't work anymore. I'm pretty sure that, as I'm writing this, there is something I've forgotten to do that I told you I'd do. *Sighs*

Nina—for also staying up late with me, pulling 12 hour shifts and helping me with my young kings when I needed to meet my deadlines. For offering to do my grocery shopping when all I had in my fridge was an egg and string cheese. For offering to cook when I'd been writing for 12 hours straight and could no longer make my arms work. For all the days when one of the boys would say "Mom, what's for dinner?" and I'd have a stricken dumb, deer-in-headlights look on my face because I was in writer's zombie mode and had no idea it wasn't morning anymore. Or when I would squint really hard at them and say "Wait..how long have you been home?" Thank you for always stepping in.

To Gram, my Momty and my mom—thank you for stepping in to help with the boys. Especially during quarantine when all writers thought they were going to die sweet, slow deaths. Not because we were stuck in the house (of course not, we love to be home). But because we actually had to be stuck there with other people. I am definitely a person who needs to be free, uninhibited and in perfect solitude in order to write. Thank you both for helping me out so that I was able to balance mothering with the things I desperately needed in order to be me.

Special thanks goes to **@tharealoutlaw** for going above and beyond with promotion and inspiration for this novel that I'd decided I wasn't going to write many, many times but started back because you wouldn't let me give up on it. For being the most positive person I know who never seems to have a bad day and is always in the best mood, you are the sunshine among all of us blessed to call you a 'friend'. And, of course, infinite thanks for gracing the cover of yet **another** Bad Boys novel. Can't have a bad boys book without Outlaw.

To Michelle, I'm thinking of you and sending love always. My thoughts, prayers and love is always with you.

To the readers who support my passion. I love you all very much. Thank you for being around for another ride. I'm not sure how many more are coming, but I'll keep writing until it feels like I'm done. I hope you'll continue enjoying the stories.

I have the best family, friends, readers and supporters. Y'all are awesome 😚

SPECIAL NOTE ABOUT THIS BOOK

I had no idea what I was signing up for when I started this book. Honestly.

I actually was writing something else in an entirely different genre. I'd decided that Bad Boys Love Good Girls 2 was the final Bad Boys book for all eternity and that Addicted to You was going to be my last 'urban' romance novel. I was playing around with the idea of starting off totally new, under a different pen name and not putting out anything else under 'Porscha Sterling' at all.

To be perfectly clear, I'd determined that this phase of my life had ended and I wanted to move on to something else. Wasn't sure what I wanted to move to. I just felt that I was done.

With embarking on something new as my focus, I started writing a novel that was coming more from my head than my heart. I couldn't feel the story at all. And because I couldn't feel it, none of the people who read the first few pages of it could feel it either. I specifically remember sending the first chapter over to my husband to give me some feedback and I can't even describe the horror in his face when Leo lifted his head, looked me squarely in my eyes and said verrrrryyyy slowly, trying his hardest not to offend me in any way, "Babe, I think you might want to take a break. Unwind. And I mean this in the most loving way. Just put the pen down. Maybe find a hobby. Just relax for a while until you get it back."

I think it was at that point that it became clear that I was doing something wrong. I already knew what I had been writing wasn't good in ANY way. Of course, I still tried to defend it—after all, I am an artist. And I'm sensitive about my shi—.

But I knew it was trash.

One day, I woke up at 4am and I just started writing. Like all of the Bad Boys books, a random scene came to me in a dream and I didn't think too much about it, I just started to write. That scene was the prologue. It wasn't until I had written the last word that I realized I'd started a story about January and Legend falling in love.

The prologue was the ONLY part of this book that came easy. Everything else came through extreme emotional turmoil, extreme highs followed by extreme lows, pain and heartache. Every bit of this book was written with me learning real life lessons and sewing them into the story one word at a time. Every book I've written has felt like a personal diary. This one much more than any of the others. It's almost hard to refer to it as fiction because so much of it is so real.

This book is really about acceptance, compassion, growth, empathy and unconditional love—for yourself as well as for others. It's about not settling, never giving up, speaking your truth, and understanding that we are alike more than we are different because underneath all of the junk, once you get to the heart of the matter, all life paths began exactly the same. Life really is all about figuring out who you were before someone told you who you should be and then loving that person, flaws and all.

And so, I present to you **drumroll** the longest book I've ever written. Ha! I guess that's only proper since this one took me the longest amount of time to write. I hope that you all enjoy it. It's much more than a simple tale of young love and romance.

I hope you love it.

SYNOPSIS

Balance.

Balance was my everything.

Growing up as a classically trained ballerina with dreams of being a professional dancer, balance was my life. Everything about me depended on it; my diet, my temper, my sleep and waking schedule. I even dedicated myself to rigorous yoga practice and martial arts training to learn how to maintain focus by balancing my breath. Balance was literally my *everything*.

Living like this came with several rules and I was the kind of person who didn't mind following them. Rules were made to protect me; they kept me safe. And I never had issues following them but, to be totally honest, I never once had a reason not to.

At least, not until I met *him*.

My name is January Luckeisha Murray, daughter of the honorable Janelle Murray and Luke 'Outlaw' Murray, the infamous leader of the *Black Bag Mafia*, an underground crime society. Most know me as the apple of his eye, a cherished mafia princess who always followed her father's rules about staying out of the public's eye. But now daddy's little girl is all grown up and I'm ready to share my story.

This is a story about the time when I decided to break all the rules... The time I fell in love.

When Stars Collide

"*Whatever our souls are made of, his and mine are the same.*"

EMILY BRONTE,
WUTHERING HEIGHTS

Download & listen to the playlist as you read.
Listen now on Spotify!

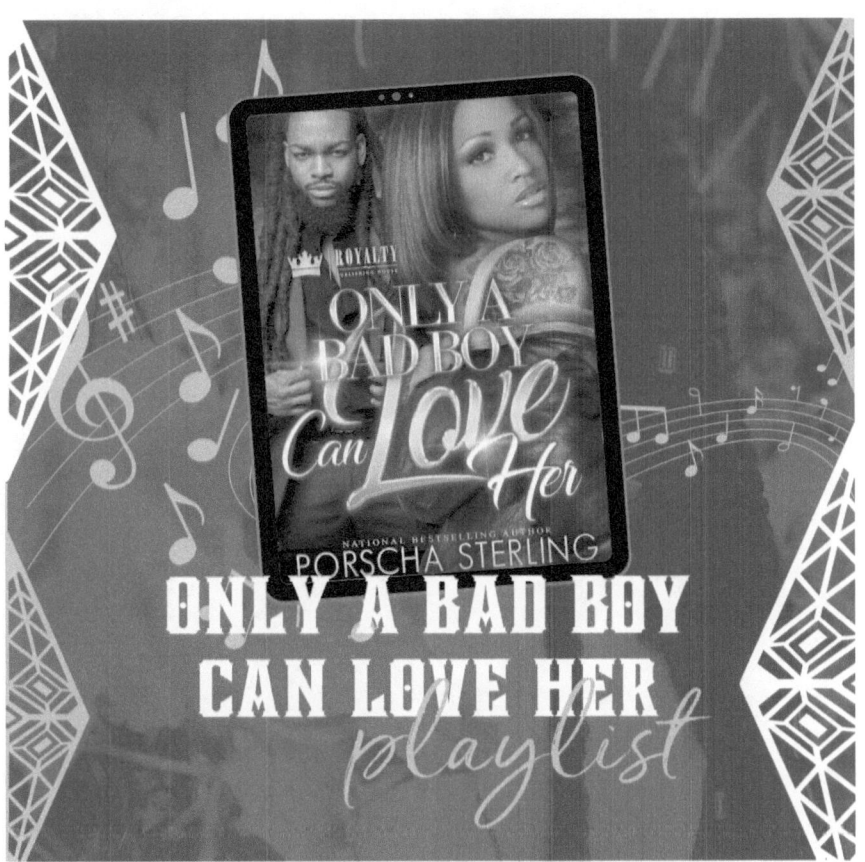

PROLOGUE

JANUARY PRESSED HER NOSE AGAINST THE TINTED WINDOWS OF HER
father's custom-made Black SUV, marveling at the scene outside.
Envy bubbled in her belly as she stared longingly at the children all
around. Girls and boys her age were enjoying the prize that the
summer in New York City gave them every July. The weather was
beautiful; there wasn't a cloud in the sky. The gentle breeze in the
air called out to kids her age—teenagers who were tired of being
tucked away in the house during a brutal winter and nearly half of
what the rest of the world referred to as spring.

Now short shorts and tank tops adorned the curves of the girls and
t-shirts and basketball shorts covered the boys as they celebrated the
start of summer with a block party thrown by her father. Known as
New York's Outlaw, January's father was hood royalty and, along
with her uncles, they commanded an underground criminal society
known in the streets as the Black Bag Mafia, rumored to be a crime
ring that had an international reach. Though its existence made her
the hood's princess, putting her parents on the level of celebrities,
and giving her the life of a celebrity child. It simultaneously made
her one of its earliest victims. She always had to be protected;
forever separated from living a normal life.

Dance was her only outlet. When it came to ballet, she met every expectation with expertise. She was something of a child protégé in the way she moved, completing formations difficult for dancers who had been training for double the time. Her life revolved around dance because there was little else outside of it. On a stage or inside of her custom-made dance studio that her father had built for her, was the only place where she could be totally free.

Eyes wide, January watched two kids talking. They looked to be about fifteen or sixteen, around her age. The girl was smiling so hard that her high cheeks nearly pushed her eyes closed as a boy whispered into her ear that made the curl of her lips wider and wider. He was 'spitting game' as January's father would say. 'Talking shit so he can hit it and quit,' is how he defined it to be exact. Somehow, though he had preached to her many lessons on how to see through a 'young niggas lies' all she could think about was the day when a boy worthy of her time would be spitting game to her.

"Mama... can't I go outside?"

Janelle bit the inside of her cheek as soon as she heard the question her daughter asked. She knew it was coming. Could see the longing in January's eyes, read the expression on her face the same way she'd been able to over the sixteen years of her life. Guilt twisted her gut. She would have to say no—though she wished she didn't. The streets weren't safe. Not anymore.

It was safe when everything was normal; but nothing was normal anymore. Once an assistant DA, trying to make her name in the world, Janelle was now a Federal judge. And her husband who was once the first name on New York's list of most wanted, was now one of the most influential men in the world. Luke Murray, formerly known as the Outlaw, was now something like the Black Godfather. His name was whispered in the streets, for a different reason than before, but still a reason, nonetheless. Things were too risky; the power they gained also left them vulnerable. Outlaw's ambition had made them a trophy, in life, to their friends and a trophy to their enemies, in death. In order to keep January safe, she had to be untouchable. To be untouchable, she had to be locked away. There was no other way. She *had* to be separated.

It was an agreement that Janelle made with her husband the day they agreed he would establish the BBM, an international ring of powerful Black families who controlled their territories and influenced local and national law. They knew there were risks but they'd determined that the good outweighed the bad. However, in times like this, Janelle hated that the bad affected their daughter.

"January, you know you can't be out in public at events like this. It's not safe——"

In a flash of adolescent rage fueled by the threat of rebellion, January whipped around towards her, tears pooling in her eyes.

"How not?" She shot back. "Daddy has security all over this place. If they are good enough for him and the other kids here, how isn't it good enough for me?"

Janelle swallowed back her emotions and straightened her back. This was a battle that she'd been fighting with January for most of her life, but she knew at some point, they would have to go to war. Every year that passed, January grew older and Janelle came closer to the inevitable defeat.

"January, we have already discussed this. Things are different for you. You can't do things that the other kids can do because you aren't like them. There are bad people in the world who know the best way to get to your father is by getting to you. We protect you for a reason."

"And for how long?" January pushed, summoning fears that only a child could pull out of her parent. "How long do you think you can keep me trapped here?"

A stab to Janelle's heart nearly took her breath away. She understood the real intention behind January's words. Time was winding down on the amount of control they had over her. In only a few years, January would be eighteen and no matter how much she'd convinced herself that her daughter would choose a university close to home, Janelle knew all of her prayers were of no use. January was her child and, like her mother, she had a determined and free spirit. Once it was up to her, she wouldn't be restricted for anyone. And with that thought rooted firmly in her mind, Janelle decided to wave the white flag.

"Okay," she began, letting out a deep sigh. "You can go out for a little while but stay close by where I can see you. Don't wander off and—"

"Thank you, mama!" January shouted, tossing her arms around her mother's neck. Grinning through the kiss that she planted on her cheek, she gave her one last squeeze before turning away. Though Janelle called out for their driver to open the door, there was no use because January was already stepping outside.

The sun overhead beamed down without resistance on the top of her head as she surveyed the world around her as if seeing it for the first time. It wasn't that she had never been outside before or that she hadn't played with other kids—mostly her cousins—but she'd never been able to do *this*. Her uncles and father were always talking about their glory days in the hood, but she'd never been able to experience it first-hand. The 'hood' was like a mystical land to her, a fairytale where instead of waving wands or changing fates by a simple kiss, the heroes carried guns. Danger loomed, but with her upbringing, it always did. The presence of it didn't stop her from wanting to experience the other side of how people who looked like her lived. Now she finally had her chance.

But what was she supposed to do with it?

Just as quickly as the high of it all had arrived, it was gone. She stepped away from the car taking cautious steps, working against her nature because her every thought was trying to get her to change her mind. What she'd forgotten was that she didn't *know* anyone. And she wasn't the type to easily make friends. Her mother said it was because she was always too stuck in her own head, too busy talking to herself instead of the people around her. Maybe it was true, but it did nothing to change her presence circumstance. Everyone around was caught up in their own lives, reconnecting with kids they knew from school or familiar faces they'd seen before. She wasn't one of them. She was still alone.

Sucking in a breath, January felt her shoulders begin to drop under the weight of sheer disappointment at the anticlimax of something she'd wished on for so long. An empty feeling in her gut further confirmed the feelings that she didn't belong, but her mind wouldn't let her turn away. Dragging the soles of her designer sneakers across the cement, she walked down the sidewalk, heading for the swings. Thankfully, they were empty and would provide as the perfect distraction from feeling out of place. She sat down and slowly reeled her legs back, swinging just enough to feel the wind in her long, curly hair. Her soft waves were the one thing that she'd gotten from her father, as her dark cinnamon complexion, pebbled nose and round, expressive eyes were gifts from her mother.

"What kind of chick wears $800 sneakers to play in the park?"

The sudden question brought on a myriad of unexplainable emotions. The most obvious one being alarm but the longest lasting one being a subtle familiarity that struck her as odd. Though she knew better, she felt like she had heard this voice before.

Without saying a word, she drug her shoes deep in the dirt below her to slow her movement and then turned towards the voice. Her eyes landed on a figure behind her that both captivated her attention and fully commanded it at the same time.

Wow.

He wasn't someone she knew but she instantly felt like she wanted to. Maybe it was lust at first sight. He was a boy, who seemed to be around her age, but everything about his aura was that of a grown man. He was tall, had to be almost six feet or maybe more, with an athletic and expertly toned physique, much more muscular than she'd seen of any boy in her class. His hair was cut low, fading away into a light goatee expertly trimmed to precision. Though his words felt playful, the contemplative, brooding stare in his eyes made her feel as if he were studying her, just as interested in her as she was in him.

A few seconds more than she'd wanted passed of her staring at him in awe before the edges of his lips curved into a knowing smirk.

"You like what you see?" He joked, finally breaking her spell. "If you want, I could come closer to give you a better view."

Remembering herself, she rolled her eyes.

"Don't flatter yourself," she snapped, blowing a burst of air through her nostrils. Although she was able to briefly look away, not wanting to further swell his growing ego, she couldn't resist turning back to get a second glance. Her annoyance only deepened when she saw him standing with gloating eyes on her and his arms crossed at the chest.

"Don't flatter yourself?" He parroted, mocking her words. "Seems like something a princess with $800 'play shoes' would say."

"I'm not a princess," January snapped, hating the way he made it sound. Her father called her a princess all the time but the way *he* said it was different from when her daddy did.

"And these aren't *play* shoes," she added. "They are specially made for dance. They are made to help me maintain balance when I'm not training."

"You're a dancer," he surmised. "What kind of dance?"

She didn't want to answer him. In fact, she wanted to ignore him and pray that he'd go away. She wanted him to leave her alone to deal with whatever this new thing was that she was feeling. Something about him made her feel off-center.

Instead of following the urgings of her mind, she found herself muttering out an answer to his question.

"Ballet."

He lifted one brow. "Ballet? Damn, that's what's up."

He took a seat in the swing next to her and she sucked in a breath, feeling her heartbeat react to their close proximity. The smell of his cologne caressed her nostrils, like an elixir specifically spellbound to entrap her.

Why do I feel like this? She couldn't help but wonder.

This wasn't the first boy she'd met, definitely not the first one she'd spoken to. Not even the first that she'd been alone with—if being surrounded by security and many other people who were paying them little attention could classify as being alone. Even with January's carefully protected and controlled life, she'd been around other kids her age from rich families who lived her same life of privilege, but none of them were like *him*. Their obvious differences frustrated her, making her feel out of place or naive in a way, but also left her intrigued. Although his sense of style showed that he was used to the finer things, his demeanor revealed that he had worked hard for every possession he had. Nothing had been given to him, that was for sure. Like her father, he held a dominance in his gaze that spoke of his unwillingness to accept anything he hadn't fought for.

"Who are you anyways? And why are you bothering me?"

Biting back a smile, Legend cut his eyes at the girl sitting next to him, catching her icy-cold glare. Her anger only incited him further because he could see through it to what lay beneath. She was trying to ignore it, but she couldn't. Neither could he.

Their energy was electric. Their chemistry was unavoidable.

He'd felt it the second that she stepped out onto the sidewalk. In fact, he had been talking to another broad, some chick who had been trying to get his attention for a while, when he saw her. He'd finally been convinced to give her some play but all that changed the second he looked across the street and saw the beauty who was now beside him. It wasn't just the fact that he had never seen her before. It wasn't even the fact that she was the most gorgeous girl he'd ever seen in his young but experienced life. She drew her to him, and he couldn't deny it.

His father used to always talk to him about vibes when he was younger. How a feeling from a vibe someone gave off told you everything about a person and whether they were good or bad for you.

Maybe that nigga was on to something, Legend thought, introspectively massaging the hairs on his chin.

"So, is that your way of sayin' that you wanna know my name?" he teased, turning to her. He was having trouble controlling his eyes. He wanted to stare at her, but his mind was telling him that he needed to play it cool. After a while of fighting it, he decided there was no use and stopped resisting the urge to pretend she didn't have him fascinated.

She shrugged with indifference at his question. "I guess so."

"All you had to do was ask." He laughed at little at the frown that crossed her face. "It's Legend."

January wrinkled her nose and peered at him. "Excuse me?"

"Legend. That's my name."

"What kind of name is Legend?"

"What kind of name is January?" He countered.

"My *real* name."

She was a bit of a smart ass. Legend chuckled at that. "And so is mine."

She pursed her lips, eyeing him up and down in a haughty way that she didn't know made her even more appealing to him. "It sounds like your street name," she summed up her explanation with judging scrutiny that made him smile.

Not many had the power to do what she could easily do without trying. She had him showing more of his teeth in five minutes than most had been able to get him do in his entire life. She was pulling out a softer side that he didn't know he even possessed.

"For my pops, it was just a street name," he explained with a shrug. "Let him tell it, he was a thug, so I guess it fit for him."

"And does it fit for you?" January asked, more from out of her desire to keep the conversation going than anything else.

With another shrug of his shoulders, he said, "I guess."

"So, then that means..." She began her question with apprehension, first piecing together the words in her mind. "...that you're a thug too?"

The sudden laugh that burst from his chest first made her feel uneasy but the sound of it was too contagious to fight back her nervous smile.

"If you're asking if I'm a dangerous man, the answer is yes. I'm the boogeyman."

January's eyes shot to him and he held them within his mischievous stare, leaving her to wander whether or not he was serious. In that moment, she knew that it didn't matter either way. She was captivated by him and, she knew that if the opportunity presented itself where he would be the one 'spitting game' in her ear in order to find his ways between her thighs, he wouldn't have to try too hard. Her daddy had warned her for most of her life about men like this... bad boys who always found a way to garner the affections of a good girl.

There was something about that saying of how opposites attract that rung incredibly true, especially when it came to situations like these. The appeal of something outside of the norm added to the spice of life and January wanted some of that. She was tired of the norm, the safe and the mundane. She wanted excitement, thrill and spontaneity. Who wanted Carlton when you could have the Fresh

Prince? Urkel when you could have Stephon? How could you appreciate being good when you'd never been bad before?

"You want to get some ice cream?" He asked, regretting the question as soon as it left his lips.

Ice cream? What kind of childish shit was that? Not once in the history of his life had Legend ever asked a girl on a date to get some ice cream. To be real, he'd barely ever asked a girl on a date. He didn't have time for that kind of shit. His days, hours, minutes and seconds were taken up by other things and, because of that, earning the true affection of a woman had to be pushed to the side. He had time to fuck but little space for much else aside from what his duty to Outlaw demanded.

Growing up In Miami where his father reigned supreme, he'd had to keep his fascination with the things Outlaw was doing in New York a secret. Not only did the two cities have natural tension based off the old north vs. south unspoken but widely accepted beef, his father and Outlaw actually had history that had kept them at odds for a while.

Before Legend Jr. was even a thought, both Outlaw and Legend Sr. had their intentions set on expanding their empire into Atlanta. They battled relentlessly to take over the city but, in the end, it was Outlaw who claimed the victory after pulling in help from powerful families in other locals who eventually joined with him to create the *Black Bag Mafia*. Even with all of Outlaw's resources, he'd lost a lot in the fight and realized that there was no way that Legend Sr would ever back down or join the *Black Bag Mafia* without there being a lot of bloodshed in the process. So they decided on a truce. The fighting had ended decades before but the bad blood between the two was still in the background of every one of their semi-peaceful conversations.

There was little doubt that they would ever get along.

And for that simple reason, the last girl in the world that Legend should ever think of speaking to, smiling at or even making the focus of his curious stare, was January Murray. She was Outlaw's most prized possession and, though this was his first time laying eyes on her, he known long before that it was forbidden. It was forbidden for anyone but especially for him.

"I would love to get ice cream, but I can't," January said suddenly, snapping him out of his thoughts about how out of bounds he was at the moment. Then again, as he looked around, he noticed that she didn't have a guard tending to her, which wasn't the norm from what he'd heard about Outlaw's safety protocols for his family. Maybe that could be his excuse. He was there with her to keep her safe.

"Why not?"

He kept the conversation going but watched their surroundings carefully, trying to pick up on whether they were being watched. So far it, looked like no one was paying them much attention.

"Because I have to watch everything I eat. I take dance very seriously. It's the only thing I know that I want to do with my life. I'm going to be a professional dancer one day with my own studio. I keep a strict diet—no dairy, no meat, low carbs, lots of fruit and veggies. You know." She shrugged as if whatever she could have said after was obvious. Like a ballerina's diet was common knowledge to niggas like him.

"You mean like no burgers, no chicken wings or shit like that? What *do* you eat? Celery and grass?"

She sputtered out a laugh at the ridiculousness of his question. "There is a lot you in the world that you can eat outside of carbs, meat and cheese, Legend."

His chest tightened. He loved the way his name rolled off her pretty lips.

"All I know is steak and potatoes. That rabbit food shit ain't for niggas like me."

"It's a sacrifice that I make in order to achieve my dreams," she replied in a quiet voice. "I bet you sacrifice a lot in order to be a dangerous man."

Ignoring the sudden reminder that it was impolite to stare, January forced herself to not look away, probing into Legend's eyes as he did the same to hers, each of them studying each other in a way that words didn't allow to describe. In a way that can only be understood by the rumbling desires of one's soul. She didn't know if she would ever see him again... ever talk to him once more after this day was gone. But somehow meeting him felt like an omen—a sign that life as she knew it would, from this point on, forever be changed. She wanted to know more about him, had to ask more questions. She wanted to keep him there, cement them both in that moment, in hopes that it wouldn't escape too fast.

But then it did.

In a flash so sudden that January barely had a chance to react, Legend's eyes narrowed into a glare, focusing on an object in the distance behind her. The vulnerability and sincerity in his expression was seemingly snatched away, giving way to a menacing coldness that chilled her to the core.

It was then that she also noticed the shift in the atmosphere around her. Though the engagement of the youth remained the same, the soldiers standing around were now at attention, all of their eyes focused in on the same object as Legend, something behind her. Before she could get a chance to have a look for herself, a thunderous noise cracked the sky; one that January knew all too well.

Pow! Pow! Pow!

Snatching her body into his, Legend pulled January into his chest and then dove to the ground, scouring the scene as she trembled beneath him. His right hand reached for his pistol and his senses sharpened as he prepared for war.

He'd heard from a source that there was a possible threat to Outlaw's annual *Summer Madness* summertime fling but because of who the source was, he hadn't been able to give any warning of it. Legend was in a complicated situation being that he was the first of his family to be welcomed into the BBM organization. His father and Outlaw had been longtime rivals for all of his life, only to make amends because it made sense politically. However, the hatred between the Dumas and the Murrays still ran deep. The only one exempt from their disgust for each other was Legend Jr. who had earned Outlaw's trust through years of working with him over the summer.

"Stay down and don't move," he ordered January before roughly pressing her back further down into the grass to illustrate his point. She did just as he asked and didn't move a muscle as he stood, running away with his pistol outstretched in his hands.

January's blood was cold in her body as she listened to the shots sounding off around her. She took the chance of moving to lift her arms, pressing her palms against her ears to mute the noise. Her chest was constricted, making it hard to take in air. Panic gripped her entire body, expelling the little oxygen that was still in her lungs. She wanted to cry, wanted to run, but instead she remained frozen in place, crumbling under her fear.

The sound of bullets oscillating overhead, mixing with the panic-filled screams of mothers and daughters running fro cover, brought on fear that threatened to unravel the fabric of January's mind. Her sanity was up for grabs.

Violence was always a threat to her reality. It was the constant, invisible and ignored elephant in the room, a side-effect of their life of luxury. Never had January had to confront it like this. Murder, betrayal and the threat of sudden death surrounded them daily like an invisible membrane enclosing their world. Her parents tried to protect her from it but nothing was promised.

Especially not life.

The gunfire continued to erupt all around her, thundering in her ears like a steel-toe drum so powerful that the vibrations of it echoed in her bones. She didn't move a muscle, hoping that it her obedience would be what saved her life.

But then she heard a voice that made all the difference

"January! God, please, not my daughter! January!"

Her mother's panic-filled screams sent a jolt through her spine that awakened every muscle in her body. She looked up and saw Janelle trying to run towards her, fighting against the two men, hefty body-guards with little regard for anything other than their charge to keep her safe. January could see it in her mother's eyes. She was afraid, devastated and panicked by the thought that something could happen to her daughter and she would continue to put herself at risk, wouldn't stop fighting, until she had her within her arms.

But then, from the peripheral of January's eyes, she saw the barrel of a lift and it was pointed right at Janelle. Time slowed to almost a stop as the will to preserve her own life faded away, leaving January only with concern for the safety of her mother. Jumping to her feet, she ran at top speed, shouting and screaming for Janelle to get back into the SUV she'd escaped from, the one that was custom-made to keep them both safe. She was desperate, focused and light on her feet as she charged across the field of grass, running as if she was suspended in the air, her footsteps carried by the wind.

Pow!

A searing pain burst through her thigh, sending her body jerking into the opposite direction as if she'd ran into a brick wall. She landed awkwardly on her ankle and the force of gravity mixing with her body weight shattered her bone. Her mouth opened to scream out in agony but no sound left her lungs. The heat from the bullet radiated through her entire body until it was the only sensation that she could feel. White noise curdled her eardrum, blocking out every-thing from around her.

Except for the sound of more bullets.

Pow! Pow! Pow!

Three more shots were fired but January didn't even have the will to react. Her body had grown faint, her vision was blurry, and she was so weak that she could barely breathe. No one had to tell her that her life was over because she felt it. Whether or not she lived past this moment, this would forever be the day she died.

She would never dance again.

Spark

GLITTER-TOPPED BULLSHIT.

Not all storms come to disrupt your life.
Some come to clear your path.

THE WORDS GLOWED ON THE SCREEN OF JANUARY'S PHONE LIKE AN omen. One that felt oddly like a warning of something unexpected to come. Something like a huge load of bullshit topped with glitter to add a little pizzazz. Who in their right mind would choose to suffer before getting to the good? And, in her experience, she'd found that those so-called 'good moments' were always fleeting, giving you a quick burst of satisfaction before you got bored and wanted to search for more. The bottom line was: suffering never _helped_ anyone. And whoever said it did could go directly to hell.

Do not pass go. Do not collect two hundred dollars.

She stirred a little, wiping the sleep from her eyes before sitting up in her bed. A frown created deep indentations in her forehead as she swiped the screen of her phone to look ahead at her horoscope quote for the next day. Each one was based on a full birth chart, so it was supposed to be much more precise than the regular ones most people checked. Spiritual by nature and superstitious by birthright

—thanks to her uber-superstitious father—January didn't get out of the bed until she checked her astrology apps each day. In a way, she felt like it prepared her for whatever was waiting for her.

Your heart must break before it opens: It's the heartbreak that teaches you how to love.

Her frown deepened and her lips twisted to the side of her face as if she'd eaten something sour. Yet another message predicting gloom and doom. She squinted hard, reading it again under bended brows. January had no idea who all this was for, but she knew one thing: This didn't have *shit* to do with her. Obviously, it was for some other girl who had her same exact birthday.

And birth time.

And birthplace.

Yeah… maybe that didn't seem *exactly* likely, but the bottom line was, these message weren't for her. For one, her heart had never been broken because she'd never even been in a real relationship. And it wasn't because she never cared about someone enough, it's because she never had the chance. With the father she had and the life she lived, it was hard as hell to get close to anyone—*especially* a boy. She barely could get close enough to people in order to like them, let alone love them. She had cousins growing up but, outside of them, she couldn't really say that she had close friends. Being the daughter of an alleged mafia kingpin kinda worked against that.

Being that her reality had forced her into a loveless life up until this point, the only conclusion she could draw from this current quote was that she should look forward to a future full of heartbreak in order to open her heart. Only through pain, she'd learn to earn the love she wanted.

Another promise of happiness at the end of suffering.

The Universe was trying to hand her yet another pile of shit with glitter on top.

No thanks. No ma'am and no sir. She didn't want it.

I'm good, God, she thought, locking the screen of her phone and setting it to the side. *You can keep that…but we still good.*

After splashing water on her face and brushing her teeth, January rolled out her yoga mat and completed two full practices on her yoga app before sitting for a quick meditation. Anxiety had been a constant in her reality ever since she could remember. It rode her back like a second skin becoming a permanent part of her, but she'd learned to live with it—or at least control it—through practice. However, even after completing her normal morning routine to quiet the nervous whispers in her mind, she still couldn't shake the ominous feeling sitting at the edge of her consciousness.

She groaned, and fell flat on her back, lying on the floor.

And that's why you shouldn't read that shit first thing in the morning.

January knew perfectly well that the reason for the anxiety bubbling in her belly was the messages that she'd read earlier. But she couldn't help but think that something was coming to uproot her world; something or *someone* she needed to be prepared for.

With nothing else to do, she decided it was the best time to head to the campus bookstore to grab everything she needed for class. She'd been pushing the trip away, waiting for her roommate to move in so they could go together, but classes started the next day and her roommate hadn't arrived. Knowing her father, her roomie probably hadn't passed the full background check and security clearance measures Outlaw had demanded the school put whoever it was and her family through. January's parents had promised her they would allow the University to pick her roommate for her, but she wasn't convinced they didn't lie and comfort themselves by being convinced it was all for her safety.

THE L.A. WEATHER was easy to get used to. The warmth from the sun mixed with the calm and cool summertime breeze just enough to balance out what January would normally consider scorching heat, making it the perfect day for shorts. Nearly everyone was wearing them, but she preferred to hide her long, perfectly sculpted dancer legs in tights or yoga pants. With her thick thighs and rounded ass, unarguably one of her best assets, she could rock booty shorts with enough sex appeal to have niggas on the streets drooling like dogs in heat. But tights and yoga pants were a staple in her closet, and she clung to them as if they gave her life. Regardless to how it downplayed her style, the fact of the matter was, the big, ugly scar on her right thigh couldn't be seen through yoga pants.

Just as she was about to grab the handle to open the door to the bookstore, a notification chimed on her phone. Unlocking it quickly, she swiped up to check the message.

You were born with wings, why prefer to crawl through life?

January squinted hard, feeling an icy, tingling sensation travel down her spine as she read and reread the quote. It didn't matter which one of her many apps this had come from, she was convinced that this was a message sent directly to her. Crawling through life was exactly what she was running from. It was everything she'd been doing since the moment she slid her ass through the birth canal. She'd always felt like her soul didn't understand what was in store for her when choosing the parents she had. Her soul had probably opted for the life of jewels, riches, luxury and comfort, without really considering all that came with being a real princess.

In the world, every girl wanted to be a princess.

But every girl in New York wanted to be *January Lukeisha Murray*.

The problem was that they didn't realize everything she had to give away because of the mafia life. Yes, they had endless money, but what she missed out on happened to be all things that money couldn't buy.

Like privacy.

And friends.

… Or love.

"Welcome to Campus Books, how can I help you?"

Looking up, she caught the eager gaze of a youngish boy around her age, sporting a blonde mohawk with the tips dyed dark green. On his face were glasses fashioned after something the singer Prince probably wore back in the 80s. He had on a *Boy Meets World* shirt, a clear nod to the 90s, and completed his look with glittery black pants that hailed straight from the 70s and Vans with a photo of Tony Hawk on the right side and Lupe Fiasco on the left. His style was suspended between three different decades and, truthfully speaking, he looked a *hot ass mess* by normal standards. But he worked the look like he didn't have a care in the world what anyone thought and had long ago run out of fucks to give.

Being that 'unapologetically you' must be nice, January couldn't help but think, smiling.

Still smiling politely, she shook her head. "No, I think I'm good." She lifted her phone, flashing the copy of her schedule before his eyes. "I have all the books listed here. I don't mind finding them myself."

The guy nodded, his lips curving into a smile that revealed an icy gold grill. He was like Paul Wall's nerdy, disco-loving, skateboarding younger brother.

"Okay, well, let me know if you need anything!" he said before walking away.

Phone in hand, January read off the title of the first book on the list and then took a moment to browse the labels on the shelves searching for her first class. The bookstore was big with multiple rows of shoulder-high bookshelves arranged throughout, each one marked with a label on top ordered alphabetically by course name. Although it had gotten a recent facelift, with a fresh coat of paint on the wall and freshly waxed tile floors, there was still something that felt 'old' about it. Familiar, even. Or maybe it was something else about this moment that had her suddenly feeling nostalgic. In that moment, a conversation she'd just had with her mother on the plane ride to L.A. came to her mind.

"January, are you sure you want to go all the way to Los Angeles? Why can't you just stay in New York? You've already completed two years."

"Because I don't want to stay in New York," she said, shaking her head. *"I want to live my own life outside of being 'Outlaw's daughter'. I want to be my own person and do my own thing."*

"You can do your own thing in New York," her mother, Janelle, had said.

January gave her a pointed look, smothered over in pure doubt. *"You're kidding, right?"*

"You could still live on campus," she continued, pleading her case. *"You could still do your own thing without us around to cramp your style."*

She had to be joking.

"You're kidding, right? My own thing? In New York?"

Everyone knew that New York belonged to Outlaw. There was no way January could ever 'do her thing' in Outlaw's city.

"Not everyone knows your dad, January," Janelle reasoned, before crossing her legs and turning away to look out the window.

She was as regal as a queen, sitting with perfection like royalty in Nelly, the private plane her husband had named after her. Her gentle brown eyes were clouded by emotion that she was trying to hide... and was failing at that terribly. Once again, her daughter was exercising her right to be free, but Janelle didn't want to let her go. The last time she had, it almost ended in tragedy. She knew she couldn't force her to stay home any longer than she had already, but it was just too hard to let go.

"You're right," January replied, her tone just as stubborn and strong as she was. *"Not everyone knows Daddy and I want to make sure that I'm surrounded by as*

many of those people as possible. The least people around, judging me by who he is, the better. I love him, but we are not the same."

Taking her mother's lead, she reclined back in her own seat and looked out the window, fixating her eyes on the clear blue skies. It was a beautiful day; the perfect day for flying with the clearest sky they'd seen in days after dealing with so much rain. For her, that was a sign that she was making the right decision. Besides, they were almost to Los Angeles by now. It was too late to turn around and, even if they were just leaving the runway at JFK, she wouldn't be changing her mind.

"Wait," she started, just as another thought occurred to her. "Did Daddy hire someone to follow me around? He doesn't have anyone planted on campus to watch me, does he? You'd tell me if he did, right?"

With her eyes poised on Janelle's face, she felt her mood quickly begin to change. Her leg started to jump, bouncing as her body filled with anxious energy. It was a nervous habit she'd developed long ago. She hid it well except in the moments when her mind was so fragmented with thoughts, she couldn't.

"January, calm down," Janelle started, making a clicking sound with her teeth as if she was being ridiculous. "Contrary to your belief, your dad can't do any and everything that he wants to do. He's not Jesus."

Her neck jerked back, and she cocked her head to the side, staring doubtfully at her mother.

"Some people think the only difference between him and Jesus is that no one argues about what Daddy looks like."

Pulling out of thoughts and back into her sinking reality, January looked around at the shelves and shelves of books, suddenly feeling overwhelmed. Even a little homesick. Her anxiety bubbled in her gut. She'd never gone out in public without a security staff around her to not only keep her safe but also provide as accomplices, friends even, so she never felt alone. She felt small and helpless now that she was by herself.

Needing something to settle her mind, she reached in her bag and pulled out a fortune cookie from the Chinese food she'd eaten the other night. Tearing off the wrapping, she split the cookie in two and popped half of it in her mouth. She was about to toss the remainder before then deciding to read the message inside. Pausing to open it, she didn't even realize that she was holding her breath while she unfolded the message. Words appeared before her eyes and her anxiety prickled like tiny, ice-cold fingers through her gut.

Calamity brings forth peace. You must endure the bad for the good.
The road ahead will be hard... But worthwhile.

Endure the bad? Hard road ahead? Oh, *hell*, nah!

Without giving it a second thought, she tossed the message in the closest trash bin, and deleted all astrology and psychic apps from her phone, telling herself that all the doomsday messages about enduring bad days for an exchange for better was a load of shit. None of the messages pertained to her.

Not a single one.

"Excuse me, I think you dropped this. Is this your phone?"

January nearly jumped out of her skin before turning to look down into a pair of thick bifocal lenses. Knowing she'd startled her, the girl smiled.

"I'm sorry if I alarmed you." She held the bedazzled pale pink and gold phone out in front of her. January shook her head.

"It's okay. And yes, this is my phone. Thank you for grabbing it for—"

January stopped short when she went to grab her phone, noting the number 11:11 tattooed on the girl's wrist. She frowned when she noticed it also matched the time showing on the inside corner of her phone.

If you ever see 11:11, make a wish and get happy! It means true love is on the way, she could almost hear her grandmother's voice in the back of her mind.

"Don't mention it!" the girl said, cheerfully before walking away.

She tried to write everything happening this day as just a coincidence. But, for her, there were no coincidences. They simply didn't exist.

There just was *no such thing.*

She believed in omens, fate, and karma. She truly believed that the Universe worked in ways that the human mind could never comprehend, but that we were constantly sent signs, coming from the stars in the sky or in the form of what people *thought* were coincidences or other synchronicities. The signs were there to let us know when we were fucking up bad and needed to change course or to prepare us for whatever was coming next.

She took a deep breath and forced her thoughts away, focusing back on her schedule and the materials she needed for class. The only thing left for her to do in that moment was relax and get ready for whatever was coming next.

Unfortunately, what she didn't know was that not even her free-flowing philosophy on life could have readied her for what was coming ahead.

There was no magic 8-ball, no fortune cookie or astrological quote that could have prepared her for the way that her entire life was about to change. There was no preparation at all for the moment her heart would truly burst open, making room for the perfect love.

The kind where you loved to the point that your souls became intertwined.

The kind of love that transcended lifetimes.

A love that was like meeting someone for the first time, and some-how, knowing it's *not* the first time. You'd loved each other deeply and unconditionally for many, many lifetimes.

It was a love she wouldn't be able to deny; the kind that made her question every single rule, lesson, code or law that made up every-thing she was and thought herself to be.

Nothing could have prepared her for the moment she was reunited with *him*.

QUANTUM PHYSICS.

THE ROBUST AROMA OF COFFEE PERCOLATED FROM A KIOSK IN THE center of the store, where two smiling employees served everyone who approached. Next to it, January caught the sight of a sign with the abbreviation for her sociology class, pointing to a few rows of books towards the back.

Crossing by the kiosk, she headed towards one near the back where the books for her class should have been. Eyes tight, she scanned over the top of each row, checking for the one that read SOC 101.

"There it is…" she whispered once she spotted it.

She was about to slide right onto the row when she stopped short, noticing that there was someone else standing right at the entrance of it, blocking her path. Someone who also looked *especially* out of place.

Dressed like the star love interest in a teenage girl's favorite rap video, complete with a body that would put every guy in the store sporting 'dad bods' to shame, and a side profile that showed her just enough to know he was *sexy as* hell, he was a GQ model in trap god's clothing. Pure, sexy thug in a gentlemanly way… if that made sense.

Does *that make sense?* January thought, judging her assessment of him with a slight frown.

What *didn't* make sense was how he could be so fucking fine. Especially for someone like him. He wasn't even her type. In *no* shape or fashion.

She took a moment to catch her breath and, most importantly, find her voice which had, somehow, gotten lost somewhere in between her mental tug-of-war between lust and desire. A ragged "excuse me" was all that she could muster out before quickly crossing his path. Not realizing she was holding her breath again, she sucked in a sharp burst of air and was greeted by the smell of his cologne. Notes of cedar, hints of musk, and a small bit of cinnamon tickled her nostrils. She nearly swooned on her weakened knees.

His scent was *intoxicating.*

"You're excused, princess," he replied, his tone soaked and dripping with obvious dry sarcasm.

January's brows crinkled and the fine hairs on her arms stood up on end.

Something about what he said made her feel some kind of way. It caught her off-guard. Or maybe it was his mocking, somewhat condescending tone. She wasn't quite sure what it was really, but something was tugging relentlessly at her senses. She felt like she should've been defending herself, but she didn't know why. So instead of popping off at the mouth, she simply turned her attention to the bookshelf.

Though she was right where she needed to be, the book that she was looking for right in front of her face, her mind felt saran-wrapped around the presence of someone else.

Glancing down, she noticed that the fine hairs on her arm were still standing straight in the air. She mused, pausing to quickly assess her environment. There wasn't the least bit of a chill in the air. She'd realized fairly quickly that most places of business in L.A., especially the ones on campus, seemed to prefer the warm west coast climate and rarely used air condition to regulate the temperature. The chilly sensation in her body was there, but not because of the air. It was something else.

Or *someone* else.

Lifting her eyes momentarily away from the books ahead, she twisted slightly and peered at him under a single lifted brow. He didn't look like anyone she'd ever seen before, not that she *remembered* meeting. Still, there was something about him that felt so familiar to her, and she wasn't sure why. Shoulder-length locs hung to his shoulders, somewhat hiding the warm butterscotch complexion peeking out from beneath. It was perfect and smooth. He was definitely easy on the eyes, but there was something else about him that called out to her soul. His aura sparkled like diamonds under the L.A. sun. It eclipsed her in its essence; she couldn't ignore the effect.

Her body felt warm, recognizing something in him that her mind hadn't been able to place just yet. Completely unaware that she was now officially staring, she narrowed into him, scrutinizing each detail that made up the glory of him in hopes that it would jog some distant memory.

"Shorty, something wrong with your fuckin' eyes, or are you going to ask to 'be excused' before bumping into me again?" he asked with grit and without bothering to even glance her way.

January's jaw nearly dropped to her feet. She couldn't think of a single moment in her life when someone had the audacity to talk to her in that way. In fact, she couldn't think of a moment in her life when she'd been disrespected in *any* way. No one in the world had the chance to even think about it without the threat Outlaw somehow figuring it out and taking their life. They didn't even dream it for fear that he would snuff them out in their sleep. Men twice January's age treated her with more respect than they did their own mother.

Who the hell does he think he is?

"Excuse me?" she snapped, shocked to the absolute max. Taking a step back, she looked at him from head to toe. "Do you know who you're talking to?"

It wasn't arrogance. And she wasn't being rude because she thought that she was somehow better than everyone just because of her family and connections. This was every bit about the common decency and respect that should be given to any human being. *Especially* a woman. It didn't matter who you were, how much money you had or how sexy you thought you were, you just *didn't* talk to people that way.

Sighing heavily, Legend snapped the book shut that he'd started flipping through and took a stance that further illustrated his obnoxious attitude. He was being rude—he knew it and the chick who seemed eager to get on his nerves knew it, too. In fact, it wasn't something he was being, it was something he was. He *was* rude as hell, an asshole by nature, and he didn't give a fuck what anyone thought about it. He wore his asshole badge unapologetically, wishing he could wave it around like a flag, so he didn't have to deal with situations such as this.

It was bad enough that he was in a city he hated, doing the last thing on Earth he wanted to do and in the last place on Earth where he wanted to be. A fucking college bookstore, searching for books to help him get a degree just so his moms could hang the paper on the wall and have something to be proud of him for. This wasn't what he'd thought he was agreeing to when he promised to take a break from the streets. This wasn't what he thought he'd be swearing to when he held his grandmother's hand and swore to grant her one last dying wish.

"I'm a street nigga, grandma, I don't do the school shit," was what he wanted to say.

But he saw the fear in her eyes as she panted through her last breaths, holding on to the final fragile threads of life as she waited for him to give her the comfort she so desperately needed. She couldn't rest in peace until he committed himself to it. She wanted him to be a better man than his father, father's father, and father's father's father had. To be a man of substance; a good example to his future children as to what it meant to live with honor and morality. To be an example of what it meant to give love and be loved.

How could she expect him to be something he never had?

The question was one he'd have to figure out the answer for himself because, as soon as he made the vow to his grandmother that he would earn a college degree and prove to the world that he was more than a product of his environment and circumstance, she smiled and released her final breath. He sat there cloaked in his thoughts, bound in his solitude, holding onto her hand until it went cold. Still feeling the essence of her in the room, reminding him of what he'd vowed to do. Telling him that she wouldn't move on, wouldn't cross over, until his promised was delivered.

The days passed by in a blur. He was in cruise control, present only in body for his grandmother's wake, funeral and burial. All the while, the promised he'd made sat in the back of his mind, haunting him to the point that he couldn't sleep.

Legend was a hitta. He'd separated many souls from many bodies; watched the light fade from many eyes. He'd done it so many times that he was comfortable doing it. Feeling haunted came with the lifestyle and he welcomed it. He was used to his demons. But this was something different. It literally felt like his grandmother was riding his ass. And when he tried to return to his former life only for some niggas to show up busting shots on him and his cousin, Nico, he realized that her crazy ass meant business. Nico and Legend had been in the streets for a long time, but they'd never been so close to meeting death.

"Fuck this shit," he'd said, finally giving in. His aunt pulled a few strings, called in a few favors at her alma mater and both Legend and Nico were enrolled to start the next year. And just like that, two street niggas, hittas, former mafia fixers were enrolled in college to

get a business degree. The streets had already said enough about Legend due to his past fuck-ups but the tongues were really wagging with good gossip now.

"I don't know who you are, and I really don't give a fuck," he said without bothering to look at the girl standing not too far away from him. If she had any sense, she would take the opportunity to leave rather than waste her time trying to teach him manners and get her feelings hurt.

He didn't have time to make nice.

He had a lot of other bullshit to deal with.

The girl audibly gasped, as if she couldn't believe what he'd said. Of course, she didn't; she was probably one of Cali's finest: a pretty girl who thought niggas would fall at their feet after taking a single look at her. It was yet another reason why Legend hated L.A., women out here thought that everything was earned with a pretty face. Some of the men, too. Motherfuckas didn't believe they had to work for shit. It annoyed him like a constant pain in the ass because the evidence of it was everywhere he went.

The only reason he even decided to go to Cali was because he had to. As a former hitta for the *Black Bag Mafia* who had been stripped of his position, he wasn't welcome in any of their territories without Outlaw's permission. The *BBM* ran worldwide and had total control over almost all 50 states, California and Florida excluded. Legend's father resided in Miami and had total control of Florida while a mutual friend of both Outlaw and Legend's controlled California.

There was no way Legend could stay in Florida without being in the streets, so Cali was his only choice. Which meant he'd continue to bump into chicks like the current one he was dealing with.

What an asshole, January couldn't help but think. She was completely repulsed by him. It was a new feeling. In her life, everyone catered to her every whim. She'd never *not* liked anyone after first meeting them.

"You don't have to be so rude," she scoffed, beyond agitated. "I haven't done anything to you."

"Nothing but waste my time," the guy responded.

In a matter of seconds, she'd gone from being so turned on by him that she couldn't think to being completely and utterly turned off. She couldn't understand why she was even still standing there, outside of the fact that she felt pressed to stand up for herself.

A brief stroke of curiosity made her glance at the cover of the book he'd been reading before he had the chance to put it down.

Quantum Physics?

Her brows rose in question.

Was she being punked? Standing here in expensive sneakers, 'hood-luxury' designer apparel, and his neck wrapped with chains that could probably pay for the average person's salary for the next ten years, he looked like the *last* person on Earth to be interested in anything like Quantum Physics.

Suddenly something else occurred to her. Before she knew it, her attitude shifted and her body tensed, becoming as rigid as stone. Squaring her shoulders, she placed both hands on her hips and narrowed her eyes into him, glaring with conviction before she'd even gotten a chance to ask the question.

"You work for my Daddy, don't you?"

"Huh?"

His body went oddly still, and he lifted his head from the book that he was still holding in his hand. With a slight frown, he stared ahead of him, the edges of his eyes were pulled tight as he considered her question.

Don't try to lie, January thought, a smirk threatening the edges of her lips.

She fought to keep her expression even, though on the inside, she was already rejoicing in her victory. Her parents had tried to outsmart her, and she'd discovered it on Day 1. That'd be 100 points for her and a big, fat zero to the Infamous Outlaw.

Game *over*.

A BEAUTIFUL DISTRACTION.

SEEMING BEWILDERED THAT HIS COVER HAD JUST BEEN BLOWN, THE guy turned, and his eyes finally met hers for the first time since they'd been standing there. Upon seeing her, they rounded, forcing his dark, full, bushy brows to the ceiling. It was at that moment when she got the exact sign she'd been looking for. An emotion flashed through his pupils, one that was easy for her to pick up on. She read it crystal clear because she'd seen it many times throughout her entire life whenever people had enough time to really take a look at her.

He knows me, she thought, still holding back her smile.

She detected it the second the recognition hit his eyes.

And then, quite to her absolute and utter delight, that expression was quickly followed by another that she also knew well. It was the '*Oh, shit… Outlaw's gonna fuck me up*' look. Because of the consequences of crossing one of the most merciless men alive, this expression was much more intense than the regular 'oh, shit' look. It was another that January could pick up on with ease because her father didn't fuck around. People were always worried about whether or not they'd done something that would land them on his bad side.

"Wait… what did you say your name was again?" Legend asked.

In his heart—or the space where his heart would have been if he had one—he already knew the answer.

January Motherfuckin' Murray… in the flesh.

She was just as much a dream now as she had been back when he'd seen her for the first time. Still elegant in a way that didn't need the prepping used by other girls her age. She stood before him completely natural, not a hint of makeup on her face, save for lip-gloss that made her lips appear dripping wet. His imagination got the best of him as an image of her doing something explicit flashed through his thoughts. Something she would deem as dirty and unla-dylike if he said it, rolling her eyes and curling her pretty lips upwards in disgust.

Cutting his eyes away, he suppressed the feeling that awakened immediately in his loins. He didn't have time to waste fantasizing on bullshit—especially bullshit that would get him killed. In his last run-in with Outlaw, he'd made it perfectly clear that he wanted Legend to leave him and his family alone. The only reason Outlaw had even bothered to spare his life was because he thought of Legend as the son he never got the chance to have. Even still, he made it clear that he wouldn't hesitate to end his life if he ever found him near January or anywhere in *BBM* territory again.

It was nice to see her after all this time but that wasn't why he was here, and he couldn't fuck with her on any level even if he wanted to do. His goal was to get through the last two years needed to complete his degree as quickly as he could and then move the fuck on with his life. Considering her in any way was a mistake because nothing could come of it. She could be nothing to him but a distraction.

But what a *fuckin' beautiful distraction* she was.

Against his better judgement, he allowed his eyes to drift over curves that were more pronounced than they had been the time he'd seen her before. A sweet thickness was there that hadn't been there. The

January he'd met had been totally focused on dance, explaining to him all of the sacrifices that she had to make in order to maintain her slim physique. Trying to get him to understand the benefits of eating nuts, berries, lettuce and fruit instead of dairy and meat in order to stay light on her feet. Back then, he'd let her talk to her heart's content just so that he could continue staring at her, just as he was now. Years ago, her slim sexy had him tripping hard, but he was nearly drooling over her curvy thick now.

Thick thighs matched with a tight, juicy ass that bricked his dick seemingly beyond repair. And it didn't stop there; her beauty was inside and out. It was felt so clearly he could almost see it, even through the screw-face she was currently delivering. January was a sight so magnificent that she could make a thug cry.

She was pure magic.

"I *didn't* say my name," January replied, snaking her neck with pure attitude. "But I'm sure you know it. Don't you?"

She waited, leveling her weight to one side, balancing it on her left hip as she tapped her right foot, impatiently waiting for his response. His eyes tightened and his lips pressed firmly against each other, but he didn't attempt to say a word.

Which means I'm right, she quickly surmised. Letting out a breath, she tried to expel all of the disappointment she was feeling.

Although part of her felt victorious in that she'd discovered the ruse, another part of her wanted to cry. Her parents lied to her. They didn't trust her to be responsible enough to live in the city on her own. But even above that, her father had promised that he wouldn't have her watched by any member of his security team and still did. He'd *lied* to her.. something he'd never done before. That realization crushed her more than anything.

But wait... she paused, temporarily delaying the pity party she was about to throw herself.

Frowning hard, she allowed her eyes to wash over the man chosen to carry out her father's dirty deeds. His style wasn't flashy, but it definitely wasn't toned down in any shape or form. Besides all that, he was so good-looking, he stood out like a sore thumb no matter where he was.

This is who they thought to pick? Did they really think he would blend in? Or that I'm too stupid to have noticed?

"When you call to let my dad know that he failed, do me a favor and let him know that he might want to pick a replacement who can do a better job at knowing what it means to be undercover." She had to bite down on her bottom lip to stop from going further.

If there was one thing she hated more than anything, it was for someone to think she was stupid. In her life, it happened all the time. People always assumed a pretty face only came with an absence of brains. As if you couldn't be pretty *and* smart at the same damn time.

They assumed she leaned on her money, family connections, and beauty to get her everything she wanted in life, as if she couldn't possibly want to work hard. She hated to be stereotyped. She hated when someone didn't think of her as important enough to truly get to know. As if she wasn't worthy of their time, they dismissed the real person and chose instead to hold on to their idiotic and inaccurate assumptions. Even though she was trying to stop herself, she couldn't help it and, like she'd contracted diarrhea of the mouth, the rest of the words in her head spewed like venom from her lips.

"And *another* thing," she began, stepping in closer to him while lifting a finger in the air. "Tell my father that it might be good for your replacement not to call me 'princess' and not to think that the way to fool me is to be extra rude." Disgusted, she rolled her eyes at that. "There are better ways to try to make it seem like you don't know who I am than to be rude. You would've been better off at least giving me the respect you would give any other human being."

Legend chuckled a bit at that. He wasn't sure whether or not she remembered him, but it was obvious that she hadn't heard much about him or his dealings in the street scene since the last time they'd seen each other.

"I did give you the respect I would give any other human being. I really *don't* give a fuck about any—"

"And *lastly*," she continued, interrupting him, lifting her finger higher in the air. "The *Fundamentals of Quantum Physics* textbook was a nice touch but—" She paused to let out a dry cackle and then shook her head incredulously. "—that was *quite* obvious, too."

With a quick wink, she shot him a fake smile before turning her back to him, which, in her mind, meant she was giving him her ass to kiss. She prayed he was smart enough to pick up on the symbolism because, though she wanted to, she was too much of a 'good girl' to actually say it. If she hadn't been, she'd definitely be giving her middle finger to the world right now.

This shit was *ridiculous.*

She was a grown ass woman and her parents still felt the need to keep tabs on her as if she was incapable of taking care of herself.

"Yo, I don't know why you thinkin' whatever the fuck you thinkin'. I ain't workin' for nobody."

"You are," January replied, speaking at him from over her back.

Legend shook his head. "I'm not."

"Are too. I'm not stupid."

"Am not. I'm not a liar."

The raging fire of anger inside of her had been reduced to a slow burn until Legend's refusal to back down poured gasoline on the flame.

Her body tensed, and she knew right then she wouldn't be taking the higher road. She wasn't the type to leave a blatant lie hanging in the air.

She *hated* when someone lied to her. Hated it above any and everything else.

To her, it showed sheer disrespect. A lie was someone's way of telling you that you're too stupid to figure out the truth. In other words, he was calling her stupid. Basically.

Or, at least, that's how she reasoned it in her mind.

"You know I'm not stupid, right? I've never seen you before and I don't know who you are, but I definitely know who and what you're *not*. You're not just here by coincidence. For one, there is no such thing."

Legend paused for a moment to allow her words to stew in his mind for a minute. He agreed with her; he knew she wasn't stupid, and he had to agree that he didn't believe in coincidences either. Which brought something else to his mind worth considering.

What was she doing here, so far away from home, in *this* city, in *this* bookstore, *at the same exact moment* that he was?

"Did you hear me?" January pressed for a response, further annoyed by his lack of interest in giving her one.

He didn't speak to affirm or deny her question for the moment. Instead, he paused, taking a moment to simply gaze into her eyes, wondering to himself how it was that she didn't know him. The intensity of the moment, the immense amount of emotion that she'd awakened in him—it all couldn't be one-sided. She had to feel it, too. Didn't she? The more he stared at her, trying his hardest to read into her soul, pick up on any bit of anything inside of her that remembered the bond formed in the brief moments they'd shared years ago, the more he realized that she didn't feel a thing he felt because she didn't have a clue. She didn't recognize him at all.

Damn, he thought for a minute, giving in to a brush of disappointment. Then again, he wasn't in the position to be fucking with her like he wanted to anyways. Maybe the fact that she didn't recognize him was actually a blessing in disguise.

"Alright, I'll play this game with you. I'll tell you the absolute truth," Legend said finally, shrugging his shoulders as if he was giving in.

January crossed her arms in front of her chest. "It's about time."

"Like I said, I'm *not* working for your father," he said it without blinking. "Or anyone else."

Narrowing her eyes, she looked him over, reading his body language. He didn't appear to be lying at all.

"And you're telling the truth?" She widened her eyes, for the first time coming to terms with the fact that she might actually be mistaken. "I mean, are you telling the *absolute* truth? Hand on the Bible?"

Reaching out for a book beside them, she pulled out a copy of the King James Bible from the shelf. It, apparently, was the required for a *Sociology of the Bible* class and was perfect for the current moment.

Legend recoiled, taking a couple steps back, as if the Bible was covered in skin-soluble poison. If he were honest about it, technically, it *was*. If any nigga could drop dead from touching the holy book, it would be him. The thought was hilarious when he thought about it. He nudged his nose, fighting to suppress his laughter but there was no use. Before long, he found himself having the first genuine laugh that he'd had in a long time.

Silent for once, January watched him with intense curiosity. She hated to admit it but he had a gorgeous smile. One that lit up his face in a way that totally transformed it, giving way to a boyish and carefree nature that was a total contrast from the 'complete asshole' vibes from before. Seeing it made her feel privileged in a way—like she was witnessing something that not too many others had a chance to see.

"Real shit, me and the Bible ain't been vibin' heavy for a minute.

Ain't tryin' to get burned. It'll fuck up my fingertips." He chuckled as he said that, lifting his hand to wiggle his fingers for emphasis. "But I assure you, I'm telling the truth."

January's jaw nearly dropped to the floor.

He was telling the *truth*.

Mortified, she thought quickly back on everything that had just transpired between them. All the things she'd said.

Oh God…

She probably looked like a crazy lady.

"Shit, I'm so sorry." She slapped her palm against her forehead. "I'm sorry, seriously. I really thought—"

"That I was working for your daddy?"

Her cheeks scorched at the way he said it, an extra flare of something accusatory in his tone.

What did he think she meant when she said 'Daddy'?

"That's *not* what I meant when I said 'daddy.'"

"What's not?" Legend smirked, teasing her with his head cocked to the side. "By the way, there's no point in lyin' to me, princess. I can see right through those."

January's cheeks flamed. She placed her hands over them, feeling them literally pump heat into her fingers.

"I mean that I'm not a—"

"I ain't trippin' so why should you?" Legend said, cutting her off with a wave of his hand. "Everybody gotta get it how they live, shorty."

Saying that, he slightly shrugged his shoulders and took a step back. Fucking with her simply for shits and giggles, he slowly wet his lips with his tongue before lowering his gaze, scrolling from her face to take in the rest of her body. If January wasn't so deathly mortified, she would have swooned. She felt totally caught up by the intensity in his eyes.

"Shorty, it's your body and you can do whatever you want with it," he added, wetting his lips once again before returning his eyes to her face.

"No—no—no, that's not it. I don't have any problem with what people choose to do with their bodies, I'm just saying that's not what *I* do." She pressed a finger into her chest for extra emphasis. "I'm not the type to give myself away for free."

"I feel you…" Legend nodded. "Can't blame you for putting a price tag on it. Gotta be a paid nigga to get it. Well, you in the right city now, shorty. Lotta paid niggas out here."

January gasped, feeling the blood drain from her face.

"I've never let *anyone* get it, whether they are willing to pay for it or not. Like I said, I'm *not* that kind of girl!" She finished, completely flustered, and with much more volume than she'd intended to. If a single person on their side of the store hadn't heard her, it was only because they were totally deaf in both ears.

"Listen… one thing you should know 'bout me is that I don't judge," was all he said, shaking his head. "I've fucked up too many times to feel any kind of way about what the next person chooses to do."

Dread pooled in her gut. He *didn't* believe her. And for some reason, she felt so pressed to make this man, who she'd known all of about ten minutes, not think that she was a whore.

He said he didn't judge, but she knew better. He probably thought she just another chick like Diamond from the movie *The Players Club*; student by day and baring it all for whoever could pay for it at night.

She was horrified.

"No, I mean—"

He shook his head, cutting her off. "Nah, shorty, it's all good."

One last smile passed over his lips and he lingered for a few seconds longer, probably watching to make sure that she wouldn't go crazy on him anymore. January didn't move a muscle. Trust, she wanted to get the moment over as quickly as possible, and that desire was even stronger than her need to be understood.

After deciding that it was safe to leave without her running up on him from behind again like a crazy woman, he turned around. And left.

With her still standing there looking like a damn fool.

And not just *any* kind of damn fool. She looked like a very special kind of fool. One who had mistaken a random Black man in a college bookstore as working for her pimp. It was like some kind of weird spin that had her looking like a Black version of a 'Karen.' She'd stereotyped him without much evidence and managed to make herself look like an idiot in the process. For someone who hated to be misunderstood and stereotyped herself, she currently sucked at giving others the same benefit.

In other words, her first day out and about in L.A. was a complete and utter fail.

A NEW DAY.

THE WORLD SEEMED SO PEACEFUL WHEN YOU WERE LOOKING DOWN on it from the sky above. All that you could see were beautiful landscapes and crystal blue ocean. You didn't see any of the chaos that lay below. Or the ways so many of its inhabitants were held captive, unknowingly made into victims of their environment or social constructs. You didn't see that, sometimes, no matter how hard you tried to make your own way, one simple fact remained: *Life was a hateful bitch who spent all her time making sure you stayed in your place.*

And no one knew that better than January did.

"AFFIRMATION OF THE DAY: I am brave. I am bold. I am fearless. Let's say it together…"

One hand gripping the strap of her boho bag, January repeated the chant along with the voice speaking through her headphones.

"I am brave. I am bold. I am fearless. I am brave. I am bold. I am…"

The declaration continued and she took a moment to close her eyes and visualize the words in her mind as the vibrations rolled off her tongue. The calm-inducing low chime of a Tibetan bowl signaled the end of the day's affirmation and she slowly opened her eyes, feeling a peaceful calm replace the anxiety that had the pit of her stomach bubbling.

It was either the anxiety or hunger pains that was responsible for the bubbling, being that she'd been up since 4 am and, like an idiot, skipped breakfast before leaving for class. She was starving but couldn't eat a thing no matter how hard she tried.

Her nerves were a mess.

"Heads up!" someone shouted, bringing her back to the present.

She flinched, her peripheral catching the sight of a football sailing overhead. A shirtless guy around her age ran up, catching the ball in his hands before greeting her with a dazzling, pure white smile. Sculpted body with chiseled abs became the new center of her focus while she watched as he trotted off to continue his game of catch with a couple of his equally sexy friends.

Damn... you most definitely aren't in high school anymore.

He caught her stare and winked before tossing her another smile, and she felt her cheeks warm. Tucking her head, she retreated from the flirtatious exchange and decided to focus on her schedule instead. She only had a few minutes left to make it to her first class. Like her father always said, when you're in the middle of achieving your goals, all boys could be was a distraction. Not only that, besides being cute, there wasn't much about them that interested her anyways. Little did, these days.

Squinting hard, she chewed on her bottom lip while staring at her class schedule, trying to make sense of it and the directions she'd scribbled off to the side.

"Two rights and then a left once I pass Shepherd Hall," she mumbled, taking a second to look up in the direction where Shepherd's Hall should have been. But instead of the large brick building that she was expecting after pulling the image from the website, there was an empty field of grass with a few students either sitting or sprawled out on blankets, soaking in the early afternoon sun.

Taking a deep breath, she adjusted her silk red scarf to smooth down her gelled and toothbrush-sculpted edges before pursing her lips. Mentally, she knew it was her time to shine—to seize the day. But her nerves? They were on some other shit.

This isn't the first day of ninth grade. So why are you on this high school shit?

"Hey, you're looking for Shepherd's Hall, too, huh?"

January's eyes darted to her right, settling on a kind, brown face with gentle eyes. A girl who seemed to be around her age, maybe a little younger, with long box braids hanging low over her shoulders and cherry lip-gloss smothered over her smiling lips stared back with expectation, waiting for an answer to her question.

She had friendly, inviting eyes that looked January over briefly in a nonjudgmental but curious way, as if trying to quickly assess the type of person she was. There was no spark of recognition as she stared—a clear difference from how it was when January met someone new in New York. They always knew who she was before she had the chance to get to know them. Being normal for once felt refreshing.

"Yes, I wrote down the directions straight from the email that they sent over the weekend. It's supposed to be right here," January answered, pointing towards the field before checking the directions once more.

"Yeah, they made a mistake. Shepherd's Hall is actually another two blocks down. Over there."

She pointed somewhere behind them and, sure enough, the building she was searching for was there. Feeling a nagging in the pit of her stomach, January grabbed her phone to check the time.

Shoot.

She had about two minutes to get to class if she was going to have a chance in hell of getting there on time.

"Thank you!" she yelled out to the girl who, for whatever reason, came right in the nick of time. She seemed friendly, and it would have been nice to stay and chat, but she was not the kind of person who showed up late for anything. Especially not class.

This is the moment you've been waiting for your entire life. It's different from what you expected but you were born to adjust. To refocus. And regardless of anything that's happened before, you are still following your dream.

For the first time in her life, she was truly free. It was something that she had wanted for a long time, even though it wasn't quite on the terms that she'd originally planned. She wasn't majoring in professional dance as she'd thought she would. And she had long ago accepted that she wouldn't own and operate her own studio for a living. In order to succeed in life, you had to be flexible and make adjustments. She was doing just that, adjusting while still living a life that she defined for herself. Without security detail or constant supervision and, most importantly, without any mafia ties.

If she'd stayed in New York, she could never be her own person. Too many people knew who her father was. Too many people recognized her no matter how much she tried to blend in, which meant that she was always accompanied by a full security detail for her own protection. Or for the protection of anyone stupid enough to try and hurt her, as Outlaw put it. At any rate, there was no way she could be normal there. It was Outlaw's city and, after getting shot and nearly losing her life, she knew that staying meant she had to follow his rules in order to be protected and survive. If she wanted to live her own life, she had to leave; she couldn't take any chances.

The *BBM* was known everywhere but, in L.A., the people and the media weren't as interested in her existence. Besides a couple of photos sent to *TMZ* and *The Shaderoom* showing her moving into her dorm—both stories Outlaw had promptly killed before they had a

chance to even make it on either site or social media page—
January's presence in L.A. was already old news. For once, she had
an opportunity to blend in.

"I couldn't help but notice the symbol on your bag. Are you a
Capricorn?"

Blinking back into the present, she frowned and glanced to her
right, shocked to see the girl from before speed-walking alongside
her while clumsily juggling several books in her hand as she struggled to keep up with her quick, long strides. It was almost comical
and, had the question she'd been asked not brought such painful
memories to her mind, she might have laughed.

"Yes," she answered, nodding her head. "Capricorn sun and ascen-
dant. Leo moon," she rattled off, hoping that all questions were
answered.

"Wow!" the girl let out in a breath. "I've never heard about
ascendings—"

"Ascendants," January corrected her.

"Oops! I mean, I've never heard of *ascendants* and moons. You must
really like astrology. I'm a Capricorn too, but I don't know about all
that other stuff." She shrugged. "I guess I should look into it. I turn
19 on the 8th. What about you?"

"Twenty on the 17th," she mumbled before glancing at the time. It
was almost time for class to start.

"Twenty?" she asked. "Oh... I thought you were a freshman.
Like me."

January could clearly hear the frown on her face through her tone.

"Well, no, but this is my first year here," was all she said, offering no
further explanation. This was not the time to go into how she'd
taken a year and a half off for physical and emotional therapy after
recovering from a gunshot wound.

"So... What's your major? I'm in psych but I'm on the pre-med track. My father is a doctor, so I really had no choice in the matter. Since the first day that I can remember, it's always been drilled into my head that I'd do the same thing, but what do you know? I actually like it! My name is Carmen, by the way."

"My name is January. And I'm pre-law," she replied, ignoring the stinging sensation in her gut as she spoke those words aloud. It still hurt to admit that she'd given up on dance.

Thankfully, their arrival in front of Shepherd's Hall gave her something else to focus on. Filling her lungs with air, January took a moment to look down at her phone once more. She had about a minute to spare. Not ideal, but she had at least made it on time.

She grabbed onto the handle of the door and took another deep breath, enjoying the excitement fluttering through her as Carmen chittered on, not missing a beat.

"Pre-law? That's impressive. I feel like I could have been a lawyer in another life. I love to talk so my parents always told me that. In fact, that's the exact reason why I didn't choose it. I think I need to calm my mind, learn how to focus more and talk less. You know what I mean? That's why I went into medicine. You have to be quiet to be good at that. And you gotta focus. Both things I could use some help with. Anyways—" She rolled her eyes. "—you seem kind of quiet for pre-law. What made you choose it? I mean, not that I'm saying you wouldn't be good at it or anything, I just—"

"My mom," January cut in as she pulled open the door to the lecture hall. "My mom is a judge. That's why."

It was a half-truth. But much easier than dishing out personal details of how she'd always dreamed of being a dancer until a gunshot wound to the thigh forced her to make a quick change of plans.

"A judge!" Carmen balked with a gasp. "That's *so* awesome."

January stepped inside the building slowly, almost cautiously, feeling like she had just walked through a portal leading into the next chapter of her life.

Though the outside of Shepherd's Hall looked like one large building filled with multiple rooms, the inside was one single auditorium. She stood at the top of the tiered auditorium seating, looking down over the students already seated as well as the teaching area situated below where she stood, right smack-dab in the center.

Welcome to college, she thought, soaking it all in. *Where all your dreams can come true.*

From the smell of the freshly painted walls down to the faint smell of mildew from the worn carpet floors, so far, it was everything that she'd imagined it to be. The room was nearly silent outside of the sounds of shuffling paper, bags being zipped or unzipped, and occasional chatter as other students began to make their way to their seats. Something she would be doing—should be doing—if her feet weren't firmly cemented in place.

She wrung her hands in front of her as she searched for the perfect place to sit. Fold-down seats with adjustable desks lined the outside wall of each tier, but she was hard-pressed to find an empty space that felt right. She had always sat right front and center in class before, when she had the choice. But something about being in foreign territory around people she didn't know felt different, like she shouldn't bring too much attention to herself.

"We should exchange information," Carmen was saying, oblivious to the fact that January was barely paying attention. "I heard that this professor is tough. She's not like the other ones who recycle the same curriculum each semester. She comes up with something new, so you never know what you're going to get from her. We should all work together. We'll need all the help we can get."

January nodded, unable to find words just yet.

Maybe it wasn't the first day of high school, but it definitely *felt* like it. Especially with Carmen's constant chatter nearly catapulting her into an anxiety attack. Being homeschooled for all of middle school and most of elementary, her first day of high school had been just as exciting but much more terrifying.

A civil war had erupted in the Murray home before the moment she even stepped out of the house that day. Outlaw had hired a security fleet to escort her and her mother to the new school, but Janelle wasn't having it. She demanded that he call off the security brigade. At the time, January didn't see what the problem was; in their world, *everyone* traveled with security. The first life lesson that her father had taught her was that the world was a grimy place, and you couldn't trust anyone in it. It was the first law of *The Family Code*.

The *BBM* lived by a code created and made official by Outlaw. He designed it based off his experiences and life lessons. From before the moment she could talk, he drilled these lessons into January's head, one at a time, revealing them on the evening of every one of her birthdays. He said the first one was the most important because, if it was false, there was no need for the others that came after it.

"The world is a grimy place. Trust no one but family. And sometimes, not even them."

She eventually learned that each part of the code was about as ominous and dark as the one before it.

"Wonderful thing to tell a one-year-old," Janelle had said at the time.

"Mind yo' business, Nell," Outlaw had replied. *"I don't know 'bout you, but I'm raising a baby thug."*

She rolled her eyes at her husband but didn't object. She knew that there was more benefit to her daughter knowing the code than not knowing it when it came to the life they lived.

"A friend of mine is saving a seat for me up front," Carmen said, interrupting January's search for a seat by standing squarely in front of her face. "So, I'll catch up with you after class. We have to stick together!"

With that said, she gave her one last smile and then darted away, seeming to bop as if dancing with each step. She was graceful in the way January was used to seeing with other dancers. She may have been a good one if she wasn't so short.

Adjusting her bag's strap over her shoulders, she steadied herself and then headed to a row right before the very last one in the back, deciding to sit close to the wall.

Knowing who is doing what and what moves they're making could be a matter of life and death. Another one of her father's rules. One she never paid the slightest attention to, being that a full security squad followed her everywhere she went, a motorcade of armed guards drove her to and from school and even stood outside the bathroom while she peed. She didn't worry about where she sat when she entered a building or who may or may not be walking in, because they decided all that for her.

The need to look out for herself didn't become real for her until after that day at the park. That was when she realized that it wasn't enough to have people around watching out for you. You had to look out for yourself.

The double doors opened with a loud creak, and in walked an average-height, plump black woman who appeared to be in her 30s with her hair styled in a long mohawk, with dark purple tips that hung low to one side. She was casually dressed in a Nike sweat suit and matching sneakers that were spotless and expensive. In her arms was a stack of papers and a couple books. Her teaching assistant, was following behind her with a laptop in her arms.

January sat up straight in her desk, watching as they descended all the way down into the bowels of the lecture hall. The teaching assistant took a seat right in the front row and the woman stood behind the podium, pausing for a few moments to organize her materials in front of her. She had a laid-back, eclectic vibe and a style that was all her own.

"Hello, everyone, and welcome to *Self & Society*. My name is Professor Stubee but I go by Ms. Bee because I love Beyonce more

than life and I am the self-proclaimed president of the Beyhive."
She flipped her hair for emphasis.

Without knowing it, January found herself smiling from ear-to-ear.
She could tell that she would like Ms. Bee. The fact that she loved
Beyoncé, possibly as much as she did, was an added benefit.
Relaxing into her seat, she began to feel her anxiety melting away to
make room for the excitement it had replaced.

Ms. Bee began to speak again, and January leaned eagerly forward,
giving her full attention.

"First off, I want to thank you all for being here," she began, looking
around to catch a few eyes. "I can tell by the fact that there are so
many students here on time and ready for class that most of you
must be freshmen, even though this is technically considered an
upper-level class."

A low rumble of laughter cut through the silence as half the room
chuckled at that. January cracked a smile, feeling even more relaxed
by that. Though she wasn't a freshman, it was nice knowing that she
was among many others who were new to campus.

Taking a moment to observe her surroundings, she began to quickly
analyze the others around her. It was a fairly diverse mixture, with
students from multiple backgrounds present. The room wasn't very
large, probably had about a hundred seats. The front was full and
the back, closest to her, had been somewhat vacant but was starting
to fill out quickly with students who were coming in late. A group of
guys took up almost a whole corner in the back rows. January would
normally assume that they were athletes, based on their physical
appearance paired with the lazy and indifferent 'I don't want to be
here' look in their eyes, but considering that she'd been wrong in her
assumptions the other day at the bookstore, she held out on her
judgment.

Towards the front of the class, where Carmen sat, were the nerds.
The overachievers. It was obvious, not only because they chose to sit
nearly right up under Ms. Bee's chin, but also because they were

overly prepared for the lecture. Carmen, for example, had covered her desk with everything she could even *think* she may have needed for class. Along with a notebook placed in the center, she had a pencil and two backups, a highlighter, a spare eraser, and a pencil sharpener placed on her right-hand side. On her left-hand side, she had hand sanitizer, a pack of tissues, Chapstick, and a small bottle of baby lotion, in case her hands got dry from all the notes she planned to write. Even with all that, she was steadily searching her backpack for something else.

January couldn't judge. Though only an iPad and Apple pencil was on her desk, her bag had everything that Carmen had come equipped with, along with a couple back-up chargers for her iPad, a backup iPad, Post-It notes, flashcards, and a mini first-aid kit.

Yes, she was most definitely a nerd, but she hid her nerd tendencies well.

She was a nerd with finesse.

"In about a month or so, your innocence will be shattered, and many of you will start to believe that you can arrive to class late. Some of you may decide to not even arrive at all," Ms. Bee continued. "For that reason, attendance is mandatory."

A collective, shared groan sounded off around the room, most of the despair coming from the students around where January sat in the back. Ms. Bee narrowed her eyes, settling her attention to the rear of the room.

"Ah. So, the few athletes who bothered to show up earlier than the customary 'fifteen minutes late' don't like the attendance requirement. What a surprise!" Ms. Bee faked her astonishment with pure sarcasm oozing from her tone as she stared pointedly at the group of guys who January would've been correct in assuming were athletes.

"There is a project for this class that requires me to have an accurate count of who signs up and attends. As you know, the name of this class is *Self & Society* and you will learn about this subject through our lectures as well as direct field experience," she explained, allowing her gaze to drift around the room as she spoke to them all. January's eyes widened and she sat totally still, soaking up every word that fell from her professor's lips. She was so excited already and she'd barely had a chance to fully explain.

"You will complete a class project as a major percentage of your grade for this course. Think of it as a case study, if you will. You will be assigned a partner and your job is to seek out to experience important aspects of their life, which are totally different from yours. This could be a religious, cultural, or economical difference, or even a difference in hobbies or individual passions. You are to find some major quality that separates your life experience from theirs and then dive headfirst into it. If you're a hardcore Republican, you could attend a Black Lives Matter rally. If you're heterosexual, you might choose to join in on the parade during Pride Week. The point is that you must *fully* immerse yourself in the experience by being an active participant in a major way. It's not enough to simply be a passive observer of what is happening around you. You must completely dive in, seek to fully understand whether you agree with the viewpoint or not, and then offer your full support for that contrasting view in some way. In doing this, you will not only discover things about society that you never knew before, but you'll also learn a lot about yourself."

It took every bit of effort January could muster to stop from jumping up for joy. Her energy was on a million. It was all she could do to stay in her seat and nearly impossible for her to sit still.

This.

Is.

Fucking.

Amazing.

She said the words over and over inside her mind like a chant.

All her life she'd daydreamed about what it would be like to experi-ence a life outside of her own. To plunge into another reality to see who she would be and how she'd feel if she ever had the chance to choose for herself. And now she was being assigned that exact opportunity. It was like the Universe was conspiring to please her. In her mind, that was *literally* the only plausible explanation. Prayers were finally answered. Her #1 dream was being manifested into her reality.

"That brings me back to my attendance requirement," Ms. Bee continued, focusing back on the guys at the back. "In order to give your all, you need to learn the tactics that you'll apply outside of class for the project. You'll need to be present for every lecture. If you can't commit to that, you might as well leave now. There is no point in faking through the rest of our two hours together in order to not appear rude."

Pausing, she lifted a single brow, staring with question at the guys in the back. January followed her gaze, with bated breath, wondering what they would choose to do. This moment was so intense for not only her but seemingly for many others in the class. In high school, you didn't have these options. They were *grown* grown now.

Finally, one of the guys shrugged before standing up and walking straight out the double door exit. Two of his friends followed quickly behind him. One gave a quick salute to Ms. Bee before letting the door close behind him. January rolled her eyes at the disrespect.

"Anyone else?" Ms. Bee paused and took a moment to look around.

The room remained silent. No one moved nor said a thing.

"Alright, then let's begin with attendance."

January wiggled in her seat and then reached up, running her hand over her hairline to smooth down her edges, suddenly feeling antsy. Why? She didn't know, but an unsettling feeling had come over her. All of her senses were on edge and the fine hairs on the back of her neck were standing on end. For her, that was an omen that something was about to happen. She wasn't the typical girl who might have ignored things like that. To her, *everything* was a sign.

Swallowing a bitter taste forming in the back of her throat, she looked down at the screen of her phone for no other reason than to ease her discomfort. Her eyes washed over the screen, settling in on the time.

It was 11:11. From there, her eyes leveled on the notifications for her email. She had 1,111 unread emails.

Whoa. Synchronicity. *Again.*

The fact that this had happened twice in a row meant something *big* was about to happen.

January was extremely superstitious. It was a trait that came directly to her from her father. He had superstitions about some of the craziest things, and he believed in them the same way people believed that oxygen was necessary for life.

Crazy enough, his superstitions were never proven wrong. He had a theory about women riding in the front seat of a man's new car. It was a theory specific for their family alone. He always said that whichever woman was the first to ride in the front seat of a Murray man's new ride ended up being the one he got pregnant.

According to him, Janelle was the first woman to ever sit in his front seat—she forced him, is what he claims—but he said that was the moment he accepted that she was the one he would marry and have kids with. It all was proven correct when Janelle came up pregnant with January.

Superstitions were an essential part of the mafia lifestyle. Most things she initially thought were just normal traditions were rooted in superstition. Every Sunday, Outlaw made a point of spending the entire day with their family. It wasn't until she overheard her uncles speaking amongst themselves about some friend of theirs that January understood why.

It was against *BBM* rules to do any business on Sundays unless it couldn't wait. If debts had to be collected, none would be collected on Sundays. If it was decided that someone had to die, they would have to stay alive until Monday.

For them, Sundays were holy. Like the super-religious, they dedicated every Sunday to God. But unlike the super-religious, they didn't believe that God was some ghostly white man in the sky, regarding them all like pawns He'd created in an entertaining game of right and wrong. The essence of the Creator was in *everyone*, but the most cherished representation of God was in your family. And God was jealous about quality time. The ones you loved had to be highest priority in life. If you didn't honor your family with your time, attention, and affection while they were around, you would grieve over your mistakes once they were taken away by way of one of the three Ds: death, divorce or distance.

Before January could do a quick internet search on the synchronicity and meaning behind seeing 11:11 twice in the same moment, the double doors to the lecture hall flung open. Natural light seeped into the room and she felt her body suddenly warmed by the sun, which was pointed directly at her. With a resounding creak that made her spine tingle, the door whined as it came to a close, and she tore her attention away from her phone, feeling the urge to look up.

And the second that she did, her heart just about stopped, and her blood nearly froze in her veins.

With brooding, smoldering eyes tucked under hooded lids, a familiar face scanned over the room with a slight scowl, seeming much too pissed off for so early in the morning.

Oh. My. God. It's him!

Turning to face the front, January shrank down in her seat, wishing that she'd been the one reading about quantum physics that day in the store. Maybe then she'd know how to flatten her body into two dimensions and become one with the floor.

Unable to resist the urge of her curious nature, she slowly peered out of the side of her eyes to make sure his head wasn't pointed in her direction before taking the chance to glance back at him. Her body went warm once again, but this time it didn't have a single thing to do with the sun. Her cheeks prickled with embarrassment as she came to terms with her feelings of attraction.

This nigga right here *everything*.

He didn't fit her typical type of man in any way. But even with his arms covered in tattoos and gold jewelry in his ears, wrists, and wrapped around his neck, he was magnificent to look at.

"Well, hello, and thank you for finally joining us," Ms. Bee greeted from the front. "You can find a seat once you tell me your name. I want to add that attendance is mandatory for this class, so if you intend on staying, and being present for every lecture, feel free to find a seat. If not, there is no harm in leaving."

He paused, as if weighing her words, and January turned away, dropping her attention down to her desk. She felt on edge as she waited to see what he would do, whether he'd walk right back out like the other guys had done. What she didn't understand was why she cared and why she felt like if he left, she'd be disappointed. Based on their run-in at the bookstore, she should've *wanted* him to leave. God knows the last thing she wanted was to be forced into reliving that moment again.

He isn't that *fine.*

With a neck sporting three icy, Cuban-link chains, a single diamond stud earring in each ear, and sneakers that probably cost more than the chains combined, he had the aura of a rapper. The ones who were every teenage girl's celebrity crush and usually had 'lil' in front of their name. In fact, January could see many of the other freshmen girls in the class nearly salivating over him already. Even Carmen. She wasn't surprised in the least. It was a well-known fact that good girls couldn't resist that type of guy—not a rapper; a 'dangerous' man. And this one right here appeared to be the full embodiment of that.

The *ultimate* bad boy.

Falling victim to her desire yet again, she looked back just in time to see him nod and then open his mouth to moisten the sexiest lips that she'd ever seen with his tongue. Moisture built up between her legs and she shuddered, squeezing her thighs together.

Okay… maybe he *was* that fine.

He looked oddly familiar… and not just because of the bookstore. But she couldn't place where she may have known him from. He had a subtle sex appeal that almost seemed accidental in a way. It oozed from every part of him in a way that didn't seem intentional but was even more alluring because of that simple fact.

Struggling to compose herself, January had to turn away again. The intensity of it all was getting to her.

What is wrong with me? she thought.

She'd never been the kind of girl who was crazy about guys like that. Rappers, rockstars and the young boyish celebrities that most girls loved did nothing for her. Thanks to her parents, almost every one that girls gushed about, she'd met personally. Most of them had made-up personalities curated through expert branding. January liked her men low-key. Maybe a Kendrick Lamar or J. Cole as far as rappers went. So why did she feel like a silly thirteen-year-old girl over this flashy 'what's his face'?

"My name is King Dumas," she heard him say to Professor Bee. The deep and gritty tenor of his voice sent waves through her gut.

Scrunching her nose, she stared down at her iPad's black screen.

King Dumas? The name didn't seem familiar.

"Ah, I see you right here. Thank you. Find a seat where you'd like," Ms. Bee continued, looking at her attendance sheet before turning back to address the class. "Okay, everyone, I'm going to pass a few papers around to explain the requirements of your assignment. Pay attention as I go over it all with you. This project is 70% of your total grade."

January tried her hardest to focus on what Ms. Bee was talking about, but it was damn near impossible because her body was reacting to something else—another presence moving not far from her. In fact, she could sense that it was moving closer. The fine hairs on the back of her neck seemed to stretch to max capacity when she realized that he was coming her way. She was both horrified and delighted by the thought. Out of the corner of her eye, she could see him turn onto the row behind her and, although she was mentally praying for it not to happen, her prayers were unanswered when he settled right into the seat behind her.

Her nerves flared. Of all seats, that's the one he chose. The one *right* behind her.

A peculiar feeling swirled in her stomach as her entire body became more aware of his proximity to her. It was like every nerve ending in her body was coming alive. Instantly, she regretted not following her father's rules to the letter and positioning herself where no one could sit behind her. To have some random guy she'd found herself oddly attracted to sitting directly behind where she couldn't see a thing, made her feel vulnerable in some way.

"Okay, so my awesome teacher's assistant, Sonya—Sonya, stand and wave to the class." Ms. Bee paused as Sonya stood to deliver a small curtsy. "Sonya will be assigning the partners for your project. The assignments will be posted at the end of class. Until then, I want to take a few moments to allow everyone to create a list of the things you believe. The things that make you the person you are with the values, goals, and moral codes that you've set for yourself. If you're religious, put that down. Any and everything that makes you who you are, and defines your core beliefs, write it down. It'll be from this list that you'll begin to plan the activities your partner will accompany you on."

January snapped to attention, the nerd in her instantly forgetting all about the guy behind her and whatever attraction she thought she had. She was so *hype* about this project—her first as a college student. And it was about a topic so close to her heart.

Until that one day years ago at the park, she thought she knew exactly who she was and who she wanted to be. But when that all changed, she felt like she'd lost her identity. She loved dance, but there was something about being so close to having your life taken from you that made you want to rethink your choices. She wanted to do something meaningful. She wanted to give back. She wanted to separate herself from the dangerous lifestyle that her parents had created for her.

She would always yearn to dance, but she felt the need to prove herself, to make her mark in the world in a different way. She wanted to prove that she wasn't a bad person, even if her family did bad things.

Scribbling out her list as fast as her hand would allow it, January couldn't wait to get started on this project. She couldn't wait to find out who her partner would be. Deep down, she knew that this project would change the entire direction of her life. She could *feel* it.

I am going to love *this class.*

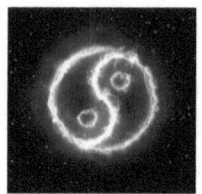

KING LEGEND DUMAS.

I AM GOING TO HATE THIS CLASS.

"Hello? Do you hear me?"

Reaching out, January jabbed the massive waste of space sprawled across the desk in front of where she stood. As fate would have it, the object of her private daytime fantasies ended up being assigned as her partner.

Initially seeing that they were paired sent a ripple of nervous energy through her. She'd always been a fan of romance novels, and this seemed like the perfect intro to one:

Girl sees boy in bookstore.

Girl mistakes boy for an undercover mafia bodyguard.

Boy and girl have same class.

Boy and girl become partners in class.

Boy and girl fall in love and *live happily ever after.*

Unfortunately, this was real life. And real life was *nothing* like a romance novel.

When Ms. Bee asked everyone to meet with their partners to exchange contact information and decide on a time to meet outside of class, she was both nervous and excited, but it was quickly replaced when she found her partner slumped over on top of his desk, headphones over his ears, hoodie pulled over top of him and arms pooled around his head, tucked comfortably in the center. He seemed to not have a care in the world and definitely wasn't bothered at all about the class or the project.

Just my luck, she thought, rolling her eyes.

It was the best project ever—better than anything she could have thought up herself—and she was matched with the one person in the room who didn't give a damn.

Reaching out, January poked him once more in the shoulder, this time much harder, and then stood back to wait. Slowly, he raised his head and peered up at her, his brows bent into a low frown. Standing to one side with her arms crossed in front of her chest, she glared down at him as he scowled up at her before finally pulling the headphones from his ears.

"What do you want?" Legend barked, rudely. The right edge of his lips curled up slightly as he eyed her over.

"Sorry for interrupting your nap." January didn't bother trying to hide her annoyance. "But we are partners for the class project." Leaning over, she picked up his copy of the information sheet that the professor had passed out to everyone and placed it just about under his chin. "It's 70% of our grade so we have to get started on it."

Snatching the paper from her hand, Legend frowned down at it for a few seconds before folding it up and stuffing it inside his backpack.

"Yeah, okay. Just put your number in my phone and we can talk about it later," he said. Before she could object, he shoved his phone towards her.

January's frown deepened as she felt her body begin to go warm. It was insane how quickly she went from being turned on to completely turned off.

To her, it was clear that he was the type of guy who was used to the world kissing his ass, giving him no need for manners. And though she'd grown up with the world kissing hers, she never let it affect the way in which she dealt with the world. She treated everyone with respect. But this nigga here? He thought it was perfectly okay to go around treating people like shit. His attitude was *disgusting*.

There is no way this is going to work, she thought, with a shake of her head.

Turning around, January was about a second away from requesting a different partner, but that option faded when she saw that Ms. Bee had already left the room. She was stuck. At least for now. There was always the option to track her down during her office hours, fall to the floor and grovel at her feet until Ms. Bee matched her with someone else.

"You gonna put your number in the phone or not?"

Her attention snapped back to the rude ass in front of her, pointing his phone out towards her chest. He felt familiar to her in a way that she couldn't explain but pushing past the current level of disgust she felt in order to figure out why seemed impossible at the moment. And, even if she *could* push past that, she'd have to somehow see through the perpetual scowl that only deepened the more that he looked at her. It was unsettling. Unnerving the way that he glared at her like she wasn't worth the effort.

In the dark recesses of her mind, somewhere past the consistent nagging urging her to give him her ass to kiss and find a new partner, she felt in a way that he might make the perfect one. There was no way they could have anything in common. If she was going to have an experience completely different from her normal with anyone in the class, it would be with him.

But working together would mean that they'd have to actually get along, and that was something that would require divine intervention. As it was, they'd only been in contact twice for about five minutes each time and the thought of being around him any more than that made her skin crawl. There was no way that they could be partners. She'd just have to beg Ms. Bee for another one.

"Listen, King. I don't think that it's a good idea for——"

"It's Legend," he corrected her with a grumble that sounded more like a bestial growl than actual intelligible words.

Legend?

January's heart skipped a beat in her chest. There was something so familiar about that name, but she couldn't place it just yet. As if going through a rolodex of memories, she mentally searched for the one that would make sense of what she was feeling in that moment.

The chatter of the students around them seemed to fade. Her shoulders tightened as a sharp jolt of an intense emotion tightened her chest and her mouth went dry. She couldn't understand the reaction; it was like her body knew a secret that her mind had yet to discover. She wanted to know what it was but every time she searched her mind, all she came up with was a blank.

It had taken many therapy sessions for January to get over the trauma that came after her first near-death experience. The damage to her body was easily seen, but the damage to her mind, not so much. It had taken every bit of her mental strength and determination to move forward in a healthy way, and the only way she'd been able to do that was to ignore the pain. She had to repress it—completely forget.

Once it became clear to her that forgetting that day was necessary in order to heal and move on, her mind cooperated with ease. Before long, she was able to tuck the final moments surrounding that painful, tragic incident deep down within her subconscious and pretend it didn't exist. The sweet memories of the boy that she'd met had been a casualty of her need to recover and soon, she was able to forget that he'd ever existed, too.

It took a while but eventually, over the years, she forgot his face, the way it felt being in his presence, the way he smelled and the intensity of how he made her feel—like no one on Earth had ever done before and hadn't been able to since. It had taken months of meditating and covering up her memories of that day by making new ones, months of allowing other experiences to take her time. She didn't want to, but she had to in order to save herself. Because every time she thought of him, she had to consider what came after. She had to think about how that one moment in time had completely ruined her life. The high he gave her was followed by her ultimate low.

"Legend," she repeated, swallowing hard.

There was aa sour taste in the back of her throat and no matter how much she tried to force it back, it returned. "Aye… are you okay?" she heard Legend say.

With her eyes still closed, January expelled a long breath through her lips, rubbing the deep scar outside her thigh that had begun to ache.

It had taken only a few months to fully heal the gunshot wound in her leg. Much longer to heal the feeling of despair, guilt and loss that had accompanied it. The one decision that she'd made for herself had been the decision that killed her dreams in an instant. She'd spent so much of her life wanting to be normal, just like the other kids, not locked up in her luxurious estate living the infamous life of a mafia princess. They say be careful what you wish for and she knew more than anyone how true that saying was, no matter who the 'they' was that said it. Now she was normal. She'd never dance again. She had no talent; there was nothing special at all about her. The person who had shot her made sure of that.

"Do—do we know each other?"

It wasn't a question that she'd planned to ask but there it was, falling off the edge of her lips anyways. She sucked her lips into her mouth, biting on them, wishing that she could take the words back.

She considered that maybe he hadn't heard her, but the moment he looked up, narrowing his eyes into a hard squint as he scrutinized her face, it was clear that he had.

"When I saw you at the bookstore, I was thinking that you looked kind of familiar." Legend cocked his head to the side, still observing her. Then a hint of a smile crossed his face. "Hold on a minute, did we ever…"

His words trailed off but the suggestion that followed showed clearly in his eyes. Instantly, January's ghostly feelings were replaced once again with utter disgust.

"Ew, no!" She snapped, wrinkling her nose at the thought. "We have *never* slept together, I can promise you that. Wait… are you telling me that you've slept with so many women, you don't remember who you've been with?"

He didn't answer but the satisfied smirk that curled her lips told her everything she needed to know. January scoffed, shaking her head to push away the feeling that there was more about him that she needed to know. She knew enough.

Folding his brows back into the glare that was the permanent expression for his face, Legend sat back, once again observing the woman standing before him from head to toe. He knew her alright. There was no way that he could forget her, even though it had been so long. However, he didn't want to unearth the past. It was clear that she'd forgotten that day, had no idea at all who he was, and it needed to stay that way for a lot of reasons. For one, he had seen how just the mention of his name had affected her. He'd watched her rubbing her scar, seen the pain flickering through her eyes. Her knees had seemed to go weak and he had prepared himself to catch her if she were to faint. Somehow the mere mention of his name had undone a part of her healing and he didn't want to unravel the rest.

And then there was the issue with Outlaw. Though the high-level members of *BBM* knew that he had nothing to do with January being shot, to everyone else, he was public enemy #1: the man who had betrayed the king and tried to murder the princess. To the world, he was just as guilty whether or not he'd fired the bullet from his own gun. And Outlaw never spoke a word to quiet the rumors because he'd made it clear that if Legend ever came near January again, he would punish him as if the rumors were true.

"Nah," he said, shaking his head to answer her initial question. "We don't know each other, princess."

January flinched slightly. Something about him using the same name her father gave her when she was only a child felt wrong. Like he was muddying up a precious memory.

"My name is January," she firmly corrected him. Though not loud, her voice seemed to echo throughout the room.

Legend chuckled. "Noted."

She took a moment to look around them and realized that the room was completely empty. Everyone had left and they were all alone. She checked the time and realized she only had about fifteen minutes to find her next class.

"Well, I have to get to my next class," January said, shifting her weight back and forth in her sneakers, feeling uneasy all of a sudden.

Turning she began to walk away, heading behind Legend towards the double doors. The atmosphere in the room suddenly felt thick and she felt the need to bring fresh air into her lungs. Once she got to the exit, she placed her hand on the knob to leave but remembered there was something else she needed to say.

With her back turned, she spoke while forcing herself not to meet his eyes.

"I don't know if it's a good idea for us to be partners. It's obvious that we have an issue connecting. I guess I can ask Ms. Bee if she can reassign us," she said with a shrug.

"Your choice, princess."

January gasped when she felt his breath on the nape of her neck. He was *right* behind her. She could feel the warmth of his presence without even seeing him. He moved without even making a sound. Snuck up right behind her with the expertise of a trained hitta, with silenced steps undetectable to the untrained ear.

A trait that she'd only picked up on when it came to her father's expertly trained soldiers.

Whipping around, she turned to face him and nearly loss her breath when she saw how close he actually was. Their noses were nearly touching. The electricity of attraction sparked the blood in her veins, making her feel high as she absorbed his scent, losing herself for just a few seconds until she asked herself the question that she may have seemed trivial to the average person but could be the key to everything when it came to her.

How *did* he get there so fast?

"I didn't even hear you walk up behind me."

Legend heard what she said but he also heard what she hadn't said. There was an accusation hidden in her comment that she was waiting for him to affirm.

"I'm a light walker," he replied, toying with her in way that he might later regret. But at the moment, he didn't care to think about it. He wasn't used to playing it safe when it came to anything in his life and his craving for all things dangerous only intensified when it came to her. She was something he would desire anyways, but the fact that he couldn't have her— *shouldn't* have her—made him want her even more.

And that's why you got to pull away and distance yourself from her. Being around her makes you act reckless.

Two voices spoke daily into his mind: one reasonable and one reckless. One an angel, the other a demon. Legend sided with the demon every time.

"A light walker, huh?" The squint in January's eyes revealed her true thoughts. "That's an interesting skill for a *college* student. How does a *college* student learn to move around like that? I mean…" She paused to tiptoe on the old wooden floors beneath them, illustrating how even the most subtle and careful steps set off a chorus of creaks and whines from the floorboards. "… you'd have to be a *really* light, or expertly trained, walker to avoid making a sound on these. From my experience, being able to move around undetected is an asset for maybe the military, CIA, FBI… you know, *dangerous* men." She pretend-shuddered, shaking her shoulders sarcastically.

Her final words sent off a jolt of electricity through Legend's body, bringing to his mind a statement that he'd said to her many years before.

"If you're asking if I'm a dangerous man, the answer is yes. I'm the boogeyman."

At the time, he'd been joking. He was talking shit—or so he thought. What he didn't know was that he had actually been speaking a prophecy. He didn't know that, in only a few minutes, that statement was about to come true, and that organization he'd promised his life to full of people he regarded as family, would turn their backs on him. The word would go out declaring him as the most dangerous man. January's attempted murdered. Her personal boogeyman.

Taking a few steps back, this time Legend was the one to retreat. He needed to distance himself in order to fall back into his senses. The scent of her was like kryptonite to his brain, making him temporarily go dumb. He had to remember his place.

Right before January's eyes, Legend became a Transformer. His entire countenance began to change. He retreated back into the cold aura that enveloped him before, tucking away his human side to become a creature only a mother could love. He gave her a hard stare, full of irritation, like he was pissed off that he even had to waste time looking at her. Like he'd have more excitement watching paint dry. Or a snail trying to roll up a hill.

"Something must be fucked up in your head because I told you this shit before." His lips twisted as he spoke to her under smoldering eyes. "Whatever you think you know about me, is wrong."

That said, he pushed by her, nearly taking off January's shoulder with the force at which he bolted through the door. Had she not had such extensive training in dance, though that life seemed so long ago, she might have lost her balance.

It fucked Legend up inside that he had to treat her that way, but it was necessary in order to make sure that she would stay at arm's length. Further than arm's length, was preferred. He didn't trust himself to remain in control if she came too close so his only choice was to push her to the point where she would stay far away.

He had to make her *hate* him. He had to make it so that he had no other options than to stay out of her life. It was the only way. And it had little to do with saving his own life. He didn't fear death; in fact, many times he welcomed it. But he had respect for Outlaw and his wishes. He saw him as a father, and he knew Outlaw saw him as a son. He didn't want to take actions that would lead to Outlaw being forced to have him killed.

The thought of pushing her away when he wanted the opposite was devastating for a short moment, but January had been raised to adapt quickly when it came to the people in her life. She'd learned not to get too attached to anything or anyone. When it came to the mafia life, no one's presence was permanent because if they made one wrong move, Outlaw would end their entire existence. Even when it came to her bodyguards, she'd learned early on not to grow too attached to the men charged with watching her. She wanted to consider them family, pretend they were her uncles, but too often they'd been inexplicably replaced for the simplest mistakes. Over time she realized that the payment for these mistakes was their lives. January eventually learned that when it came to people, the best form of protection from the grief of losing them was to avoid becoming too attached.

Which Legend knew she would do to protect herself from him. She'd avoid becoming too attached.

We aren't the same people anymore, he thought as he walked away from her. *We are living different lives than what we had before.*

There was no substitute for the truth. He wasn't the same boy from back then and she wasn't the same girl. They both survived a life-changing experience that day, set in place by the motion of a bullet, and the outcomes were different but also very much the same.

Their lives had been completely altered in every way. They were wounded by trauma, destroyed by dreams left unfulfilled and changed by conquests left unconquered. They would never be the same again. Any love that could have been born out of their past moments together were now only another casualty of a bitter tragedy.

A CLUMSY, RUDE ASS TODDLER.

Holding her cellphone out in front of her, January pulled her legs up onto the brand-new leather sofa that had been delivered to her dorm. Digging her toes firmly into the cushions, she waited impatiently for her mother to pick up. With each ring, she ran through the way that she was going to approach the reason for the call, but the second that she heard Janelle's voice on the other line, all of her prior preparation went right down the drain.

"It's about time you called! How was the first week of school?"

"Mama, did daddy hire someone to watch me?"

The question rolled right off her lips before she really even knew it. Though she'd planned to start with a much less aggressive approach, feeling that it was the best way to get to the bottom of things, it wasn't in her nature to beat around her bush. It wasn't how either of her parents were and, in that way, she was definitely their child.

"January, he wouldn't do that. You made him promise not to and you know he never breaks a promise."

He doesn't break a promise unless he feels an exception has to be made in order to fulfill one of his rules, January silently combatted, rolling her eyes.

She'd gotten a response to her question but, somehow, she still wasn't convinced. The only way to get to the bottom of this was to go directly to the source.

"Where is he? Can I speak to him?"

"He's not here. He left about an hour ago with your Uncle Cree and he said that they would be out late… handling some things."

The tone her mother used for the last few words told her everything she didn't want to know. In her lifetime, there had been plenty moments when her father had to 'handle some things' and it was never anything good. He'd left to 'handle some things' the day after she'd gotten shot at the park and didn't return home until three days later.

While in the hospital, she vividly remembered watching news reports of brutal killings, rumored to be gang-related and in retaliation of some unknown crime. The word 'brutal' could barely describe the carnage that took place in those days.

Three men were found hanging from three different traffic lights in the neighborhood where they stayed. Their bodies were bloodied, beaten nearly to a pulp and dismembered. The skin on their faces hung in an unnatural way that could only be accomplished by having every tooth removed from their mouths and their jaws broken into two.

Though the police tried to have the bodies removed quickly, their bodies were so severely mutilated that it was extremely difficult to do without pieces of their skin falling to the street below. Whoever had killed them made sure that, even in death, the gruesomeness of it all would be a constant reminder to anyone and everyone that you didn't want to end up like them. Whoever had killed them was a monster.

There wasn't a single person in the city who didn't know what the killings were in retaliation for and it was unspoken but common knowledge that Outlaw was behind it. However, with the media, the local government along with its key officials and the police force on his side, there wasn't a single thing that could be done against him. Other than reporting on the murders to deter any others from being bold enough to challenge him, there was very little else said. He had made it clear many years prior by use of other acts such as this one, that it wasn't wise to get on his bad side.

There was a dark side to her father that January had never seen and never wanted to. It was hard for her to imagine that he could be responsible for doing some of the things that she'd heard he'd done. It wasn't until after that day at the park that she cared to even think of it or to look into Outlaw's past. She knew that her family was special in some way that required them to be protected but she never understood why. In her mind, it was just because they were very rich and because her father was a businessman, and her mother held a top position in politics. She had no knowledge of the *Black Bag Mafia* or Outlaw's criminal past. She didn't know how they'd earned their money in the beginning or the actions currently required to maintain it.

As she sat in the hospital nursing both her physical and emotional wounds, she began to dig around for the first time and that's when she learned why people referred to her father as the Outlaw. Reading everything written by several journalist, reputable ones at that, opened her eyes to a dark side of his life that she wished she'd never stumbled upon. Sure, each article held the disclaimer that what they were reporting were only 'rumors' but she knew better. Disclaimers were only to protect the storyteller from being harmed for sharing something that was definitely true.

It was during that time when January realized that no matter how much she loved her family, she had to leave and go on her own way. She didn't want any ties to any criminal organization. Her mother's way of dealing with the fact that she was a Federal judge married to a man with little disregard for the law outside of the one he made for himself, was that the good things he did outweighed the bad. It was why she covered for him, stood by his side and looked the other way when she knew that he was responsible for things that any other person could be locked up for life for.

For January, the good didn't outweigh the bad and she would never choose that life for herself. She didn't want a bad boy. She knew that she could never make the decision to marry a dangerous man.

"I have a project for my sociology class," she began, wanting to tell her mother about Legend in some round-a-bout way. "We were matched with a partner. We are supposed to find out something about their life that's completely different from ours and experience it for ourselves."

"Really? That sounds fun. Did you get a good match?"

Pausing for a moment, she thought about her mother's question.

"Technically speaking, yes," she admitted begrudgingly. "He's completely different from me in every way. Rude, arrogant, thinks he knows everything…"

Janelle chuckled. "Sounds a lot like your father."

"He's *nothing* like dad."

"Well, if the point is for the two of you to be different, then this should be a great project for you. But… I'm guessing your professor probably means 'different' as in lifestyle, not personality."

"Trust me, mama. He's different from me in *every* way. Designer clothes, expensive shoes, gold chains, gold bracelets, Rolex watches, gold rings. Gold *everything.* Soooo flashy and materialistic. It's ridiculous." January scoffed, rolling her eyes as she thought about it.

Listening to her, Janelle couldn't help but laugh again. "Gold everything? Are you *sure* we aren't talking about your father? It's so funny listening to you… You remind me of someone I know describing a man she met and eventually fell in love with."

Janelle was speaking of herself, thinking of the day she'd met Outlaw and immediately described his full gold grill as a 'yuck mouth'. Her reaction to him that day mirrored her daughter's reaction to her partner.

"We can't even talk without arguing," January complained. "How are we supposed to do an entire project together?"

"Through patience and understanding. That was the only way I was able to get to know your dad. And I'm glad I did."

"And still there are some things about dad that you don't understand. He does things that you, as a judge, can't possibly agree with. How can you love someone who sees the world so differently from you?" January asked, reviving a topic that she'd battled with her mother about since she was a child. How could she, a Federal judge, be married to a man whose entire life is a contrast to every one of her fundamental beliefs? It made *no* sense.

"Because I know that your dad has a good heart," Janelle replied with honesty. "People go about doing things in different ways. They show their love and support for others in ways that are specific to their upbringing. You and I were raised based on love. Your father was raised on survival. You'll never fully agree the way that he does things, but his intentions are good, so you should understand that and accept him for who he is. Same as you should do with this partner of yours." she added the last part assuming that her daughter's partner was more like Outlaw than January cared to admit.

"I don't think I'll *ever* be able to do with him what you've been able to do with dad."

"Well, if it bothers you *that* much, why don't you try asking your professor for a new partner?"

She laughed and January shook her head, releasing a smile in spite of it all. She knew there was no point in arguing the point further. Her mother didn't see things the way she did. She would always take her father's side. Janelle said that was what love was—always having the back of the other person no matter what.

January paused, thinking about that. Could she see herself being with Legend in that way? Was there a chance that she could have his back and love him no matter what?

And then, as if she'd called his name, Legend's face appeared in her mind's eye and she found herself thinking about him. He was just as different to her as her father was to her mother. Her parents were complete and utter opposites but still they found a way to make the love work.

Could I do that with him?

Just as quickly as the thought occurred to her, she shook her head and forced it away. Not only was it ridiculous to even think about something like that with someone she barely knew, but it was also obvious that Legend wasn't interested in her in the least.

And even if he was, she wanted *nothing* to do with him. Not only was he rude, but he was careless and a complete bum when it came to any of his classes. If anything could make her write a nigga off, it was that. She couldn't see herself with someone who didn't care about school, learning or his grades. Even with all the things her dad had done, he still was college-educated. With all the street running he was doing, he managed to get a bachelor's in computer engineering and a master's in information technology.

Legend on the other hand? School didn't seem to interest him in the *least*.

After seeing him in her first class, January also found him in her second class, third class and, by some stroke of bad luck, he happened to be enrolled right across the hall from her fourth class. It was too much to be a mere coincidence and with each class, she suspected that her father had involved himself in her life once more.

However, by the end of the day, it was clear that if Legend had been hired to watch anyone, he was failing miserably. Not only did he sit dead center in each of the classes outside of the first one, completely unaware of anyone walking in or anything happening behind him, he wore headphones over his ears and sat with his head buried under the hood of his sweater, totally oblivious to the world around him.

The stealthy, light way he'd walked after their first class seemed to be a fluke on January's part because ever since then, she'd observed him clobbering around like a clumsy toddler. In fact, she distinctly remembered thinking to herself how true the description was. Legend was, in so many ways, a clumsy, rude ass toddler. He thought the world revolved around his big head.

Then, as if he hadn't shown his clear disdain for school enough already, on the second day of class, he came in with red-rimmed, glassy eyes—an obvious sign of a hangover. A closer look revealed the faint hint of glossy, red lips on his neck which made January roll her eyes with disgust.

Probably came straight from some random girl's bed and rolled his dirty ass right into class, she had thought, feeling a hint of jealousy that she couldn't explain. *It's quite obvious what kind of experience he really came to college for.*

"Mama, I have to go. My roommate is supposed to arrive today. I have to get the place… ready."

It was a half-truth. She did have a roommate on the way but there was nothing wrong with their place. However, thinking about Legend had put a sour taste in her mouth and she now had something in mind that she needed to do.

"I hope you end up with a great one," Janelle said as the call was about to end. "My first roommate was…not the greatest experience. But anyways, I think you should try to stick with your partner for the class project. I have a strong feeling that you can learn a lot from him. And him from you."

January snorted her disdain and rolled her eyes after ending the call.

There is absolutely no chance in hell of me learning anything from Legend.

DESTINY'S CHILDREN.

EYES CLOSED, JANUARY TOOK A DEEP BREATH TO GATHER HER
nerves, calming them as much as she could before raising her fist to
knock on Ms. Bee's office door. She hadn't made an appointment
but after stewing for a few days with the idea of keeping Legend as
her partner, the conversation with her mother made her realize
there was no way she could do it. Beyond him being unlikable in
every way, he was lazy, and she couldn't risk compromising her
grades by dealing with a partner who couldn't care less.

"Come in."

Once she heard Ms. Bee's voice welcome her from the other side,
she twisted the knob and opened the door to walk inside the office
that appeared to be a shrine to Beyoncé. Posters of the singer was
all over the walls alongside what appeared to be autographed
albums enclosed in expensive glass cases. She had the cover of every
one of Beyonce's albums, even back to her Destiny's Child days, in
small frames that made up a photo collage right above where she sat
at her desk with her hands folded together on top of her desk.

"How can I help you?"

"H—Hi, Ms. Bee. I'm January. I'm in your *Self & Society* class—"

"Yes, I know who you are, January," Ms. Bee interrupted and then nodded her head towards the front of her desk. "Take a seat. I've been waiting for you."

Wrinkling her brows, January frowned into her confusion, wondering what Ms. Bee was talking about. She hadn't made an appointment or emailed her about meeting with her, and she'd only just decided for certain that she wanted to change partners.

"I see you're confused so I'm guessing you haven't gotten a chance to speak to Legend yet," Ms. Bee continued with a smile. "I'm going to tell you the same thing I told him when he came in here asking for a different partner: the answer is no."

Stunned, January's mind hadn't even had the chance to process the fact that Ms. Bee had told her 'no' before she'd gotten the chance to ask her question. She was still stuck on the first thing she'd said.

Legend came in here before me?

Something about the fact that he had beat her in asking for a new partner bothered her. It was offensive. She had a lot of reasons to want a different partner, but she'd given him absolutely none. *She* wasn't the one sleeping in class, *she* wasn't the one acting like a pure asshole, *she* wasn't the one who seemed to hate him simply because he was still breathing. She was a good person and a model student in all of her classes. Anyone would be lucky to have her for a partner. Especially someone like him.

"I know it wasn't what you wanted to hear but I think the fact that the two of you seem to have such strong dislike for each other—strong enough that you can't put your simple differences aside to complete a project that is a major part of your grade—tells me that you'd benefit the most from this experiment."

Fluttering her eyes as she fought to find words, January couldn't let go without putting up a protest.

"But, Ms. Bee, it's not only about our differences or dislike for each other," she began, pleading. "I know you've seen the way that he sleeps through your entire class. We have three other classes together and he does the same thing in *all* of them. He doesn't care about college at all but being here is *very* important to me. I take my grades seriously and I can't depend on him as a partner when this project, as you mentioned, is a major part of our grade."

Instead of answering right away, Ms. Bee leaned back in her seat, placing her hands on top of her head with her fingers laced together and palms down. She twirled on the wheels of her chair, rolling her eyes over the many posters and other memorabilia on her wall.

"Whenever I've heard a student make a case to me about how someone else's behavior or attitude could affect the outcome of their grade, I find myself thinking of Beyoncé."

January felt the edges of her lips tug downward as she suppressed a groan that was working its way up from inside. She loved Queen Bey just as much as anyone else, but this was *not* the time to be discussing her. She already had her husband, her children *and* her billions. She had the life of her dreams and everyone else's, too. January's only concern was fighting for hers.

"In an interview, back when she was in Destiny's Child, both Michelle and Kelly were discussing Beyoncé's work ethic. Both singers credited her dedication to perfection as the driving force behind how they were able to reach their own full potential. Even once they went their own separate ways, they still said that thinking on how hard she worked towards her goals and how dedicated she was in meeting every single one fueled them to meet their own. It's quite remarkable actually," Ms. Bee added, pushing her glasses further up the bridge of her nose. "Anyways, January, I said all that to say this…"

Pulling her hands down from her head, Ms. Bee leaned forward, placing her arms back on her desk and stared straight into her eyes.

"Everything is energy. And energy is shared. What I want for every student in my class is to understand how we are all connected through the transfer of energy. It's a scientific fact."

Not seeing at all how any of this connected to her having to put up with Legend's energy, January sat quietly and gave her teacher a pointed, blank stare.

Sighing, Ms. Bee decided to take another approach to prove her point. As a professor passionate about her studies, she took a student's understanding to heart.

"Let me break this down for you," she eagerly began again. "There is a system that NASA uses to measure the electromagnetic field of the Earth every moment of every day. It tracks it the same way that a EKG machine tracks your heartbeat. Your heartbeat is electricity, same as the Earth's electromagnetic field. It's just a tinier bit of electricity because it's in your heart."

I did not come here for this science lesson, January thought, fighting not to roll her eyes. She respected Ms. Bee to the max but thus had not a thing to do with her dealing with Legend's ass for the next few months.

"Keep up with me, January. Don't let me lose you." Ms. Bee snapped her fingers twice in front of her face, jarring her attention.

"So, the machine that NASA has is like a big EKG machine that tracks the heartbeat of the Earth, the electromagnetic field. *Every* second of *every* day, it measures the electromagnetic field surrounding the Earth, because it's the *only* thing that protects us all from being zapped by a solar flare from the sun and burnt to a black crisp. It's *very* important because just like if the line on the EKG goes flat, you're dead, if the line on their machine goes flat, we *all* are dead. I mean… do you want to be burnt into a black crisp?"

January's eyes widened and she shook her head. "No, ma'am."

Ms. Bee cocked her neck and looked at her sideways. "You like living, don't you? You wanna stay alive, don't you?"

January's head wagged. "It's been pretty nice so far. Don't mind if I do."

With a cut of her eyes and a satisfactory purse of her lips, Ms. Bee nodded her head.

"So, anyways. One day, scientists noted that the graph measuring this field showed a huge spike, a drastic increase in that field. They were stunned. They wanted to know what, literally in the world had happened on that day to make it that the Earth electromagnetic field, its *heartbeat*, had increased such a drastic amount. When they did research to figure out the day and the time it had occurred, guess what they found out?"

Ms. Bee paused, most likely for dramatic effect because January was completely clueless. However, the anticipation was definitely killing her.

"The scientists found out that the spike happened on 9/11, about 15 minutes after the first plane hit the first tower. It happened at the exact time when images and videos of the tragedy began to circulate throughout the world. The moment the images started circulating around the world, the Earth's heartbeat spiked. Do you know how *incredible* that is? Do you understand what that means?"

Feeling completely lost as Ms. Bee tried to explain to her a scientific concept that she had absolutely no background knowledge to comprehend, January simply stared at her under raised brows. It wasn't until she realized that Ms. Bee was actually waiting for a response that she shook her head.

"*That* is a testament of how connected we all are. Your heart's elec-tromagnetic waves, your heartbeat, keep *you* alive and your emotions affect it. You can feel it. When you're excited, scared, feeling loved… you might say your heart skips a beat. Too much stress can give you a heart attack. Feeling and giving love makes you live longer. Your emotional reactions create heart responses that affect your life."

Nodding slowly, January was finally beginning to understand where Ms. Bee was going with her story. And she also understood why there was no chance in hell of her getting another partner.

"Here is the connection," Ms. Bee continued, bringing her analogy to an end. "When those images of 9/11 circulated throughout the world, many people had an instant, *powerful,* emotional reaction to them. Whether it was fear, pain, sadness or grief… they had a sincere *heart* reaction. Most people felt empathy, love for others. They empathized with the people killed, the ones having to choose whether to jump to their deaths or be burned alive, the families and people below who could do nothing but stand in one place and helplessly watch. The world empathized with those images. Collectively, we all sent love to each other. We had an emotional heart reaction that caused a simultaneous spark in our heartbeat and it caused a spike in the Earth's chart. Empathy and love for one another is the *only* thing that is protecting us all from being burnt up to a deadly crisp by the sun. "

Whoa…

The more Ms. Bee spoke, the more excited she became, waving with her hands as she explained a scientific theory that had January wondering if she was teaching the right subject at the university.

"Do you see the depths at which we are all connected to each other? Connected to Earth? Our collective emotions can change our planet. Science have proven that when the Earth's field is low, it alters weather patterns, cause earthquakes, hurricanes. But scientists have also noted that these times also coincide with times of war, and events which led to an increase in murders. The Earth's heartbeat was lowest during the darkest moments of history: slavery, the holocaust, the World Wars, Hiroshima… I could go on. Killing each other almost led to the sun killing us all. Our lives literally depend on our decision to empathize with and love each other. And this is only on a large scale. It works the same way on a small scale, too. In our every day life."

January thought back to 9/11 and how it had affected everyone around her. What Ms. Bee was saying was true. Even in her world, where tragedy, death and loss were a normal part of their existence, the terrorist attack had completely altered the world around her. She lived in New York and though she'd only been a child at the time, the terrorist attack was one of two things that happened in her life and changed her entire world.

"Everything is energy, and we are all connected. And we never know how the way we vibe might help the way someone else vibes." Pulling her hands back up over her head, Ms. Bee leaned back in her seat, reclining comfortably again.

"Stick with Legend. Get the chance to know him. Make an effort to understand him. Empathize with him and show him love. You'll begin to see that being around you will create a shift in him. You'll see and understand things differently the more you're around him and he'll change his perspective on life the more he spends time with you. You might assume he's lazy, but I'll tell you this: I've never known a student to come here completely for academic reasons who is lazy and doesn't care about grades. UCLA isn't an easy school to get into. And it for damn sure *ain't* cheap. Because, honey, *my* checks are popping."

Blowing out a breath, January nodded her head in agreement. Ms. Bee had a point. If you didn't give a damn about college, why waste the time and money at a school so competitive and so expensive? There were a lot of others you could choose.

"I guess I can try to make it work with him," January reluctantly said, shrugging her shoulders. She might as well have agreed; it wasn't like she really had a choice.

Smiling her approval, Ms. Bee nodded her head. "You'll be happy you did. Though 9/11 was a terrible tragedy, the emotional response it triggered from the world, those heart reactions, led to an immense amount of cooperation, care and understanding for each other afterwards. Much like the death of George Floyd led to the riots and the Black Lives Matter movements which joined people all over the planet together for a single great cause. I wouldn't be surprised if the videos of his death circulating around the world caused another spike, based on how the world's response. What looks like a bad situation at first can sometimes end up teaching us our greatest lessons. These experiences can become your greatest blessings."

January grimaced a little on the inside, immediately thinking about the messages she'd received on the horoscope apps and the fortune cookie only a few days before. The 'dooms day quotes' promising her better days after all the suffering. Obviously, dealing with Legend was what all that had been trying to prepare her for.

"There can only be *one* Destiny's Child, but we are *allllll* destiny's children," Ms. Bee said, snapping twice as if she were her own personal 'amen' corner.

With a sigh, January stood to leave. Ms. Bee's point was clear. We were all children of destiny. We needed these heart reactions to prevent the sun from burning us all into a black crisp, so the Universe was constantly meddling to forced us into positions to understand, empathize and love one another in order for the Earth, and us, to live. Oh… and all things worked together to bring us to the moment of accepting and expressing unconditional love. With all these lessons learned, January felt like she had all the knowledge required to earn her minor in sociology. Or at *least* ace the class.

Wrinkling her nose as she exited her professor's office, she paused for a moment to think about Legend.

Where in the middle of her annoyance, aggravation, and icky, blood-curdling disgust for him, could she see through the devil horns on his head and ungodly level of assholery to summon even a *fraction* of empathy—much less unconditional love? Was such a miracle even possible?

I guess I'll find out, January thought with a twirl of her eyes.

There was nothing left to do at this point but dive headfirst into her destiny.

A BABBLING BROOKE.

HOURS LATER AND JANUARY STILL COULDN'T FIND HERSELF TO remedy her feelings over having Legend as her partner. It was almost the end of the first week of class and he hadn't hit her up once to discuss when they would meet. All the other students had met with their partners multiple times already and she hadn't even had a chance to speak with hers.

"Stick with Legend. Get the chance to know him. Make an effort to understand him. You'll begin to see that being around you will create a shift in him."

"Highly unlikely," she scoffed and then began to pout. Like a child. Legend was a child. Maybe he was rubbing off on her already. Definitely not in a good way.

"Ugh…" January groaned, feeling trapped.

After only a few days, she was ahead in all of her classes except the one that was the most difficult and carried the most weight. She couldn't help but think about who was the one to blame.

She understood what Ms. Bee had said and it made perfect sense that being kind and showing love to someone would rub off on them. It felt workable with *normal* people.

But Legend wasn't normal.

January couldn't say that she knew where Legend was during the 9/11 attacks or when George Floyd had been killed and the world was collectively rioting in protest of police killing unarmed black men, but she'd bet money he wasn't all that concerned. His type only knew what was happening because the riots and curfews interfered with his club schedule on the weekends. Or because the block was hot and he couldn't hit the streets.

Nothing about Legend's rude ass behavior and repulsive attitude screamed 'humanitarian'.

In the middle of her doing her best and childish version of cursing Legend out in her mind, her phone began to ring. She grabbed it and glanced at the name on the screen quickly before answering.

"Hello?"

"Hi, January!" Carmen's voice was just as cheerful as it had been the day they met. It was like the girl never had a bad day. "I just wanted to check on you. I didn't get to talk to you after class the other day because I had to meet with my partner. I'm so lucky to be matched with her. We have the *best* things planned for our project. I'm so excited!"

I wish I could say the same, January thought, rolling her eyes.

"I'm happy to hear that," is what she said instead. "I didn't get your same luck with partners, unfortunately. I haven't even had the chance to meet with mine."

"Oh." For the first time, Carmen's voice went to an octave somewhat close to the normal range. "Who did you get?"

Sighing, January pushed the notebook she was working in from her lap and leaned back on the sofa behind her. She'd been in the middle of synchronizing her schedule for the semester with her planner in order to silence the thoughts roaming through her mind, but it was becoming clear that Legend was meant to be at the forefront of them for the moment.

"You know the guy who always comes in and sits in the back? The one who sleeps during the entire class?"

"Um, yeah! He came in late on the first day, too. I think his name is King or something."

"Legend. King is his first name, but he goes by Legend."

Pausing, she frowned, wondering why it had felt so important to her at the time that she correct Carmen about his name. As if he were lurking around somewhere and would care what she referred to him as.

"Anyways, yes," she continued. "That's him. He's my partner."

Carmen gasped. Loudly. As if him being January's partner was the worst thing she'd heard all day.

"I feel *so* sorry for you! You should ask Ms. Bee to swap you with someone else. I mean—I don't know *who* would want to trade part-ners with you when they would be getting someone like *him*, but there has to be something she can do."

"I already went to her earlier today and she said no. She told me that our differences actually make us great partners for this project and that I could affect him in a positive way."

Carmen's sudden burst of laughter was so loud and unexpected that it sent her eardrum rattling. January almost dropped the phone.

"I'm *sorry* but Ms. Bee either wants you to be miserable or she's delusional," Carmen said once she was finally able to speak through her uncontrollable giggles. "There is *no* way you could do anything to change him. He's a loser. I know the type."

January pinched her lips between her fingers, feeling her brows furrow as Carmen continued to speak. A burning sensation set off in her chest and she felt strangely uncomfortable, wanting to say something in Legend's defense, even though she didn't really under-stand why. All of the things Carmen was saying were all things she had either thought or said herself. It just felt different coming from someone else.

"He's probably only enrolled because he has to get a degree as a requirement of accessing his trust fund. Or he's an athlete. I'm sure he's never had to work hard a day in his life! Just sleeps his way through everything so other people can clean up his mess. In this case, 'other people' is you."

"He's not *that* bad," January finally spoke up, unable to let her continue. "I'm sure he's taking classes because he wants to. Ms. Bee says he's here for academics only. He's not on an athletic scholarship."

"January, trust me. I *know* what I'm talking about. You're not from Los Angeles but I am," Carmen battled back. "When I first saw him walk into class, I was like 'oh here he goes… one of those little thuggy guys that only come to college to party, get all the girls and have a good time'. L.A. is full of those types!"

Something about the way Carmen was stereotyping Legend without even speaking to him once bothered January beyond explanation. She had done the same thing to him, but it was different. She'd at least interacted with him prior to forming opinions. She frowned, feeling her temperature rise. It was one thing when *she* talked shit about Legend but Carmen doing it was something else.

"Actually, he's *not* that type, Carmen. You really don't know anything about him, and you shouldn't judge someone before you get a chance to meet him."

Glancing at the digital clock ahead of her to check the time, she was just about to make up an excuse to end the call when Carmen began to speak again before she had the chance.

"I don't have to meet him to know him, January. It's clear," she said, pausing briefly before speaking again. "I just wonder what sad, silly little girl will fall for him only to get her heart broken when she realizes that he tells all the girls the same things he told her and that he has commitment issues."

January's brow lifted at that. Her ears burned as her anger began to boil. If she'd taken the time to examine her reaction, she would've known that she wasn't angry at anyone but herself. Deep down, January felt that Carmen had just prophesied the destiny she would fulfill. The 'silly little girl' was her.

"Carmen, you sound a little bitter," she said, calling her out. "Do you know so much because you had a run-in with your own bad boy before? Just because you may have been that sad, silly little girl in your *own* experience doesn't mean it's like that with everyone. Don't project *your* situation on everyone else."

As soon as the words left her mouth, January knew she was dead ass wrong for saying them. It wasn't Carmen that was doing the projecting; it was her. She was the one feeling some kind of way about what Carmen had said. She was the one offended about being silly for feeling a connection to Legend that she couldn't understand and hadn't even admitted to herself that she felt just yet. A connection that he obviously didn't have to her.

A gasp much louder than the one before came through the phone. "No! It's not that, January. Really! It's just... I've seen it happen and... I mean, I was just talking, it wasn't meant to be serious. I'm sorry if I... offended you in some way?" She said the last part like it was a question and it only made January feel even worst about her aggressive reaction.

She knew that Carmen had only been talking; she was a gossip, she loved to talk—that much was obvious from when she'd first met her. She was the type who just said whatever came to her head and was certain that she was right, whether or not she really was. She meant no harm, but January had taken offense either way. And the only reason a woman took offense over anything negative said about a man was if she had feelings for him. Whether or not she wanted to admit how she felt about Legend, her actions spoke for themselves.

"I mean, he might be different. It's not impossible. Isn't that the point of the class anyways? To prove that everyone isn't the same and that we should accept each other and not judge?" Carmen started again, trying to ease back on her comment now that it was obvious January was in her feelings. "He might not be the woman-izing type. He might actually be a good guy. I think that—"

"It's okay, Carmen," January said, interrupting her. There was no need to continue the misery. "It's not even about him, really. I'm just on edge about the project. It's a big part of our grade and I hope that he can get it together and be a decent partner for me."

"Of course. No worries. I completely understand," Carmen replied.

Her tone was noticeably less upbeat and light-hearted than her norm. Yet another thing that made January feel guilty for her sudden mean-girl outburst. Not only that, but it was also very obvious that Carmen didn't believe her one bit. She might have been off base about Legend as a person, but she was spot-on about some silly girl falling for him. *That* much was crystal clear.

"Um… I guess I'll see you in class?"

"I'll be there," January replied with a sigh. "I'll see you then."

The call ended and she dropped the phone to her side, lying back on the sofa cushions as she fought to reign in her emotions. Legend wasn't even hers to feel possessive or defensive about. She wasn't even sure she wanted him to be, even if that was an option.

Which… it wasn't.

"He doesn't even want you to be his partner for a class project. What makes you think he'd want you to be his girl?"

It took only a second for the absurdity of the moment to hit her. As if she hadn't already been acting crazy enough on the call with Carmen, now she was talking to herself. Slapping the palm of her hand to her forehead, she groaned when she thought on the insanity that Legend's entrance into her life was causing. And this was only after *two* actual interactions. What the hell else could happen next?

She sat up to gather up her planner and start back with organizing her schedule when she heard a key slip into the front door. Her body instantly tensed. Was her roommate finally arriving after being almost a week late?

The door opened, creaking to a halt, and in the space between stood a girl with a cute baby doll face and pretty brown, oval eyes. Long box-braids, reminiscent of Janet Jackson's in the movie *Poetic Justice*, were pulled up into a high ponytail on her head and wrapped with a multi-colored, mostly blue, scarf that perfectly matched the rest of her casual, but couture, outfit. Her skin was rich and brown, the color of hot chocolate, and the warmth of her complexion manifested in her smile. January liked her instantly.

"Girl! You don't understand how hard it was carrying all this shit up three flights, even *with* the elevator," she said as she kicked a large red suitcase through the entrance with her leg. "But here I am. Your new roommate!"

In both arms, she was struggling with two duffle bags. January effortlessly flowed from crossed legs to a full stand and offered her assistance, hastily crossing the room to move away the suitcase and grab one of her bags.

"Well, welcome home!" She held her arms out and smiled. "I'm January. And… I guess you must be Celia?"

She wrinkled her nose. "Ew, no. Not Celia. I mean, I am *Celia*, but call me Brooke," she corrected, extending her hand out to January. "Celia is my mama and I will never understand why she decided to pass that ugly ass name down to me, but I'm not claiming it."

Sidestepping by where January stood, lightly chuckling at her state-ment, Brooke walked into the dorm appearing stricken, as if trying her hardest not to let her jaw hit the floor.

"This shit is *laid!*" She paused for a few moments to allow her eyes to roam over her new home, taking it all in. "Damn... are you, like, somebody special?"

She was about to respond when Brooke suddenly stopped short—so short that she nearly tripped over her own feet. Slowly, Brooke turned, nearly completing a perfect pirouette before locking eyes with January.

"Wait...are you related to the Obamas? Because that's the only way I can see how someone could pull off some shit like this."

"I'm *not* related to the Obamas," January replied, laughing hard as she watched her continue to explore.

With her hands flailing in the air above her head, Brooke ran from room to room, screeching at everything she saw like a contestant who had just won on the game show *The Price is Right.*

"Oh my god! Do we *literally* have the entire floor? Is that an indoor pool? Shit, is that a *jacuzzi*? A treadmill! Listen... I don't even do the gym like that, but I'll tell you right now, a bitch is ready to try new thaaangs!"

Sticking her tongue out like Megan Thee Stallion, she watched as Brooke did a little dance, dropping it low.

January doubled over in laughter for the first time in what felt like a very long time. Brooke's personality was electric, and she had the best kind of vibe. Being around her for only five minutes was enough for her to feel like she was reuniting with an old friend, someone she'd met before.

Brooke wasted no time making herself at home once she'd had a chance to explore every part of the dorm. Connecting her phone to the surround sound speakers installed throughout the dorm, she turned on her favorite playlist and before long, January was bobbing her head to *The City Girls* while helping her unpack.

"So, I'm guessing you're 420-friendly?" Brooke asked, peering at her from under a lifted brow. As if she'd planned it, a Snoop Dogg song began to play as a song by Lady Gaga ended. The variation in her taste of music wasn't unexpected; she had a style that was all her own.

January shook her head. "No... I mean, I don't smoke personally, but I don't have anything against it."

Her eyes widened in surprise. "You don't?" She frowned just a bit before continuing. "I was just wondering because you've got a lot of stuff around here that gives off that kind of feel."

Brooke paused to look around, studying the decor as she searched for the perfect way to describe the theme.

"Incense holders, those energy stone, crystally thingies." She lifted her nose in the air and took a sharp inhale. "You got the sage smoke burning, got my chakras all popping... a yoga mat in the corner." Turning to January, she gave her a sideways, pointed stare. "Are you one of them new age, extra woke types? I mean, you giving me some serious Jhene Aiko, Erykah Badu vibes. A little hippy, mixed with a little witchy. No offense."

January literally laughed out loud at that. Brooke's direct nature caught her off guard. Where she was from, most people who she'd just met, even some who had known her for years, rarely spoke their mind when it came to her. They were always careful to not offend, which just made every interaction superficial. Brooke was about as real as they came.

"I'm no Jhene Aiko or Erykah Badu. I love them both, by the way," she couldn't help but add. "My dad actually had this dorm laid out and designed this way. But, yeah, he picked up my style when it came to it. I'm not religious at all but I'm very spiritual. I've been through a lot and I used my spirituality and things like meditation and yoga to keep myself focused and on track."

"Damn, that's kinda dope, actually." Brooke nodded slowly as she thought on it. "I mean, I don't know shit about meditation except that it seems boring, but people swear by it so there has to be something to it. I'm a Leo and it's hard as hell for me to even shut my mouth for five minutes. There is no damn way I can do that *and* sit by myself all at the same time. But yoga is something I've always wanted to try. Who can't use a little more flexibility? I sure can!"

The mischievous smile on Brooke's face lingered and January definitely caught her drift. The boy-crazy gleam in her eyes was a definite giveaway that her plans for yoga had a purpose outside of her own personal wellness and fitness goals.

"What about the portrait over there of the girl in the dance studio. Is that you? Are you a dancer?"

"Yeah…that's me." January paused, ducking her head a little to look down at her hands. She swallowed hard before shaking away her emotions with a shrug. "I used dance to express myself creatively. In the past."

"In the past?" Brooke caught her eye and held it with an intensity that felt like she was looking deep into her soul. "Something tells me that there is a story behind that."

"A story for another day." She grabbed a hanger.

Catching the hint, Brooke didn't push and simply raised the volume on the speakers, winding her hips in rhythm with the melody of a song from her favorite artist of the moment, *H.E.R.*

There was no doubt in January's mind that she would be sharing her story with Brooke one day. It was clear that she was the type who had a knack for getting people to open up eventually. She just had that sort of vibe.

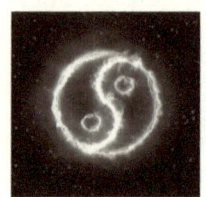

CELIA BROOKLYN MCCLYDE.

Celia Brooklyn McClyde.

THAT WAS HER BIRTH NAME.

Given to her by her mother and a reluctant father who gave up on fighting his wife over the subject. But by the age of three, Brooke realized for herself that 'Celia' wasn't what she was going to be called for the rest of her life and she demanded to be called Brooke.

Growing up, she was always the type who didn't take 'no' for an answer when it came to anything she put her mind to. Her grandmother told her it was because when God made her, he used too much water; making her uninhibited, mellow in some cases but forceful, overpowering, mighty and emotional.

Brooke wasn't sure water had anything to do with it, all she knew was that she had a low tolerance for bullshit. Unfortunately, that low tolerance didn't extend to men.

"Where are you from?" January asked as she rummaged through Brooke's things, trying to make sense out of how she'd packed them, which was basically to throw any and everything everywhere it would fit.

January was a neat freak; that much was obvious by the fact that not one thing was out of place before Brooke entered the dorm.

Wait until she realizes I'm a fuckin' slob, Brooke thought once she had a moment to calm down from all the luxury surrounding her.

She had a lot of good traits but plenty of vices—the main one being that she was a complete and utter mess 90% of the time. It wasn't something she was proud of, just an indisputable fact. Brooke was a creative spirit and that came with its own level of disorder. And laziness…

But when it came down to doing what really needed to be done, she eventually got the job done one way or another. She blossomed through procrastination.

"San Diego. Not too far from here," Brooke answered. "Where are you from?"

After a brief hesitation, January replied, "New York."

Brooke's brows lifted as she eyed her, noting a weird expression on her face. There was something hidden behind it and she could tell January didn't want to expand on her statement.

Too bad. Brooke was the type that was just pushy enough—and nosey enough—to have no problem getting all up in her business.

"What brings you all the way out here? You running away from something?"

January frowned. "Why I have to be running away from something just because I decided to come here for school?"

With a shrug, Brooke replied to her. "You don't *have* to be running from anything. But are you?"

January pursed her lips and busied herself with fiddling with a shirt that she was struggling to put on a hanger. She was stalling; trying to decide whether or not she was going to answer Brooke's question truthfully. Or whether or not she was going to answer it at all.

Might as well get to talking, homegirl, Brooke thought to herself, watching her closely. *Ain't no dodging me. We live together now.*

"It's a man, isn't it?" The edges of Brooke's mouth curled up with the question because she knew she was right.

Give her any problem that a woman was facing—especially a beautiful and intelligent one like her roommate—and Brooke would bet a million dollars that the reason behind it was a man. In her experience, it *always* was. Women could run the world, figure out the most daunting problems to any crazy situation, run Fortune 500 companies, countries and families all at the same time, but there was something about the male species that always seemed to throw them for a loop. Brooke included… but that was a story for later.

"No…" January hesitated and then frowned again before shaking her head. "I mean, yes, but not really. Not in the way you think."

Rolling her eyes, Brooke grabbed her purse and pulled out a bag of materials that would perfectly assist her in a time such as this: her bag of weed and other things, which she referred to as her 'medicinal supply'.

It was obvious to her that January was a little uptight, definitely the good girl type, but based off the vibe that Brooke was getting from her, she had reason to believe that she would become a different person after a puff or two. She claimed she didn't smoke, but maybe a few inhales would help her loosen up.

"Are you sure you don't want to hit this with me? It's mild… a good introductory strain," Brooke asked, lifting a joint that she'd rolled earlier in the air.

January lifted her eyes and then stared pointedly for a few seconds at the weed before shrugging and shaking her head.

"I've smoked weed before, I just don't anymore. But I don't care if you do."

That was all the permission she needed. Brooke wasted no time putting the blunt to her lips and lighting the tip.

"What happened to make you stop?" she asked, standing to open a window and blow smoke outside.

"It was only once." January thought back to that day. "My dad gave it to me while I was recovering from surgery. It was to help me deal with the pain."

"What?" Brooke exclaimed, plopping back down on the floor next to where January sat. "Your dad is cool as hell. Let *me* have surgery. My parents would give me some Ibuprofen and tell me I better pray my way through the pain."

It wasn't clear to her whether or not she was getting a contact high or not from the smoke but, for some reason, January laughed hard as hell at that.

"No, my dad did not make me *pray* the pain away, but I kinda wish he had. My mind was so messed up over the surgery… I was in such a depressive state that I had a bad reaction. Started tripping so bad that he had to call my mom to come and calm me down. I've never seen her so mad at him in my life." January paused for a moment and then shrugged. "But he was only trying to help."

Nodding slowly, Brooke took a long pull of the weed before exhaling out easily. She wasn't even bothering to blow the smoke out the window anymore. It was intentional. January was right in thinking that Brooke had a way of making people talk because she did. A little weed smoke, whether they were smoking it for themselves or not, did the trick every time. Not only did she think it was necessary in order to have January loosen up and relax some, but Brooke wanted to know what type of person she was dealing with. When it came to females, especially one that she had to share living space with, she preferred to know what she was living with.

"So, I'm guessing this was no simple surgery to remove your tonsils or some shit like that," Brooke began making moves to push for more. "It had to be big for you to be so depressed."

Instead of answering, January's eyes dropped to her lap and she simply nodded her head. Sadness enveloped her and it was almost as if Brooke could visibly see the dark cloud that was now hovering above her, cloaking her in the same depression that she must've been going through the day she was revisiting in her mind.

For some reason, Brooke found herself glancing back over at the portrait on the wall of young January dancing in ballet shoes. She couldn't say exactly why, but she had a nagging feeling that what-ever reason January had for being in surgery was connected to the reason why she didn't dance anymore. Brooke saw the sadness in her eyes when she asked her about the portrait and the same gloomy look from then matched the one in her eyes now.

"Well, I've got an idea," she said, clapping her hands together. "I know exactly what we need to do tonight."

Lifting her head slowly, January stared uneasily at her roommate, having an instant feeling that whatever idea she had in mind was not going to be something she would have come up with herself.

"Don't worry about it right now. I'll tell you after I make a few calls," she said. Holding her hand up, she made a motion as if she were making a sworn statement before placing the hand over her heart. "You don't know me all that well yet but, trust me, I'll never steer you wrong."

HO SHIT.

Legs long.
Heels high.
Skirt short as hell.
Tank top barely there.

TO SOME, THAT MIGHT SOUND LIKE A RECIPE FOR A GOOD TIME, BUT for January… these were all the ingredients for ho shit activities.

In fact, that was exactly what Brooke had told her that they would be up to tonight. At the time, January didn't really understand what she meant, but it was currently becoming crystal clear with each passing second.

The pungent odor of premium quality weed perfumed the air, making her feel light-headed although she'd opened every available window to avoid a contact high. It wasn't the weed that bothered her. But, at the moment, she had finally finished helping Brooke and was trying her hardest to focus on getting some class work done. But the effects of the second-hand smoke had gotten to her, making her ability to concentrate nearly impossible.

"Take off those glasses, put those books up, and change out of them boring ass clothes," she had said right before trying to snatch the glasses from January's face and swiping one of said books out of the way with the tips of her toes. "I'm about to take you out tonight. We about to be on some ho shit."

January frowned, turning around from where she sat, Indian style, with all of her various syllabi surrounding her and pointed her eyes in Brooke's direction.

"Excuse me, I don't think I heard you right," she said, peeking at Brooke from over the top of the glasses she'd tried to pluck from her face. "We're about to be on some what?" She raised one brow in question as she stared up at Brooke's tall, model-thin body hovering over her as she sat crisscross applesauce in the middle of their dorm-style living room.

"Ho. *Shit*," Brooke clarified, looking squarely at her. Then her eyes widened in disbelief when she realized January didn't have the slightest idea what she was talking about.

"Wait… You sincerely don't know what it is?"

January shrugged indifferently. "I mean, I know what a 'ho' is, and I know what it means to be involved in some shit but… I've never heard the phrase used together." She wrinkled her nose, trying to take a guess at what Brooke was talking about. She couldn't possibly think January was about to go out with her to find a one-night stand. It had to be something else because January knew damn well *that* wasn't it.

"'Ho shit' is just another way of saying that we are about to go out to somebody's club, looking sexy as hell, showing off all our best assets while we dance and live our *best* lives the way we want to live it."

Curling her nose at Brooke, January squinted. "That sounds like a message for how you should live everyday life. Nothing close to what I was assuming from what you called it. Whatever you're talking about, 'ho shit' is probably not the phrase you should use." January turned back, squinting at the printed copy of the syllabus in her hand.

Letting out a heavy sigh as if January was getting on her last nerve, Brooke rolled her eyes just as she looked back up.

"Girl, stop being all…" She raised her hand and dramatically waved it over January's body from head-to-toe as if to illustrate whatever word she was looking for to describe her. "…Extra. Let's just stick with that. Stop being extra and get dressed. I'm going out and I want you to go with me."

"First of all, I don't do clubs," January said, pulling the glasses from her face. "And second of all, I don't dance. But out of pure curiosity, how do you dress for 'ho shit'?" she asked with a little bit of a laugh. The concept that anyone would intentionally set out to do anything deemed 'ho shit' was hilarious to her.

"How do you dress for it, you say?" Brooke's mischievous spirit birthed a sly smile across her chocolate brown face. "I'm glad you asked!"

After showing January a few examples, she knew right then and there: No way in *hell* was she going to allow Brooke to dress her.

"One thing you'll learn to do while living with me is how to have fun. And one thing you'll learn *about* me is that I don't take no for an answer," Brooke reasoned, cocking her head to give January a sideways look with that statement. "Look, I just got moved in, this is the end of your first week of college and we need to bond since we will be roommates for the next few months. What better way to do that than to go out together and have fun tonight?"

Tension and inner conflict were present all over January's face as she sat in silence with her head bowed, looking at all of the papers, notebooks, and textbooks surrounding her.

Standing, Brooke walked over to January's closet, rummaging through her clothes, without invitation, fully helping herself. It was becoming obvious that she did most things in that way: without invitation and fully helping herself.

"Do you not own a single dress?" she asked, frowning deeply as she ran her fingers through January's wardrobe. "Or heels? I mean, I see flip-flops, sandals, sneakers, and boots, all designer, which is nice, but not a single heel in sight. This is just *sad*."

"More reason for me to not go," January chimed in, watching her from the entrance of the closet.

"Oh no, you're definitely going," Brooke replied. "You'll just have to wear something of mine." She bent down to grab one of January's shoes. "Luckily, we wear the same size."

A groan passed up from January's throat and she stepped to the side as Brooke flew past her to look in her own closet. Anxiety filled her stomach, but January said nothing because it was obvious there was no point. Brooke was on a mission, and the only thing left for her to do was fall in line.

Maybe this won't be so bad, she thought with a subtle shrug. She had wanted to experience new things and her wish was unavoidably being granted. Not quite in the way that she'd expected but, in her life, things never went according to plan.

"You'd look perfect in this!"

January was almost afraid to look up and when she finally did, the short, black silk dress in Brooke's hands definitely caught her by surprise.

"You can pair this with a jean jacket and some cute heels that I just bought the other day. I don't have the labels that you're used to wearing, but I promise you won't die," she added, and January rolled her eyes.

"It's not the label that I'm worried about killing me," she said as Brooke held the dress in front of her. The lacy hem barely covered her thighs. "You don't have anything with a little more material? This is definitely more like a shirt than a dress."

She held the dress in her hands and looked from it to the full-length mirror across the room. It did seem to complement her rich mocha complexion, and the soft fabric felt nice against her skin. But it was just too much. It would draw the kind of attention that she didn't want. January wasn't that kind of girl; she liked to blend in, be behind the scenes. She liked to observe. She wasn't the type that was comfortable being watched.

"This is your dress now. It looks like it was made for you, so you can have it." Brooke patted her once on her shoulder before walking away. "Hurry up and get ready so we can go. I already scheduled a ride to come get us, so don't take all day."

"Yes, ma'am," she replied, rolling her eyes.

With a sigh, she sat the dress on her bed and walked to the bathroom to start the water for a shower. Not even a week in, and she was already doing things she'd never done.

Once again, January… welcome to college life.

"THAT IS *DEFINITELY* NOT what we agreed that you would be wearing."

Hands on her hips, Brooke looked down at January over the bridge of her wrinkled-up nose as she sat on the edge of her bed, tying up the laces of her black rhinestone sneakers.

"*We* only agreed that I would go out with you tonight. What we *didn't* agree on was the dress," she said, looking up to meet her eyes.

January stood and, just as Brooke was about to object, she clamped her mouth shut. January had swapped the dress out for something more casual, more her style, but it definitely showed off all her assets, whether or not she was really trying to make it that way.

"It'll work," she gave in with a shrug. "Give me five minutes and then we need to leave. Our driver is on the way."

Thankful that Brooke had decided to fold on that battle, January grabbed her small backpack, checked for her ID and then sat down on the bed to wait. The second her mind settled; an image of Legend's face crept into her mind. Almost immediately, it set off a burst of nervous energy in her gut and she took a deep breath as an attempt to settle it. He was nowhere around, but just the thought of him was enough to set her nerves in motion.

What is it about him that I can't shake?

January wasn't the type to be boy crazy and he wasn't even her type. Still, there was something about him that excited her, and she couldn't understand why. She thought about the first day in class when he'd looked her up and down, his eyes roaming liberally as he tried to remember whether or not they'd met before. Pure sexual wanting oozed from his gaze, setting her entire body aflame. Her emotions were conflicted as she bounced from feeling a deep, natural desire for him while feeling utterly repulsed by him, all at the same time. He unnerved her. Made her feel naked even when she was fully clothed.

January's head tilted as she fell into the memory and, before she knew it, her nipples hardened and she felt them pressing against the soft fabric of her bra. Tingles erupted between her thighs at the thought of him, and the shock of her sexual desire awakening so suddenly brought her back to her senses.

"Girl, you need to get it together," she whispered to herself as she stood suddenly, walking to the large wall-to-ceiling windows to distract from her visualizations of the man she could never allow herself to have.

Thoughts became feelings, feelings became desires, and desires became fiercely coveted realities. There was no room to allow him in her space—not even in her mind. Standing at the window, she peered down into the small courtyard in front of the dorms that was always bustling with activity. Since none of the living spaces were co-ed, the courtyard was used as the meet up spot for guys to watch girls and for girls to be noticed. She never had the nerve to be a part of that scene, though it piqued her curiosity, but one of her favorite past times was to stand at the window and observe it all from a distance. Watching as others her age had fun was something she'd gotten used to over the years.

Almost immediately, as if drawn by a magnet, her eyes went to a familiar figure sitting on the brick ledge right in front of her building. Her heart skipped a beat, recognizing him before her mind even had the chance.

What is he doing here? Of all places he could be… why is he here?

His back was to her, but it really didn't make a difference. She could recognize him anywhere. The way he sat, his mannerisms, the way his head bounced back and forth as he observed anything and everything moving around him. He had been mentored by her father, and it showed. There was no blood relation, obviously, but everything about his presence reminded January of her father. She winced at the thought.

Was that weird?

They said that girls always fell for men who reminded them of their fathers—the first men in their lives who showed them real, unconditional love. Was that the reason for how she felt? Was it because he felt so familiar to her?

He bent his head and his long, twisted locs parted around his shoulders, showing off the tattoo that covered his neck. For some reason, January found her eyes drawn there as she thought deeply about the real source of her attraction for someone who had coined himself as a 'very dangerous man.' Was the universe playing some sinister game with her by constantly pushing her towards someone that she knew she could never have?

Then, suddenly, as if she'd called out to him with her thoughts, Legend turned around and looked up at the building behind him, right where she stood perched at the windowsill, as if locking his eyes into hers. There was no way he could see her. The windows were tinted for privacy—her father had made sure of that—but for a few intense seconds, they seemed to stare right into each other's eyes. She felt her body go warm; she wanted to look away, but it was like she was in a trance. How was it that it seemed like he could see her?

He felt your heart reaction.

It was like Ms. Bee was somewhere in the back of her head, speaking her scientific nonsense.

But *was* it nonsense?

"I'm ready!" Brooke announced, stepping up from behind her. "What you looking so hard at?" She peered down over January's shoulder and the spell was immediately broken. January jerked away from the window and curled her lips into an awkward smile.

"Nothing."

Brooke stared into her with knowing eyes before leaning over to peek out the window in the direction of the person she'd been staring at.

"Mm hmm," she hummed like a tune. "You'll open up to me one day, Jan. We're roommates so we're destined to be friends."

That said, she grabbed her sequined clutch in her hand, pulled at the hem of her short spandex dress and then locked arms with January.

"Let's go have some fun!"

January forced down her reluctance with a smile and then playfully rolled her eyes.

"Yes... let's."

WHEN THE TABLES TURN.

"Yo, I can't fuck around with you no more, nigga. I still ain't recover from two nights ago."

Legend sat on the concrete ledge and watched as his cousin slide out of the driver's side of his dark blue Camaro. It was rare to see Nico riding something other than a motorcycle these days, but it was easy to see why he'd vouched for the change today. The car was sick; much flashier than what Legend preferred—he was more low-key with his rides, though they all came with a price tag just as heavy. But whereas Nico would dress his rides up with rims, gold trims and all the bells and whistles that a true Florida boy from the Southside of Miami couldn't resist, Legend had more exquisite and simpler taste.

"Man, stop lying," Nico replied, taking a seat next to him. "The chick I left you with told me that you peeled out of there like ten minutes after I did. Said you was poppin' some shit 'bout how you had an early class."

"I do have an early class," Legend commented with a smirk. "But I don't really give a damn about that. I just wasn't telling shorty like that. She ain't my type."

Reaching into his pocket to pull out the leftover piece of a blunt he'd started smoking earlier, Nico laughed before positioning it between his fingers.

"Nigga, ain't nobody yo' type. We already established that. We don't have no types and that's just how it is. Fuck hoes and get money is how we live. Ain't no need for nothing different. We ain't got time to be catching feelings."

"Real shit," Legend agreed with a simple nod.

Silence grew around them as Nico puffed from his blunt and Legend settled into his own thoughts. The sun had abandoned the city many hours before but, in its absence, it seemed like their part of the world had come alive.

It was Friday night on a college campus, the first of the new semester. As he sat outside the freshmen dorms, he watched as girls, dressed in high heels, short skirts, dresses or even shorter shorts and skintight tops walked with intention and an extra twist in their hips. Their 'trap-fits': the perfect recipe for trapping a nigga.

One girl, a chocolate brown beauty with a complexion that shined bright under the moon-lit sky, made a point of walking right in front of where he and Nico sat perched on the front ledge. Catching his eye, she allowed her attention to linger on him just a few moments longer than what was naturally expected, a sure sign that he was welcome to put his bid in now before she gave some lucky man at the club a try.

Legend barely looked at her.

I ain't fuckin' with it.

"*Damn*, she thick," Nico spoke through a puff of smoke. "Care to shoot your shot before I do?"

Running his hand over his chin, Legend used his forefinger and thumb to smooth over the edges of his facial hair but didn't reply because, just that quickly, someone else had caught his eye.

The hell she think she goin' dressed like that? he thought before narrowing his eyes at the object of his full attention.

Wearing jean shorts that fit snugly enough to pass for spandex and just barely cupped the bottom curve of her firm ass, matched with a black cotton tee with some sort of White hand symbol on front with black and white high-top converses on her feet, January stood at the front entrance of her dorm building looking sexy as hell. There was something so alluring to him about a woman who could soak up the energy of everything and everyone around without even trying. She was an enigma; the type of woman God created for the sole purpose of fucking up the mind of niggas like him. She was a distraction, an unwanted one at that. Giving in to his desire for her would be a mistake that he couldn't afford to make.

"Yeah, actually I think I might do just that," he replied, standing as he answered Nico's question.

One last look at January was what he allowed himself, but somehow the weight of his stare summoned her mind.

JANUARY LOOKED UP, taking a brief reprieve from pretending to be interested in the pointless conversation that Brooke was having with some girl she had just said that she couldn't stand, and found herself captured by Legend's probing eyes.

Damn...

Her lips parted and she exhaled softly as if audibly speaking the word. Thankfully, she didn't so Brooke had no evidence of her thirst, but the evidence of the sexual pull she felt was all in her eyes. It wasn't until Legend turned away, slipping his arm around some girl's waist, that she was released from his spell.

The cool night air all of a sudden felt suffocatingly thick as January fought against the natural urge to look back at the sight that was causing the sharp pain coursing through her chest. She couldn't even understand the reaction; there was no reason for it. Not only was he not hers to feel possessive over, she didn't want him to be. He represented everything she was running away from. Falling for him would make the changes that she'd made to her life a waste and who had the time to be hustling backwards whether it was in love or life?

"Well, like I said, let me know if you hear anything about Rush because I do plan on being part of it this year for sure," Brooke was saying, finally ending her conversation. "Jan, you ready to go?" she asked, using a nickname that January wasn't sure she liked but wasn't bothered enough to correct.

She had more pressing matters to tend to—like putting as much distance as she could between herself, Legend and his new, boda- ciously-shaped boo. It really didn't matter. They could have been going to shake hands with Satan and she would've been just as amped to ride shotgun. Anything was better than seeing Legend laying down the preliminary work for his next dick appointment.

"I *didn't* say," Brooke replied, linking arms with January as a broad smile took over the entire bottom-half of her face. "It's a surprise. And the fact that I was able to be mature enough to have a whole conversation with that bitch Racquel, we have something to celebrate."

January cut her eyes at Brooke giving her an easily read response in her expression.

"Okay, okay. I only spoke to her because I wanted info on when Rush will start for the AKAs but now that I know everything I needed to, we both have a way in."

The second she opened her mouth to let Brooke know that she had absolutely no desire to be in any Greek sorority, especially if it meant that she would be signing up to be a slave for how many ever weeks to prove she was worthy, she stopped short when she saw Legend lean over in close to the girl—who she had already decided she hated—and whisper something in her ear. The amount of envy that swarmed over January in that instance was both annoying and repulsive to her.

In response to whatever lie Legend was telling in order to get in her pants, the girl flung her head back and let out an obnoxiously loud laugh that was sickening to January's ears. she was doing way too much.

There is absolutely nothing on Earth he could have said that could be that damn funny.

Her frown deepened, and she continued walking alongside Brooke, with utter disgust showing clearly on her face, completely unaware that she was staring. Also, completely unaware of the trash-can ahead of her until it was too late. The length of her long, graceful stride was cut short when the front of her sneaker collided with the aluminum can, throwing her completely off balance. The momentum of the energy exchange tossed her forward and it was only her quick reflexes that saved her from sailing head-first over the can and landing clear on the other side.

"Shit! Jan, are you okay?" Brooke asked, reaching out to steady her.

The only thing she could do was nod her head through the embarrassment. Even if by some miracle, Legend might have missed the spectacle, the resounding drone that came from when her foot hit the aluminum had definitely caught his attention. It was like a gong, signaling the start of the show; there was no way he had missed it. And when she looked up, unable to keep herself from turning towards the subject of her misery, the first eyes she saw were his. He'd seen the entire thing and, of course, he was grinning from ear-to-ear. Just like the asshole he was.

"Girl, come *on*—he ain't worth it and you know it." When she saw January open up her mouth, she held up her hand to cut off the lie she knew was coming. "And *before* you say it, I saw how you were looking at Ms. Bad and Bougie over there with the Brazilian Remy weave, who I know for a fact that you *don't* know, so you can't tell me the reason for your attitude isn't Prince Charming Dreadhead."

Brooke expertly read the situation leaving January with no other choice than to clamp her mouth shut. Maybe she didn't understand *why* she felt the way she did about Legend, but she definitely knew *how* she felt. She wanted to be the one in his face right now, soaking up all his attention, giggling over whatever stupid shit was coming out of his mouth—because it was definitely stupid shit, she was sure of that. She wanted to be the one whose simple existence made him look at her and smile. But, instead, he was giving all of that to Black Becky-With-the-Good-Fake-Hair. Life was anything but fair.

"Jan, there are plenty of guys where we are going and, trust me, they are paid and better looking than he is." Pausing to press her index finger to her lips, Brooke thought for a quick moment. "Scratch that. They might not be better looking, but the drinks will be strong enough to have you think they are… at least for the night. Now, let's go. Our ride is here."

Forcing herself not to look anywhere else but straight ahead, while simultaneously swallowing her pride, January gave in as Brooke tugged her towards the intersection where the driver she'd called was waiting.

Regardless to what Brooke had said earlier about not knowing if clubbing was her thing if she'd never done it, she couldn't get over feeling like her night was already ruined.

DIOR.

"WHAT YOU 'BOUT TO GET INTO?" LEGEND ASKED, NOT CARING IN the least about what the answer would be.

His words were to the girl standing in front of him, but his attention was on the one who was practically running in the opposite direction. As the chick replied to his question, completely oblivious to the fact that he couldn't care less what she said, he watched as the over-enthusiastic driver of the car January was heading towards jumped out as soon as his eyes fell on her. Though it was obvious that he'd been called by the girl with her, being that she was the one checking the information on her phone against the number on his license plate, the driver was barely giving her the time of day.

Kinda like how Legend was doing with the girl he was only entertaining as a distraction from the one he really wanted to be talking to. It wasn't until the car had taken off down the street that he even realized the girl was still talking. He'd been so caught up thinking about the shirt that January was wearing. He dropped his head to look at his own shirt and realized he was wearing one just like it—minus the glitter. Her shirt was literally the girl version of his. All black, with 'Dior' spelled out in big letters on the front. Instead of the bold font on his, hers had large curvy letters for the logo, covered in what he would call 'glittery shit'. He frowned, scrunching up his entire face as he thought of it.

I fuckin' hate that glitter shit.

"... I mean, that's what I was *going* to do but I can cancel if you had something else in mind."

He cut his eyes at the girl just in time to note the seductive way she licked her lips, openly suggesting that she was willing to do things he hadn't even bothered to ask for. She may have thought it gave her extra points to be so forward, but he just thought it was thirsty as hell.

As a man who had been brought up on the notion that nothing in life worth having came easy, he enjoyed the thrill of the chase. He didn't live a regular life because he didn't do regular shit. Nothing about him was regular; not his car, his clothes, not even his hoes—if they could even be qualified as his.

"Nah, I got some place to be. See you around, shorty," he said dismissively before turning back to Nico who was steady puffing on his blunt with a big ass grin on his face. From the humored gleam in his eye, he could tell that Nico had watched all of the action unfold and thoroughly enjoyed the show.

"Aye, I'm about to go check up on Onyx."

"Yeah, I already know," Nico replied. Quickly putting out his blunt, he stood to clasp hands with his cousin before they parted ways. "You ain't have to do that to ole girl though," he added with a smirk. "You ain't see the way she looked after you told her it was time to exit the stage left. Chick looked sad as hell. Probably had to walk sideways just so she wouldn't trip over her bottom lip."

Legend laughed at that as they slapped hands. Nico was always the one with the jokes. Out of the two, he was the one everyone liked from the start, a benefit for men in their lifestyle to have. Both of them were raised in the streets—born, raised and trained to be hittas—but Nico's natural charm always worked in his favor. He was the one who made everyone around him instantly feel relaxed. A mark never even know he had been sent to end their life until it was too late.

On the contrary, people intuitively knew to be on guard around Legend. They could sense his dangerous nature as if it were spelled out in his aura. It was hard for someone to ignore unless he cared to make them feel otherwise. Something he rarely did, which was why, outside of the people he considered family, he had no friends. In Los Angeles, Nico and Onyx, Nico's twin sister, were all he had.

The engine of his 4-door Porsche Panamera roared to life as he pulled out onto the main road, heading to the same destination he always did every Friday night. Being a student with a car worth more than the President of the University's yearly salary, one of only a few Black ones at that, gave him a good deal of attention as he drove through campus, but most just assumed he was the son of some celebrity or star athlete. No one would've ever believed he made a fortune hustling in the streets.

Never concerned with the need to impress others, everything Legend bought he purchased for himself. Everyone had a vice and for him, his was that he liked nice things. Very, very nice, *expensive* things. But the luxury he enjoyed came at a price beyond material currency. His fortune had been paid for in blood.

Had he never left his position working under Outlaw, he would have quickly become a senior member of the *Black Bag Mafia*. At this point in his life, he would've been making more money than he could ever spend. He was in line to be Outlaw's right-hand, and he'd earned his position by being an expert at what he did but also because of loyalty.

Once he gave his word, it wasn't broken, and that same thing was true when it came to the pledge he'd made once he swore his service to *BBM*. The issues between Outlaw and his father didn't concern him and both parties knew that Legend wouldn't cross them for the other. Outlaw trusted him as much as Legend's father did and he never gave either one a reason not to.

Until that one day at the park that fucked it all up.

As a matter of reflex, his muscles grew tense and he found himself gripping the steering wheel even tighter as his thoughts reversed back through time, Channeling memories and feelings he'd tried, and failed, to leave behind. He hadn't known for sure that the shoot-out would happen. He'd suspected it only. Which was what he told Outlaw later that night when he'd asked.

The message came in that Outlaw was looking for him and Legend was lying back on the trunk of his drop-top Cadillac, staring up at the night sky, when he got the call. He was parked in the lot of an old and forgotten about storage building that had a perfect view of the night sky and the Brooklyn Bridge. The downside of living in the city that never sleeps is that there is too much light to get a good look at the stars. This was the place where he went when he needed to be alone with his thoughts. It was the perfect place to stargaze.

As he lay there, Legend contemplated if this was the best way that he could make use of the last night of his life. He already knew that Outlaw would figure out that his father had knowledge of the hit that had almost killed January. Though Legend, Sr. hadn't been behind it, he knew that gunplay was a possibility at the *Summer Madness* event, and he had mentioned as much to his son who then warned Outlaw of the threat in a roundabout way but didn't *exactly* mention it.

That simple fact was enough to end his life.

The fact that Legend hadn't been part of it, didn't know for sure that it would even happen or the fact that January had gotten shot by someone who had been given strict orders not to harm any member of the *BBM* and definitely not anyone in the Murray family, was of no relevance. The bottom line was that someone *did* get harmed and it was one of the only two people in the world who Outlaw lived his entire life for. There was a list of names for who had to pay for that mishap and Legend's was at the top of the list.

"You called?" was all Outlaw heard as Legend walked up on him from behind.

He was sitting alone in an alley near the hospital where January was currently undergoing surgery. Outlaw looked nothing like himself; hunched over, sitting with his shoulders nearly enclosing him like a shell. The white linen designer suit and matching leather loafers he'd had custom-made for the earlier festivities were now stained red by his daughter's blood. His forehead was resting in his hands, clasped together so tightly that his knuckles appeared white, stretched to max capacity by his grief. He'd been so deeply involved in his own miserable thoughts that he hadn't even picked up on Legend's presence nearby until he revealed himself. Had Legend been a different man, Outlaw would have found himself being tossed over into a shallow grave. Getting caught slipping was the easiest way to get snuffed out.

Through all the rigorous training that Legend had gone through to make his body movements completely silent so that he could move about unaware, none of that shit had ever worked on Outlaw. At least not until now. His grief over January's pending fate had his mind in another place.

"You knew what they were planning today, right?" Outlaw asked, lifting his head.

The dim lights in the alley partially illuminated his face, revealing the devastation in his expression. The formation of new worry lines in his forehead made him appear older than he actually was. His caramel complexion looked ashen and dull as a consequence of his tortured disposition. It was a tragedy to see.

In spite of wanting to accept his fate like a man, standing strong and tall like the soldier he'd trained his entire life to be, Legend dropped his head. Not long after, his shoulders followed suit.

"They were coming for Emmanuel. The only reason he was even asking you for protection was because he raped some nigga in Jersey's daughter—"

"You told me that," Outlaw interjected, his voice dangerously tempered though a vein protruding out the side of his neck clearly showed his agitation. "I let everyone in BBM know that Emmanuel wasn't welcome and I told Emmanuel

that myself as soon as I saw him. What I'm trying to understand is how the fuck my daughter ended up in a fucking hospital bed."

Legend parallel parked on the side of the road in a spot sectioned off for VIP. It was Onyx's doing. He hadn't even spoken to her all day, but she knew that he was coming because he always did. Since her freshman year, she had been singing at this club, gracing their stage every Friday night, so every Friday, Legend graced their VIP. And, in the event he couldn't make it or had to leave early, he made sure Nico took his place. It wasn't that he was a fan of her singing— she was *alright*, but definitely not his taste—it was because experience had shown him the things that could happen when he wasn't around. There were only two times in his life when a woman he cared for had been hurt badly in his absence. He lived every moment of his life making sure it never happened again.

"Legend... it's so good to see you!" Rachel, the club's hostess sucked in a breath and straightened her spine, effectively pushing up her breasts nearly to her chin in the process.

"Likewise," he replied, giving her a wink that caused the edges of her smile to nearly reach her eyes.

For over a year she'd been trying to get him to pay her even the least bit of attention, but it never worked. Though cordial, he barely gave her a second glance. what she didn't know is that he never would. The only thing he had time and patience for that she could offer was a quick fuck before sending her on her way. But Rachel seemed like the type to want to retaliate if she detected anything she considered disrespect. He didn't want his actions bringing bullshit on his cousin.

"Onyx should be up in about another twenty minutes. Should I just bring you your usual drink?" Rachel asked after personally showing him to his seat in VIP. As hostess, she was also the manager; she had employees available to tend to the guests, however, she always let it be known that when Legend came, addressing his needs was reserved for her.

"Yeah, that'll work." Kicking back in his chair, he flashed her a rare but award-winning smile. Her pale cheeks blushed red as she nearly stumbled over her own feet to retrieve his drink.

He snickered. "White chicks," he said under his breath and then turned to scan the crowd.

Rather than at the front, the VIP section was against the back wall of the club, which he loved because he could see any and everything in the building. It was elevated just enough for him to see the stage over the heads of the people dancing on the dance-floor. He couldn't have paid for a better view. Though had there been one better, he would.

It took less than a minute for him to find Onyx. She was hard to miss. Not many women stood at nearly six feet tall, and that was *before* the six-inch heels that she currently wore that had long velvet straps wrapped like tentacles around her model legs. Onyx's beauty was peculiar, in an exotic way that made anyone with a working pulse take notice. Legend had never thought anything of it. She was his cousin and they'd been raised like siblings so, in his mind, she like an annoying little sister who happened to actually be older by a few months. Nine, to be exact.

Peeking over the velvet ropes, he watched as she grabbed a drink from the bar and then made her way to a table where two other girls sat. One of which, put the first genuine smile of the night on Legend's face. The second he thought about how he probably looked stupid as hell, sitting alone, smiling at the sight of a girl he was trying his hardest to hate, the grin was washed away.

Get a grip, nigga. Don't got time for this girl and her goofy shit.

Sighing, he ran his hand over his face and sat back as Rachel came with his drink: water with a freshly cut slice of lime.

The DJ had dropped what must've been her favorite song because, before he knew it, January was on the dance-floor, winding her hips and making love to the music. She was dancing in a way that almost made him feel disrespected by the fact that others had the pleasure of seeing a sight that he felt should have been reserved for his eyes only. He knew that she had been a dancer, but ballet had nothing on the this.

Times like this, he wished he were the type to drink. Nico always seemed more focused with alcohol, but others told him they used it to loosen up. He could definitely benefit right now from loosening up. January had all of his muscles tense. Especially one in particular that was pressing firmly against the crotch of his jeans. And the more she moved her body, the more pressure was applied. He shifted to ease the discomfort and then pulled out his phone as an alternative visual to busy his eyes from roaming over the curve of her thighs.

And hips.

And breasts.

Damn, she is sexy as fuck.

He leaned forward, placing his elbows on the tabletop and pressing his fingers together as if in prayer. Or maybe it was more like meditation, being that he'd somehow managed to block everything around him out and focus solely on the woman that he had been trying so hard to ignore. Just the sight of her equally intrigued, excited and burned him to the core. She was the epitome of everything he wanted, beautifully gift-wrapped in a package that had a lit stick of dynamite waiting for him inside. It didn't matter how right she was for him, the second Outlaw found out Legend was anywhere around her, he would kill him.

Never in his life had Legend ever wanted a woman this badly and now that he did, she happened to be the one woman in the world he couldn't have.

The realization of that only infuriated him even more.

ON SOME SQUARE SHIT.

"What did you say this place was again?" January yelled over the music.

Brooke smiled back at her with a knowing look in her eyes. "It's a club called *Entanglements*! You like it!?"

January smiled as she continued to bob her head to the music. "It's not bad."

"Told you!"

The smile on Brooke's lips curved into a smirk. She knew that if she could get January's nose from in between her textbooks and out of the house, she would loosen up. The second January mentioned that she was a dancer, she knew it was the remedy to snap her out of the dull, stiff and fun-repellant person that she was pretending to be.

The smell of liquor wafted up January's nostrils as more dry ice crept its way onto the dance-floor. She smoothed her hands over her t-shirt, suddenly feeling out of place as she observed everyone else around her. The girls in the club were dressed in short skirts and tight crop tops or mini dresses that could have passed for a top. They all wore heels to match, mostly stilettos, including Brooke. She was severely underdressed but somehow it didn't bother her as much as she initially thought it would. Honestly, she was used to sticking out in crowds and she'd never felt quite like she belonged on any scene she roamed. It was her normal.

"Come on! Let's get a drink!" Brooke yelled, cupping her hand over her mouth to be heard over the music.

January nodded her head. "Yeah, I could use some water. Or maybe a Sprite."

She was so caught up by everything around her that she didn't even notice the look that Brooke had given her.

"A Sprite?" Brooke echoed under her breath, ogling her as if she'd grown a second head from her neck.

Who came to the club and ordered a Sprite? She was convinced that January had lost her entire mind. This was the time to be young and dumb. They had their entire life to be responsible and use good common sense. Right now, they could afford to make mistakes and Brooke intended to make plenty of them in exchange for living her life.

Linking arms with January, Brooke led her over to the bar, nearly dragging her as she stalled taking in everything around her. Her surroundings spoke to every bit of her, like a shock to her senses.

"Is it always this loud in here?"

Brooke beamed pure light. "Isn't it great? It puts you in the mood to have fun. *Real* fun, which is just what you need. Oh…and the guys in here ain't bad either," she added with a shrug. "You should find one to dance with. Just for the night, nothing too intense."

January raised her brow. Just the thought of dancing with a guy, any guy, seemed intense. How was that supposed to work? Was she supposed to approach one? Or would one approach her? What would she say?

"Don't think too hard about that," Brooke said, reading right into her expression.

"What can I get you two ladies?" the bartender yelled, centering his attention on them as soon as they approached the bar.

He was cute, had a smile that probably earned him plenty of tips. Brooke leaned over the bar, taking him in with a look that should have been reserved for the bedroom, and spoke without a moment's hesitation.

"I'll have a strawberry margarita with an extra shot. And so will she."

January gasped. "What? No, I just want a Sprite... or 7Up."

"Actually, scratch the second margarita and just bring her a Sprite along with the shot," Brooke cut in rolling her eyes although she'd fully expected January's response. The girl had to lighten up and have some fun.

With a nod and a special wink for Brooke alone, the bartender left to make the drinks and January cut her eyes at her roommate.

"I didn't know you meant a *drink* drink. We aren't old enough to drink! How did you know he wouldn't ask for ID?"

With a roll of her eyes, she answered while simultaneously waving at someone behind January's back.

"Because they never do. Hey, Onyx, over here!" She touched January on her shoulder. "One second, my girl is finally here. Let me go grab her and I'll be right back."

Pursing her lips into a straight line, January nodded but said nothing. Truthfully, she needed a second alone just to come to terms to how much of a shift from her previous life she was experiencing in such a short amount of time.

If my parents could see me now, she couldn't help but think.

Had she been in New York, this would be the talk of the city. Young January, the precious, secluded and viciously protected daughter of the infamous Outlaw, was in a club taking shots without security, accompanied only by another young teenager who didn't seem to give a damn about life. What was the world coming to? In her mind's eye, she could already see her father's face. This whole scene would give him a heart attack.

Or would get somebody killed, January thought frowning.

Flashing lights against the wall caught her attention and she whipped around just as Brooke jotted off. The DJ up in the booth was slinging heavy-hitting songs around while strobe lights made everyone look as if they were moving like robots. All around her, people were bumping and grinding on one another, letting the rhythm run through their veins, and manifest in the movement of their hips, lips and other parts they chose to rub against each other.

Brooke was right; the music did seem to take them away. It was like they didn't have a care in the world.

January felt someone shove into her and she stumbled forward, catching herself against the bar. The place was getting crowded, and quickly. The DJ switched to a summertime jam that must've been everyone's favorite song and even more people rushed to the already packed dance-floor. There were people working the area, carrying what looked like Jell-o shots on a tray, but the more the crowd gathered on the floor, the more those workers were pushed off to the side.

For the first time in her life, January was surrounded by people she didn't know and who didn't seem to recognize her at all. The only curious stares came from people who were wondering about the reason behind the fearful expression on her face. Swallowing hard, she tried to relax, just as the bartender set the drinks that Brooke had ordered down in front of her.

"Here is your Sprite but I also made you the strawberry margarita, just in case," he said with a smirk that was obviously his signature. It was the type that would most definitely make a girl drop her panties.

Grabbing the Sprite, January took a long sip as her eyes scaled the wall. There were levels that she hadn't even seen yet. She counted two balconies above her head.

"The top level is V.I.P. only," Brooke murmured in her ear, returning to her side. "Snag the attention of the right one and you might get an invite."

"I'm most definitely *not* trying to snag anything."

Ignoring her comment, Brooke stepped to the side and a girl who appeared to be around their age stepped up beside her.

"January, meet my friend, Onyx. Onyx, this is my roommate, January. But I call her Jan."

"Which sounds like something you'd call an old lady," she quickly corrected her. "January is what I go by."

Onyx smiled and replied with a simple nod. Like Brooke, she was dressed in what most would call appropriate attire for going out; a silk, olive-colored dressed that hugged her model frame and high heels that accentuated her long legs. She was tall and naturally beautiful, although she presented herself in a way that suggested she wasn't all about looks and didn't quite understand just how gorgeous she was. The hue of her dress perfectly complemented her warm mocha skin tone, her make-up was flawless, bearing a natural look with just the right bit of a gold highlights on her cheeks and eyelids that gave her a radiant glow. Her eyes were soft and friendly, giving off an inviting vibe that you wouldn't normally see when it came to girls like her. She was elegant in a subtle way that drew people in, and the effect was no different when it came to January. Same as it was with Brooke, she liked her instantly.

"I was telling Jan on the way over here all about how you're the best singer they have come here," Brooke continued. "When she gets up there, you'll see. My girl shuts the club down."

Bashful, Onyx dropped her head, hiding another bright smile before rolling her almond-shaped brown eyes.

"Whatever," she replied, laughing lightly at the compliment. "I just do what I love." She shrugged. "Anyways, what happened to the shots? Brooke, I thought you said you ordered some."

"I did, but now we need one more," she said. Turning towards the bar, she signaled to the bartender. "Hey, can we get one more? Actually, make that four. We are celebrating life!"

After giving off one of his signature smirks, which Brooke soaked up like a wet paper towel, the bartender wasted no time pulling out four additional shot glasses and filling them with Brooke's clear liquor of choice.

Cringing, January watched in pure horror as Brooke grabbed the two shots that had already been poured and held one out to her.

What was she so afraid of? Living? She really didn't know. What she *did* know was that she didn't want this night to end with her plastered across the floor or leaning over the toilet as one of the girls held her hair back while she vomited up all of the contents in her stomach.

Relax, January tried to coax herself. *This is one night, and I'm with good company. I'm in college now and it's all I've ever wanted: to be free and have fun. Now's the time.*

"You ready?" Onyx whispered to her, giving a knowing look. "You've never had alcohol before. I can see it all in your eyes."

January's eyes widened. "Am I that transparent?"

Onyx giggled and nodded her head. Her gold chandelier earrings wagged their agreement at the same time.

"Yes, you definitely are. But you're our girl. We would never let anything happen to you. You're always safe with us. Just relax."

Relax.

January inwardly groaned. *There's that word again.*

Interrupting loudly, Brooke waved her hand in the air. "We can leave these conversations for when we're back at the dorm, drunk, and spilling our guts out to each other. Right now, though, is dance time."

January's brows jumped. "Dance time?"

Brooke took her hand. "Come on! This is the perfect place to lose your clubbing virginity, and I'm going to make sure you have a good time. To friendship, good grades, fine ass niggas and making mistakes," she toasted, lifting her glass.

Onyx and January followed suit, even though January wore her discomfort all over her face. Brooke suppressed a laugh, loving every minute of it. She knew from experience that the most controlled people were the ones to really let loose once the liquor set in. January didn't even know what she was in for.

Placing the glass to her lips to take a sip, January winced as the pungent smell of the liquor singed her nostrils, before opening her mouth and taking it down quickly like a dose of medicine. She cringed as the liquid burned before settling in her chest. She squeezed her eyes closed, absorbing the warmth that followed, and then slowly opened them once again to find two pairs looking back at her, full of excitement and expectation.

"Not bad, right?" Brooke smirked.

She paused for a moment to think and then shook her head. "Actually, no… It wasn't."

"Great!" Brooke replied before collecting their glasses. "Now we dance."

As Brooke tugged her onto the dance floor, January didn't put up much of a fight. She was getting used to the atmosphere. The place was wild. Untamed. Raw, and teeming with energy. There was something brutally honest, primal and free about *Intrigue*. Everyone around wanted one thing only: a good time. No matter how they obtained it. And there was something about that concept that appealed to her.

A slow, melodic, and familiar tune began to spill from the speakers. The effect of the alcohol began to take over and January felt all of her inhibitions push to the wayside. For the first time in what felt like forever, she wasn't worried about anyone in the room, who they were, or what they might think if they were looking at her. Her only focus was on the music and how it spoke to her, the way the rhythm seemed to course through her veins, the way the words fell off her lips as she worked her hips, feeling the rise and fall of the bass.

Closing her eyes, she let the music move her, surrendering to the vibe around her in a way that felt so natural. As if this was what she was made to do.

She had always felt that it was. Dancing was her form of self-expression. For someone who was always so controlled, so obedient, and who suppressed so much of herself in order to please the ones around her, dancing was the only way she could be free. She made her own rules, put her all into it and allowed her will to freely flow through the music.

Ballet had been her avenue of choice because it fit perfectly in the narrative of the life story that she'd been born into but, honestly speaking, she enjoyed all types of movement and had training in all areas of dance. There wasn't much she couldn't do—in one moment, she could go from performing the steps of *The Black Swan* or *The Nutcracker* to working her hips like Beyoncé.

Sex ain't the only thing that's on my mind
But you get me so excited, whoa
Irreplaceable

Tattoos from your neck that drop down to your ankles
Droptop in the rain
Shawty, you wanna feel good, I wanna feel good too
Don't I make you feel good?
You get me so excited

With her eyes closed, January let her intuition guide her and fully surrendered to the guidance and desire of her body. For her, it was like a deep meditation, and she didn't even realize how many eyes were on her. Some were in awe and, of course, a few women were hating severely at the fact that a chick wearing some sneakers and a simple t-shirt with cut-off shorts had managed to capture the attention of most of the most-sought after and available men. If they paid enough attention, they would realize that January didn't even want their attention, she was just being herself, happy and satisfied in her own lane. But that was the point the other girls weren't understanding—seeing a woman happy and satisfied on her own was like a magnet. Every nigga on the planet wanted a piece of that.

Suddenly, a different feeling entered her consciousness, a stronger connection that sliced right through her making love on the dancefloor. An image, a perfect visual of Legend, flashed through her mind, birthing tingles of excitement and sweet seduction up her spine. Though she held him only as a visual in her head, January's thoughts captured every essence of him, so completely that she could nearly smell his cologne. It was so real, as if she could reach out and touch his skin.

Her heavy eyelids opened, drunken by her emotions or some strong substance that had fully enraptured her mind, and lifted, connecting immediately with a stare so filled with intensity that it was almost as if it had been calling out to her.

Legend?

Though her hips didn't miss a beat, January's heart skipped right through a couple before accelerating to nearly slamming in her chest. She and Legend locked eyes and the energy between them was so electric that it seemed to change the atmosphere. It definitely changed everything about how she felt, in a good way, if she were to admit that to herself, and thanks to a little bit of liquid courage, she was willing to do just that.

Giving in for once to the feelings that had overtaken her, January tilted her head to the side and slowly licked her lips, showing Legend a side of her that he wasn't sure he was quite ready to see. With a smirk on her lips, she lifted her hand in the air and beckoned to him with one finger, calling him down to her, silently laying out a spell that she completed with the seductive thrust and rhythmic wave of her hips.

Legend was caught all the way off guard.

PLAYING GAMES.

"Fuck…"

Leaning forward, he placed his arms on the top of his legs, hoping the movement would create some space for the throbbing muscle between his legs that seemed to be communicating directly to the woman he desired dancing down below.

What the fuck is she doing? He thought, watching her.

She was in full stripper mode, dick-teasing him to the max. He blew out a hot breath of air and ran a weary hand over his face to force his eyes away. This shit was all bad and he knew right then that whatever the hell was going on between him and January would not end well. Or at least, not like how he'd initially planned for it to.

On second thought… nigga, what the fuck are you doing? he asked himself, bringing his eyes to her once again.

She was down there, nearly throwing everything he wouldn't admit that he wanted right at his feet. And instead of claiming it, he was sitting up in V.I.P. trying to ignore her fine ass while she gave the rest of the club a show. If he continued to delay, it was only a matter of time before one of the lame ass niggas standing around watching got enough courage to shoot his shot. Shit would really go sideways at that point because, whether or not he was ready to make his move, letting another man make a play for her attention was out of the question. He wasn't having it.

Standing, Legend walked to the edge of the balcony and beckoned to January in a less subtle and definitely more aggressive way.

"Get your ass up here!" he gritted, giving a signal with his hand that made it clear exactly what he meant.

The expression on his face was enough to make grown men on the street fold instantly. He knew it because he'd used it enough times to fully observe its effects and only conjured it when absolutely necessary. It worked every time on the most fearless soldiers, grown ass men who had body counts more than twice his age. So why the hell did it seem to have no effect at all on a little ass college girl who had never done gangster shit?

A short few seconds of hesitation mixed with January playing games was all it took for a young, brave nigga to set himself up to lose his life. Under Legend's watchful stare, someone he surmised as an athlete, basketball no doubt, swiped his hand over his face, steadied his shoulders and began to walk towards her with his lustful intentions all in his eyes. The kid was totally oblivious to the fact that, though he had plans of toying with her body by the end of the night, what he was really playing with was his life.

Bracing himself by placing his hands on the outside rail on the balcony, Legend leaned forward and cut his glare right into January, giving her a real deal warning to cut it out. But her coy expression told him that she was still with the shits. The totally oblivious college kid walked up to her side, reaching out to grab her hand in one swift motion that was still slower than the time it took for Legend to strengthen his grip around the handle of his gun, tucked firmly at his side.

"Shorty, don't do this stupid shit," he whispered under his breath, speaking directly to her as if she could hear.

Instead of snatching away, the single thing that Legend wanted her to do, January allowed her hand to linger and glanced up, catching the guy's eye before giving him a seductive smile.

Legend was seething.

January had never seen a nigga really get fucked up before and that much became obvious to him right then. If she had, she would have told ole boy where he could put his hands and sent him on his way. But nah… Instead, she was laying the foundation for all three of them to be caught up in some bullshit.

With his cell in his hands, Legend placed a call that he knew was necessary in order to get him out of making a mistake that would cost him. Never before had he ever contemplated being this reckless, his every move was carefully thought and planned in every way because there was nothing more that he hated than to make mistakes. He hated paying consequences for some shit that could be avoided. But here was January, testing him in ways he'd never been tested before.

"Nico, you on your way?"

With his eyes still glaring into January's skull, he spoke to the only person who could stop him from walking headfirst into a situation that wouldn't end well. He couldn't take that kind of heat at the moment and, in normal circumstances, he was able to control himself, but January was presenting a test that he wasn't sure he would successfully pass.

"Yeah, I'm pullin' up now. Late as hell and for no damn reason. I tried to talk up that chick you left hangin' but that shit was a waste of fuckin' time."

"Why?" Legend asked, not from interest but from a need to busy himself with the conversation.

"Don't get me wrong, we was vibin' heavy. She seemed like a decent chick but that was until I leaned in and caught a whiff of dragon breath. I can't fuck with that under no circumstances."

"Wait... what?" Legend momentarily lost his train of thought. "Did you just say 'dragon breath'?"

"Hell yeah," Nico replied. "Breath so hot, she bout melted the fuckin' eyebrows off my face. She's one of them broads that brush their teeth but forget they got a whole damn tongue that needs some special love. That's an automatic 'yuck' for me, nigga. I can't fuck with it."

Chuckling to himself, Legend turned to exit from the V.I.P. area, relaxed now that something had gotten his mind off January acting crazy as hell down below. To be real, she wasn't his to feel some kind of way about so if she wanted to spend her time letting broke niggas push up on her for attention, that was on her.

"I should be pullin' up in five," Nico said just as Legend was on the main floor of the club, quickly approaching the doors.

"Good, I'm 'bout to head out. Shit too thick in here for me tonight. I'mma go somewhere I can lay low and chill."

"Lay low and chill?" Nico echoed, chuckling to himself as he said it. "That's all you do anywhere you go, no matter how many people are around. What's the difference about tonight?"

"A lot," Legend replied simply as he pushed out the exit doors, fighting a ferocious battle in his mind, though his tone was as cool as ever.

Under the surface, he was boiling hot coals under his skin. He wanted to turn back to see what January was up to, but he knew better; it wouldn't be good for anyone involved if he saw the wrong thing. And so, with as much mental fortitude as he could muster, he walked through the club doors and left everything that frustrated him behind.

Or so he thought.

Before he could properly gather his thoughts, he heard the creak of the heavy glass door behind him, followed by a voice that made him feel anything but calm.

"Are you following me?" January snapped, glaring at Legend as if she had razors coming from her eyes.

"Love, you're the one runnin' up on me," he said nonchalantly turning around to face her. "I should be asking you that exact thing."

Frowning, she curled her nose to the sky and gave him a hard stare.

"Me? You're the one who keeps showing up where I am. First, my class. Then outside my dorm and now here."

She lifted a brow and placed her hands firmly on her hips, inadvertently causing him to follow them to the curves he couldn't help but find irresistible. Clenching his jaw, he forced his attention to her face. She gave him a sideways look, narrowing her eyes while peering into him.

"Are you sure you aren't working with my father? Are you watching me for him?"

"Here we go with this shit again."

Sighing, he turned fully towards her while running a hand over his face before catching her gaze with his eyes.

"Yo, I know you're used to all the niggas around you treatin' you like you're something special but this ain't that. You're not important enough for me to follow around, princess."

It was a lie but the way that she winced as it hit her ears let him know that she bought it. As much as she tried to study him for answers on his inner thoughts, searching for hints on how he really felt and why he made certain moves, it was obvious that she really couldn't read him at all.

Legend watched with pleasure as his words put her completely off-center, fully understanding why and loving the effect he had on her entire being. January was used to being in complete control of every situation, or at least feeling that way, whether she actually was in control or not. The problem was, when it came to him, she was absolutely clueless. He continuously threw her for a loop and nothing frustrated her more than that simple fact.

"Fine. Just stay away from me then," she snapped, her voice becoming icy to force gravity in her tone.

She was putting on. But it didn't matter because Legend saw right through her act.

With a deadpan expression on his face, he stepped forward, closing the gap between them. He was close; dangerously close. she wanted to move away—to take a step back for some air—but that felt too much like retreating so she steadied herself, cementing her feet firmly into the ground. He thought he scared her, and maybe in a way he did, but she would rather die than to let him know that.

"That's what you want?" he challenged her.

She took in a subtle breath in an effort to clear her thoughts.

Big mistake.

All it did was force her to take in a whiff of his cologne. It was a powerful elixir, like a hypnotic drug, forcing her emotions into a battle of tug of war with her thoughts. Her mind battled her heart. She wanted him close but at the same time wanted him far. Her brows furrowed and she pursed her lips. She couldn't answer his question. Truthfully, *she* didn't even know what the hell she wanted.

"Yes," she forced out in a single breath. "That's what I want."

"What is?"

She licked her lips and strengthened her tone. "For you to stay away from me."

A smirk teased the edge of his lips. "That's a motherfuckin' lie. What I told you about tellin' me those?"

Her shoulders dropped. Her response to his question came out as if she were on autopilot. "That you could see right through them."

"That's right."

Then he dipped his head, bringing his lips down into the crook of her neck. He was fucking with her mind, but what January didn't know was that she was fucking with his as well. She was trying to resist him, pretending that she didn't want something they both knew she did. To be real, he wanted it just as much. Maybe even more. Both of them were just too stubborn to admit it.

The warmth of his breath tickled her skin and January closed her eyes just as he did the same and took in her scent. The world around them melted away and, in that infinite moment in time, it was just the two of them standing there. Raw in their emotions, vulnerability on display—a rarity for them both. Neither was the type to allow their feelings to show.

"You gotta stop," she whispered when she felt his lips touch her skin. "Please."

As expected, he didn't listen. Legend wasn't the type to follow the rules. And he definitely wasn't the type to follow commands. Especially ones said but not really meant to be followed.

"Do you want me to?" he asked so low that she could only barely hear the words as they fell off his tongue.

He cupped an arm around her waist, pulling her lightly into him with the tips of his fingers. Her balance wavered and she fell into him. It was an effortless movement, deepening their connection in a way that felt so natural. Like magnets that could do nothing else but attract. In one swift moment, he swiped under the thin material of her shirt and allowed his fingers to find her skin.

The contact set off a series of electric shocks to his spine.

Damn, he thought, feeling the sudden but foreign energy course through his body.

She was *pressure*.

It quickly brought him to his senses. And she was also right. He did have to stop. It would take the last remaining bit of his will to do it, but it had to happen now. If he allowed this to go on any further, it would be impossible not to.

Just as he was about to pull away, January pressed her body even more into his and said something that changed the game.

"Actually, no. I don't want you to."

The blood in his loins quickened to a boil. He flexed his hands and tested her, cupping firmly around her ass. She let out a soft gasp which gave him the permission he needed.

That was it. There was no turning back now. Only the Creator could stop was about to happen. But so far, it seemed the Universe was working in their favor.

Giving into his most primitive sexual desire, he began to toy with the waistband of the shorts she was wearing but stopped cold when he caught a whiff of cheap off-brand cologne, making the image of her entertaining the lame ass nigga in the club come to his mind. His muscles went rigid and he backed away, scowling at the thought.

Feeling cold air replace the warmth that their bodies had created, January's eyes fluttered open.

"What?" she asked when she saw the agitated expression on his face.

"A real nigga don't run up behind a lame." His eyes bore into her as he spoke. "Meditate on that when you're doin' all your peacemakin' shit tomorrow morning. Maybe then you'll remember it next time you feel like shaking your ass for a broke nigga in the club," he added and then turned to walk away. Thinking twice, he stopped just long enough to deliver a blunt warning.

"Matter of fact, dead that shit altogether. Have all the fun you want with your dumb ass friends but if I catch you entertainin' these niggas out here again, you'll have a problem on your hands that you don't want to be responsible for."

Her skin seared as if under a flame.

What?

Her brows bunched up nearly to the center of her forehead. January was thrown. Once again, Legend had built her up just to let her emotions come crashing down over some fuckery.

What was his deal?

One second he was acting like he didn't want her, didn't care what she did and was annoyed by her existence and the next he was telling her what to do with her body and her life. He was a walking contradiction. It was bipolar disorder at its finest.

Marching up behind him, she didn't hesitate to give him a piece of her mind. Whether he wanted to hear it or not, she was determined to put him in his place.

"You can't tell me what to do and who to talk to. It's not your business. You don't own me, Legend!"

Dry chuckles was the only answer he gave her, mentally tossing her words to the side as if they meant nothing. Pure rage engulfed her soul, forcing blood to her head.

In an act of rebellion, January took a moment to look around at the few people standing outside of the building, talking, chilling, drinking, smoking and minding their business as pure drama unfolded in her life. And then she saw the perfect specimen to use for a quick uprising against him. He wanted to have the final word and believe that she would be obedient to him. But he didn't know that she was the type of woman who refused to be owned.

Smiling sweetly, she caught the eye of a guy standing a little ahead of where Legend had parked his car curbside. When she saw him respond to her with a simple nod and crooked smile, she knew that his attention was hers for the taking.

"Sup, shorty?"

"Not too much," was her simple reply, but it was enough to grab Legend's attention, just as she'd planned.

Looking up, Legend released the handle of his car door just in time to see her taking off in a seductive strut towards yet another corny nigga and instantly saw red.

How in the fuck *does she keep finding these goofy ass dudes?* he silently fumed.

Slamming the door shut, Legend ran up on her and grabbed her tightly by the wrist, snatching her so hard that her chest crashed into his.

"What the fuck are you doing?"

January squirmed, trying to pull away but his grip was too firm. The more she tried to get away from him, the tighter he held her in place. There was no use.

"Stop it, Legend! You may be working for my father, but you are *not* him. You can't tell me what to do. Now get away with me!"

"Oh yeah?" His brow curled and his upper lip followed suit, lifting into a devilish sneer. "Keep playing with fire and see if I don't burn this whole bitch down."

The pupils in his dead eyes seemed to sparkle in the moonlight. They danced, as if he were actually excited at the thought of setting some shit on fire. January felt the weight of his words in her bones. Common sense told her to stop testing him—but there one thing about common sense: It *wasn't* common. She was still determined to fight.

"Whatever," she scoffed, kicking up dirt with the tip of her shoe.

Such a fuckin' baby, Legend thought, but still didn't waver in the least.

"Try me."

Silence enveloped the two of them and he watched as she weighed her thoughts.

Scanning her brain as to whether she wanted to test his gangster.

See if she really had what it took to go toe-to-toe with a thug.

Once he saw her lower lip push forward in a slight pout right before her body went limp, it was apparent that she had learned the lesson. That was fortunate. The last thing he wanted was to have to make an example out of some unlucky nigga just because January was trying to play it bold.

"You didn't have to do all that. I was *just* playing." She rolled her eyes. "And having fun."

"Well, get your playful ass in the car. I'm taking you home."

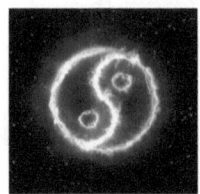

LOVE WOUNDS.

"Um...No, you're not," January replied stubbornly crossing her arms in front of her. "I came here with my friends and I'm leaving with them."

Agitated beyond his max, Legend ran his hand over his face and blew out a sharp breath. She was testing him like no one ever should. Because if there was anything that Legend knew how to do, he could prove a point. And, in that moment, it looked like he was going to have to prove a point to January that when he said something, he fucking meant it.

It wasn't the fact that she was out with her friends, dancing and having a good time that got to him. It was the fact that she was drunk as hell which made her more apt to doing some reckless shit with niggas who were game to make a decision they wouldn't live long enough to regret once he got involved. Legend wasn't the jealous type, and he had no problem letting her make her own decisions if she were making them with a clear head. But the only thing perfectly clear in that moment was that she was on some other shit.

"You go back in there and I'mma be right behind you like a fuckin' second skin," he said, speaking to her through clenched teeth. "Ain't shit happening so ain't no point in stayin'."

Still standing chest-to-chest with Legend's hand firmly wrapped around her wrist, they glared into each other without saying a word. It was a vicious stand-off of some sort, with both unyielding and waiting for the other to back-down. Each one mentally called the other stubborn, not even realizing that they mirrored the same traits: both were hard-headed, strong-willed and stubborn to a fault. Ungiving in the least once they became set in their ways.

Deep down, January wanted to leave with Legend, but she wouldn't admit it. He was too commanding of her and she was unwilling to fold. After being under the rule of a domineering father who set the law and expected her to follow it without question, the last thing she was about to do was trade out one master for another. Her freedom meant everything, and she would defend it until the end, even in instances such as these, when it positioned her against the one thing she truly wanted.

She wanted him to want her. She wanted his attention, his affection, his time. She wanted to feel important in his eyes. But now, when his full attention was on giving her the exact thing she wanted, she was pushing him away. And to be honest, she didn't fully understand why. She was a walking conundrum, a puzzle that was impossible to solve—for him, and even for herself.

But then again, so was he.

Whether he realized it or not, Legend was just as much of a puzzle as she was. He wanted her but didn't want her at the same time. He needed her close but pushed her away. He wouldn't have her but didn't want other men to have her. He had his reasons and so did she. Their emotions wanted one thing, but their mind wanted another. They were sending mixed signals to each other and sending mixed signals to themselves. Neither one could decide whether to listen to the message that came from their head or the one coming from their heart.

"Let me *go*, Legend!"

Giving in, something that he didn't do often, he released her wrist just as she snatched away from him. The force of her pulling nearly sent her catapulting in the other direction and Legend had to reach out to grab her arm once again, pulling her towards him in order to avoid a fall.

"You need a nigga, even though you think you don't," he said as he steadied her to her feet.

Smart ass, January thought, glaring up at him. With her lips pressed into a straight line, she pulled away from him once more, rubbing her wrist.

"I don't *need* anyone. I can take care of myself. I don't *need* saving."

"Could've fooled me," he replied, snorting a burst of air through his nose. "Looked to me like you was 'bout to bust yo' ass."

Before she could answer, the sound of someone calling her name stopped the words from falling from her lips.

"January!"

Turning, she saw Brooke rushing towards her, diving through the crowd of people standing outside. Behind her, Onyx was struggling to keep up, tiptoeing as fast as she could in her stiletto heels, being extra careful not to fall. Brooke, on the other hand, was a pro. As if she were wearing sneakers instead of stilettos, she made strides with very little difficulty.

Frowning hard, her eyes circled back and forth between January and Legend in an attempt to figure out what was going on. As far as she knew, one second, they were all dancing together and having a good time and the next, January had disappeared. Being that it was Brooke's idea to go out in the first place and that she'd been the one who practically forced each shot of liquor down January's throat, she felt it was also her responsibility that she made it home safe and in one piece *without* becoming a date rape victim.

"What's going on?" she hissed, her voice just low enough so only January could hear her.

After backing away a few paces to give them some space, Legend stood stoically watching and waiting for January to fill her in. Regardless to what happened here, his word would still stand. Either he was leaving and he was taking January with him or she would be shaking her ass with a shadow standing by her side. All the dick-teasing and grabbing up on niggas was a done deal for the night.

"It's okay. I'm good," January replied, annoyed as she cut her eyes over to Legend. "I was actually just about to walk back inside."

Nodding slowly, Brooke followed her eyes over to Legend as well before back to January, a question sparkling within them. It wasn't until that moment that she recognized him from earlier, sitting outside the dorms. It gave her some comfort knowing that he wasn't some local who was picking up college girls at the club, however, she didn't know him and wasn't sure how well January knew him either.

"Oh my *God*, I've never moved so fast in these heels in all my life!" With her hand over her chest, Onyx leaned forward, giggling in between gasps for air. "Brooke, you ain't tell me you were a track-star, bitch! Somebody call 911. I need an oxygen tank!"

"I was trying to make sure January's drunk ass hadn't been kidnapped," Brooke replied, rolling her eyes before glaring down at Onyx who was still holding her chest. Legend, who had been watching from the other side of the car until that point, finally decided to circle around to their side, positioning himself right next to where January stood. He leaned back on the trunk of the car with his arms folded across his chest. He seemed amused as he watched Onyx and all of her theatrics, heaving and gasping for air as if she had somehow punctured her lungs.

"Damn," Brooke said, under her breath, once she was able to take a good look at him.

Looking back at her friend, she had to bite back a smile. Now she fully understood why January was leaving with him because, had it been her, she would have been doing the same exact thing. Placing her back to both Legend and Onyx, Brooke turned to face January alone and gave her a wide-eyed look.

"He is sexy *as hell!*"

Laughing, January pressed her hand to her forehead, covering her eyes. This would probably go down as one of the most embarrassing moments in her life.

"Girl, go ahead and do your thing," she said, nudging January on the shoulder. "A nigga that looks like him ain't gotta drug no bitch to kick it. So, as long as you straight, I'm *good*."

"Nothing's wrong, I promise," January replied with a nod.

Onyx smiled, looking up at her once she was finally able to catch her breath. "Good. I thought my cousin was fuckin' with you. I was going to beat his ass." She gave Legend a gentle punch on the shoulder.

"Yeah, 'cause *that's* what would happen," he said back with a half-smile.

January's chin almost dropped to her feet. She was floored.

"*This* is your cousin?" She pointed a finger at him.

"Yeah, this is my overprotective ass cousin who comes here every time I have a show," Onyx explained, rolling her eyes. "I don't know how I'll ever get a man to take me home for the night with his ass lurking around."

"Not happening," Legend said with a straight face. Onyx shook her head, rolling her eyes again before placing them on January's face.

"Sooo, you two know each other or you just met here?" she asked.

Unable to resist, January snuck a peek at Legend, only to notice that he was already looking at her. Although his expression was unreadable, his eyes were soft. He watched her, not like he was waiting to hear what she would say, but like he was absorbing her image into him. Like he was studying her features, memorizing them to pull up in his mind's eye for another time.

"From school. Crazy enough, we share every class."

"Every class? What a coincidence." Onyx's smile deepened.

"January doesn't believe in coincidences," Brooke chimed in. "She says it all the time."

Legend lifted a brow as if to ask a question. Picking up on it, January didn't hesitate to reply.

"It's true, I don't."

Silence fell between the four of them with January and Legend looking at each other with such intensity that it almost seemed as if they were having a conversation between themselves.

"Well, okay!" Brooke said, clapping her hands together. Deciding it was time to make their exit, she looked at Onyx. "How about we go back inside?" She grabbed onto January's hand to tug her along with her towards the door, but the gentle pull knocked January off balance. All of a sudden, her head felt heavier than normal and her vision was blurry. Noticing that something was off, Brooke turned back.

"You good?"

January nodded, but really, she wasn't. Not only did she feel like he'd once again made her look like a fool, but she was also light-headed and nauseated from the alcohol. She had too many drinks for a first timer who had barely eaten a thing all day.

"I really just want to go home."

"Already?" Brooke whined, pushing out her bottom lip. "It's not even one o'clock and Onyx still has the second half of her show."

January shook her head. "No, you can go ahead. I can call a car. It's no big deal."

"All the way from here to campus? That's going to cost a lot."

"It's not a big deal."

"Well, what about all that you said about this not being an innocent city and—"

"Never mind, never mind. I'll just stay—"

"I'm going that way. I'll take you home."

Everyone turned in the direction of Legend's voice. His head was bent and eyes down as he pecked away on his phone. A huge grin spread across Brooke's lips and she widened her eyes at January, wiggling her eyebrows suggestively. Legend was, hands-down, one of the sexiest guys on campus and if January played her cards right, she could get a chance to really see what he was working with. They weren't even two weeks into the semester and already her girl was winning.

"Oh?" Onyx said, looking at Legend. "You're going to leave me alone to fend for myself for once? How fun!" She clapped her hands together dramatically.

"Nico is about to pull up because I have business to tend to," he told her before turning his eyes to January. "And since I gotta go by campus, I'll take you home."

"Of course," Onyx sighed, rolling her eyes. "You called big brother to watch over me. I should've known. Well, goodnight, January. It was nice meeting you."

"Nice meeting you, too," she said, before shaking her head. "Wait, I—"

Before she could finish objecting, Brooke grabbed Onyx's hand and began to tug her away.

"Bye, January. Text me when you get home… if you make it there before I do," she tossed over her shoulder before she and Onyx took off back across the street.

"You've got to be kidding me," January said under her breath, watching them leave.

Wasn't there some girl code against this?

"Let's go, princess," Legend said, tucking his phone into his pocket.

"Nothing has changed." January crossed her arms back over her chest, fully falling back into her stubborn nature. "I'm not going *anywhere* with you. I'm going to call a ride to get me."

"So you'll call some random nigga to pick you up, but won't get in the car with me? That's backwards as hell."

She rolled her eyes. "So is paying for classes just so that you can sleep through all of them."

"Damn. Yo, can you talk to somebody without all that extra shit?"

"It's not something I can do for you personally. But it's something I can do in general."

Legend furrowed his brows. "And why not for me?"

"Because you might be some crazy criminal. How do I know that I can trust you?"

His frown deepened. "The fuck? You're the crazy one with a pimp you call 'daddy' who is always sending niggas lookin' for yo' ass. I should be the one askin' if it's safe letting *you* ride around in *my* shit."

In some roundabout way, January guessed he had a point.

"I'm not a prostitute." She was still fuming, her tone dipped as some of her anger faded to make way for embarrassment. "I told you that at the bookstore. I don't have a pimp."

A cocky half smile crossed his lips. "I know," he admitted. "I knew it back then when you first said it. But it was funny as hell fuckin' with you."

Something about the way he said it, the way he took delight in teasing her, made her pause. Looking at him hard, she felt a nostalgic feeling haunting her. She *had* to know him, *had* to have seen him somewhere. It wasn't something she could place in her mind, but it was definitely felt in her soul. He was someone she'd met before and, for some reason, she felt like he was important in some way.

Legend's breath stalled in his chest as he watched her watching him. He could see the wheels turning in her head. He could see her trying to figure it all out.

It's only a matter of time before she does, said the voice in the back of his mind. He knew it was true. He was playing with fire and the heat was getting deadlier with every second he spent in her presence. The craziest part of it all was, even though the moment she recognized him could lead to him suffering some drastic consequences, he hoped that she would. Although he knew it was stupid to think so, somewhere inside he felt like her memory of the moments they shared together, the feeling he knew they'd both felt even in those brief moments, would overshadow the disaster that came behind it. His grandmother always used to say that love could heal all wounds, but he'd never believed it. In this moment, he hoped that it did.

LESSONS.

"I REMEMBER YOU," SHE SAID, STOPPING THE BEATING OF LEGEND'S heart. With bated breath, he pressed his teeth into his bottom lip, waiting for whatever she would say next.

Nodding, she narrowed her eyes into him, lifting a single finger in the air to accompany her accusation. "I don't know from where, but I know I've seen you before. You *are* working with my father, aren't you?"

Legend expelled a harsh breath. All hope faded away and disappointment flooded in.

"Yo, I don't have time for this shit. I'm 'bout to leave. What you wanna do is on you. Either get in or get left."

With that said, he took off, leaving her behind to make her own decision. He was done fighting her. Over playing this little game of hers. He'd already wasted too much time fucking around with her as it was. In some strange turn of circumstances, the fact that he no longer cared to force her against her will anymore was all it needed for January's mind to change. Walking behind him to his car, she crossed over to the driver's side, opened the door and then slid in.

"You promise to take me home and nowhere else?" she asked once he started the engine and pulled off onto the street.

Legend lifted one brow in the air, glancing at her quickly before returning his attention to the road.

"Where else would I be taking you?"

She shrugged. "I don't know. To the river to execute me?"

"Eh, I prefer sailing out into the ocean for something like that. Much more room to play with."

Her jaw dropped open in shock. The way he nonchalantly offered up that information completely threw her for a loop. Unless he had been joking? He didn't laugh, though. He didn't smile, and he didn't backtrack like someone would if they had just made a joke like that.

Who *was* this guy?

"But, to answer your question, no. I'm not taking you straight home."

"My roommate's going to want to know what happened to me," January said. "I'm supposed to text her when I get home."

He came to a stop at a light and turned to look directly at her, cradling her eyes in his. "Then you tell her a very good-looking man took you back to his place before dropping you off at home."

January rolled her eyes to the sky. "I'm not sure 'good-looking' is the word I'd use, but whatever."

She was lying. And from the way he seemed totally unfazed, he definitely knew it.

"All this talk 'bout how you don't know a nigga…" He chuckled. "You know more about me than you've told me about you. Is January even your real name? Or is that your *street* name?"

Smirking, he added the last part as a tribute to their first conversation. It still made him chuckle when he thought of it.

Did he just ask me a personal question? January wasn't sure she'd heard him right.

She stared at him, feeling her brow furrow deeper by the second. Why was he even acting like he gave a damn about her? Or her name? He definitely didn't seem to care in class. Now he had her in his car, and he was all of a sudden interested.

January, you're being paranoid. Just chill.

She was trying, but there was something about him that made her feel like there was more to him than meets the eyes. He was more than just a college kid. There was a dangerous, bad boy vibe that she couldn't ignore. Especially now that they were alone, she couldn't stop the alarms in her head from ringing.

Legend was the type you had to watch out for. The kind people gave a pass because he was nice to look at. In January's experience, those were the men who were the deadliest. Getting in the car of someone she barely knew, especially this late at night, wasn't smart. That seemed like the prologue to an especially gruesome episode of *Forensic Files*. Or *First 48*.

And yet, here she was…

She had to swallow down bile at the thought.

"Aye… you hear me?" he asked.

January turned her gaze away from him. "I did."

"Are you going to answer me?"

"I haven't decided yet."

He chuckled, flicking the bridge of his nose with his thumb. "You're hardheaded as fuck, you know that?"

She lifted her chin in the air, stubbornly. "Only when it comes to people I don't know." Fire in her eyes, she stared pointedly into him at that.

"So now you don't know me?" He smiled in response to her attitude, and her insides turned to mush.

"No, I definitely *don't* know you.

"That sucks." He shrugged. "'Cause I'm not a bad nigga to know."

January couldn't say that she disagreed with that, but she kept her mouth closed anyways.

"There is one sure way to tell if you can trust somebody," he said, changing the subject.

"How?"

"Their vibe."

"Um... what?" Her brows wrinkled.

"Look at me. Do I give off a bad vibe to you?"

She stared Legend in the eyes and hesitated, genuinely taking him in. A calmness flooded her body, shooting a cool feeling through her, like liquid gold through her veins. Peace completely enveloped her, but the beating of her heart accelerated the more she looked in his eyes. It was an odd feeling; something she couldn't place but couldn't help but feel comforted by. Before she could completely register what was happening, she found herself shaking her head.

"No... you don't give out a bad vibe," she replied.

"Everything you need to know about a person is in the energy they put out." Legend spoke with complete sincerity as he stared gently into her eyes. "Always trust your vibe."

The car went silent for a few moments as they both retreated into their own thoughts. Both of them trying to decide in that moment whether they were going to side with the commands coming from their heads or the ones coming from their hearts. January was the first to come to a decision.

"Yes, January is my real name."

Testing how much she truly trusted him, Legend decided to push her a little further.

"January what?"

She paused, not wanting to share. A different level of feeling came with giving someone your full, legal, government name. Then again, what was the use? They had almost *every* class together. If he really wanted to know her name, there were several ways to find it.

"My name is January LuKeisha Murray."

"Yeah?" he asked and then nodded his head. "That's pretty dope."

"I guess so."

"You don't like it?"

She scrunched up her nose. "No, not really."

"Why not?"

"I don't know, it just… sounds so ghetto."

He chuckled. "What does a girl like you know about the ghetto?"

"What do *you* know about it?"

"More than you think."

January rolled her eyes and snorted air from her nose. "Typical."

"What's that supposed to mean?"

"You just sound like so many other rich boys I know. Their trust fund is the reason for their expensive cars, flashy jewelry, and designer clothes, but because they like rap music and hang out in the hood every now and then, they think it makes them street. Meanwhile, they have the luxury of going to Ivy League schools and sleeping through the class because it's on their parents' dime and they have too much money to worry about a stupid degree."

Legend's brows bounced high. "So you really got me all figured out, huh?"

"I guess you just give off that vibe." Purposely being a smart ass, she turned her stare to look out the window. "And I was told to *always* trust my vibe."

Looking at her, Legend held in a smirk by pinching his lips between two fingers.

Pretty ass lips and a smart ass mouth, he thought, staring at her. *I can dig it.*

"Ask me something that we went over in our classes. Anything."

January sat back in her seat, feeling confident that she was about to prove her point she'd been dying to make: that Legend didn't give a damn about class because he slept through each and every one and didn't learn a thing.

One point for January and for Legend? A big fat, ugly ass zero.

"Something we went over this week?"

He shrugged. "It's up to you. Ask whatever you want to ask me."

She couldn't help but grin. "What is 'cognitive dissonance'?

Legend smiled, squeezing the bridge of his nose. "It's the law you live by."

January sucked her teeth and rolled her eyes. "Explain it."

"It's when someone holds on to two competing beliefs or attitudes, which creates imbalance." Turning to her, he licked his lips slowly and looked her up and down. "Like how you like to pretend that you ain't got a thing for thugs, but I know you feeling a nigga."

Ignoring the sexy ass smirk forming over perfectly straight, pretty white teeth, she moved right on to her next question.

"Okay then… what are the four clairs of intuition?"

"Clairvoyance, clairsentience, clairaudient, claircognizant," he replied. "But I would argue that there is a fifth clair. Clairavoidance:

when you clearly avoid some real shit your intuition is telling you. That's something *you* like to do."

Ignoring that, January fell right into her next question. And the next. And another. And yet another. Each one, Legend answered perfectly and completely, even when she pulled out questions pertaining to the quantum theory class he took during her lectures on dance theory. Each question he answered without hesitation or even the slightest bit of difficulty, while making sure to add some kind flip comment about her at the end.

She was dumbfounded. *Utterly* dumbfounded.

"Whether it looks like it or not, I pay attention to everything. Where I come from, watching, listening, and analyzing is the only way to survive."

"Makes perfect sense, I guess," she replied, shrugging.

"What are we going to do about this project?" he asked, changing the subject. "We're supposed to get to know each other, right?"

January nodded. "Yeah, that's what the rules say. I'm supposed to experience something about your life that makes you different and vice versa."

Fiddling with the hairs of his goatee, Legend nodded his head, thinking to himself as he drove. "When you wanna start?"

She shrugged. "I guess whenever you have time."

"I've got time now," was his reply.

The air between them felt thick so January settled into the silence, clearing the thoughts running through her head. Her spirit calmed as she relaxed into the cool leather seats, forcing herself to wonder why they were heading in the opposite direction from the university, clear across the city in the other way from the dorms. The scenery outside changed, becoming most unfamiliar.

There was a subconscious tugging at the back of her mind wondering if it was smart to trust him, but she tucked it away and allowed him to drive to some unknown destination that she would have no idea or way to escape from. Doing so didn't make sense; she didn't know him and had only seen him a few times in her entire life. But the fact of the matter was, that currently nothing in her life made sense and she was tired of trying to figure out why. If Legend was someone who couldn't be trusted, she would find out one of these days. Maybe this one.

"You trust me?" he asked in a way that made her body suddenly grow chill.

Taking a deep breath to calm her nerves, she took a minute to look around, realizing they were pulling into a vacant lot with an abandoned building in front.

"Should I?" she asked, answering his question with one of her own rather than revealing her current thoughts.

Instead of giving her a reply that would put her worries to rest, Legend let out a dry chuckle and pulled the car into an empty spot before silencing the engine. Reaching behind them into the back seat, he grabbed a small duffle bag and sat it on his lap.

"You're going to learn to trust your intuition one day."

Saying that made her mind retreat to something her mother told her all the time whenever January frequently asked her how someone like her mother could fall for someone like her father. How did a good girl fall for a bad boy? It was the greatest mystery to her; one that she always wondered if she could ever solve. She didn't understand how love could grow between two people who had absolutely nothing in common outside of the love they shared for each other. It didn't seem natural and lasting. With nothing in common, how could you form anything other than a fleeting emotion built solely on infatuation. How did she feel safe to surrender into her emotions and form something real?

I trusted my intuition, was what her mother always said. *You'll understand what I mean one day.*

"Get out," Legend said suddenly and then opened his own door to do the same.

January watched him, taking even breaths. Her mind told her that she was crazy as hell to trust a man that she could clearly see had the makings of a killer. Everything about him reminded her of someone who had formal training in her father's mafia. Especially in this moment, holding a duffle bag full of mystery items in his hand after driving her to some secluded area in the middle of the night. He looked every bit like a fixer; the mafia's fixer. But what did her intuition say?

You can trust him.

The voice didn't sound like hers, but it was clear. She did as he asked and got out. She took slow steps to the back of the car where Legend had sat the bag on the back of the trunk and was unpacking the items inside. A soft gasp escaped from her lips and she stopped short when she saw an array of various weapons perfectly lined up below the bag. She didn't know the names but recognized a Glock .9 and peeped the silencers on each gun.

Narrowing her eyes into a squint, she looked up from the bag into his eyes, feeling icy fingers creeping up her back. But it wasn't from fear. It was one of recognition.

I know him, she thought, looking at him closely, seeing him somewhat clearly for the first time.

Flashes of images came to her mind of a teenage boy, maybe around eighteen years old at the time. She closed her eyes for a moment, trying to pull up the fullness of the memory, trying to fully remember the experience she had with him. She could only see parts of it, but even in those small bits, she could feel an intense amount of emotion.

Longing and desire. *Instant* and pure love.

There was something about him that she couldn't shake. A remembering started in her mind and, little by little, she could remember fragments of time they spent together when she was younger, but she hadn't been given enough pieces to put the entire puzzle together. All she knew was that Legend was someone she'd met; someone she'd known and felt that she loved the moment she laid eyes on him for the first time.

But does he remember me? she wondered.

"You ever shot a gun before?" he asked, picking up the Glock. He checked the cartridge and then brought his eyes to January just as she shook her head.

"No," she spoke slowly. "My dad wanted to teach me about guns and stuff, but my mom wouldn't let him. She doesn't like having them around."

Legend nodded, knowing what she was saying to be true before she had even said it.

"Pick one." He nudged his head towards the line of guns and then took a step back to give her space.

With brows pointed to the sky, January walked up, slowly eyed each one, accessing the feeling inside of her as she observed each one. After short contemplation, she reached out and pointed at the Glock, feeling like it was the least threatening since she at least knew what it was.

A smirk fell on his lips. He already knew that she would bypass the AR-15, AK, Desert Eagle and -45 for the 9. It would be the most familiar to her, and she was used to playing it safe. He took it as a personal challenge to force her to live a little. Live life on the wild side. January was so sweet, so careful and so responsible all the time. She liked to live safe. She didn't even know that living the safe life was the most dangerous of all. It was in the chaos of the jungle where savages were built. The survival skills required to protect yourself when it mattered could only be learned from submerging yourself in the most turbulent and unpredictable situations. If she kept living the same way she always had, she would easily fall prey to the worst people in the world. Niggas like him.

Grabbing the other guns, Legend packed them back in the duffle and placed it back in the car before coming back to her.

"Grab it and follow me."

She did as he asked and winced at the weight of the steel object in her hands. Fear prickled at the back of her neck and she hesitated for a moment before dragging her feet as she walked behind him heading to the abandoned building.

"I guess I trust you, too, shorty," he said.

January furrowed her brows at his back, wondering what he was referring to.

"Gangstas never turn their back on someone holding a gun," he explained. "That's a dumb ass mistake that's ended a lot of lives."

Once they were at the entrance of the building, Legend keyed in a code to the digital lock on the door to open it. The inside was nothing like the outside. Sucking in a deep breath, she slowly lagged behind him, taking a moment to soak it all in. It was set up like a shooting range but not any that she'd ever seen or imagined.

The luxury of it all was over the top. No expense was spared. For someone as low-key as Legend, it was obvious that he had an affinity for the finest things. With heated marble floors at their feet and large canvases of abstract art on the walls, January felt more like she was in an art studio than a gun range. Lounge seating filled one part of the room, along with a pool table, a custom dart board and a large chess table with large golden chess pieces made up a game area in the far-right corner. There was a small kitchen area with stainless steel appliances and another area to the left of that with a weight bench and gym equipment.

"I guess this is your idea of a man cave?" she said, lifting one brow while smiling at him.

Though he tried to keep his expression neutral, he couldn't help but fold and sheepishly shrugged his shoulders, delivering a half-smile of his own.

"Something like that," he replied. "This is where I go to get some shit off my mind when needed. Consider yourself special… I don't let anyone in here."

Playing it cool, she didn't respond, but her heart blossomed. It was easy to see that Legend was the private type; he didn't open up to many. The fact that he allowed January into a space that seemed so personal to him definitely made her feel special, among other things.

He walked over to her and held out a hand for the gun. She eagerly handed it over to him, feeling relieved to rid herself of the weapon.

"Let me show you a few things," he said. "It'll help."

Doubtful, she pursed her lips. "I don't think I'll ever feel okay with holding a gun."

He snickered and shook his head. "You're the type that needs to understand what you're dealing with in order to feel comfortable. I peeped that a while ago. So, I'm going to give you a quick lesson and then you're going to shoot the shit out of that target over there." He nudged his head towards the space behind him where the image of a zombie resembling something from *The Walking Dead* hung on a back wall.

January teetered on her feet, shifting her weight from side-to-side as she watched him intensely. She still wasn't convinced.

"Relax," he coaxed me. "You'll be fine."

Closing her eyes, she took a deep breath, steadied her stance and squared her shoulders.

"If you say so," she said, giving in. "I guess, let the lessons begin."

NICO.

On one end, Brooke felt guilty for letting January leave with Onyx's cousin, but the other part of her felt like he was exactly what she needed. In her mind, January was uptight, rigid as hell for her first time on her own, and the most obvious remedy was that she needed some good dick to light up her life. Or at least a distraction to keep her head from out of the books all the damn time.

She understood the need to be responsible, especially in her case, being that she was only able to afford college due to her scholarships, but January's family had *bread*. She could afford to make a few mistakes and there was nothing wrong with living a little and enjoying some freedom.

That said, Brooke needed to give herself the same damn advice because, for whatever reason, her mood took a nosedive into the depths of depression as soon as she and Onyx walked back into the club. Actually, it wasn't for *whatever* reason. She knew the exact reason why she was in her feelings and it all boiled down to one word.

Trevor.

With her phone to her ear, Brooke listened once again as it rang twice before going straight to voicemail, just as it had a few minutes before. The fact that it happened again only pushed her emotions from despair right into anger. She was at the brink of the highest level of pissivity. Which, technically, wasn't a word, but it described perfectly every emotion she felt.

"Still no answer?" Onyx asked, looking at Brooke with an expression that clearly said she already knew the answer.

Pursing her lips, Brooke shook her head, unable to speak for fear that she would start crying. Trevor was her boyfriend, or at least, that's what he was in her mind because they'd never quite made it official. She hadn't really seen him in weeks before moving into her dorm because he'd been so busy working. That was the reason he told her that he would meet up with her at the club so they could spend time. Well, at this point, the clock on her phone marked two hours from when he was supposed to have been there and not only was he nowhere to be found, but he also wasn't answering her calls or texts.

To be honest, she wasn't all that surprised. Trevor was known to flake on their plans at the last minute and that was why, in the back of her mind, she doubted that he would show up. However, the fact that it had been so long since they had a chance to kick it made her hopeful that he would come through. Turns out, she was wrong in that assumption.

"Brooke," Onyx began with a sigh, which was an obvious clue to Brooke as to what was about to come out of her mouth next. "Why do you even—"

"Onyx, stop," Brooke interrupted, holding her hand up. "I told you that Trevor has a lot going on in his life. He didn't grow up living the life that you live. His family is dysfunctional as hell and he grew up basically raising himself. He doesn't understand things the way we do. He just operates differently but he's learning to be better."

Onyx gave her a doubtful look. One that said, 'that nigga ain't learning a damn thing'. Though the words didn't come from her lips, they were definitely felt. Deep down, Brooke felt the same exact way. But she also understood the pressure that Trevor was working his way through. He didn't grow up surrounded by love and therefore he operated on survival mode. Brooke felt like if she showed him what it meant to be loved unconditionally, he would change for the better. She wanted to believe that her love could heal everything.

"There's Nico," Onyx said, looking somewhere behind Brooke before glancing at the face of her phone. "Perfect timing, too. It looks like it's about time for me to hit the stage. Let me get him so I can introduce you before I go."

Nodding, Brooke barely paid her any attention as she left the table because she was so caught up in her thoughts of wondering what Trevor was up to and what he was doing.

Or who *he's doing*, she thought, feeling her gut churn.

This was bullshit at all levels. She looked good as hell. Smelled good as a motherfucker and was wearing a dress that she'd been dying for him to see. But instead of popping her ass for a real nigga—namely the one she'd given her heart and soul to, she was sitting in the club, alone, caught up in her feelings. To make things worse, her roommate who hadn't even wanted to go out in the first place, was getting more action than she was. So far, this night was a complete and utter waste.

After battling it back and forth in her mind for several seconds, Brooke finally gave in and grabbed her phone to send Trevor yet another text message asking where he was. She waited for the message status to show it had been delivered but after a few more seconds, it still hadn't updated.

I know damn well he didn't turn off his phone!

Brooke's heart seared with hurt and she bit down on her bottom lip, closing her eyes as she tried to talk herself down from the emotional cliff that she was about to tumble over. The fact that he'd stood her up once again was one thing, but the sheer embarrassment that she felt was another. Onyx had been her friend for months now and she'd never even gotten a chance to meet Trevor even though Brooke had made arranged multiple meetups with him. It never failed; Trevor wouldn't show and then always hit Brooke up later with some lame ass excuse which she would eventually accept after working through her 'stank ass attitude' phase. She was never one to hold grudges when it came to the ones she cared for and, unfortunately, Trevor understood that well. Each time he let her down, he would just give her a few days to get over it—long enough for Brooke to be worried to the point that she was simply happy he was still alive—before he appeared again.

"Nico, this is my friend, Brooke. Brooke, this is my little brother, Nico."

"I ain't your *little* nothing," a soothing deep voice said.

"By two minutes, yes, you are," Onyx replied back with a laugh.

With a sharp inhale, Brooke pried her eyes open and reluctantly turned towards their voices to meet the twin brother who Onyx had told her so much about since the day they'd met. Though this was their first time meeting, she felt like she already knew what to expect. From Onyx's descriptions, the two looked nothing alike, acted nothing alike and pretty much had nothing in common. Nico was her aggravating, overprotective younger brother who was always telling her what to do even though he barely had *his* shit together. Truth be told, Brooke was in no mood to meet yet another man who was free-falling his way through life but, for the sake of her friend, she forced a smile and lifted her head to meet Onyx's twin.

"Nice to meet y—"

The last word hung somewhere suspended between her throat and her open mouth as she stared with wide eyes at the most gorgeous man on the face of the planet.

Daaaaammmmmn! This can't possibly be Onyx's brother.

Dazzling white teeth greeted her with a knowing smile, one that said he fully understood and might have even expected her reaction. This man *knew* he was fine. His warm mocha colored skin was smooth and richly wrapped around the most desirable, muscular frame Brooke could have imagined for a man. He was dressed to impress, in nice grey slacks, a black turtleneck sweater and black dress shoes—definitely designer. His neck was adorned with various icy, gold chains to match the diamond in his ears and the ones decorating the Rolex watch on his wrist.

"Great! Soooo, you've finally met," Onyx said, clapping her hands and somewhat pulling Brooke from her trance. "Now that's done, I need to get ready to go on stage. Nico, please remember what I said." She gave him a pointed look, narrowing her eyes.

"I got you," was his reply, smirking as he looked at his sister. Brooke's body reacted so suddenly and strongly to him that she had to squeeze her thighs together to stop the waves flowing from in between.

Hell… can you have me to? was what she wanted to jump in and say but, fortunately, she was able to keep her mouth from revealing her current level of thirst.

Though he was dressed like a business professional, the street side of him clearly shined through and it ignited every bit of Brooke's desire. He was a bad boy to the core—that much was obvious when a man passed by a little too close to Onyx as if he were trying to 'accidentally' swipe his arm against her ass. Nico lightly touched her back, nudging her away and gave the guy a glare that should have resulted in immediate death.

Brooke's heart fluttered. She was in insta-love.

"I need a favor," Onyx said, leaning down close so that she could speak directly in Brooke's ear. "Remember that guy I told you about? He's coming tonight to watch me. Can you try to keep Nico entertained so he doesn't welcome himself in my business?"

If there was a meme with an image on it to depict sheer horror, Brooke's face would've been on it.

"You want me to *entertain*... him?" She whispered back, cutting her eyes briefly to Nico who was bobbing his head to the track the D.J. was spinning and scrolling through his phone.

He wasn't doing much at all, nothing that would normally draw attention from any other man, but Nico was soaking up all the female energy in the room like a dishrag. At one time or another, all eyes in the room that were attached to a woman's head made their way over to him. He had his pick of the room.. what could Brooke possibly do to keep *him* entertained?

"Yes!" Onyx spoke with desperation, speaking through her teeth. "I already told you how my brother is. He's not as bad as my cousin but he still has no intentions on letting me live. And I really like this guy..."

"Fine, fine, fine!" Brooke agreed, waving her off. "I'll do my best. That's all I can agree to do." She mumbled the last part under her breath, not feeling positive about it in the least. After pulling her into a tight hug around the neck, Onyx said her thanks and tiptoed off in her heels to prepare to grace the stage.

Cradling her hand in her chin, Brooke took a deep breath, sighing heavily with its release. The D.J. switched the music to another track and she began to bob her head to the beat. An edgy feeling rippled through her. Anxiety? Nervousness? She couldn't place it because it wasn't something she was used to. Brooke was bold, outspoken, expressive and confident. She didn't shrink for anyone because no one and nothing ever made her feel small. But in this moment, sitting across from a man who appeared to be the epitome of every woman's late-night fantasy, she was at a loss for words. She was shook; she wasn't used to dealing with men like him.

"How long have you known Onyx?" Nico asked. Or at least, she thought that was what he said. With the music so loud, the bass thumping heavily nearly rattling her eardrums, she couldn't be sure.

Lifting her eyes, Brooke leveled her gaze on Nico who was still focused on whatever was his phone.

"Did you say something to me?"

Moving nothing but his eyes, Nico glanced up and caught her stare, instantaneously igniting a spark in the space right between her legs. Like warm chocolate, she began to melt.

"Yes," he replied. He paused to place the phone down on the table and then moistened his lips with his tongue. Lips slightly parted, breath coming out in soft pants, Brooke followed the movement across his lips every bit of the way. It wasn't until he placed both of his arms on the table, clasped his hands together and looked back up at her that she was able to force herself to regain her composure.

"I asked you how long you've known Onyx."

He grabbed a stick of gum from his pocket, opened it and pushed it between his lips in a way that seductive. *Everything* that he did felt sexual. It was easy to get lost in him and start feeling some kind of way even though he was only doing regular shit. It just didn't seem regular the way he did it.

"Um, about a year," Brooke told him once she was finally able to find her voice. "We met during a campus tour last year for incoming Freshmen and kept it touch since then."

Nodding his head, he chewed on the gum a little, looking back down at his phone. It seemed pathetic as hell, but Brooke found herself wishing that she was the stick of gum that he'd pushed between his lips. Oh, how badly she wanted to be what he was rolling around on his tongue.

Get a grip, girl, she thought, giving herself a quick reality check. *He's probably texting his girl right now. Or at least one of them.*

There was no way on God's green Earth that Nico didn't have a whole basketball team worth of women at his beck and call, ready and willing to do whatever he desired. Brooke knew how niggas like him rolled; they had a starting lineup *and* benchwarmers waiting for the day the coach would put them in the game. Pussy came too easy for men like him to even consider being faithful. It wasn't even a consideration. Men as sexy and paid as Nico and Legend were expected to play the field, break hearts and not give a fuck about a bitch's feelings. In fact, most people would consider it a waste if they *didn't* take advantage of everything they could. To commit themselves to any woman would be like giving God their ass to kiss. That was the shit that made up a side bitch's nightmares. A sexy, young rich nigga with big dick energy who is… dedicated to *one woman?* Side bitches all around the world would join together to cry and shout out to the sky: *How the fuck* dare *he be faithful and not want meeeeee?*

"What you drinking? Can I buy you another one?"

Finally, finished with texting whoever had his attention before, Nico placed his phone in his pocket and then leaned over placing his full attention on Brooke. The only problem was, she didn't want it. In her mind, she already had him all figured out. And it hadn't taken long at all.

"Why?" she asked, rolling her eyes.

Smiling, Nico's brows crinkled into a slight frown, not really catching the reason for her sudden change in mood.

"What you mean? You're almost done with that one… I figured you would want another one and I want to pay for it. A woman shouldn't have to open her purse to pay for shit when a man is present."

Oh, he's smooth *smooth*, Brooke thought, pulling away from him to let her eyes grace the stage. They were setting up for Onyx to begin her show. She decided to focus there instead of in Nico's eyes. The way he was looking at her, watching her every movement and change in expression made it hard for words to form in her brain. He was studying her, and she could feel it. It was catching her off-guard. Making it hard for her to think up some slick shit to say.

Nico felt his phone vibrating in his pocket, and he pulled it out already knowing who it was before he had a chance to check.

Legend, what the fuck you want, man? He thought when he saw his cousin's name on the screen. Unlocking his phone, he pressed on the message he'd sent.

Legend: *Onyx got some nigga coming to see her. Don't say shit. She don't think I know.*

Chuckling a little to himself, Nico shook his head before replying back.

Nico: *Sis think she slick as shit.*

Legend: *Hell yeah. He there?*

Taking a moment to look around, Nico turned a little to look over his shoulder and saw a man sitting at the table a little behind where he was sitting. He took a moment to make a quick assessment. The man was alone, flicking through something on his phone with his head down, not paying attention to anyone in the room. From the glass of water on the table, it was obvious that he wasn't there for drinks.

This nigga is a square, Nico quickly summed up. Sighing, he ran his hand over his face and shook his head. This was the kinda shit that niggas did when they had too much time on their hands.

Nico: *Legend, the fuck you got me watching this goofy ass nigga for?*

If it were one thing that Nico couldn't understand, it wasn't his cousin's obsession with making sure that Onyx was safe. If he didn't know better, he'd think that Legend was the one who was her twin instead of him. Ever since they were kids, Legend made it clear that his little cousin wasn't to be fucked with. There were plenty of lil niggas who thought they were going to push up on her, but the second Legend made his presence known, all that was a done deal. Now that she was a 'grown ass woman' as she often reminded them both, Legend gave her some room to make her own decisions, but he still kept a close eye on whoever she dealt with until he felt like he could be trusted.

Legend: *He ain't goofy. Watch him.*

Nico: *Nigga, watch some pussy. Handle yo' business. I got mine.*

Putting his phone up for the final time, he took a quick glance behind him again just as Onyx walked out on the stage. This time, the guy was no longer sunken down in his seat, staring at his phone. Sitting up, he had his full attention on Onyx, full tunnel-vision, like he couldn't see anything else.

This nigga got stars in his eyes. Nico almost laughed at that until his expert eyes caught the sight of something else. The imprint of a gun tucked at his side.

Ain't as goofy as I thought, he thought, turning back around. *Lil sis stay fuckin' with them goons.*

He couldn't blame her. As pretty and innocent as Onyx appeared to be, all she knew was thug life. She was a hood chick at heart; born and raised in the county of Dade. She grew up shaking her ass to Trick Daddy and Trina while still in diapers, shouting in baby talk about how she was a 'trues and vogues hoe'. He should've known better than to think she would fuck with a square. Only a hood nigga could handle a hood bitch.

"You still ain't told me about that drink," he said, resting his eyes on Brooke. If Legend had anything else to say, he'd have to tell it to himself because Nico's attention was tied up for the night. With her sexy, chocolate smooth skin, soft eyes and perfect pebble-nose, Brooke was hands-down the only woman he wanted to watch tonight. After Onyx another singer was scheduled to perform but Nico didn't give a fuck what was happening on the stage. All of his focus was on the woman he planned to take home tonight.

To *her* home, not his. Or even a hotel. He didn't chicks in his shit. That was his number 1 rule: *Never let a bitch know where you lay your head.* Those were wifey privileges and, since Nico never planned on having a wife, no woman would ever get that info.

"I can order my own drink," Brooke replied with attitude, not even bothering to look his way. "Obviously, you have *other* things to tend to."

The fuck?

Nico stalled. He wasn't one for the bullshit and he didn't do attitudes. Any woman who dared to give him one was quickly dismissed. He was a conqueror and loved a challenge. He had been fighting in some way or another his entire life. Knocking niggas out with his fists or through the barrel of a gun. He had never turned down a battle in any shape or form. But one thing he did *not* fight was a chick. Not physically and not verbally either. If a bitch wanted him to fight for her for the pussy, she could have it. In normal circumstances, Brooke's attitude would have been an automatic turn off. But for some reason, in this case… it wasn't.

"What you mean?" he found himself asking, surprising his damn self.

"What do I mean?" she snapped rolling her eyes.

Running his hand over his mouth, Nico fixed his eyes on her, staring with all seriousness. Brooke felt a flutter ripple through her gut as the vibe changed. The conversation went from playful to serious real quick.

"Yeah, shorty. That's what the fuck I said," he told her, his tone dangerous but low, carrying just enough volume to be heard over Onyx singing in the background.

"Well, you've been on your phone the entire time so it's obvious that you got other things to tend to," Brooke replied, trying to stand firm in her attitude. It wasn't easy.

Something about Nico's rawness unnerved her. He looked like a player but something about his vibe didn't quite strike her as one. He didn't seem like the type of man who had time for childish games. Or anything childish at all.

Sensing that he was losing her, Nico decided to fall back on his aggression, which was an incredible feat in itself. It was just something he didn't do. Changing course in order to comfort a female? Taking the time to *explain* himself? Even the thought of doing something like that was foreign to him. But here he was... doing it.

"Listen, I know what you're thinkin' but that's not what it is. My cousin kept hittin' me up about some nigga out here tryin' to see Onyx."

Still cradling her chin in the palm of her hand, Brooke moved only her eyes to look at Nico, wanting to see the expression on his face. What he was saying was obviously the truth because, according to Onyx, he wasn't even supposed to know that anyone was coming here to see her.

"Mmhmm," she hummed, not really wanting to lose ground by giving in so easily. Regardless to who he was texting, he was still a player. All men like him were.

"Real shit," Nico said. "Now about that drink?"

Brooke shook her head. "No, thanks. I'm done drinking tonight." Then, as if proving some other point to him, she turned back and added. "And if I *do* get thirsty, I can buy my *own* drink."

Caught off guard by her response, Nico suppressed a chuckle and settled on a smile as he squeezed the bridge of his nose.

Shorty stubborn as hell, he thought, watching her as she turned back to the stage, dancing in her seat as Onyx continued to sing.

He wasn't used to a woman refusing him. Especially not when he was offering to buy something for her—some shit he wouldn't normally *ever* do. And in the very few cases one had, he never wanted her enough to really give a fuck. There was something different about Brooke, but he couldn't put his finger on it. Something about her piqued his curiosity and spoke to the warrior in him. She was playing it hard, but he was going to match her energy.

For the first time in his life, Nico had actually found a woman he felt was actually worth putting up a fight for.

RAYS OF SUNSHINE.

GOLDEN SUNLIGHT PIERCED THROUGH THE OPEN BLINDS OF THE window across from January's bed as she sat with cross legs on her yoga mat, eyes closed, in deep meditation. Or at least meditating was what she was attempting to do. Unfortunately, clearing her mind was becoming an issue. Every time she drew a deep breath and then expelled it through her lips in a *whoosh*, forcing away every thought in her mind, an image of Legend's face entered into the eye of mind, clouding access to her third eye.

Frustrated to the max, her eyes shot open and she stared at the rays of light peeking through the window, reveling in the warmth that danced on her skin. Was this how it was to have a crush?

Definitely not, she thought to herself.

She'd had a crush before. In middle school, a boy named Kyle Banner had moved into the area and started attending her same school. He was cute and mutual attraction existed between them from the beginning. They shared many of the same classes and she was always excited the second she saw him walking into the room. In fact, she always arrived early; eagerly waiting for the moment when Kyle would arrive. Once their eyes met, they would always exchange smiles and would sit next to her every time.

When he asked her to be his girlfriend, she happily agreed, and it was at that moment that the entire school knew they 'went together'—a childish way of expressing their perceived exclusivity in whatever kind of relationship they had. January wasn't allowed to date, and they never spoke on the phone. Their relationship only existed within the confines of the school walls, during class and in the brief moments when he would walk her from one room to the next one, carrying her books as they engaged in small talk. Though it seemed so important and real at the time, the feelings she had for Kyle were never as intense as what she felt for Legend. Everything she felt was extinguished the second the last bell rang and the school day ended; she never thought about him outside of the moments when they were together.

Kyle never invaded her consciousness the way that Legend's presence did. It annoyed her to the max. It almost felt like an intrusion of the worst kind because it was completely unwelcome, and she was totally dumbfounded on how to rid herself of it.

Staring at the sun, her mind went back to a moment from the night before, after Legend had taught her everything she could ever know about a gun: loading, unloading, applying the safety, cocking and shooting. As he'd stated, she definitely 'shot the shit' out of the target once she was comfortable. Either she had a natural talent for wielding a weapon or he was an incredible teacher. He stated that it was the former although she felt it was the latter.

When the lesson had ended, Legend packed up everything and took down the bullet-ridden paper target before handing it to her to keep as a keepsake. Holding it in her hands, she stared at it in awe; every bullet she'd shot had gone into vital areas. If the zombie had been a real, live person, he would have been deader than dead now.

"Damn, you gave ole boy a nose job," Legend joked, pointing at a small hole in the center of the zombie's head, right through the nose. "Very nice."

The inside of the building had no windows, so she was shocked when they stepped out of the door and was greeted by the orange and red hues of the sunrise. It hadn't seemed like she had been there with him that long, but when she thought about it, she shouldn't have been surprised. Time always seemed to a non-factor when they were together. The world around them always seemed to go through its natural cycle and routine while they two of them were oblivious to it all, only focusing on each other.

"Yo, you should let your hair out more often," he said as they walked towards his car. "I mean, wrapping it up in that cloth shit or that cinnabon style you're always wearing is nice, too. But I gotta admit… it's sexy as hell when you let it hang down around your shoulders."

Flinching, January muttered a quick 'thanks' before snatching up her thick tresses and winding it up to place it back into the 'cinnabon' style as Legend had named it. She'd taken it down sometime throughout their time in the range in an effort to loosen the tension she'd felt when learning to deal with the gun, but that was over now and she felt the need to get back to her normal self.

"Why do you do that shit?" Legend asked frowning deeply as he looked at her. She returned his stare with a frown of her own.

"Do what?"

"Why do you hide yourself, the things you know people love and like about you. The things that make you special?" When she didn't readily respond, he continued. "Your body is bangin' but you always wearing big ass shirts and black tights. I mean, I ain't complainin' about the tights but them big ass shirts make it hard for a nigga to see what you really workin' with in them tights. I was shocked as shit that you came out dressed like this, to be honest." He paused for a beat to take in the fullness of her attire. "Pleasantly surprised, but still…"

"Oh my God!" January gasped, smiling hard as she wound her arms around her body to hide whatever he was staring at. It was ineffective because he was still staring and saw everything that he wanted, none the less.

She was cute in the way that she tried to hide from him even though she could never. He smiled at her natural coy nature; her entire being was addicting, but he didn't allow himself to get caught off-guard in his thoughts of how much he wanted her. Straightening his composure, he centered his focus back on her face and pierced her with his eyes.

"Answer me," he prodded once more. "Why do you do it?"

She shrugged. "I don't know. I guess to blend in. In my experience, standing out hasn't always been a good thing."

He watched as she bowed her head and retreated into her mind. Somehow, he seemed to go there with her. It was like he could read her thoughts. Pain showed subtly through the expression on her face, clear as day, though she tried to hide it. The ache in Legend's chest intensified, growing into a boulder of guilt that temporarily blocked any words from escaping his throat.

She didn't have to say anything more because he understood her exactly in what she wasn't saying. She blamed herself for the bad things that had happened to her. Told herself that there was too much risk and vulnerability in her beauty, too much danger in being unique. These were all the excuses she used to convince herself to dim her light. To blend in.

"Nah, baby girl, that ain't what's up," he said finally. "You by yourself in a new city, your folks ain't here. Nobody watchin' you because people ain't jocking for you like that, but your ass still trying to hide. That's not in your nature. What you're doin' should be considered a sin. It's unnatural."

"Huh?" Her brows bent as she tried to catch his angle. "What's unnatural?"

Mouth closed, Legend ran his tongue over his teeth and looked away from her for a few moments before taking a seat on the hood of his car. He patted the space beside him, urging her to take a seat as well. She did as he asked, still frowning, wondering why she felt like she was about to go to school, to learn a lesson in the class of life. And none was a better teacher in giving a lesson in life than a gangster.

"Look at the sun," he said lifting his head. "Look directly at it and don't blink."

Squinting, she slowly lifted her head and did as he asked. The rays of light beamed through her eyes, burning her pupils in a matter of seconds. There wasn't a cloud in the sky and in the short time they'd been talking, it had already risen to its fullness in the sky. She strained her eyes to do as he'd requested but couldn't last very long. Giving up, she winced and looked away, but Legend placed his hand under her chin to lift her head.

"Nah, don't do that. Don't look away. Stare at it."

"I can't," she replied, forcing his hand away. "It burns. You already know that no one can stare at the sun. We'll go blind."

"Right," he said and then turned to look her right in her eyes with a blank but pointed expression on his face. "And do you think the sun gives a fuck about you goin' blind?"

Confused, she released a nervous chuckle before replying.

"Um… no, I don't think it does." She laughed even harder at the ridiculousness of his question. "Legend, where is this going?"

With a sigh, he shook his head and pulled his focus away from her to look back up at the sun's shining magnificence above them.

"The sun knows its purpose is to shine. And it don't give a fuck about who it blinds in the process, it just does what it came to do. You don't see it asking niggas to put shades on if the light is too bright. The sun doesn't wait until we are comfortable with the heat or ready for its light. The sun literally says 'Fuck y'alls eyes' every single day and does what it came to do. It shines and whoever don't like it can either adjust or get the fuck out the way."

January laughed harder than ever at that. In fact, she couldn't remember ever laughing as hard as she did then in her entire life.

"HEY, do you have any more classes today? I need your help."

Taking the textbook from her last class out of her bag, January looked up, pushing pause on the thoughts in her mind. The words that Legend had spoken to her still ruminated there although it was hours later.

Baby girl, shine bright.

She didn't even know if he understood the effect, they had on her or if he would ever know, but she felt a shift inside.

"No, I only have three this morning, but I'm done by noon," she replied, looking at Brooke who stood across from her, pecking at the screen of the phone in her hand.

"Perfect," Brooke said. "One of Onyx's friends needs my help with her makeup and her hair stylist is out of town so I was wondering if you could do her hair. You remember those videos that I showed you the other day on Instagram?"

Scaling her eyes to the ceiling, January thought for a minute and then nodded as the memory came to mind of some videos Brooke had forwarded to her while she was in class.

"The one with the couple and the two twin boys? Yeah, what about them?"

"That's the friend. They got some sponsorship, and she has to do a quick promo for it but apparently, she looks a hot mess. She doesn't need much, just someone to blow out her hair. Both of you have the same hair type so I told her that you should be able to do it."

January's eyes grew wide. "I do *my* hair but I'm not a professional. Why would you tell her that?"

With a quick roll of her eyes, Brooke sighed. "Girl, stop. You are good enough for what she needs. It's just a quick video and it's not that serious. She's not the high maintenance type so I'm sure anything you can do will work just fine."

With that said, Brooke walked away to her side of the dorm, leaving no room for any rebuttal, as always. And though January still doubted that she could do much to help, she decided to comply.

"What time?"

"Now. I'm about to get my stuff and then get dressed. Whenever you're ready, we can leave."

"Thanks for the advance notice." January's tone dropped with sarcasm.

"You're welcome!" As usual, Brooke didn't even seem to notice the sarcasm. Or maybe she didn't care.

Emptying her bag of the rest of its contents, January walked to the dresser and opened the drawer where she kept her favorite hair products and started stuffing them inside. As she reached for the jar of coconut oil, she paused for a beat when her eyes landed on the ballet shoes that she'd pushed into the far corner. Her gut tugged as she contemplated for the first time in what felt like forever how it would be to put them on her feet again. She'd kept them; even though she didn't think she would ever wear them again, she couldn't force herself to throw them away. Now she wondered if it was for a reason.

As she stared at the slippers, her mind fell on Legend once again. Every time he rolled through her memory, she felt breathless. She didn't feel scared, though. Not like she thought she would, at least. She felt shame because of that, too, because every time his face popped up into her mind, she realized something.

I want to see him again.

Pushing her thoughts away, she grabbed the rest of her products and dumped them into her bag, forcing herself not to look back at the slippers. Once she was done, she pushed the drawer closed firmly and let out the breath that she had been holding inside. Before she could make another movement, her phone chimed, and she quickly grabbed it from where it lay on top of the dresser.

It was a text. From Legend.

Swallowing hard, she unlocked the screen to read his message.

You know what you want to do. I don't even need to tell you, because you know. Don't overthink it.

Her brows furrowed. The fact that he'd sent that message at that exact moment had an eerie effect on her. But most things concerning Legend did. It was the reason she couldn't rid him of her mind. It was like a fusion of the souls that allowed for things to be communicated. Things that had yet to be said.

Whatever, she quickly replied back with a smart-ass comment. *You don't know me. You think you do but you really don't.*

A smirk on her lips, she hit send and then waited, almost seeing the smile that would fold his lips once he read it. Once the phone indicated that he'd read her message, she waited, watching the bubbles on the screen as he typed his reply.

I do know you.

She rolled her eyes. "I hate his arrogant ass," she scoffed before placing the phone in her bag.

"Whose arrogant ass?"

Turning around, she tossed the bag over her shoulder and shook her head at Brooke who was fully dressed with her make up bags in hand.

"No one," she replied.

Brooke smiled, picking up on the distress an angst in January's expression. The look that was only there when she spoke about a certain person. She didn't understand why January played this push and pull game with herself.

"Could it be…Legend that you're referring to?" she teased, knowing the answer before she'd even asked the question.

Although she didn't give a clear answer of yes or no, the sheepish expression on her face said enough.

"Tsk, tsk, tsk." Brooke shook her head as if fake chastising January as she clicked her teeth. "You know they say 'Da Nile' is more than just a river in Egypt."

January's brows lifted in question. "Isn't it 'The Nile' is more than just a river in Egypt?"

"Honestly, I don't know how the hell the saying goes, but I *do* know what 'denial' is and I know you're rolling around in it. When are you going to admit to yourself that you have a thing for Legend? It's obvious that he's feeling you!" Brooke ended her statement with her hands out, palms up and eyes stretched wide open as she waited with full expectation for a response. And she wanted an *honest* one at that.

"It's more complicated than you think," January said and then paused for a beat, biting on her bottom lip. "I've met him before, but I can't remember everything about it. There was a time in my life when something bad happened and the only way I could move on from it was to forget it. I met him during that time, but I can't remember all of it. Only flashes." Her frown deepened and she tried to shrug away her frustration. "There were a lot of bad people around me at that time. What if Legend was one of them? On top of that, he's not the type of guy I see myself being with. I want a guy like President Obama… Or even Jay-Z. Legend has more in common with 2-Chainz."

Brooke opened her mouth like she was about to say something and then snapped it shut before releasing a heavy sigh. Dropping her bags to her feet, she walked over to January's bed and flopped down on top of it.

"January, I wasn't going to say anything until you brought it up, but…. I Google'd you and—wait!" She held her hand up to stop January from interrupting her before she was done speaking. "Before you get mad, I *had* to do it! You're so damn secretive all the time. And then look at this fucking dorm room!" She held her hands out and rotated her head around the room to dramaticize her point. "Who the hell wouldn't Google you after this? I had to see who the hell I was living with!"

Smiling, January let out a deep sigh and nodded her head in under-standing. "Yeah, I guess it makes perfect sense."

"Exactly," Brooke said, with widened eyes. "So, anyways, I know why you're so guarded and why you're so private and responsible and…"

"Boring," January completed for her.

"I was *not* going to say 'boring'! But…" Brooke squirmed a little, scanning her brain as she tried to think of what to say. "…Yeah, some people might call it boring."

Smiling, January rolled her eyes. "Responsible people are always called boring."

Brooke shrugged in response and threw her hands up. "We can call it that. But anyways, I just said that to say that I understand where you're coming from and why you're so guarded and afraid. Especially when it comes to someone like Legend. Onyx hasn't told me much about her family…" Pausing, Brooke's eyes rotated to the ceiling as she stopped to think. "Actually, she's a lot like you in that way. But what she's told me about her cousin and her brother lets me know that they aren't bad people. Not in the way that you have to be concerned with. I mean, niggas will be niggas," she added with a sigh. "And you can look at them and tell that they're from the streets, but they are better than most niggas I done run into. I mean, what motherfucker you know is going to skip out on a night at the club to watch out for his lil' cousin?"

Brooke cocked her head to the side and waited for an answer. Blowing out air, January rolled her eyes slowly to the ceiling before bringing them back down to Brooke's face.

"I can only think of one," she admitted with a shrug. "I guess you have a point."

"I *know* I have a point," Brooke said. "Be smart. He *is* a man. A fine as hell man, at that. So just remember that all men are dogs and niggas ain't shit. As long as you keep that in mind, it's okay to have fun."

January almost choked on a laugh. "Wait… 'all men are dogs and niggas ain't shit'? That's the advice you're going to leave me with?"

Brooke shook her head. "No, that's the *best* advice I can leave you with."

Standing from the bed, she went to gather up her things so they could leave but then stopped suddenly when an image of Nico's face dropped into her mind. Placing a finger to her lips, she took a moment to access how she felt about her conversation with him the night before. The jury was still out as to whether he was a dog or not worth shit, but she had to admit that he didn't come at her the way that most guys their age did. He had a vibe that she hadn't picked up on when it came to any man she'd ever dealt with, to be honest. Not only that, he was so raw and authentic. He had said and done all the right things, but it wasn't because he was putting on or trying to fool her. Everything about him felt totally honest.

With her finger lifted in the air, Brooke swung around, turning back to January who was picking up her bag of supplies, and decided to clarify her statement.

"Actually, let me make a small change," she began slowly, carefully thinking it through as she said it. "All men are dogs and niggas ain't shit *until* you find the one who isn't."

"Okay," January replied, nodding. "And then, what happens once you find the one who isn't?"

"Honestly, I hadn't thought it out that far," she admitted, shrugging. "But I guess when you find the one who isn't a dog and is *actually* worth more than shit, you'll know which one deserves your heart."

January laughed so hard at that, her head fell back. "You should package all this up in a book and sell it," she said between giggles. "You're better than Iyanla Vanzant."

"I know," Brooke replied draping her arm around January's shoulders once they'd locked up and began walking down the hall. "Somebody should tell Oprah. She should give me a show on *Own*."

"She *most definitely* should."

RELATIONSHIP GOALS.

SKYLAR GREETED THEM AT THE DOOR IN A KIMONO ROBE WITH HER shoulder-length natural hair in damp coils hanging just above her shoulders. She smiled warmly, radiating a calm and cool energy that seemed to grow with each passing second. January immediately felt relaxed in her presence—a new feeling for her being that she was naturally resistant to making new friends.

"Sorry, the house is kinda a mess. I've been trying to clean it but with the kids home, it's a mess."

"Girl, we ain't worried about that. Your house is gorgeous," Brooke said, echoing January's exact thoughts.

Skylar's smile deepened and she stepped to the side to let them both in.

Brooke wasted no time stepping in as January followed slowly behind. "I'm Brooke and this is my friend and roommate January. She's going to help you with your hair."

"I hope you're up for the challenge." Skylar pulled at one of her tight curls with a light laugh. "I've washed it but that's about all I can do as far as hair. I don't need anything fancy though. Maybe just straighten it out and I should be good."

"I'll do my best," January promised with a smile of her own. "I'm no professional but I've learned a few tricks from dealing with my own hair." At that, Skylar nodded and then motioned for them to follow her through the foyer of the house.

"Onyx is already in the living room, with a glass of wine. If you'd like a drink, feel free to make yourself at home."

"Got any Henny?" Brooke joked with a laugh.

"Actually, I do and it's already out on the counter," Skylar replied with a giggle. "The bar is fully stocked so pick your poison."

Natural light shined through the living area draping them in an ambient glow that provided warmth and a feel of relaxation.

This is the life! January couldn't help but think. *True relationship goals.*

Skylar was barely a few years older than they were and she seemed to already have life completely figured out. She was doing what she loved, married to her soulmate and they'd created a beautiful family. This was exactly the kind of life January was looking for.

"Aunty Onyx, I'm thirsty," January heard a tiny voice say just as they fully entered the grand living room and saw Onyx, who was sprawled out on the white leather cushions of an exquisite sectional most likely custom-designed for the space.

The voice came from a little girl, no more than about four years old, who was the spitting image of her mother. Like Skylar, she had a chestnut complexion and the most expressive eyes January had ever seen on a child so young. Her thick black hair was tightly pulled into a bun on the crown of her head as she eyed the wine glass in Onyx's hand.

"Baby, you gonna have to get a juice box out the fridge because you can't have any of auntie's drink. This is red wine spiked with Red

Bull and a splash, or five, of Vanilla Crown. It's for grown folks with emotional trauma and man issues."

"Shit, I'll have what *she's* drinking," Brooke said, tossing down her make-up bag on a large island with granite countertops before making her way to the bar. "Jani, you want me to make you one?"

This time, January smiled at Brooke's newest nickname of the day for her. 'Jani' was what her aunts called her mother. She made a mental note to call home as soon as they were done for the day. It had been a minute since she'd heard her mother's voice and, not only did she miss her, but she could definitely use some love and relationship advice.

"No, I'm good. I'll just take a can of Sprite."

"Mixed with what?" Brooke asked pointedly with her hands on her hips. January rolled her eyes.

"Mixed with *ice*," she replied.

"Fine." Brooke shrugged. "Suit yourself."

"I'll take a refill," Onyx declared, waving her empty glass in the air.

Brooke gawked in her direction as Skylar handed a juice box to her mini-me and grabbed Onyx's glass.

"Damn, lil' mama, what you going through?" Brooke asked. "You seemed fine when I spoke to you earlier."

Skylar pursed her lips as she walked over to where Brooke stood at the bar filling two glasses with ice.

"She's having man problems," Skylar whispered, giving both Brooke and January a look.

Rolling her eyes, Brooke huffed hot air through her nose.

"Shit, ain't we all," she said under her breath. "I mean, except you," she added, glancing up at Skylar.

January frowned. "And me," she said, to which Brooke once again rolled her eyes.

"Girl, please. You're denying your feelings. Actually, fuck the feelings, that's a whole other topic in itself so we aren't even going to get into that yet—you're denying your very *attraction* to a man, who you obviously want, just because he doesn't fit your ridiculous requirements."

January wanted to rebut the statement but, for whatever reason, her mouth felt glued shut.

Brooke's lips twisted to the side, showing pure satisfaction with being right, and then she directed her attention back to Skylar.

"So like I said, you're the only one winning in the man department so maybe you can give us some advice. From what I see going on around here, you got it all together."

Dropping her head to focus on the drinks she was making, Brooke totally missed out on the sadness in Skylar's eyes as her expression shifted.

"You'd be surprised," Skylar said so low that the words barely escaped her lips. January was the only one who heard her clearly, being that Skylar seemed to forget that she was sitting in a bar stools right next to her.

Light tingles passed down January's spine as she watched Skylar drop her weight into a bar stool at the other end of the island. Her energy had suddenly shifted, making her appear weary. Frown lines settled into her forehead and she seemed to age several years right before her eyes.

Empathetic by nature, January absorbed her emotions, feeling a well of sadness in the pit of her stomach. She felt compelled to get up and give Skylar a loving bear hug. It just felt like the girl needed a warm embrace, but January didn't know her like that. For that reason alone, she decided not to pry and chose to mind her own business, focusing instead on pulling the hair products from the bag she had packed.

"Onyx, I'm waiting," Brooke said, interrupting her thoughts by forcefully placing a glass of Sprite on the counter in front of her. "What happened? I'm guessing this has to do with that sexy ass nigga who came to see you at the club."

"Yes, girl," Onyx replied, snatching the refilled wine glass from Brooke's outstretched hand. She paused to take a few liberal gulps from it before beginning again. "He's perfect. Literally, everything I thought I wanted. As you know, we've been talking for a while now, started dating exclusively about three months ago after only mainly talking to each other on the phone for three months before that. He comes to all of my shows at the club even though he doesn't even live in town. He's sweet, thoughtful, romantic, caring and has made it perfectly clear that he doesn't want anyone else but me."

Confused, Brooke held out her hands and gawked at her with her eyes wide. "So... what's the problem?" she asked. Then, as if a light-bulb went off in her head, she clapped her hands together. "Oh, I know. The dick must be bad. Damn!" She looked at Skylar. "Don't you *hate* when that happens?"

Closed eyes, while shaking her head, Skylar pressed her glass to her lips and mumbled, "Mmhm." Next to her, January sat, looking bewildered and lost as Brooke continued.

"I mean, how come just when you think you've found the perfect man who has it all together, you find out he's working with little bitty sausage meat? Then it'll be the ones like mine with no job, no car, no ambitions, three baby mamas, who's sleeping on an air mattress in their mama's attic who can properly slang the big ding-a-lang just right to make you wanna let them fuck up your credit?"

"Ones like yours?" January piped up with a frown. "Now whose been keeping secrets? Brooke, you have a boyfriend?"

"Real talk, I can't even call him that. He's *supposed* to be my boyfriend, but he *acts* more like my son. I'm nineteen years old with a nineteen-year-old son."

"Damn!" Skylar chimed in, scrunching up her nose. "How the hell did you let *that* happen?"

"Long story for another day. I'll let Onyx finish telling us about the fine ass man from the club with the lipstick tube worth of dick."

She pressed a hand to her forehead and drained nearly half her glass before pulling it from her lips to sulk silently, looking in the distance, as if retreating into her thoughts. Shaking her head at Brooke's dramatics, January stood to check the heat on the flat iron that she'd plugged in before plugging in her blow dryer and motioning to Skylar.

"Let me start on your hair," she said. "It looks like Brooke is going to need a minute to get herself together." She pointed over to Brooke who was now fully spread out on the sofa with her hand propped over her forehead, palm up, like a damsel in distress. Skylar laughed and the warm glow from before returned to her face.

"It's not his dick," Onyx continued looking at Brooke. "I mean, I don't *think* it is." She looked down at her hands, wrinkling her nose. "I mean, he doesn't *look* like he has a small—hell, I don't even really know." The room went completely silent and, outside of January busily detangling Skylar's curls with a big tooth comb, everyone around her froze. Noticing the sudden change, she glanced up to see what had happened.

"Wait..." Brooke began, rotating her entire body on the sofa so that she could look Onyx directly in her face. "You mean to tell me that you've been talking to this man for six whole months, exclusively dating him for two and you ain't gave him none yet?"

Onyx's head dropped nearly between her shoulders and she nodded sheepishly, her butterscotch-toned cheeks flushing with a tinge of red.

"Bitch, *what?*" Brooke screamed and then caught herself, clamping her mouth shut once she suddenly remembered Skylar's daughter, who was quietly putting a puzzle together at a table in the center of the room.

"I'm sorry," she apologized to Skylar and then dropped her voice to what she thought was a whisper. "Bitch, *what?*" she repeated. "Why haven't you given this man no pus—" She cut her eyes at Skylar's daughter again. "Vagina. Why haven't you given him no vagina yet?"

Stifling a laugh, January shook her head. Brooke was crazy as hell.

"Adia, go play upstairs with your brother and sister, please," Skylar said to her daughter. "This conversation has gotten too juicy for us not to be able to speak properly."

"Okay, Mommy," Adia said, and they all waited impatiently for her to clear the room before starting again.

"I want to... *Really,*" Onyx affirmed directly into Brooke's doubtful eyes. "But my last experience seriously dating a man was..."

Voice trailing off, she closed her eyes as she took a pause, and January could almost feel the weight of her grave emotions clear across the room.

"It wasn't a good one."

The pureness of her complicated emotions seemed to be lost to Brooke, who still appeared utterly confused. Eyes still stretched wide, she nodded her head to beckon Onyx to continue.

"Okay... but what does the old got to do with the new? New man, new dick. The only way you'll know if it's bad is if you sit on it and give it a test ride."

"Brooke!" January hissed, motioning for her to cut it out.

"What?" Still clueless, she lifted her hands to plead innocence.

She motioned to Brooke, with two fingers pinching her lips, to keep her mouth closed.

"My last boyfriend was my first," Onyx continued, clearing her throat as she sat up straight in her seat. "We were childhood sweet-hearts, if I can even say that because shit definitely was *not* sweet. We started dating when I was eighteen. I was a virgin because my daddy is crazy. If you think my brother and cousin are bad, they can't even come close to him. In the streets, they call him 'Murk,' and he didn't earn that name by doing nothing."

Still making herself busy combing Skylar's hair, January didn't say a word. She knew all about crazy fathers. With a name like 'Murk', she understood exactly what Onyx meant. No further explanation was needed.

"The first time we had sex was in a car. I didn't want to do it—I was scared but he was pressuring me. We had been kinda dating for about a month and it was the first time I'd seen him outside of school. He was impatient and didn't want to wait any longer."

She paused to wipe at her teary eyes at the exact moment that January felt her own eyes fill with water as well. She knew where this story was going and so did everyone else in the room. Sadness engulfed them all as they listened intently to Onyx as she spoke.

"He didn't force me, but he made me feel like I had no choice—"

"So he *did* force you then," Skylar cut in. "Doing something because you felt like you had no choice is not the same as doing it because you want to. Trust me… I know the difference."

January glanced at Skylar, once more getting the feeling that there was more to what she was saying than what it seemed at surface level. As perfect as Skylar's life was, it was obvious that, like all of them, she had her own struggles and her own secrets.

Onyx nodded somberly. "It hurt like hell, but he didn't care that I was crying. After a while, he stopped to check for blood but there was none. He got so angry at me because he thought I'd tricked him. He didn't believe I was a virgin and blamed me for making him wait all that time. I tried to tell him that I was eighteen and I could have broken my hymen any number of ways. He didn't believe me. He grabbed my neck so hard that I couldn't breathe and forced himself into me. This time, he was much rougher than before. He said since I wanted to pretend to be a virgin to make a fool out of him that he would make me bleed. And he did."

There wasn't a dry eye in the room by this time. No longer able to pretend that she was combing Skylar's hair, January placed the comb on the counter and took a seat, giving Onyx the full, undivided attention that her story deserved. For someone so beautiful, so perfectly put together and talented, she'd had such ugly experiences that you would never guess at from looking at her outside. It was easy to take one look at her and feel like you wanted her life, but that was only because you didn't know the trauma that plagued her under the surface level.

"The relationship was incredibly abusive from there, but I felt trapped in it. Every time I tried to leave, he threatened to kill me. And then when I no longer cared about my own life enough to stay, he threatened to kill my family. I tried to pull away, but I didn't know how, so I told myself that college would be my ticket out. When I went away to school, I thought I was finally free from him when a few weeks passed, and I didn't hear from him. But he still refused to let go. One night, I came home to my apartment to find him there. He'd tricked my friend into giving him the address and when he saw me, he beat me so badly I couldn't see through the blood in my eyes. I had to tell him that I was pregnant to make him stop. He was so deranged and crazy that he actually went from beating my face in one second to smiling and planning our wedding in the next."

Several moments of silence passed as they all settled into the void, embracing Onyx with their loving thoughts while sympathizing with her struggle at the same time. She'd given them each a piece of her story and though January knew they all felt privileged to hear it, it devastated them all the same.

"What happened to him?" Once again, Brooke asked the question January, and most likely Skylar as well, had been thinking to herself.

With a deep sigh, Onyx shook her head. "I don't know. The only one I told about any of this was Legend. He randomly showed up at my apartment after my ex had left from almost killing me and I couldn't make him leave. I made him swear not to tell anyone else and also swear not to hurt my ex for what he'd done. I've never seen Legend so mad in my life. Seeing him that way scared me even more than thinking of what could have happened to me that night. He wanted to kill my ex, and I could tell that he wasn't thinking straight because he wasn't worried about the consequences at all. I couldn't let him do it because I didn't want to be the reason he took a life. That's why he comes to all of my shows... to make me feel safe. I never know if my ex might come across a flyer or something and show up to pay me back for disappearing after that night and for lying about being pregnant."

January folded her lips into her mouth and bit down hard on them to keep quiet. Maybe Legend had fooled Onyx, but she knew better. There was no way on God's green and blue Earth that he'd heard the same story January had just heard and actually saw the result of the abuse Onyx had endured but didn't make sure that his cousin's ex paid in blood for the things he did.

She didn't have to remember anything else about the time they'd met before to know that. It was obvious to her from the night at the range that Legend was a hitta, through and through. The way he held a gun, the pure confidence he exuded when he bust shots, the way he seemed to come alive as soon as the metal was in his hands... all of those were tell-tale signs. The fact that Onyx had confirmed that her father was a hitta as well was the icing on the cake. Legend was the kind of man who didn't take assaults on his family lightly.

Coming to Onyx's shows to protect her was all a ploy to cover his secret and to make her feel safe while finding comfort that he'd kept his promise in not killing on her behalf. But it was all a lie just to make her feel at peace, because January would bet her life that there was *no way* in hell that Legend hadn't taken care of it. Onyx's ex would never show up at one of her shows because that nigga was deader than dead.

January's heart grew in the pit of her chest, as if making additional room for the man she was steadily trying to keep away. Somehow, something about the fact that Legend would go to such great lengths to take care of someone he loved made her feel some type of way. To not only avenge her honor but vow to go out of his way to give his cousin peace of mind spoke volumes of the man that Legend was. Though he pegged himself as a dangerous man—which he most definitely was—he also had a good heart. January couldn't say that she agreed with his decision to kill, but she also knew that every single man in her life—her father, and his brothers, her uncles— they all would have done the exact same thing that Legend had.

He's a good person, she found herself thinking. *Maybe he's not the man for me, but I at least know that. He has a good heart.*

In her heart and soul, she had already known it. The only difference was that now she was allowing the truth to settle in her mind, no longer denying what she felt, what her intuition told her. Or, as Legend would say, she was no longer clinging onto her clairavoidance.

BACK TO THE STREETS.

GET DRESSED. COME OUTSIDE.

The words glowed on the screen of January's phone created an instant tingling sensation in the pit of her stomach. For what felt like the millionth time, she looked up from the screen and peered outside the sheer curtains over the window, the only thing separating her from the man who was waiting outside. That and her conflicted feelings.

Legend was the ultimate bad boy. He was the epitome of everything she always said she never wanted. Why was it that she couldn't get him out of her head? Why couldn't she have this connection with someone else—anyone else—but him?

January took in a breath and held it for as long as she could before letting it out slowly as she dropped her eyes to the phone once again. This time, to her surprise, she saw that text bubbles had formed, indicating that Legend was about to send another text.

I know you saw my message. Stop overthinking. Get. Dressed. Come. Outside.

A smile formed on her lips, one so natural, she hardly knew it was there. He wasn't even in the room with her, but it didn't matter.

Even when they didn't share the same physical space, he occupied her mind. It was so... frustrating. January really wanted nothing more than to get him out of her head.

"January, just go already. *Damn!*"

Brooke's voice broke through the silence, startling her to the point that she nearly jumped out of her own skin. Brooke yawned loudly, closing her eyes before reaching her long arms over her head in a long stretch. When she opened her eyes once again, January was still standing in the same exact place but facing her this time. The inner turmoil she was creating for herself could be read on her face like a book. Whereas Brooke lived life on the cuff doing whatever felt good to her at that particular time, January was the captain of *Team Too Much*. She was introspective to a fault; too stuck in her own logic to even consider the most loudly spoken and obvious intuitive thoughts.

"January, we both know what you want to do. Make a decision so I can go back to bed. All that damn sighing you're doing over there is fucking up my sleep."

With that said, she opened her mouth with another obnoxiously loud yawn and rolled over in the bed, complete with all the dramatic fanfare that was expected. January once again expelled a long, protracted sigh and then rolled her eyes. As annoying as it was to admit, Brooke was right. She already knew what she wanted to do. She needed to just go ahead and do it.

There was no use denying it; her chemistry with Legend was electric and couldn't be ignored. Their mutual attraction was palpable.

On my way out, January texted, finally giving in.

She wanted to see him. Needed to. There was no point in pretending otherwise. It was so easy to let ego get in the way, but there was no real happiness in it. There never was when it came to running from the truth because the truth was that, though it went against everything she'd planned and everything that made sense to her, she wanted Legend.

Crisp, fall air tickled her cheeks in a refreshing greeting that opened her heart the second she stepped out of the building, fixating her eyes on the dark blue Lamborghini parked curbside, yet another one of his exotic playthings. As usual, Legend didn't follow any rules, always preferring to make his own lane as evidenced by the fact that he was positioned directly in front of a 'no parking' zone and pulled in horizontally at that.

His face was down, hiding the apprehension in his expression as he waited, wondering if January would come to him. She was feeling him—that much he could easily see. But she was skittish, prone to running from any and everything she didn't understand. At the present, he was the prime object of her fight. The second she stepped out of the dorm's double door, her energy awakened his consciousness, and he lifted his head, immediately aware of her presence. The hardness in his eyes faded as soon as they connected with her face. There was a sweetness inside of her and it seemed to ooze out of her pores, drawing him to her like a sweet, pheromonic seduction.

Shit, he thought, dropping his head. *I'm trippin' hard over this girl.*

Lifting his hand, he pressed two fingers into the middle of his forehead, right between his eyes as if to release some pressure. As much as he wanted this, wanted her, alarms were going off in his mind.

This wasn't just another random broad that he had somehow developed the hots for. This was January Murray, the one woman he could get stretched out in a grave for fucking with.

He had to focus on the task at hand and put the other shit to the side.

"Good morning," January said once she opened the passenger door.

"Great morning," was Legend's immediate response.

He didn't turn his head to look at her. His body language was stilted. If the thoughts in his head showed in his eyes, he made sure that she couldn't read them.

"Where are we going?" she asked as he pulled out of the parking lot, whipping every turn like he was trying to toss her through the windshield.

"To work on our project."

"I figured," she replied, rolling her eyes. "But *where* are we going to work on it, might I ask?"

"No, you might not," he said coolly. Before she could object further, he turned on the radio, blasting some rap song she'd never heard before over the speakers.

Rude ass, January thought.

Sitting back in her seat, she crossed her arms in front of her chest and fell into a full sulk—complete with a drooped, stiff bottom lip. Legend was aggy as hell; in fact, part of her was convinced that he may have been clinically bipolar. There was no other way to describe the kind of man who could go from hot to cold in a matter of hours... minutes or seconds, even. And yet, in so many ways he reminded her of her father.

Growing up, she'd seen it plenty of times. It was part of why people feared Outlaw—he was so unpredictable. He could go from telling jokes like some famed comedian with someone eating out of the palm of his hand, to calling in a command that would have that same someone's life come to an early and tragic end. He was not the man you wanted to cross. The line separating his sane from his insanity was very, *very* thin. In some cases, it seemed like it didn't even exist based on how effortlessly he flowed back and forth between crazy and not crazy. He was *insanely* sane. *Sanely* insane. And Legend was just like that.

All the more reason why I'm done with him as soon as this class is over, January thought.

She didn't have time for this. Her heart would never belong to a thug. Especially not a crazy one. She preferred her man to be exactly like the life she desired: safe, predictable, and careful. Everything that Legend was *not*.

With her attitude on one hundred, she stared out the window, forcing herself to observe the scenery outside rather than further acknowledge his repulsive behavior by verbalizing all of the things she was calling him in her mind. It was obvious that he preferred when she was pissed off since he so clearly enjoyed pushing her buttons, and she wasn't about to give him the satisfaction of knowing he could control her so easily.

Only fifteen minutes into the drive, the scene outside began to drastically change. Gone were the prestigious and plush landscapes that she was used to. The manicured lawns, high-priced, luxury homes and expertly designed sidewalks and walking trails had been replaced with graffiti-covered stop signs, distressed and abandoned buildings, and visible power cables. In only the span of four blocks, they passed three liquor stores—yes, she counted—and nearly a dozen wanderers who were most likely homeless as they ambled aimlessly down the street.

Ducking her head to look above as they passed under a streetlight, her nose and brows crinkled into a frown when she saw three pairs of shoes hanging from it. They passed by a building that had the doors and windows boarded up with wood that had gang signs spray-painted all over it next to 'No Trespassing' signs.

Where the hell is he taking me?

January clutched her butterfly necklace and bit the inside of her cheeks as she continued to observe her surroundings under furrowed brows.

"Relax, princess," Legend told her. "You're not in Kansas anymore, but it's still all good."

He could pick up on her fear and apprehension as easily as if it were his own. It oozed from her. No matter how much January tried to give off the vibe that she was just like everyone else, she *wasn't* like everyone else. At least, not anyone he'd ever been around. She had heart, a lot of mouth, and more than enough attitude, but the fact remained, she wasn't 'bout that life.

"What does this have to do with our project?" she asked, hoping that he'd answer and give some type of hint as to where they were going and what he had in mind.

"You said you wanted to be a lawyer like your mom, right? Except that you wanted to help the people in the hood and not the ones who get over on them." He cut his eyes over to her and watched as she slowly nodded her head. "Well, you can't properly do that if you don't know shit about who you're helping."

January wrinkled her nose, feeling her pride begin to rise. "I *do* know who I'm helping. Single mothers, children, black men who can't seem to catch a break when it comes to life. Innocent people who live in trauma because of racist systems and institutions put in place to keep them down."

"And how will you decide who deserves your help and who doesn't?" he asked, looking at her straight as they came to a stop sign.

She shrugged. "I'll just know. I'll listen to their case and decide whether they are good or bad. I only want to help good people. The ones who deserve it."

Legend shook his head. "It's not always that easy, Princess."

Her lips puckered into a pout, but she resisted the urge to fold her arms across her chest and give away just how annoyed she really was. Legend tested her in ways that she wasn't prepared for, but in the deep crevices of her mind, she felt that she needed it all.

Pulling into a neighborhood of buildings that all looked the same, he parked his car curbside in front of one of them and killed the engine. January lifted her head to let her eyes roam, taking in the new scene that surrounded her. It was still pretty early but there was so much activity around. Each building had a front entrance where some were posted up, talking and laughing with each other, children were outside at play and though there didn't seem to be anyone in particular looking after them, everyone outside seemed to be conscious of their presence, watching out for danger anyways.

Everyone had seemed to be in their own little world, wrapped up in the normality of the day until the moment when the car had stopped, grabbing the attention of everyone on the block. Nervous energy filled her belly when she noticed that all eyes were on them. Their curious but excited glances alarmed her, cementing her body into the cushions of Legend's cool leather seats.

"Time to get out," he said, with a half smirk on his face.

January gave him a look, a desperate plea, that he chuckled at.

"Don't tell me the girl who hated having bodyguards around all the time is actually afraid to be somewhere without one," he taunted, shaking his head. He'd expected this reaction but seeing it in person was much more fulfilling than when it had only been a figment of his mind's eye. But then, in a moment so sudden that she barely had time to react, his expression changed—going serious in a way that shocked her to the core.

"You never have to be afraid of anyone when you're around me, January."

She bristled at the rarity of hearing her name on his lips rather than the nickname she'd gotten used to him using. Closing her eyes, his words brought a deeply buried memory to the forefront. Everything around them seemed to fade, giving way to a silence that allowed her mind to travel back down memory lane. Her shoulders stiffened and a sharp jolt of an emotion ran through her chest. Her mind returned to a moment that she'd long ago tried to forget.

A sour taste settled in the back of her throat and, no matter how much she tried to swallow it down, it returned. Her breathing became stilted and the tension in her body only inhibited her even more, stopping the flow of oxygen to her brain. Her ears rang with the blood-curdling screams of women and children swirling all around her. The metallic, rancid scent of blood commanded her nostrils. Her legs weakened as she was mentally transported to a place that she desperately wanted to leave in the past.

Take a deep breath and relax, January began to mentally coax herself, using the instructions that her psychiatrist at the time had given to her. Over the span of more than a few months, she'd endured therapy after therapy session to get her back on track after the incident.

January, be present. Think of only this moment. Too much focus on the past will depress you. Too much worry about the future will worry you. Both are emotions that will cripple you. Stay in this moment.

With her eyes still closed, she expelled a long breath through her lips, absentmindedly rubbing the deep scar outside her thigh.

It had taken only a few months to fully heal the gunshot wound in her leg. Much longer to repair the feelings of despair, guilt and loss that had accompanied it. The one decision that she'd made for herself, to finally stand up to her parents when it came to something she deeply desired, had been the decision that killed her dreams in an instant.

January had spent so much of her life desiring to be normal, just like the other kids, not locked up in a luxurious estate living the infamous life of a mafia princess. It's been said to always be careful what you wished for and she knew more than anyone what the warning was behind the statement. Now she *was* normal. The one thing that made her different, her talent, was stripped from her forever. The person who had shot her made sure of that.

As Legend stood in front of her watching intently, he fully understood every bit of what was happening then. He saw the emotions coursing through her, picked up on the horror, the fear, the anger and the devastation at the exact moments they were felt. Giving her time, he allowed her to process her remembrance, lending her space while also making sure that his presence was felt. She wasn't alone, there were no looming threats. She had nothing to fear.

"I fucked up once and I'll never get over that. But it'll never happen again. I don't make the same mistakes twice."

Somehow, that declaration was all she needed to calm the beating of her heart. Opening her eyes, she trailed her eyes up from where they were aimed at Legend's face, all the way up, meeting his eyes. So much had been answered now that her memory had been fully restored, but it only left more unanswered questions. The main one echoed continuously in her mind.

Why was Legend here?

It seemed like too much of a coincidence that he was at the same exact college she'd chosen, clear across the country from where they'd first met. And it definitely was too much of a coincidence that they'd ended up in the same class and partners on the first project, at that. If there was one thing that she didn't believe in, coincidences were it. There just simply was no such thing. Every 'coincidence' was set in motion either by people meddling in the circumstance or the Universe expressing its mythical powers. Nothing *ever* just happened by accident.

And this right here had her father's fingerprints all over it.

"Did my dad send you to watch me?" she asked once again. Steadying her stance, she crossed her arms in front of her chest. "And I want the truth."

She watched him carefully, needing more to gather her answer through his body language than whatever words would come through his lips. There were many tell-tale signs of deception. Natural things the body did to betray even the best liar. Like a subtle tilt of the head. A sudden abnormal flutter of the eyes. A difference in the rhythm of breathing. Legend might have been trained to kill, but he didn't have the patience for perfecting his skills of deception. His trigger finger was too quick; he didn't have a need for tricks.

As expected, his expression did shift at her question, but not in the way she was prepared for. There was a slight curl to his lips, a dark twinkle in his eyes. The air around him changed, becoming colder, more intense, making him less inviting.

"Do you think I would be here if Outlaw still had me on the payroll?"

He let out a harsh chuckle to hide some other sentiment she felt lingering beneath his aggression.

"I stopped working with Outlaw many years ago. It wasn't a choice," he added, biting down on his back teeth, his jaw flexed as he looked away. "I wish I was on some mission, but I'm not."

His words seemed to be truthful enough, but there was something else hidden there that she couldn't pick up on. She could feel it, but she couldn't place the emotion just yet.

"You weren't the only one who had their dreams taken away that day," he continued, piercing her with a look that steeled her body in place. "After what went down, I went back to Miami and got caught up in the lifestyle. But that's behind me. Now I'm here, trying to get this degree so I can do something with my life." He shrugged with the last part as if he didn't actually believe it. Like he was regurgitating something that someone else had said.

"I'm no longer a dangerous man, princess," he added with a sideways smirk accompanied by a slight twinkle in his eyes. "But that's a good thing. As far as I'm concerned, this line of work leaves less room for error."

The distant look in his eyes returned and this time January could clearly read the emotions that lay beneath.

Guilt and regret.

But why?

Legend was still about as much of a mystery as he had been the day they'd met. That day when she'd told him almost everything about her life and he'd listened intently without giving up much about himself. He was an unopened book. A suspense mystery thriller.

"C'mon," he said, positioning his hand at the base of her spine, right above the curve of her ass. "I have someone that I want you to meet."

A simple nod was all the response she could muster. His touch on her back, so close to an intimate spot on her body, stole every coherent word from her lungs. Her brain didn't even seem to register literate thoughts. Nothing, outside of the love-drunk emotions she felt.

What am I doing right now? she thought when the act of thinking was finally made possible.

His touch was electric; it created a warm sensation that radiated through her entire body, settling right into her core. If January didn't know better, she would've thought she was falling in love. But she couldn't be. Not this soon.

Legend led her down the sidewalk and she couldn't help but notice how mostly everyone happily greeted him by name with familiarity, as if they'd known him a long time. It was boggling. With his gold chains, Rolex watches and expensive cars, she was shocked at how someone who lived a life as privileged as him would seem perfectly at ease in a place like this.

She, on the other hand, stood out like a sore thumb. It was obvious that January was somewhere she didn't belong, but not because of anything she had on. Her discomfort was plastered all over her face. No mirror was necessary for her to know that she was wearing her anxiety like a badge. Crazy enough, no one would have even noticed her if she didn't look so damn uncomfortable in the first place. She was a walking self-fulfilling prophecy.

"Where are we going?" she asked, unconscious about the fact that she was closing the distance between Legend and her with each stride. If she walked any closer to him, they would merge into one.

"I want you to meet someone. I think it might help you understand a few things."

Her brows raised and she turned to him, eyeing him curiously.

What is he up to this time?

Following behind him, she stayed silent until they came to a stop in front of one of the apartment buildings. It was different only in that it wasn't as clean as the others surrounding it. Children's toys were scattered all over the front entrance in complete and utter disarray. Soiled diapers collected in a small mop bucket outside that was long overdue from being emptied. The stench in the air was over-whelming to all but the flies circling around, enjoying the disgusting smell.

"Shit, I knew I should've been here sooner," she heard Legend whisper under his breath.

January wasn't sure what he meant but she didn't ask, somehow knowing for sure that it wasn't something that he wanted to explain right then.

Standing at the front door, Legend knocked, and she held onto her breath for dear life, waiting with full apprehension for whatever would answer on the other side. It wasn't just the scent of the stank ass dirty diapers that had her holding her breath, but the fact that his whole presence had completely changed. His jaw was tight, his shoulders were tense, and his brows were furrowed; there was a lot on his mind that he was leaving unsaid. January wanted to ask ques-tions but stood next to him in silence instead.

Finally, the door swung open to reveal a short woman dressed in a large t-shirt, not appearing to have a damn thing on underneath. Her hair was a total disaster on top of her head, resembling some-thing January would describe as a dusty, rusty, crusty bird's nest. The woman peered at January from under heavy eyelids, appearing fully disinterested, bored and a bit annoyed as if wondering who she was and why she was there. It wasn't until her eyes shifted to Legend that she reacted. Her face lit up like a stick of dynamite and then blood flooded her light caramel cheeks making them appear crimson red.

"Glenda, what *the* fuck?"

The words flew out of his mouth so fast, January almost jumped from shock. She snuck a glance at him, and her brows shot in the air. Legend was pissed. His anger couldn't be ignored. It was rolling off his body in waves. Though his tone was calm, and his expression was the same, the strength of his emotions was plainly felt.

"Legend, don't even start with that shit. You know I'm doing the best I can do," Glenda replied with a sheepish expression on her face.

He didn't immediately respond, allowing his eyes to cast down, raking over all the filth around where they stood. When he stared pointedly at the bucket of dirty diapers, his nostrils curled in pure disgust.

"This ain't the fuckin' best you could do," he snapped, slightly raising his tone. "Yo, for real shorty, this is some *disgusting* shit. Even for you. You think it's okay letting yo' kids live like this?"

January grimaced at his words, feeling uncomfortable as hell even though he wasn't even talking to her. Legend didn't hold back. He was rude as hell. Looking down, she found herself wishing that there was a hole in the ground big enough to gobble her up. If there were, she had no doubts that both she and Glenda would be fighting each other for it.

Standing silently, Glenda began fumbling with her hands, shrouded in her embarrassment as Legend waited for her to explain herself. She couldn't. And wouldn't. Honestly, there wasn't a damn thing she *could* say. And then, as if the moment wasn't already tense enough, Legend then decided to open his mouth and ask the one question that had already been at the forefront of January's mind.

"If you got all this shit happenin' out here, what the fuck kinda bull-shit you got goin' on in there?" he asked, pointing inside her apartment.

Not bothering to wait for a response that he already knew he wasn't going to get, Legend pushed his way through the door, forcing Glenda to fall to the side in order to let him in. Almost losing her balance, she fell flat against the door and had to grab the door handle to catch her balance. Legend didn't even bat an eye or move to help her. He gave no fucks at all.

"Legend... wait!" Glenda yelled with her hands overhead, trailing behind him as he helped himself to a full exploration of her home.

Shocked to the max, with January stood in silence, like the out-of-place sack of awkwardness she was. The only thing stopping her from letting her jaw fall to her toes was the fact that she didn't want to risk one of the diaper-flies diving inside.

"January, come in and close the door. Trust me, she ain't got room in here for one more motherfuckin' fly." Legend shouted her name, making her jump to attention. "Glenda, this right here... this is some *bullshit*!"

Huffing out a breath, January sighed heavily before dragging her feet over the threshold of Glenda's home. The first thing that stood out to her as soon as she entered was the smell. The soiled diapers were outside... so why the hell was there such a repulsing smell *inside*? She thought that it would be an unexplained phenomenon until she took a moment to look around and realize that the answer to her question was staring her right in the face. From *all* angles.

The place was *filthy*.

Dirty clothes covered the floor in heaps, old plates of food sat on top of the dining room table, a highchair and the coffee table in the living room. And every single plate was swirling with gnats and flies.

"Oh my g—" January covered her mouth, feeling her stomach jerk.

A wave of nausea washed over her when she saw a small cockroach helping itself to the food left on the table, munching away as if it didn't have a care in the world. And why would it? Obviously, Glenda didn't give a damn! It wasn't like she was doing a thing to get rid of that roach or any of his friends. Her living room was a free-for-all for any and every creature that survived off filth.

Her nasty ass included, was January's thought.

Shaking her head at it all, she stood in one place, with her arms wrapped around her body, careful not to touch a thing as she listened to Glenda and Legend's voices coming from down the hall.

"Legend, you know how it is…" Glenda started, trying to explain. "It's a lot and I can't—"

"You can, you're just lazy as fuck!" Legend battled back. "Ain't no fuckin' excuse for this stanky ass shit. This shit right *here*—nah, look at it. No, open your eyes and look at it—this shit right *here* is why no nigga on Earth will fuck with you. All this Bath & Body Works spray you got on the dresser… And what the hell for? That spray ain't fuckin' with this pissy smellin' shit."

"Oh my *god*, Legend, you're so damn rude," January whispered. She slapped her palm to her forehead, feeling like she wanted to die.

Lifting her head, she turned just in time to see Legend walking down the hall holding a small, half-asleep little boy in one arm and a sleeping little girl in the other. Both appeared to be around the same age, maybe three years old. January's heart fluttered. They were like sleeping baby angels; the cutest kids she'd ever seen. Especially the little girl, sleeping soundly with her mouth open, a little string of drool connecting from her mouth to Legend's shirt. Like she didn't have a care in the world. Her body shifted as Legend stomped angrily down the hall and, as an automatic reaction, the little girl reached her tiny arms up and gripped around his neck in her sleep, hugging him tight. January's heart fluttered in her chest.

"Well, what do you want me to do? You can't take them from me!" Glenda ran behind Legend, desperate. With tears in her eyes, she was imploring him about children that, regardless of her current antics, January didn't feel like she even cared about. To her, it was clear from the environment she raised them in. Even their pajamas were soiled, and the bottoms of their feet were dirty and black, as if they hadn't been bathed in days.

Maybe even longer, January thought, curling her nose. Any bit of sympathy she may have felt for Glenda was gone.

Desperate to make him look at her, Glenda reached out to Legend and grabbed him by the shoulder, just as he had finally made it to January.

"Legend, *please,* just listen to me—"

Turning towards her, he shot her the most callous, threatening glare; one that gave Glenda very clear instructions on what she'd better do next. Clamping her mouth closed, Glenda tucked her hands back to her sides and quickly moved away from him. With tears in her eyes, she bounced her gaze between him and her babies, watching with longing.

January was totally confused as she watched Glenda in that moment. She seemed to be a mother who sincerely loved her kids. Why was it that she had them living like this?

"Aye, I need you to do me a favor and bathe the kids. I'm going to go to the store and find some shit for them to wear. They got clothes in the drawer back there but from the smell of 'em, I'm just gon' burn that shit."

Hearing that, Glenda's head hung even lower between her shoulders. It was like she was sinking into herself, crumbling into nothingness.

"And yo, Glenda," Legend said, turning to her. "While we're here doin' the shit *you* should be doin', you need to clean up this fuckin' place. And don't try to bullshit me with that fake ass cleaning you tried to do last time. Clean this shit up like you do when them white ass motherfuckas from the government be out here inspecting shit to decide whether or not to let you keep gettin' that check."

Nodding somberly, Glenda swiped a tear from her eyes and then did an about-face to a closet where she pulled out a mop and broom.

Of everything in the apartment, the mop and broom were the only things that looked sparkling clean. After watching her for a moment to make sure that she was following his demands, Legend laid both kids on the sofa, took a moment to make sure they were asleep and then pulled something out of his pocket.

"Yo, here you go," he called out, holding a small bag in his hands. January wasn't sure what he was holding, but what she did notice was when Glenda saw it, her entire face lit up. Like Scooby Doo being offered a Scooby Snack, she grinned radiantly from ear-to-ear, running to Legend as if he was the savior of her life.

"Thank you! This is *just* what I needed." She snatched the bag from his hand and opened it immediately, dumping a single pill into her hand. Wasting not a single second, she popped it right into her mouth and swallowed it dry.

"I didn't think you would give them to me this time because..." She let her eyes fall pointedly over our surroundings.

"Just don't let this shit get this bad ever again. Call me before it gets to this."

Happily wagging her head, Glenda went back to cleaning with an extra pep in her step, leaving Legend looking down at the kids on the sofa, and leaving January attempting to glare a boulder-sized hole into the side of his skull. She couldn't *believe* what she'd just witnessed.

Humming a little tune to herself, Glenda danced her happy ass down the hallway, sweeping away like a blissful Cinderella. As soon as January assumed she was out of earshot, she took the chance to address Legend.

"Did you just—"

He quickly silenced her by lifting a single finger in the air and then turned that finger towards the door, signaling for her to walk outside. With her lips balled up, eyes narrowed and her hands in fists on her hips, January stomped towards the door with Legend right behind her. As soon as her feet hit the pavement of the sidewalk and she heard him close the front door, she was ready to go in.

"Did you just give her *drugs*, Legend?" she hissed at him with disbelief. "Like, what is this? Congrats for being a shitty mother to your kids, now go get high and keep doing it?"

Like a soldier made of pure stone, he stood in front of her with a straight face, not at all responding in any visible way to her anger. Or her unspoken accusation of him and how she felt that he was enabling a woman who didn't even deserve the children God had given to her.

"You should get to know people before you judge 'em," was all he said with a shrug.

January's eyes widened. Was he seriously defending Glenda? Like, actually suggesting she was wrong for judging her? After he'd just trekked back and forth through her house doing the same?

"Excuse me? Were you in the same house that I was in?" January asked, pointing her eyes back towards the front door. "It was disgusting in there! I am perfectly in the right to judge. It's really easy for people to lay down to make kids but when it comes to taking care of them—" She scoffed. "I guess that's a different story."

Shaking her head, she crossed her arms in front of her chest and waited for how Legend was going to position against her when it came to this. There was no way, in no world that Glenda's actions, or his, could be justified.

"You said you wanted to get in law to help people who needed it but couldn't afford to get it, right?" Legend asked after a few moments of silence.

Nodding, January cut her eyes to him, wondering what he was getting at. No way on no one's planet would Glenda qualify as the type she would want to help.

"Three years ago, Glenda decided to break up with her ex when she realized she was pregnant. He was abusive but she dealt with the shit because she was afraid of him. Every time she tried to leave, he threatened to kill her, so she stayed. When she got pregnant with the twins, she left for good. Then he started stalking her, showing up at her job, church, wherever he thought he could find her. She tried to get a restraining order but couldn't get the courts to approve it, so she just forgot about it and tried to move on."

January pressed her lips together in a straight line, knowing what he said to definitely be true. Her mother always talked about how hard it was for the people who needed a restraining order, Black women especially, to get one. For this reason, domestic violence ran rampant in many Black neighborhoods simply because the women decided to just deal with the abuse.

Wrapping her body in her arms, January let out a sharp breath as Legend continued.

"After being denied that, she moved in with her moms and little brother so that she wasn't alone."

Pausing, Legend ran a hand over the top of his head, as if smoothing down the top of his locs and then let out a breath. His eyes went dark and his face went cold and distant, letting January know that whatever was coming next would make her regret every-thing she'd said.

"On New Year's Eve, Glenda and her family were celebrating. Drinking, dancing to music and shit. She wasn't drinking, she was almost eight months pregnant with the twins. Her ex had finally found out where she lived. He broke in, shot everyone in the house, including Glenda, and then killed himself right in front of her eyes. The only ones who survived were Glenda and the twins. She gave birth to them the same night of her mother and brother's murder."

With that said, Legend let out a long sigh and shook his head before beginning again. This was about the most emotion and empathy she'd ever seen him display for anyone.

"She's a great mother to her kids but certain days for her are triggers. She goes into deep depression. When that happens, she doesn't do shit but exist, and barely that. The only thing that can kick her into gear is when I give her something to numb the pain. It's a temporary fix, a short escape, but it's enough for her to make it through the hardest days in her life. The twins' birthday is this weekend so I knew that the depression would be kicking in, but I just ain't expect it to be this bad already. I should've been over here... but my mind's been caught up in some other shit."

January stood there in silence, with her gut twisted and her body cold as ice. A haunting feeling washed over her before giving way to grief. For the life of her, she couldn't understand how Glenda had endured what she'd been through and been able to keep it together *at all.*

If it had been me... her words fell off. She couldn't even bring herself to imagine it.

Looking back towards the small duplex apartment, January saw Glenda through one of the windows, dancing to the music she'd turned on as she swept with a smile on her face. After hearing of her background, her thoughts of the woman morphed completely, and she saw none of her faults; only her strength. To have gone through all that she had and then to be left living completely alone without any help to get through it... it was amazing that she could get out of bed at all.

"Does she really have no one?" January couldn't help but ask, feeling as if her heart was being squeezed by a fist in her chest.

"After burying her mother, brother, and the twins' father, she tried to go to a therapist but couldn't. She had to get back to work to make money to support herself and the kids. She didn't have time to grieve and she didn't have any family around to help her. When I first ran into Glenda, she was hooked on Percocet, a habit she developed after being given a prescription after delivering the twins. I started selling to her, not really knowing much about her situation. Then one day, she purchased from me, but had a request: she asked me to promise that if anything happened to her, I would make sure her babies were safe and went to a good home. She was planning to O.D. She had hit rock bottom and decided she ain't want to live anymore. From that day forward, I told her that I'd always be there for her and she could get whatever for free. I told her if she needed anything from me, to just call and ask. She never calls so I always gotta remember to swing by here and check."

January swiped a tear from her chest and felt the emotions she had for Legend grow even stronger. No matter how much he tried to deny it, he had a heart. He cared for people. Just in his own way, the only way that he knew how.

"You said that you wanted to help people, right?" he asked again, looking in her eyes. Once again, she nodded. "Well, help me help people like Glenda. Yeah, she got issues, but she tries her best. She doesn't always make the best decisions but she's working with the hand she was dealt and doing what she can with it. If motherfuckas took a chance to understand her rather than judge her, they could understand how easy it really is to be just like her. Or maybe even worse," he added with a shrug. "If *you* had gone through what Glenda did, do you think you would handle it better?"

And with that said, Legend took one look down at January's thigh, pointedly at the area where she'd been shot and then narrowed his eyes back into hers. His message was clear and once he knew it had been delivered, he turned around and walked back into Glenda's apartment, leaving her to marinate on it.

She hadn't even dealt with a piece of what happened to Glenda and she had totally given up on her life because of that. January had all the support in the world from family and friends, all the money needed to afford any therapeutic treatment in the world in order to get her back on her feet, but she'd totally abandoned the dreams of the life she wanted and her love for dance. Her dream was her baby and she'd abandoned it and herself when she didn't have to—who was she to judge Glenda for shit?

With her head down, January walked back towards Glenda's apartment like a sad little puppy with her tail between her legs. In her mind, the conversation she'd had earlier with Legend kept replaying.

"You said you wanted to be a lawyer like your mom, right? Except that you wanted to help the people in the hood and not the ones who get over on them. Well, you can't properly do that if you don't know shit about who you're helping."

"I do know who I'm helping. Single mothers, children, black men who can't seem to catch a break when it comes to life. Innocent people who live in trauma because of racist systems and institutions put in place to keep them down."

"And how will you decide who deserves your help and who doesn't?"

I'll just know. I'll listen to their case and decide whether they are good or bad. I only want to help good people. The ones who deserve it."

It's not always that easy, Princess."

Legend had been right—it wasn't always that easy to find the people who really needed help because sometimes, like in Glenda's case, they never had the chance to make it to a judge. The system canceled out on their right to live long before they made it to the courtroom.

January now fully understood what Legend meant. The only way to truly help was to get off your high horse and truly immerse yourself into the community that needed you. She couldn't help people like Glenda from Beverly Hills and Hollywood. The only way to truly help the hood was to actually be *in* the hood.

OUTLAW OR MR. MURRAY.

Emotions were a complete waste of time.

The quicker that's understood, the faster you can stop being ruled by them. It's the key to life... master your own emotions and you can master anything. You can finally stop being controlled by them. Stop making stupid decisions for the sake of how you feel at whatever particular point in time. Or at least, that's what *they* say.

As for January? She couldn't tell you if that was true or not because if there was a test on it, best believe, she'd fail it. And she hadn't failed many things throughout her life, but that would definitely be one. If that wasn't true, she wouldn't have been in the situation she was currently in. She had to figure out a way to get control of herself—to get her emotions together.

In fact, she was desperate, which was why she resorted to calling the last person on Earth she probably should have in order to help her figure them out.

.   .   .

"Your moms over here trying to make me into Mr. Murray. Got me cleaning and shit. Been fucking with me all these years and still act like she don't know I'm an Outlaw."

January couldn't help but giggle as she watched her father's face frown up on the screen.

"Well... are you doing it?"

"Hell yeah! Don't nobody wanna deal with her mean ass. But I'm doing it because I want to. Not because she told me to."

January laughed so hard at that, she snorted. Her daddy was a special kind of crazy.

"You doing it because you 'want to'?" She asked him, knowing full well that was simply something he'd said to appease his swollen ego and nothing else.

"What you think?" he stopped, staring at her for dramatic effect through the screen of her phone. "I grew up running the streets. I was a 'street runner.' In fact, I got that shit tatted on my legs in case a nigga don't believe me so he can see it over and over when I stomp his ass out for doubtin' me. What's the twelfth law of the BBM? I taught you this shit already, January. I know you know it! Say it with me: 'I *don't bow down* for no motherfucka breathin' and *never* wi—"

"Luke, are you wearin' my apron?"

January heard her mama's voice come in faintly from somewhere behind him, interrupting him mid-way through his 'I'm a thug' rant.

"Huh?" he asked, his eyes screwed tightly into a frown as he looked her way.

The camera panned down some with his movement, just enough for January to see that he *was* wearing what appeared to be her mama's apron, judging from the larger-than-life illustration of a magnolia flower, her mama's favorite, on the front.

January almost burst out laughing again as she replayed his rant from only moments before in her mind. He was saying *all that* while wearing *this*? She slapped her hand to her forehead, still giggling. She couldn't make this shit up if she tried.

"You asked me to check on whatever the hell you been in here tryin' to cook. You think I'm 'bout to do that without somethin' over my clothes?"

"What's that supposed to mean?"

Instead of answering her, he turned back to look at January with his brows pointed towards his forehead and then leaned forward into the phone as if he was trying to say something only meant for her to hear.

"Yo' mama been in here for the last three hours stewing some stanky shit that she expects me to eat." He shook his head. "I ain't eatin' that shit. Then she asked me to come in here to check on it. Soon as I stepped in the kitchen, I heard it boiling and shit on the stove. I'm wearin' Gucci up under this! The fuck I look like messin' up a fit that cost over four bands 'cause she experimentin' with that stanky ass—"

"Luke, what you in here saying about me?"

Once again, Outlaw stopped right in the middle of his sentence and snapped his head to his right where, though January couldn't see her, she assumed her mama was standing. His lips curled into a half-smile, but January could still see the mischief in his eyes from the angle of his side profile.

"I was just tellin' our daughter how you been in here whippin' this work in the kitchen."

Smiling hard, Janelle came into the camera, twisting her hands at the wrist, illustrating her 'whipping' talent while doing a little jig.

"Yeah, I been doing the damn thing," she said finally, still grinning.

"Nah, you been doing something but what you *ain't* been doin' is the damn thing, Love," he said, correcting her.

He placed the phone down, propping it up so that January could see the two of them and then turned to face Janelle, as if he needed to give her his undivided attention before he broke down whatever he was about to say next.

"Listen, Nell, and I mean this in the most loving way possible." He put his right hand to his chest. "I mean it. I'm sayin' this straight from the heart. Tryin' to save our marriage."

Rolling her eyes, Janelle let out a sigh of sheer annoyance and placed her hands on her hips.

"Luke, what the hell do you want to say?"

January covered her mouth, trying to keep from laughing. She knew her daddy very well and one thing about him was that whenever he said that he was about to say something from the heart, it always 100% meant that he was about to say some disrespectful shit... but make it seem like he was making nice.

"Love, you can do a lot of things. You can run the country—are a *powerful* fuckin' woman. But you can't cook *for shit*! Why you think I'm always out here hustlin' so you can have a full-time chef? I mean—" He placed his hands in the air in surrender. "Trust, I ain't got no problem bringin' home the bacon, but what I'm sayin' is, I don't want *yo'* ass in here tryin' to cook it! That's what I pay that French nigga to do. I know you been bored but you need to find a new hobby. Cookin' *ain't* it."

By the time he finished, Janelle was looking at him with her mouth wide open, in complete shock. She stood there, totally flabbergasted, for a few seconds before shaking her head and turning to where January was watching on the phone.

"You see what the hell I have to deal with since you've been gone?" she asked, smiling as she rolled her eyes again.

"Nigga, what you mean *you*? What *you* gotta deal with?" Outlaw parroted, gawking at her like she'd lost her mind. "What the fuck about *me*? Listen, January." He turned to look squarely at her and then jabbed his thumb to point at Janelle before he began speaking.

"Yo' mama done told the chef not to come in for the entire week and threw my whole shit off. I can't even concentrate on what I need to 'cause I been tryin' to figure out how to tell her I ain't been eatin' this shit. She got a nigga in here on struggle mode." He looked down, pointedly at his muscular body. "I been losin' weight and shit. Niggas in the streets gon' get bold and wanna try my ass… thinkin' I'm sick."

Janelle pursed her lips with her arms crossed over her chest and her eyes pointed indignantly to the sky.

"If you ain't been eating it, you could've just said that. I haven't been eating it either."

"WHAT?" Outlaw shouted so loud that Janelle and January both flinched. "If you ain't been eatin' this shit, why you makin' me do it?"

Janelle shrugged as a sheepish look fell over her face. "I thought you liked it! You kept saying how great everything was, so I kept cooking."

"Aw, hell nah!" he said, shaking his head before looking at January. "January, take some cooking classes while you at that college. I don't want you takin' some innocent nigga through this shit. My mind been fucked up all week trying to figure out how to explain to your mama that I ain't want her within a fifty-yard radius of a stove."

January covered her mouth, laughing hard. "Y'all are crazy. You know that, right?"

"Yeah, but you love us," Janelle added. "I'll let y'all get back to your conversation. Luke, give me my apron so I can finish the food."

"I hope by 'finish' you mean you 'bout to throw that stank shit out the back door…way back." He pointed. "I mean, waaaay back. As far as the eye can see."

January laughed into her hand as Outlaw removed the ties of the apron from around his waist.

After handing it over to Janelle, he grabbed the phone and started to walk away so that he could continue his conversation. Exhaling, January tried to calm her mind and bring it back to what she needed to gather the nerve to ask. She'd called him because she wanted to speak about something specifically to get his opinion on it.

Though January and Outlaw had plenty conversations about boys when she was growing up, never once in her life had she asked him about any one in particular. And now she was about to finally breech that topic about one that had taken up permanent residence in her mind. But this one wasn't a boy… he was definitely a grown ass man.

"What's up, baby girl?" he asked, stepping in his office. "I can tell from the look on your face that something is on your mind. I know you called me for a reason."

January drummed her fingers against the granite countertop of the small island she was sitting at, wondering how to best bring up the topic. Each moment that she spent with Legend, her feelings for him were growing more and more intense. It wasn't a feeling she could really place. It was too early to be love—or at least that's what she thought. She'd never been in love before to know how long it took. Or what it really was.

However, what really plagued her was that she wasn't sure what Legend thought about her. She was finally at the point where she could admit to herself that she wanted him. There was no mistaking that fact. No matter how much she tried to push it away, the truth was that no other guy on campus could ignite enough for her to even glance his way. Legend was it. He was constantly on her mind when he wasn't around and when he was around, he didn't leave space in her head for anything else. The problem was that she couldn't read him like she could everyone else. He was an enigma; different from anyone she'd ever dealt with before. But that caused a major issue for her, which only heightened her insecurity. She needed to know how he felt. She wanted to know that her feelings were reciprocated so that she could feel safe feeling them.

"How did you know you loved Mama?" January blurted the question out quickly before she lost the nerve to ask. Being that her father was about the closest to being someone like Legend from anyone she knew, it seemed to her that he would be the most obvious choice for this conversation. She'd always said she wanted to love a man who treated her like her father did while having no other similarities otherwise, but she'd ended up falling so hard for Legend: a man who reminded her more and more of Outlaw each day. It felt like a trick of the Universe—something done for a specific, divine purpose she wasn't aware of just yet. In a way, she felt like this entire situation was a test. Like she was working off some karma that wasn't her own.

"How did I know I loved your mama…" Outlaw repeated, thinking to himself as he ducked his eyes, taking his thoughts back in time. "Honestly, I always did."

January's eyes widened in shock. "Love at first sight?" She giggled a little at that. "That's a surprise. You don't take me as the type to believe in that."

Smiling, Outlaw reached up and scratched his head, his expression showing that he barely believed it himself.

"I don't… well, I didn't until you asked me this and I took the time to really think on it. I always loved her; I just didn't know it at the time." He paused for a moment to shrug. "Real shit, when I first met your mama, I just wanted to fuck."

"DADDY!" January gasped before wincing in pain. The last thing she wanted to think about was her parents doing the nasty.

"What?" He thew his hands up. "You should be happy I wanted to fuck. How the hell you think you got here? You damn sure ain't sprout out of some shit that we planted in the garden out back. I mean... I did plant some seeds up in there, but—"

January threw her hands in the air to stop him. "Daddy, I got it! I got it!"

With a slick smile on his face, it became obvious that he'd just been trying to get under her skin. Which was typical for him. For someone who was so serious—and even deadly—with everyone else, he was a kid at heart. The side of him that they saw was one reserved only for friends and family. He was a powerful man with a personality that changed the atmosphere of any room he entered in, whether for bad or good. In these moments, his best moments, it was a guarantee that he'd make everyone around smile.

"Going back to your question, I didn't know I loved her at first. I thought I only wanted to fuck, but it was deeper than that. Mainly because she made it clear she didn't like my ass, but I couldn't stop pursuing her."

Nodding slowly, January thought about that for a moment. "So that's what made her different? That she made it clear she didn't want you?"

Shaking his head, he adjusted the phone, which he had propped up somewhere on his desk, and then leaned back in his dark leather office chair, placing his arms behind his head.

"Nah, what made her different is how I reacted to it. There's been a few bad ass chicks, not many—" he clarified, "—who I tried to get at, but they played hard to get. I knew I could've still got at 'em if I tried, but I ain't have the patience for that bullshit. In my mind, you either fuckin' or you not. I wasn't 'bout to wine or dine you, make you feel like a woman, talkin' and whatnot... I ain't have time for none of that shit. For niggas like me, what you won't do, the next ten chicks will." He shrugged with that, speaking honestly.

January knew for a fact that he was telling the truth, based on the stories she'd heard about him and her uncles, but also based on how it was now. Married or not, women went crazy over the Murrays.

"Janelle was the only one who made me want to actually try. She wanted me to be the perfect boyfriend, do shit for her that I never did—dates, gifts—she expected me to be thoughtful, considerate, romantic and shit. For any other woman, my middle finger waving in the air would've been the last thing they'd seen, but I couldn't do that with her."

Outlaw's eyes were pointed to the ceiling and January could tell by the glean in his eyes that he was visualizing precious memories of the past.

"I fought against it—but she made it clear that she wasn't folding. She held her ground and that's when I realized she was my mirror. She was the female version of me. She made it clear that even though she might love me, she didn't bow down to no motherfucka breathin'… not even me." He chuckled a little at that and then tossed his hands in the air. "So, I adjusted to become the man she needed me to be. A better man, in the end, so I didn't know it, but it was for my benefit."

Pulling her lips into her mouth, January nodded her head, soaking in everything that he was saying. She had her answer.

Effort.

That's what made all the difference. The fact that Outlaw bothered to put in effort to be the man she needed was the determining factor for both of them. It showed him that he loved her, and it confirmed for her that he was a man it was safe to love.

"Is there a lil nigga you call yourself catchin' feelings for?" he asked, interrupting her thoughts. "Gon' tell me so I can get the Uzi and light his ass up."

January lifted her head to look at him and instantly felt a little off kilter by the serious expression on his face. Now that the nostalgia of the moment had ended, he was back to business, trying to get up in her business. This was the part of the conversation she hadn't exactly been prepared for.

"Um, not really. I mean…" she frowned, darting her eyes back and forth, anywhere but his face. She didn't want to admit to anything, but she also couldn't lie. There was no use; he was an expert at detecting even the best told lie every time.

"Someone has my interest, I guess," she finally said, giving in. "But I don't know how he feels about me. He's not the easiest person to read. He's guarded… He reminds me, a lot, of you so I know he's good at heart. I just don't know if he's the one for me."

Taking a moment to process the fact that she'd just told him for the first time that she was interested in a man, and not just any man, but one who reminded me of him, he took a long pause. The entire time, Outlaw's eyes never left her face, and she got the feeling that her thoughts were being read like a book. Her father had never been the 'spiritual' type, and he often wondered where January got her love of astrology, tarot and all things metaphysical from when he thought all of that was just tools people used as a cop out for taking responsibility for living their own life. However, somehow, he seemed to have expert intuition and clairsentience. He just seemed to know things even if people didn't tell him. Being that she was his daughter, his sense of knowing was extra tuned when it came to her.

Silence clogged the air around January as she waited, feeling like she was sitting on pins and needles. Then, finally, Outlaw sat up straight in his chair, looking her straight in her eyes to make sure that he had her full, undivided attention. "January, I taught you the *BBM* rules of life for a reason. It wasn't because I ever wanted you to be part of this kind of life. The mafia life isn't what I wanted for you… or your brother."

January's eyes clouded over with tears at the mention of the brother she'd never met. He'd died a few days after birth but on the rare occasions when her father mentioned him, she could see the pain in his eyes. He blamed himself for it. She didn't know all the details, but it had something to do with the circumstances surrounding Janelle's emotional state when she'd gotten pregnant. They'd been going through something and whatever it was stressed her and, according to him, stressed the baby. Her brother had been born with under-developed lungs, which made it difficult for him to breathe.

"I came up with the rules after we lost your brother. It was a code of conduct that I established based on the man I would've wanted him to be. If I'd been that type of man, he might have been alive. I did some fucked up shit—I didn't know Janelle was pregnant at the time, but it don't make no difference. The night she found out about it, it broke her." He ran a hand over his face in distress. "I remember her crying, holding her chest as she gasped, telling me that she couldn't breathe."

Outlaw paused and, for the first time in he life, January saw tears pooling in her daddy's eyes. The tears didn't fall but they didn't have to. By this time, she was practically sobbing enough for the both of them.

"She miscarried and lost that baby. I wasn't around so she dealt with that on her own. When I got her back, I think God knew that even though enough shit had been thrown at me that should've convinced me to change my ways, deep down, I was still the same. If something drastic didn't happen to make me change course, I would fuck up again." He let out a harsh breath and bent his head, taking a moment to get himself together before he could force himself to continue.

"Your brother was born, and I remember thinking 'why the fuck he ain't cryin'?' when they pulled him out. I looked over the doctor's shoulder right into his face and I saw the same expression there that I'd seen on your mama's that night. I felt like that night, the worst night of my life, was back haunting me. And then the doctor said the words that confirmed it all. He said, '*he can't breathe*'... the same *exact* thing that Janelle had said that other night. They started suctioning liquid out of his lungs. They ran some tests, did some other shit. None of it worked."

Pressing her lips together, January wiped the tears from her eyes and took a deep breath, trying to keep it together. She could tell that this was the first time he'd told this story. And with the recall, she could also see that he was living through that moment again. She didn't want her emotions to make it harder on him because she knew he needed to get this out. He'd been holding in a lot of guilt that needed to be released.

"After losing your brother, I changed my life. I knew I had a higher calling for my life that I was running from. Even with all the shit I've done, which could be called 'bad'—" He did air quotes with his fingers. "—my overall mission has always been to make a difference. To take care of my hood and all the people in it. To make this world a better place for the ones who can't do it for themselves. I knew I couldn't depend on the motherfuckas in the government or anywhere else to do that for us. You gotta have lived in the hood to see the good in it. You gotta be in the hood to understand that shit is deeper than what it looks like on the surface—to truly understand that people aren't always as helpless and hopeless as they may appear to be. And that was the beginning of the *Black Bag Mafia*."

The last part of what Outlaw said, about being in the hood or from it to see the good in it, reminded her of what Legend had said to her when he took her for her own personal field trip to the 'other side.' He'd been trying to get her to understand the same thing. He had a dark side that he needed to deal with, but his intentions were good, and his heart was pure. That side of him was just so guarded that it took damn near a miracle for him to open up enough to let a person see it.

"I said all that to say…" Outlaw continued, looking her right in the eyes. "Whatever man you decide to give your heart to, make sure he's not like the man I *was*, but like the man I *became*."

YOGA LEGENDS.

"I CAN'T BELIEVE I LET YOU CONVINCE ME TO DO THIS SHIT."

Grinning so hard that her cheeks ached, January sat down on her yoga mat, placing her water bottle and face towel to her right. She didn't look up to confirm it, but she could feel Legend's eyes boring down on her. If he had the ability to make her actually feel the heat coming from his eyes, she probably would've exploded like a bomb.

"Shhhh! You're loud," she said, chastising him with her finger to her lips. They were already late since he'd flat-out refused to come in at first. It had taken a full fifteen minutes to get him to walk inside the room once he realized what she'd picked for them to do for her part of their class project.

"I don't give a fuck if I *am* loud," Legend continued, looking around. "I want everyone in here to know I ain't doin' this shit willingly."

So, apparently he *did* have superpowers , because she was feeling all kinds of heat right then. January's cheeks flamed with her embarrassment when two ladies sitting nearby each snapped their necks to look back at her and Legend, each woman wearing shocked and utterly appalled looks on their face.

"Legend, sit *your ass* down!" She hissed, speaking through her teeth.

That got his attention.

In a matter of seconds, Legend's expression gave in and January watched as his lips dipped into something like a smile.

"Damn, princess. I ain't know you had it in you," he joked, chuckling as he finally took a seat on the mat next to her. "When you started cussin'?"

"I *don't* curse," she said, rolling her eyes. "'Ass' doesn't count. It's in the Bible."

He paused, still looking at her with a twinkle of pure mischief in his eyes. Right then, she knew he was officially on one.

"What about 'damn'? That counts, right? Say it." Legend smirked, teasing her. "Say 'damn'."

Sighing heavily, January rolled her eyes again. He was such a kid.

"That doesn't count either. 'Damn' is in the Bible, too, Legend. Duh!"

With a deep frown, he held his hands out and shrugged. "I ain't never read it. How the hell am I supposed to know?"

"Riiiiight," she mused, sarcastically drawling out the word. "I forgot you're an atheist."

Lifting one finger in the air, Legend shook it from left to right along with his head. "I'm not an atheist."

She scoffed but didn't respond, hoping that the conversation was over so he could leave her alone. The instructor had walked in already and was setting up as she waited for a few minutes in case anyone was late showing up. It was a new instructor; someone January hadn't seen before, but heard was one of the most experienced teachers. Saying she was overeager to see what this new instructor had in store, was an understatement.

"What about 'fuck'?" she heard Legend suddenly ask. "You can't tell me *that's* in there. Say it, January. Say 'fuck.'"

Mortified, she looked at him like he'd grown another head out of his neck. Was he *really* doing this?

"What?" Legend's brows shot to the ceiling. "Is *that* in there, too?"

"No, it's *not.*"

"I was 'bout to say…" He chuckled. "..if that's in there, then I'ma start callin' myself religious because I say it all the time."

January inwardly groaned. This was all her fault for thinking that it would be a good idea to take Legend anywhere in public. Especially to a place where he was expected to be quiet and courteous—two things that were apparently impossible for him to do.

"Say it," he said again, jabbing her in the side with his finger.

"Class is about to start, *Legend,* so you need to hush!"

"Well then, say it, *January,* and I'll hush."

"No!"

Another poke in the ribs.

"Princess, say—"

"I said *no!*"

Another jab.

"Legend, if you don't shut *the fuck* up!"

Nearly every person in the room turned around, focusing all of their attention on her, the instructor included. January's jaw dropped fully open, as wide as it possibly could, once she'd realized what she had done. The room went totally and completely silent. There wasn't a single noise to be heard in the room… except for the sound of Legend, sitting beside her laughing hard as hell into his hand.

"I'm so sorry, I—" she began to apologize before she realized it was no use and clamped her mouth shut. The damage was already done. This was some premium, grade A bullshit.

"Well, nama-*fucking*-ste," Legend joked from her side, smiling brightly.

Even though she was so annoyed and embarrassed that she wanted to run from the room, January couldn't help but notice how cute he looked when he said it. It was boyish in a way, no surprise being that he was currently acting so much like a child. His smile was so wide and genuine that she could see the dimples in his cheeks, something that was happening more and more while he was around her.

A few of the ladies in the room giggled at his off-color humor, and she glanced in their direction, seeing the stars in their eyes as they looked at him. Obviously, she wasn't the only one who thought he was cute.

"How funny!" the instructor said, looking at Legend. "You know, it's good to be spiritual beings, but no one said that means we have to be so uptight."

Her eyes darted towards January as she said the last comment, and January couldn't help but sulk at being called out.

"It's okay to let loose sometimes. And, by the way, you have an adorable smile," she said to Legend, who only beamed even harder at the compliment. "My name is Beta, by the way."

"Why, thank you, Beta," Legend replied, ducking his head a little as he sat cross-legged.

"You *really* do," a white girl with long blond hair, sitting right in front of him, said. She appeared to be around their age. January was not humored at all.

Blondie, I know you didn't.

"Thank y—" Legend was about to say before January leaned in to interrupt him.

"Um… class is *that* way," she informed the blond, pointing ahead.

In response, *Blondie* gave her a wide-eyed look, as if she didn't mean any disrespect, but January didn't find her innocent in the least. Legend wasn't her man, but *Blondie* didn't know that. In other words, *Blondie* considered January a total non-factor in her decision to flirtatiously grin and giggle in Legend's face, offering up the goods to him through mental telepathy. It wasn't even about being jealous—it was a clear show of disrespect, and January wasn't having it.

Out of the corner of her eye, she could see Legend staring at her and she was more than sure that he had his customary smug look on his face, completely tickled by the way she was acting. January wanted to ignore him, but he refused to look away. Even after Beta started with the first pose. After trying and failing to pretend he wasn't there, she just decided to give up the charade.

"You don't get credit just for being here. You have to actually partici—"

"Uh uh, Princess," Legend said as if chastising her, holding up his hand. Then he pointed one finger up ahead. "Don't worry about what I'm doing. Class is *that* way."

"I *hate* you," she whispered, sticking out her tongue.

And, by the end of class, January really, really, *truly* couldn't stand him.

Once again, he had managed to get one up on her, tricking her completely. He'd put up so much of a fuss about going to yoga class with her that she'd thought he'd never practiced before. Turned out, she was wrong to have made that assumption. He was nearly a yoga expert, which became evident when he did a perfect chin-stand at the end of class. Beta asked everyone to do their favorite pose and, of course, Legend had to do the absolute most. In turn, he easily nabbed the attention and curiosity of, not only Blondie, but every other woman in the room.

"How long have you been practicing yoga? You are *so* good! You could teach a class."

Shrugging as if it were nothing, he smiled before answering Beta's question.

"Thank you, Beta. I've been doing it for a while now—not in any class though, just on my own time. I do martial arts so—"

"Really?" she mused, oozing her sexual attraction out of her pores. "What kind?"

"All. I don't like to limit myself in any way so I'm always trying new things."

"That is so—"

"Sorry to break this up but we have another class to go to," January said, walking to his side. Grabbing onto his arm, she tugged him into her direction. Laughing, he gave the women surrounding him a quick salute before taking off.

"If I ain't know better, I'd think you was tryin' to cuff a nigga," he said, still holding onto his teasing smile once they were outside.

Scoffing hard, she rolled her eyes. "It's not even about you. I was just ready to go. Plus, it was disrespectful being that they couldn't be sure that we weren't a couple. I could see if I was nowhere near you, but it was obvious that we were there together."

"Nobody wants my ole and washed up ass. They just liked the chin-stand," he offered as if it were nothing.

"Right." January huffed. "I forgot all about the chin-stand. Everyone else chooses something regular for their favorite position and here you go being extra."

"I told you I'm not a regular nigga. I don't do regular shit." After a brief moment, he then added, "And why did you pick that easy ass warrior pose? You're a dancer. You've had years of practicing this shit. What was that about?"

He was right. If she'd really wanted to, she could have done a chin-stand too and she would've *killed* it.

"I don't know," she replied with a shrug. "I wasn't in there to stand out. I just like practicing with a group, I'm not trying to show off."

Stopping mid-step, he turned to her and placed his hands on her shoulders to stop her. One tug was all it took for her to turn fully around, facing in his direction. He bent his head to look her directly in her eyes.

"Legend, we had people walking behind us!" she told him, noticing the angry stares from the people who had nearly collided with them. They were taking up the entire middle of a fairly busy sidewalk, but he clearly didn't give a damn.

"January, what I told you about that shit? What have I told you about dumbing yourself down to fit in with people who don't matter?"

He waited for a response, widening his eyes to make it clear that he wasn't going to let her go unless she answered.

"You told me not to do it," she muttered, teetering back and forth on her feet. Here he was, preaching again. Making her feel like a kid.

"I'm not tryin' to treat you like a child," he said, as if reading her thoughts. "I just don't like that shit because I *see* you. You're not regular. You're not normal. Don't let anyone make you feel like you are less than you are. Not even me," he added, dropping his eyes as if something else had come to his mind. "I'm serious... Even when it comes to me. Don't let anyone make you question yourself, your worth or downplay your abilities. I know I call you a princess, but you're really a queen. You don't bow down or bow out for none of these motherfuckas. Especially them in there" He pointed back at the building they'd just walked out of. "Fuck *all* them people. Don't make me tell you this shit anymore. Dead all that 'regular' shit."

Feeling cared for in a way that she couldn't explain, January stood there completely speechless. She truly didn't know what to say. Mainly because she knew that he was speaking from his heart, telling her something that she knew he wouldn't waste time saying to anyone he didn't feel strongly about. She wasn't sure how he felt about her—whether he liked her or if it was love—but she did know that she'd never felt this cared for by any man ever before.

They stared into each other's eyes for a while, so deeply that it felt like they were looking into each other's souls. Her entire body went warm and the only other sensation she felt was tingling all over. She didn't realize that they were moving towards each other until their foreheads connected. Her lips were centimeters away from his—if that. A simple pucker or subtle lean forward and they would be sharing their first kiss. His hands dropped from her shoulders and slid down her arms until he was holding her hands. The jitters in her stomach intensified and she closed her eyes, feeling like this was the moment when it would happen.

Legend was about to kiss her.

He must've opened his mouth because she could feel his cool breath against her lips. She shuddered a little, bracing herself. She'd never been tongue-kissed before.

"Aye… Let's go get ice cream."

What?

Her eyes fluttered open as she felt him pull away. A slight frown bent her brows. That was *definitely* not what she'd been expecting.

"Ice cream?" January asked, looking at him pointedly. If he'd noticed her slight attitude, he ignored it.

"Yeah, I saw one across the street. Let's go."

With that, he took off across the street, jay-walking and dodging traffic while dragging her behind him.

"This is illegal, Legend! We're supposed to cross at the light!" she shouted, feeling her anxiety grappling at her nerves as they danced through traffic. Once they got to the other side, he let go of her hand and started to laugh.

"Yo, you looked like you were about to pee on yourself. It was just a little traffic… Why the hell were you so scared?"

She wasted no time curling it up into a fist, jabbing it right in his side.

"Don't do that again! We could've gotten hit. I could've died."

"Nah," he told her, shaking his head. "You're always safe when you're with me. In the back of your mind, that's something you already know, so trust it."

She didn't respond to that. He was right, but she was still mad.

He led her over to a small food truck that served homemade ice cream. From where it was stationed, it was crazy that he'd even seen it. Then again, it wasn't really. January was beginning to realize that Legend noticed any and everything around wherever he was. Not much escaped him. It wasn't something that he made obvious; in fact, she rarely saw his eyes focused on anything but her. Still, in some miraculous way, he picked up on all the other activity around him.

He placed their orders and, just as she'd expected, it didn't take long for her to make a mess. She was clumsy to a fault and she'd always been that way. Being that she was a dancer in her past life, she was graceful when it came to her feet, but her hands were another thing. She was liable to fumble any and everything. No lie, she couldn't help it. Especially, when it came to food. Whether it was casual dining or at an exclusive event with $500 plates, she wasted something on herself every time.

"I think you got a hole in your bottom lip."

She shot him a look to which he smiled. Legend seemed to enjoy picking on her more than anything. It brought him complete and utter joy to witness her discomfort or humiliation.

Stepping away while rubbing furiously at the huge spot of chocolate ice cream on her t-shirt, January left him sitting at a bench near the kiosk so that she could clean herself up and toss the napkin away. Once she had blotted out as much of the stain as she possibly could, she turned back around only to discover that Legend, once again, had managed to attract a group of adoring fans. This time they appeared to be teenagers, or that was her initial guess by looking at them.

"We were talking about your neck tattoo," one of them, standing closest to Legend, was saying. "Did it hurt?"

Barely looking in her direction, he shook his head slightly and let out a dry, "Nah."

The girl seemed slightly put off by his flat tone and indifferent attitude but after taking a glance behind her at her friends, who eagerly motioned with their hands for her to continue, she continued speaking again. They were all so focused on Legend, they didn't even notice January standing nearby listening.

"I—I want to get a tattoo sometime soon too," she began once she'd gathered the nerve. "But it would be good if someone experienced went with me." She let that hang in the air like bait sitting on a hook at the end of a fishing pole. When Legend didn't bite, she continued, "And can you tell me wh-what place you went to?"

"Get the fuck away from me," he replied back without looking at her, changing his nonchalant tone in any way or even lifting his head. If January hadn't heard his words so clearly for herself, she'd have thought her ears were fooling her.

Lips parted in shock, she glanced from Legend up to the girl's face and immediately felt every bit of embarrassment that she knew the girl did. Her shoulders tensed and her cheeks went from olive to ruby red.

"*Excuse* me?" the young girl snapped, forcing extra aggression. January could tell that she was putting on for her friends. Her body language said that what she really wanted to do in that moment was to turn on her heels and run away crying in the other direction.

"I said, get the fuck away from me," Legend repeated. "You and your friends. Your parents never taught you to stay out of a grown man's fuckin' face?"

January didn't think it was possible for it to happen, but the girl's face turned an even deeper red. Behind her, one of her 'friends' was stifling giggles behind her back. She had to hear it; there was no way that she didn't, and January knew it only made her humiliation that much worse. Her bottom lip was trembling and there were tears in her eyes. January knew she wanted to move but her sheer embarrassment had her muscles frozen in place. She had to intervene.

"Legend, you can at least tell her where you got yours done," she said, walking up. Sitting across from him, she looked apologetically at the girl and then leaned over to him to add, "At *least* you can do that."

Stuffing another spoonful of ice cream into his mouth, he stared up at her and shook his head indignantly.

"Legend!" January whispered, feeling sorry for the girl. "She needs to save face."

His expression turned from bored to thunderous. She watched it transform, his square jaw tightening and his brown eyes darkening until they were nearly black.

"Does it look like I give a fuck? It's not my purpose in life to be some good girl's rebellious phase."

Something about the way he said that made January wonder if he was talking about the girl behind him or about her. Since the girl was still standing there, for whatever Earthly reason that was, January decided to keep it about her.

"Imagine how she feels, Legend."

He scrunched his nose in confusion. "Why would I want to do that?"

"Because empathy is everything," she replied, not even really talking about the girls anymore. In this moment, she felt like she was speaking in defense of herself. "If you can imagine why someone does the things they do, you'll see that they aren't all that different from you. You just learned different lessons before they got the chance. You do it for Glenda. Why can't you do it for them? She only asked for the name of the shop you went to."

"January, I'm a grown ass man," he said, using her legal name for all seriousness. "Them lil' hoes need to get the fuck away."

At that point, it had become perfectly clear that there was nothing else she could do. With her head hanging down, looking like a sad puppy with its tail dragging between its legs, the girl walked away with her friends chattering away behind her.

"I *told* you he would know that you were only a teenager," the one who had been laughing said.

"Was that really necessary?" January asked him, rolling her eyes. "You just sat there and answered all of those ridiculous questions from the women in the yoga class, openly flirting as they eyed you up and down, all the while wishing you were their personal sex slave, but you couldn't tell a *teenager* where you got your tattoos?"

Shoving his empty cup of ice cream to the side, Legend squared his gaze at her and narrowed his eyes.

"That shit I did in there was to fuck with you. Normally, I would've cussed their asses out, too. I hate when women come at me with that shit."

She gave him a sideways look; pure skepticism was shooting from her eyes as she pushed her lips to the side of her face. He seemed bothered that women would be attracted to him in a sexual way. What man on Earth has *ever* been angry about that?

"You mean to tell me that women coming onto you for sex pisses you off?" she tossed him a teasing smile as she called his bluff.

Knowing that she was about to catch him up, she ran her tongue over the outside of her teeth, giving him her sexiest look for extra effort and maximum appeal. His eyes never left hers, but January saw a twinkle pass through them. It was the same twinkle that appeared right before the moments when it became painfully clear that she'd met her match. Somehow, in some way, she knew right then that Legend was about to hit her upside the head with something she wasn't prepared for.

"So, I guess you wouldn't have a problem if the only thing I wanted you for was a quick fuck?" he asked with a slight tilt of his head, licking his lips as he looked her over. "If all I wanted to do was stick my fingers deep into your pussy, get a quick taste of your sweetness, have my way with you and then leave?"

Sitting back a little, Legend fell totally into character. Letting his thighs fall open, he put his hands in between and gave his dick a hard squeeze, all the while staring at her like she was a piece of meat. She felt the blood drain from her face, leaving her feeling like she was nothing more than skin and dry bones. Everything and everyone around them faded away, becoming non-existent. In that moment, she had tunnel-vision. It was just her and him.

And she was on *fire*.

"You mean you wouldn't have a problem if all I wanted was to bite on your nipples until they turned red or suck on your clit until you screamed? And at the moment when you were certain you couldn't take any more…once I'd sucked so hard and long that your pearl felt swollen beyond repair, you would cry out for me to stop, writhing and twisting your body to get away, while unknowingly only pressing my face into you further and further, you'd be forcing me to suck harder and harder. But I wouldn't stop, even as you begged and pleaded, fighting against the leather straps on your ankles and wrists that were stopping you from getting away."

Damn.

Damn.

Damn.

January didn't think she'd ever been that hot in her life. Never had she been so ready to toss away the v-card and hand over her virginity than she was in that moment.

Shaking his head, Legend dipped his index finger into the cup of ice cream he'd been eating from and ran it around the rim, suggestively scraping up a little vanilla still left inside. While watching January-with devilish intensity, he brought the same finger to his lips and dipped it into his mouth, sucking it clean.

She was about to lose her entire mind. January had an entire ocean gushing between her thighs. Never in life had she wanted anything as badly as she wanted this man.

"Wrong place, wrong time, wrong motherfuckin' man. I'm not in that phase anymore, Princess," he said, summing up the point she'd forgotten he was making. "I'm not in the mood to be fuckin' chicks for shits and giggles. I've gotten more than enough notches on my belt. There's more shit on my mind than being some random chick's plaything. It doesn't excite me anymore."

Beyond her need of him, somehow, January was able to see his point. Like her, he didn't want to be objectified. If he did, he wouldn't mind the attention, but he wasn't putting himself out there in that way, showing that he was open to it, for a reason.

She thought back, remembering how she'd felt that day in class when he looked her over, wondering if they'd had sex before or if they could again. She'd been attracted to him but being wanted only for sex wasn't what she'd wanted to come out of it. He'd gone through his 'plaything' phase and that was over. If he cared to bring anyone into his life that way again, it would have to be more than just a sexual connection.

"Imagine that. Legend having standards when it came to his body," she teased, breaking the tension with a joking smile.

"Fuckin' right," he replied. "I *know* my worth. Can't be giving away my body for free. You can't get *all this* without paying the right price."

Letting her head fall backwards, January opened her mouth and laughed harder and louder at that than she'd laughed at anything in a very, *very* long time.

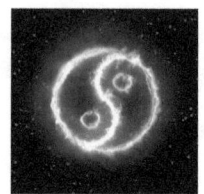

THUG MATRIMONY.

"AS LONG AS YOU SAY A PRAYER EVERY NOW AND THEN FOR ME, I'LL be safe too."

"Legend, you know I always pray for you. Stay safe and I hope to see you some time soon. Preferably in the *near* future."

Something about the way she said it made Legend feel like shit. It had been a little while since he'd been in Miami. After he stopped working with Outlaw in New York, he'd stayed home for a while and she had gotten used to him being there. His time in Cali was the longest he'd been away in a while.

"I'll be out there as soon as I can get away," Legend replied with honesty. The problem was, he had no idea when that would be.

"I can't wait until you do," she said before adding, "By the way, Nico told me that you'd picked up a new hobby. Yoga, is what he said. I called him when I couldn't get you yesterday."

"Oh, Nico told you that I was takin' yoga, huh?" he cutting his eyes to his cousin, who was sitting at his side. "What else he tell you?"

Smiling, Nico shrugged, lifting his hands and Legend responded by punching him in the shoulder.

"Well, he *did* mention that you were with a girl."

"She's just a girl from one of my classes."

"Welllll… she must be someone special for you to be with her on your birthday. We both know you don't do birthdays. Or anything else for that matter."

"Is that your roundabout way of tryin' to wish me 'happy birthday' even though you know I hate it?"

"Of course not! I know your rules, Legend. Never mention your birthday. Even though it's one of the most important days of my life. And, of course, yours, too. The day I brought you into this world… Twenty-three years ago. What a *glorious* day that was."

Legend chuckled at her wit. "Nice try, mom. But that's enough."

"I'm done talking about you, anyways. I really just want to know about this girl you were with."

"She's nothing. I was bored."

Looking up across from where he was sitting, Legend felt another stirring of some other emotion in his chest when he saw January. Her head was up as she walked gracefully with earbuds in her ears, seeming as if she was caught up in her own world. His focus zeroed in on her as he tried to understand the effect that she had on him. Honestly speaking, it was weird as hell and he couldn't understand it.

"Ma, I gotta go deal with something but I'll hit you back soon. Love you," he said before they ended the call.

"You good?" Nico asked once he saw Legend placing the phone in his pocket. He glanced in Nico's direction and nodded his head.

"Yeah, you know how it is. Moms still trying to convince me to do some shit she already knows is not in the cards for me."

His mother wanted him to become someone else's problem. She was eager for him to meet someone to relieve her of the burden of worrying about him day and night, praying that he stayed out of trouble.

Nico laughed at that. "You're a year older and another year wiser. You sure that's not in the cards for you?" he asked, confusing the hell outta Legend. Of all people, Nico knew exactly what he meant.

"What you askin' me that shit for? You already know what it is."

Reaching down, Legend grabbed his backpack, preparing to leave when he saw January walk into the building for her next class. It was some intro dance class. One of the only ones that they didn't have together.

"I know what it is, but I also got eyes and I been peepin' shit."

Legend squinted hard, narrowing his eyes at him. "What the hell that supposed to mean?"

With a loaded look on his face, Nico cut his eyes in the direction January had walked in before giving him a gloating grin.

"You feelin' shorty. I can tell."

Shrugging his shoulders, Legend shook his head. "She's not my type."

"No one is. You hate everyone."

Snorting at that, he pulled the straps of his backpack over his shoulders, thinking on what Nico said about him feeling January. Yeah, he felt something for her, but not what Nico was alluding to and not what his mother was praying for. He couldn't really explain what it was or put a label to it, but he knew what it wasn't. There were only a few emotions Legend was capable of and love wasn't one he cared to claim.

"Gone on and get yo' girl," Nico said, laughing. He already knew that his cousin was about to leave and he knew the exact reason why.

"Man, you buggin'," Legend scoffed with a frown. "You know what it is, so I ain't got to tell you. I'm married to the streets and I'm a one-woman man. Ain't no room for anything else 'cause wifey plays for keeps."

"Mmhm. That's what your mouth been sayin' nigga. But dig this rhyme: my ears ain't hearin' it 'cause my eyes ain't seein' it."

Nico shook his head before pulling a blunt out of his pocket, lighting up like they weren't sitting right in the middle of campus.

"You gon' chief that stanky ass shit right here?"

Nico shrugged. "Why not? Ain't nobody gon' fuck with me."

He was right, so Legend didn't say another word about it.

"You want to hit it right quick?"

Legend shook his head. The last time he did, the weed had him buggin'. It was the night he almost aired the whole club out over the same woman he swore he didn't give a damn about.

"Nah, last time I almost ended up doing some reckless shit."

Laughing so hard that he started choking on the smoke, Nico sputtered a few times, coughing hard before finally getting himself together.

"Yeah, you mean when you almost shot up the club behind some goofy nigga fuckin' with shorty who you really feelin' but playin' pretend with."

Legend's lips bent into a frown. He forgot he had told him about what happened that night. At the time, he didn't think Nico would read too much into it, but now he saw him putting two and two together and coming up with a load of shit.

"Don't be lookin' like that. Ain't nothing wrong with staking claim."

"It ain't like that."

"I ain't judging." Nico shrugged. "But can you ask her to put in a good word for me with her roommate? I ain't tryin' to cuff or nothin', but shorty seem cool as hell and I dig the vibe. Just wanna chill with her some time."

Hearing that made a brow raise on Legend's forehead. He stopped for a minute and took a good look at his cousin who was also his best-friend, a man he knew better than himself. The fact that Nico wasn't smiling and appeared totally serious for a change was appalling in itself. Something was up ... Never in life had he known Nico to want to 'just chill' with any chick.

"The hell you up to? Since when have you ever wanting to just vibe with a chick? And to be real, she don't even seem like your type," Legend said honestly.

No slight against him, but the girls Nico usually fucked with were surface as hell. He preferred the types who had no depth of personality at all and couldn't carry a conversation if it didn't have anything to do with celebrity gossip, weave, or which angle made their ass look good enough for the perfect thirst trap pic. It was intentional; Nico wasn't trying to get to know any of them below the surface, so he didn't care that once you pulled their wig back to see what they had up under it, you'd find there wasn't shit there.

"Yeah," Nico said with a goofy, distant look in his eyes. "Shorty look like she just need somebody in her life to show her a good time. She lettin' life pass her by."

Legend chuckled before standing up to leave. "Out of the two of us, it seems like you the one trying to make life changes."

"Nah," he replied with a smile that said he was thinking otherwise. "She just different."

Legend didn't say a word because he already knew what that meant. Whether Nico wanted to admit it or not, it looked like he was falling in love. It sounded crazy even thinking something like that when it came to him, but maybe it was true what Legend's mother said. At some point, even a street nigga had to grow up. Legend was dead-set on believing that his time for all that hadn't arrived, and he doubted it ever would.

Glancing at his watch, he saw it was time for the next set of classes to begin, so he started walking briskly towards the same building January had disappeared into. His next class was in the same building right across from hers, but he had no intention of attending it.

Circling around the corner, he slid through the open door and took a seat at the back of her class. Legend stood out like a sore thumb, looking out of place as hell—being that he was the only hood nigga present in a class full of chicks and a few dudes who looked like they were fully in touch with their feminine sides, frankly speaking. He sank low into his chair, halfway wondering what the hell he was doing in there. The professor of the class was speaking, talking passionately about dance theory—some shit that Legend didn't give a damn about, but when he looked at January, the expression on her face was the exact opposite of his.

"Nerd as hell..." He whispered with a slight grin, watching her reaction to every word that came out of the teacher's mouth.

She was on the edge of her seat, breathing slowly as if she was living life in this moment based on every word she heard. Legend sat there, staring at her for however long, not even realizing that the professor had stopped talking until the lights dimmed and a video began to play on a screen at the front of the room.

Pausing from staring at her, he took a moment to focus on the video that was playing. A skinny white woman was walking to a dance studio while the voiceover played of her speaking about her love for dance. When she arrived in the studio, it showed her no longer wearing sweats but in tights, a loose-fitting shirt and ballet shoes. His gut twisted with guilt and he found himself looking at January once again.

Through the dim glow in the room, Legend could clearly make out the pain-stricken expression on her face. He could feel the shift in her energy from clear across the room. Stirring uneasily in his seat, he leaned forward, positioning his elbows on the desk in front of him and balancing his chin on top of his knuckles as he turned his attention back to the screen. The woman was dancing now, doing a number from *The Black Swan* according to the caption on the bottom of the screen. His chest tightened as a distant memory hit his mind.

"What's your favorite routine?"

In his mind's eye, he saw young January biting down thoughtfully on her bottom lip before answering. She already knew the answer, he could tell. Her contemplation was only about whether she wanted to tell him.

"It's a routine from The Black Swan.*"*

"Which one?"

She shrugged, giving him a smile that had the same wattage of about a billion Christmas trees.

"Any of them really. It's my favorite. My dream is to dance the lead one day." She paused, squinting her eyes into a hard frown. "I've never told anyone that."

"Why not?" Legend asked, really just wanting to hear her say more. She was opening up to him—something he got the feeling she didn't do with people all that often. Somehow, he felt privileged that she was choosing to do it with him.

"I don't share my dreams much. My dad says that things special to you should be kept close to your heart. That way, you don't have to worry about people praying against them."

Legend understood that, but still, he shook his head.

"Nah, princess. You just make sure when you share them, it's with someone who cares enough to make sure that shit you dreamin' about comes true for you."

Opening his eyes, he tried to force away the image of the joy in her face when she heard him say that. In the moment, he didn't know she was actually sharing her dream with the same man who would be responsible for the same dream being taken away. It didn't matter that he wasn't the one to send off the shot that forever altered her course in life. He hadn't been able to stop it when he should have. To him, that was just as bad.

The dancer on the screen continued through the routine perfectly, putting her heart into each move she made. It was captivating to watch, even for him, someone who didn't give a damn about ballet. Because of that, he knew it was even more intense for January. He looked in her direction and his blood seemed to curdle in his body when he saw her wipe a tear from her cheek. The movement was so subtle, if you weren't paying attention, you wouldn't even know she was crying.

"Nah, shorty, don't do that..."

Legend's words were barely above a whisper. Definitely not audible all the way where she sat. Still, as if she'd heard him, January's head swiveled around, and her eyes connected directly with hers. Feeling awkward as ever that he'd been caught sitting in a class that for damn sure *wasn't* his, he shot her a slight nod, somewhat dipping his head in an even more awkward greeting. He didn't know what response he expected from her, but it definitely wasn't what he got. Her eyes tightened, narrowing into malicious slits that clearly said she had every desire to kill him if she could. Never in life had he ever been scared of a woman, not to the point that he wanted to hide. Even thinking of something like that would have felt foreign. But in that moment, January had him feeling some foreign shit.

Then, as suddenly as her anger had appeared, it disappeared, giving way to a sulking sadness that gripped his chest, forming a boulder in the space where his heart should've been—would've been, if he had one. January's eyes went glassy, wet from the formation of fresh tears that she was fighting away. Legend tried to suck in a burst of air, which sent a sharp, searing pain through his chest when he realized that he couldn't because he'd already been holding his breath. His face twisted with discomfort, an expression that January read incorrectly judging by the flash of shame and sheer terror he saw pass over her face right before she jumped up, grabbed her things and ran out of the room.

The doors slammed closed behind her and Legend sat frozen in his chair for a few moments, battling his thoughts as to what the hell he was supposed to do next. After a few seconds of fighting against the urge, he dragged his ass out of the chair and followed behind her. She hadn't gone far, had just barely left the building and was sitting on a small bench outside.

Grinding his teeth in frustration, he pushed through the double doors and then shoved his hands in the pockets of his jeans, approaching her slowly, feeling off-kilter the entire time and walking carefully as if he was dodging landmines.

What the fuck am I supposed to do with this? He thought, looking at January. She was sitting with her legs pulled up and her head down on top of them, quietly crying into her knees.

Running one hand over the top of his head with the other still stuck in his pocket, Legend let out a deep breath, feeling utterly exasperated.

He hadn't the slightest clue about what to do with the creature she'd currently become in this moment. He didn't *do* unhappy females. She was a Martian as far as he was concerned. Legend didn't do emotions and he didn't give a shit about making a chick feel better while in the middle of having a toddler fit. He wasn't used to a woman putting him in this type of predicament. Usually, any woman he dealt with was happy and more than eager to do any and everything to please him. Her current state of melancholy threw him for a fuckin' loop.

"The fuck wrong with you?" he asked, hoping somehow that it was the right thing to say.

It obviously wasn't—something he learned the second January lifted her head and pierced right into him with her red and swollen eyes.

"What *the fuck* is wrong with me? *That's* how you talk to people? Are you really that incapable of feeling empathy for someone else?"

Running his hand over his face, he let out a sigh, not really knowing how to respond. He wasn't raised on love; he was raised to survive. Having empathy for others wasn't a survival trait. Empathizing with others is how you ended up getting got. In Legend's life there was no room for that. He cared about January, but it wasn't in him to constantly wonder about how the things he said and did may affect her emotions or fuck with her mind. He just *was.* All he really knew to do was exist and just be. His world moved fast. He didn't have time to waste constantly worrying about whether he was saying or doing the right thing. But his intentions were good. Didn't he get credit for that?

"Why are you here?" she snapped, speaking through her teeth. "Why are you always around? Why are you always messing with me? Why can't you just go away and leave me alone?"

You're not the only one wanting the answer to that question, shorty.

Legend wished like hell that he knew, but he really didn't. All this extra shit he was doing wasn't because of any project—he could say it was, but it really wasn't. It was far beyond that. He was here with January because he wanted to be. Somehow, Legend felt like he needed to be. Like he had fucked up before and now he had to get her life back on track. Like it was up to him to make sure that she was happy.

Every second around her changed him. Even if he weren't the prime enemy of the *BBM,* January would be off-limits. He was no good for her because being around her brought out the good in him. In order to be an expert killer, there were certain things that had to be repressed. Everything that made him a good man had to be tucked away underneath a callous and murderous exterior. But that exterior disappeared when she was near.

She was like poison to the type of person he had to be. He had to keep his distance.

"Don't get it twisted, princess. I'm not the same little boy who had time to play games with you, ask you questions about your life, shoot the shit and let you waste my time. Either talk, tell me what's wrong or keep the shit in your head. I'm not about to beg and plead with you to share what's on your mind. I'm not gettin' paid this time to be a rich girl's entertainment."

Screwing up her face, January turned to look up at him like he had lost his mind. *He* was the one wanting *her* to talk and confide in him about *her* business. And, somehow in some weird way, Legend had managed to make her reluctance to share seem like she was wronging him. He was taking his role as the 'arrogant asshole on campus' to an entirely new level.

"Fine. I'll just keep the shit in my head," she huffed, mocking him. "You aren't doing me *any* favors by staying."

Letting out another long, protracted breath, Legend decided to give in this time and wave the white flag. He, somewhat reluctantly, sat down next to her on the bench, hoping that she wouldn't get up and run away. She had a thing about making him chase her and in this moment, he was already doing some shit he'd never done before. Having to chase her ass down to do it was too much new shit for him in one day.

But one look at her told him that she wasn't going anywhere. She looked too tired to move. Like a supernova, releasing her anger in a rage of energetic waves, she'd exploded on him until she had nothing left. Now she was collapsing into the darkness that was left behind, crumbling into the black hole created by her pain.

"Here," he said, digging into his pocket. He pulled out a small bag of M&Ms and tossed them at her. "That's all I got on me, but I can grab some more stuff from the vending machine in that building over there." He nudged his head ahead of where they sat.

Wrinkling her nose, she wiped a tear from her cheeks and held up the M&Ms to her eyes. "What are you giving me candy for?"

"For the pity party you're intent on throwing for yourself," he answered, trying to hide the fact that her emotions were pissing off. He shouldn't have been because he understood why she was upset. Anybody who had their dream taken away in such a sudden and violent way would be reacting as she did.

Well, any *normal* person.

He'd had his dreams stolen that day as well, but he'd covered his sadness and guilt with layers upon layers of anger and aggression. And he'd gotten very good at wearing his mask—so good, in fact, that these days he didn't even realize he had one on. His only real sentiment these days was that his mind was fucked up because so was he, and he forgot that he'd ever believed or been someone different. Legend was used to hiding what he felt and most comfortable not dealing with his emotions or anyone else's.

But like his reflection, January mirrored that extreme all the way in the opposite direction. She was nothing *but* emotion: raw, vulnerable, and erratic. She was a ticking time bomb, fluctuating from one extreme right to another, running easily from hot to cold depending on what button Legend pushed on her during the day. It was intriguing to see that someone so disciplined and controlled could lack so much self-control in that one way. In some twisted way, he loved seeing her reaction to each button he pushed—each trigger he ticked. For someone he elevated nearly to angelic status in his mind, it was less intimidating to know that she had at least one major flaw.

Rather than fighting Legend over calling her out on her shit, January simply decided to ignore his comment about her 'pity party' and ripped open the bag of M&Ms. She dumped the contents into her hand before pushing the empty bag back into his hands. Without even bothering to look his way or say a thing about how she'd just treated him like her personal trashcan, she popped a M&M in her mouth while staring off into the distance.

Legend couldn't help but smile and shake his head.

She's so cute… with her passive aggressive ass.

"That routine," he began, feeling the need to address the elephant in the room. "That was the same one you told me about way back, right?"

She paused for a moment, as if trying to decide whether to be vulnerable enough in that moment to admit something like that to him. Then, as if giving up the fight, she nodded slowly, the corners of her eyes dipping back into despair. Her emotions became so intense in that moment that she looked like she was folding under the pressure of them.

Legend couldn't feel emotions, but he could read energy in others very well. It was a survival tactic that kept him alive in the most dangerous of situations. In one look, he knew everything he needed to know about a person, just by paying attention. When it came to January, Legend could read her body language like it was written in the pages of a book. She was so open, especially when she was emotional. *Especially* in this moment.

Just that one question pushed her off kilter, as if he'd forced her to face a past that she was trying her hardest to repress. Her grief was palpable; an energy so thick that Legend could see it raging like waves around her. It was accompanied by its other companions: sorrow, anguish, and loneliness. He could tell that these emotions had been hidden inside of her for a long time. They'd taken up residence in her heart, leaving no room for anything else. That's why she didn't even know it, but she'd been operating like a zombie: not really living but just existing. Doing whatever she had to just to get by.

"I don't like to think of it," she admitted in a small voice as a tear slipped from her eye and fell down her cheek. She sniffed and wiped it away quickly, tilting her face slightly in Legend's direction, which allowed him to see more of her face. She looked tired. Completely exhausted.

He stirred, struggling to find his next words. This shit was much too intense.

"Why'd you stop dancing?"

"Because after what happened, I couldn't. The bullet nearly severed my femoral artery, the major artery in my leg. It was a miracle that I could even walk."

"Well, shit, shorty…" Legend started, shrugging a little. "If you were already performing miracles as it was, why stop there?"

Meeting his eyes for the first time since they started talking calmly, January frowned a little as she thought on that before shaking her head.

"I mean, I don't know… I guess I never thought about it like that. Once I was able to walk regularly, I felt like it was best not to push it further. That I should be grateful that I could even do that instead of trying to do more and then feeling like I failed if I couldn't."

Nodding his head, Legend felt like he finally understood what she was really saying behind what she had actually said.

"You decided to be happy that you'd been given the moon and forgot all about reaching for the stars.

She realized he was right. She lost something back then. She lost a bit of herself when she learned how to please others instead of herself. She was betraying herself to make others comfortable. Taming the wild side of her, holding it in when she really wanted to be free.

"I guess I never thought about it that way," January said, ducking her chin.

Reaching out, Legend pressed two fingers under her face to lift her head back up. He didn't want her looking or feeling down in his presence.

"You're too stuck in your emotions, princess. You're too connected to other motherfuckas out here. You feel too much. Trust me, it's not always a good thing."

"I trust you," she said, speaking honestly.

She trusted him because he was the first person in her life who was open enough to tell her the whole truth even if she didn't like it. Legend held nothing in; whatever he felt he said. If he thought it, she heard it. He was completely open with his feelings on every subject. It just so happened that he didn't feel as much as she did.

"And you should trust me, too," she began. "Feelings are for feeling, Legend. Emotions are supposed to be experienced, accepted and explored. That's why they call them *feelings*. It's what makes us human. You can't unfeel your way through life. You can't unfeel your way through pain. It's the pain that forces us to recognize our own strength and push to the next level of the best of what we can become. How we see the areas where we need to grow. You can't evolve into the best version of you if you're numb."

"Who says I'm numb?" Legend asked playfully. His lips spreading into a large smile. When she returned his smile with a chastising frown, he shrugged his shoulders.

"I'm just playin' with you. But I get it. Don't be numb. Feel the pain. Be soft as hell, like a nigga with a sensitive dick. Your advice has been noted."

January rolled her eyes, knowing that she couldn't expect anything more or less when it came to Legend.

"Why did you leave?" she asked before she knew it. "I remember the day at the park, when we met. You were there, working for my father, but then you never visited me in the hospital and I never saw you again. Why did you go?"

Legend frowned while listening to her question. He knew that Outlaw kept his family out of BBM business but for some reason he found it odd that January never heard any of the rumors that he was suspected of killing her.

"I was sent away. Outlaw dropped me from *BBM* that day," he said, deliberately telling her as little as possible. It pained him to do it.

Withholding the full story from her still felt like a lie even if it technically wasn't.

"Why?" January pressed, wanting to know more. "You didn't do anything wrong. You tried to protect me."

Legend's entire body steeled. "I tried but I failed. I *didn't* protect you. There are only two times in my life when I failed like that. Once with you and the other time was with Onyx. Each time, I made amends and set things straight as best as I could, but the damage had already done to the people I cared for."

Slipping into the quiet, January took a moment to think on what he was saying. She knew what he meant about making amends for Onyx. As she suspected, Legend was admitting that her ex was dead. But how did he make amends for her?

"The bodies they found... hanging from the streetlights," she started, watching his face carefully. "Everyone, including me, suspected my father had done that. Are you saying that was you?"

He didn't respond, didn't blink and didn't make any movement of any kind as he stared deeply into her eyes. No words left his lips to say yes or no but January didn't really need it. The more they sat with the question lingering in the air, the more it became clear. Outlaw would have done it, if he'd gotten the chance, there was no question about it. However, in this case, Legend beat him to it.

"I was supposed to leave New York the day you were shot. Outlaw dropped me from *BBM* and gave me 24 hours to leave the city. I'd never gone against an order that came from him before, but I couldn't leave until I knew you were safe."

Something about the way he said it, the roughness in his voice, the rawness of emotion she could feel in it, made her entire body come alive. Her heart thudded wildly in her chest, so rapidly that she partly wondered if the imprint of it showed through her shirt.

A cool breeze flowed through the small makeshift alleyway where they sat, sandwiched between two major lecture buildings. The scene around them was beautiful; the school had taken full advantage of the space to make a small garden of flowers, bird feeders and even a small pebble rock pond to give complete serenity to whoever had a moment to sit on the bench.

This wasn't January's first time visiting the spot. After discovering it during the first week of classes, it had become her favorite place and she visited it often. Not many students knew about it so it was a place she was guaranteed to have solitude and be alone with her thoughts. It was a place of peace. But Legend being there gave it a different vibe.

"I also couldn't leave until I let you know that you were safe." Legend blew out a hard, heavy

IT WAS the last time he'd seen January. The sight of her lying in a hospital bed broke the remaining fragments of his heart. She was so fragile. Asleep, but so disturbed. Clearly not a peaceful rest at all. He didn't want to see her like that, he utterly hated the sight. At the same time, it was hard for him to leave because he knew it would be the last time. He was risking a lot by even sneaking into her room as it was, and he still wondered how he'd been able to do it. The city's underground princess was lying in the hospital bed after being almost killed. The floor should have been swarming with security, but it was completely empty. It wasn't until a little later he found out why.

Leaning over January's body, Legend put his lips to her ear and delivered the message that he needed to believe she could hear.

"It's finished," he whispered. "You're safe."

Pulling away from her, he paused for a moment to look at her face. He wasn't sure if he'd imagined it or not, but somehow her expression seemed more relaxed. More at peace, as if she'd heard and understood his words. He allowed his lips to brush gently against her cheek, forcing himself not to plant a kiss. There was nothing more that he wanted in that moment than to place his lips on her skin, but this wasn't the way he wanted it.

"I knew you would come to say goodbye."

The voice coming from behind made his entire body freeze. Regaining his senses, he slowly stood up straight and then turned around, locking eyes with Outlaw.

"There's no security on her floor," Legend said, stating the obvious.

Eyes narrowed into slits, Outlaw clearly heard Legend's words but didn't respond. He no longer looked like a gangster but the gangsta in him could be felt. Outlaw was a very dangerous man, and it was clear to anyone blessed enough to spend time in his presence.

At the same time, he was a very smart man. A very discerning man. A man who knew and fully understood when he'd finally met his match. When he looked at Legend, he saw not only the man he was but the man he would come to be. When he looked at Legend, he saw a younger version of himself. But what he also saw was the love that Legend had for his daughter.

There was no question in Outlaw's mind when it came to Legend's innocence in the shooting that almost killed her. He had hand-selected him as one of his closest men because he knew that Legend's loyalty ran deep. But more than loyalty, he also knew that Legend had a good heart. He wanted to make a difference in the world in some way. He was a renegade, a revolutionary. If this had been the 60s, the Black Bag Mafia would have been The Black Panthers, Outlaw would've been Huey P. Newton and Legend would've been Fred Hampton. He fought against injustices in unspeakable and merciless ways. Many people wanted the guilty to pay for their sins but only a small few wanted to be the executioner. Legend was selfless enough to play that role for the BBM, without a care in the world as to the effect it would have on him.

Taking a life had dire consequences, even if it was a life that you were justified in taking. The more you watched the light leave from someone's eyes, the more you lost a little of your own light. Until, at some point, your eyes become as black as coal and your heart nothing but an empty shell.

It wasn't until Legend was sixteen that Outlaw realized the damage that had been done. It was irreparable; being a hitta was already embedded in Legend's DNA. It was all he knew how to do, and he would continue doing it whether he left BBM or stayed. For that reason, Outlaw decided it was best for Legend to remain under his wing where he could be watched and protected.

But now, Outlaw had to let Legend go in order to protect January. He'd seen the look in his eyes when she was shot. And the emotions in him when they spoke outside the hospital that night were easily felt. He knew Legend loved his daughter and he knew that January would return the same love to him. For better or for worse, women picked men who reminded them of their fathers. It wasn't just a saying; it was the truth. And Legend was a mini version of Outlaw in every way. A deadlier, more merciless, less forgiving version with a lot less regard for human life. A lot less capable of giving January the kind of love she deserved to be given and the life she deserved to live. He didn't want them together under any circumstances, so his hands were tied.

He had to force Legend away.

As the saying goes, 'we make plans and God laughs' because who would've thought that with all of Outlaw's intervening, fate would've still brought them together? Who would've thought that January would run into the one man her father didn't want her to have, inside of a campus bookstore?

"I came into your room. They had you in a medically induced coma. I told you that it was finished, and you were safe. And then I left." Legend looked up and they locked eyes. The moment was intense. January swallowed hard, trying to force calmness into her heart. The feeling was overwhelming to the point that she suddenly had the urge to increase distance between them.

"I—I guess I need to be going to my next class," she said, standing.

As she turned away, Legend reached out and grabbed her hand, tugging her body towards him. They were so close to each other that they bumped chests with each wild and violent breath. Dipping his head, he placed his forehead to hers in an embrace that was so tender and gentle for someone as normally aggressive as him. He closed his eyes and relaxed into her. The tips of their noses touched, and January felt a warm sensation fall over her. It gave way to a strange feeling, a tingling, like butterflies swarming all over her body. She knew in her heart she would replay this moment over and over again for many years to come. She doubted she would ever again feel a feeling like this.

"Can I kiss you?" He asked.

January's heart flip-flopped in her chest. The question was so peculiar to her ears, especially in the way he asked it; almost pleading,
begging her to say yes.

"You may."

Before she could fully close her eyes, Legend's lips lowered to hers
and set off explosions in her entire body. Every nerve ending inside
of her fired off an explosion of sensations like fireworks on the
Fourth of July. Or maybe a better comparison would be New Year's
Day, since it felt like they were at the start of something raw and
new. He deepened the kiss and she collapsed into him, arching her
back and opening her mouth to accept his tongue.

Legend took all the liberties she allowed him, exploring her from the
inside out. They would've stayed there forever in that moment, lips
locked, arms wrapped around each other's bodies, fingers kneading
each other's skin, doing everything they could to merge into one…
if only class hadn't ended. The sound of opening doors, rushed
steps and mindless chatter erupted around them as students exited
from class, heading to whatever was next. January began to pull
away from Legend, but he held her close, releasing her from his lips,
but holding her body firmly in place. She didn't resist him. Though
she wasn't a fan of PDA under normal circumstances, this was
different. Everything and everyone happening around them was like
something separate and outside of them. She didn't want to leave.

Unfortunately, the vibration of Legend's cellphone buzzing away in
his pocket brought an end to their bliss. He pulled away and their
trance was broken. Answering the call, Legend turned his back to
January and put a few paces of separation between them.

"What's good?"

"Not much," the voice said on the other line.

Once he recognized the caller, his bones turn to lead. His entire
body steeled, as if it went completely solid; so much so that it was

clearly visible to January who had been watching from behind. Sitting down, she busied herself by digging around in her bag for something to provide a distraction before finally settling on her cellphone.

Opening an app, she began to scroll through pictures, appearing interested when she wasn't paying any of them the least bit of attention. Her mind was on Legend and the few moments from before, when she was pressed against him, forehead to forehead, chest to chest. She'd felt his erection through his jeans, giving her a clear indication that he was both long and thick, an overwhelming discovery for a virgin.

Instantly, she began to doubt herself. She had zero experience when it came to sex, relationships and men. Hell, she'd barely even kissed a guy before. Thankfully, that was one thing she learned to do during her brief high school romance. But Legend wasn't a boy, and they weren't in high school. He'd been in between so many thighs, he couldn't even remember all the faces that went along with them. Here she was, still stuck on first base when he'd completed an infinite number of homeruns. So many that he, admittedly, wasn't all that interested in playing the game anymore. What could she possibly do to please him?

"I gotta meet up with Nico," Legend said, walking over to her once he had ended his call.

"But I thought that—"

We could spend some time together, was what she wanted to say. But the second she looked up and locked into his eyes, she knew that wasn't going to happen. The streets were calling and he'd taken the call. Everything in his life was ranked by priority and the streets would always remain #1. She'd seen it with her parents over and over again throughout her life until her father was able to get *BBM* to the point where he could afford to take a step back. It was the life of a street runner; when the streets called, you ran towards them. And it didn't matter who or what needed, wanted or demanded your time.

The streets owned you. Everything and everyone else came dead last.

"Is everything okay?" January asked, mainly for the sake of asking because nothing about Legend said he was the 'sharing' type. He said very little and kept a whole lot bottled in.

"It's all good," he replied, just as she knew he would. "I just gotta fly out for a bit. But I'll be back."

"Fly out?" she frowned. "But our project—we have a progress report on what we've been doing due at the end of this week."

Though his eyes were focused on some spot over her head, his mind was somewhere else. She could almost see the thoughts cycling through his mind. Finally, as if remembering that she was still standing in front of him, he dipped his head to stare into her. His gaze was stony, foreign and distant. Unfeeling. A total contrast from how he'd looked at her only a few moments earlier when she was wrapped in his arms. She bristled, shuddering away from him, although it wasn't cold.

"If you haven't realized it yet, when it comes to real life, all that school shit is of very little importance to me. Time for you to grow up, January. Figure it out."

Before she could respond back, or even see through the harshness of his tone to fully process the words that he'd said, he turned his back to her and jogged away.

IF IT AIN'T LOVE.

**Not all storms come to disrupt your life.
Some come to clear your path.**

A FULL WEEK HAD PASSED BY SINCE THE LAST TIME JANUARY HAD LAID eyes on Legend and she didn't know what to think. Deep down, she felt like in some way she should have been preparing herself to never see him again. With every day that passed, the memory of him running away from her, his thoughts clouded by some new distraction and his eyes bottling an unreadable emotion, cycled repeatedly through her mind. But parallel to that memory, almost as if it were supposed to be a caption for that moment, the words that she'd read on the day she arrived on campus also ran continuously through her head. She didn't know how or why but, for some odd reason, she got the feeling that Legend was the common factor in all of the quotes she'd read that day. He'd entered into her life right before one of the most tumultuous storms she'd ever had to fight through. And with his most recent exit, he'd left a storm of conflicting emotions in her heart in his wake.

Sighing, January flipped through her photos until she got to the screenshot she'd taken of the other message.

Your heart must break before it opens: It's the heartbreak that teaches you how to love.

The first time she'd read these words on her screen, her knee-jerk reaction was to reject it. But so many things had transpired in her life since then. The main thing being the resurfacing of the love she had for Legend. Love that had sprouted from the ground the instant they'd met and, over their short interactions so far, had grown into the most beautiful flower. He'd made his way into her heart so fast even though she'd been so unwilling to let him in. Things like that didn't happen by accident. It had to be destiny or fate. She was unable to fight it. After all, what chance did she stand against kismet?

Still, January couldn't shake the constant nagging inside that said she had fallen for a man who couldn't possibly be right for her. All the signs that he wasn't the Prince Charming she'd been looking for were staring her right in the face. Was it her intuition or was it her ego warning her that being with Legend was wrong? Was she listening to her higher self or the side of herself that was afraid to risk giving her heart to someone who didn't seem as if he had one to give back? What if she let go and gave herself permission to feel everything and just let her emotions for him flow as naturally as a leaf floating downstream? If she gave herself permission to fall freely in love, would he break her heart?

January's lips pinched into a thin line as she thought about that.

It definitely *seemed* possible.

When it came to someone like him, it seemed like the only thing that was promised *was* heartbreak. With his lifestyle, he couldn't give January anything else: commitment, true love, a real romance… all of that was out of the question. If she gave into her feelings and allowed herself to love him, a broken heart was all that would come of it. He would never be able to return love to her in the way that she wanted it. And definitely not in the way that she deserved it.

The streets had a chokehold on all of his emotions and the only thing left behind was an empty void. He'd made sacred vows to the streets, committing himself to thug matrimony and January could only be his mistress. He would abandon her any time the real love of his life desired his attention. That much he'd made perfectly clear. Thug matrimony left no room for real love because marrying the streets meant forsaking your heart. Real love required you to love with your heart and soul, but you couldn't give what you no longer had to give.

But the streets can't love you like I do.

Turning around in her seat, January glanced for what felt like the millionth time at the empty desk behind her. Legend's desk. For the fifth day in a row, he wasn't in class and she couldn't rid herself of the feeling that something was wrong. Sucking in a deep breath, January drummed her fingers along the wooden top of her desk, trying with immense effort to control her nerves. Grabbing her cell, she quickly unlocked it and scrolled over to the green icon, pressing it to peek at her messages once more, praying that something had changed in the few minutes since she'd checked them last.

Nothing had.

But she already knew that.

The first message she'd sent to him was two days after she last saw him. Two days instead of one because she'd spent the first 24 hours after arguing with herself on whether or not to send it.

Missed you in class. Everything okay?

After that message, she'd sent one for each of the days that followed. All of them were left unread and unanswered.

"I'm sure by this time you've gotten to know your partners rather well. At least more than you would anyone else in the class," Ms. Bee was saying. She'd been speaking for the past ten minutes since class started but January hadn't been paying much attention. Something about her tone in that moment made her lift her head.

"By now, you should have some kind of a picture about your partner's background, upbringing, hobbies, family life. Whether or not they have siblings and how many they have. Maybe not enough to pass through a CIA character profile examination but at least enough to get a general sense of who your person is."

Your person.

January's mind stalled on the phrase. Sucking in deep breaths, she let them out slowly to force herself into relaxation mode. It wasn't helping.

Legend was *her* person. In more ways than one.

Every morning, waking up for class, she couldn't ignore the light-hearted emotion in her chest as she got dressed, thinking on the moment when she'd walk into the lecture hall and be greeted with the sight of him, slumped over, lying on the top of his desk as if he hadn't a single care in the world. The very thing that had annoyed her to the max at first was now something that she was eagerly looking forward to. It was insane how the Universe could make you love the one thing you were set on hating. Life had a funny way of doing that in order to teach you some of the most important lessons about acceptance, forgiveness, understanding and unconditional love. January seemed to be learning them all.

"I look forward to reading the papers that you all turned in last night with updates on your class project for this semester. From the few that I've already started, I can see that you all are learning a lot about your fellow classmates and how differently people live their lives. It's easy to get stuck in your own bubble and assume that everyone around looks, thinks or lives the same way that you do. In order to live in a world or country as diverse as the one we are in and be accepting of others, we have to actively seek out opportunities to learn about other cultures. It's not enough to watch a TV program or the news and assume you know all there is to know."

Ms. Bee's eyes fell on January's face and she nodded, wanting to appear engaged although her thoughts were elsewhere. This was definitely her favorite class and normally she couldn't get enough of it and was literally hanging on every word that fell from Ms. Bee's lips. But this time, she couldn't force herself to pay attention. She was so worried about Legend to the point that she couldn't think.

January, just stop. He's not your man, he doesn't owe you a text back. And knowing Legend, when he finally pops up, you'll probably find out that he disappeared on some bullshit.

"Okay, class. I'm wishing everyone a great rest of the day and I'll see you tomorrow." Ms. Bee dismissed them with a wave, and January bent her head down, eagerly collecting her things so that she could leave. Deep down, she prayed that Legend had just come in from a late flight and would show up to their next class. Fat chance of that happening, being that he'd missed every single one of their classes for the last five days.

Before standing to gather her things, she grabbed her phone in her hand, her finger lingering over the green icon again before she finally gave in and pressed it. Clicking once again on Legend's name, she quickly typed in a text of only a few words and hit 'send'. She'd asked all the questions she could think to ask and waited for responses that never came. This time, she decided to release him from the burden of responding and release herself from the burden of waiting for one that would most likely never come.

Whatever you're doing, just be safe.

It was the last message she would send to him. A final, lasting demand.

Flame

KIDNAPPED.

Hushed voices speaking in strained tones invaded her consciousness, forcing January to retreat from the peaceful state of rest that she preferred. When she was asleep, she didn't have to face the music. She could pretend the moments she longed to forget had never happened. She could lie to herself about the truth until she figured out how to handle it.

"She'll never dance again... it's what they said..."

"If she can even walk normally, it'll be a blessing. But even then, lots of therapy is needed."

"So sad. She was such a talented dancer, too."

The voices seemed endless. January wanted nothing more than to sit straight up on the bed and scream at everyone to leave out of her room, carrying their pity and sympathy along with them. She didn't want it. But most of all, she didn't want to face whatever came next after they all discovered she was already awake, and she was forced to carry on with her life. So instead of shouting to the top of her lungs all of the many four-letter words she was dying to say, January continued to lie quietly, pretending to be asleep.

Once everyone left, the silence around swallowed her whole and the cup of emotions inside of her overflowed. Her rage boiled over and turned into tears too overwhelming to keep bottled up inside. The light slipping into the room through her open blinds faded away giving way to the luminous glow of the full moon but the somber, empty feeling inside her remained the same.

"I'm glad you finally let that shit out, baby girl."

January startled at the sound of her father's voice and her eyes snapped open wide. She'd had no idea that he was there with her or when he'd entered the room. But now that she saw him, it made perfect sense why, even in the midst of her mental breakdown, she'd still felt a small bit of comfort and love through her perceived solitude.

Sitting up in the bed, careful not to pull at the wires connected to various parts of her body, January stared into his eyes, feeling as though she could absorb the strength she saw within them. There was no doubt in her mind that he understood and felt her pain. Her father knew all about her love affair with the art of dance. He had always taught her about the importance of self-expression. And he'd constantly given his full permission for her to pursue it.

But in this moment, he was giving January what she needed most in her moment of weakness: unconditional love and his insurmountable strength.

"Daddy, they say I'll never dance again," January whimpered through her tears. "I heard them. They said it's a miracle if I can even walk. Or run."

Leaning forward in his chair, Outlaw placed his elbows on top of his thighs and peered evenly into her eyes.

"And since when have we ever taken the time to give a fuck about what they had to say?" he asked her.

As if by a miraculous happening, January found the will to smile and shook her head. "Never," she replied. "Law #7: We never give a fuck what a hater has to say."

"And why is that?" he pushed her to continue.

"Because they didn't give us our power and we'd be damned to let them take it away."

He sat back in his seat, relaxing with his arms providing the perfect pillow behind his head as he rested on the ledge of the windowsill behind him. Following his lead, January closed her eyes and decided to do the same. Exhaustion overwhelmed her. It wasn't physical, only mental. She was emotionally and mentally drained and she knew that she needed to build up her reservoir of emotional and mental strength in order to endure the days that were coming to greet her now that the secret was out, and he knew she was awake.

"January," her father called out to her a short while after she'd closed her eyes.

"Mmhmm," she moaned, still somewhere in between reality and her preferred dream-like state.

"I know you're tired, but I need you to wake up."

Pinching her eyes even tighter closed, she didn't reply. Though she sensed urgency in his calm tone, she wasn't prepared for whatever was coming next. She could feel that hard days were coming. It was much easier to sleep the pain away.

"January… get up!"

Much more aggression found its way into his voice this time. Still resistant, January stirred but kept her eyes closed. She never went against her father. Never disobeyed him in all of her life, but this time she was prepared to put up a fight.

"January. I said, get up…get up…"

"January! Get up…Get the *fuck* up. Now!"

January's eyes popped open and she sat straight up in the bed as she heard her name being called with the full awareness that it was a voice she recognized, but not her father's. A gasp escaped from her lips when she was able to make sense of the darkness and recognized the figure in the room standing over her bed.

It was Legend. But not only that—he had a gun, and his temperance was totally different from the person she'd gotten to know. He was brooding, serious, stealthy, skilled and the dangerous aura pooling around him was so palpable, that with every inhale, her throat felt thick. January swallowed hard and watched as he paced around the space at the foot of her bed, taking several glances out her window. He with meticulousness, extreme caution and skilled awareness. He moved like a hitta.

"Get dressed. *Now.*"

January felt her heart drop to the pit of her stomach.

"So my dad *did* send you," she said, making verbal the thought in her head.

He kept his lips pinched tightly shut. This time he didn't even try to deny it.

"Get dressed," he repeated with an icy look in his eyes. The coldness of it shot straight to the base of her spine causing instant discomfort.

January paused. "Why? What happened?"

His eyes continued to bore into her skull with unraveling intensity. "Don't make me ask again."

Without further question, she rushed to get dressed, picking up on the gravity of the situation. If she were right and her father asked Legend to watch her, especially after promising her that he wouldn't, then there had to be a really good reason for him to blow his cover. And most likely, it was a matter between life and death. *Her* life, to be precise.

Grabbing onto her arm, Legend half-dragged her through her dorm as she struggled to keep up with his quickened steps. He moved with stealth and silence; January couldn't help but once again notice his ability to make such hurried steps without making a sound.

Releasing his grip on her arm, he went over to the portrait of ballet shoes on the wall and arranged four circular metallic objects into a rectangular shape around the picture frame. January watched in awe as the metal objects glowed red right before a light illuminated the edges of what appeared to be a door embedded in what appeared to be a wall that the picture had been hanging on. The picture retracted, flattening into the fake wall before the door slid open, revealing the inside of an elevator.

What in the world?

Her thoughts merged with so many things she wanted to ask but she kept quiet and stepped inside. Before joining her, Legend removed the metal objects from outside the door and then stepped in behind her. He then placed the objects onto a spot on the inside elevator wall, once again in a rectangle and that area began to glow, revealing a digital keypad. January watched as he keyed in a series of numbers. Once he was finished, the door to the elevator closed and began to decline.

"How many times have you been in my room?" she asked, thinking that he might be more apt to answer a question now that they'd made their escape from whatever danger he was protecting her from.

"Once."

He replied in a monotone without looking in her direction. In this moment, he was all business. There was no warmth, no…anything. He spoke to her as if she was a stranger. Her heart was beating like a steel drum in her chest, her frayed nerves were on edge and she was forcing herself not to let her teeth chatter. But Legend made it clear that he wasn't in the business of providing her any comfort, no warmth. In this moment, he was her security, not her security blanket.

Time for you to grow up, January, his words echoed in her mind.

"This is the only time I've been inside. Your father gave me the layout of your room when he asked me a few hours ago to come get you."

January felt every bit of air expel from her lungs.

There it was.

Just like that, the mystery was solved after all this time and her suspicions were laid to rest.

Legend *was* working for her father, just as she thought. All this time when she was under the impression that they were making a connection by way of divinely orchestrated, but seemingly coincidental, run-ins and interactions that were the Universe's way of meddling with their destinies, he was simply obeying commands to keep a close eye on her. All along he had been playing a part. Which made it easy to see why his affections towards her could so effortlessly flow from hot to cold.

There are no coincidences.

She'd always believed that and, once again, her belief had been proven true. Legend and January didn't share all of the same classes because some divine, spiritual force was driving them to be together. There was no energetic connection that predestined their fates as lovers or soulmates. There was nothing God-given, divinely ordered or special about their connection.

She wasn't his soulmate, kindred soul or twin flame. January was his *mission.*

And the blank void that she now saw in his eyes proved it to be true. Everything that she thought she'd seen there before when he looked at her had been manufactured in order for him to remain undercover. For the very first time in her life, she had been completely and utterly fooled. For the first time in her life, she sincerely felt stupid.

A sad, silly little girl. Just like Carmen had said.

She took a long, deep breath to bridle the rumblings of rage growing inside of her.

In that moment, she didn't give a damn that he may have just saved her life by helping her to escape from whatever danger had been heading her way.

She was *pissed.*

Or maybe just embarrassed.

At any rate, she definitely felt played.

After every single one of their interactions, she'd spent hours of many days replaying them over and over in her mind. She analyzed every bit of his actions, his words and his expressions to decide whether or not he was truly into her. Like plucking petals from a flower, January considered each one while her brain cycled through thoughts of 'he loves me' and 'he loves me nots.' After exhausting her mind through multiple realities of his actual emotions, she'd always been left utterly confused for the most part, but her knack for wishful thinking pushed her to believe it was love.

Now she clearly had the answer she'd been looking for. But it definitely wasn't the one she wanted.

The elevator doors opened to what appeared to be a dimly lit underground area and January bottled up her emotions, setting them temporarily to the side while she focused once again on getting to safety. They stepped out into the large parking garage, but there was only one car. She hesitated, wondering how in the world her father was able to arrange for all of this to be underneath the school.

Did he really coordinate construction of all of this just for her to go to school? This was pure insanity.

"Let's go."

Legend's voice sounded almost like a growl and it quickly snapped her to attention. Rushing to the point of tripping over her own feet, she struggled once again to keep up with his long strides. He walked to the back of the car and opened the door, appearing calm as he waited seemingly patiently for her to climb in, but urgency was all in his eyes. Unable to help herself, January bent her brows into a frown, glaring into him before she slid into the backseat. Appearing completely unbothered by her emotional display, he simply shut the door behind her before getting into the passenger side.

A guy she'd never officially met but had seen a few times before was sitting in the driver's seat. January recognized him as Onyx's brother, Nico. The few times she'd seen him, he was always laughing or playing around but, like Legend, his countenance was now entirely different. Though he didn't move at all to acknowledge her presence or even look in her direction, she peeped his expression through the rearview mirror. It was steeled like concrete, tense but controlled at the same time. All business.

She couldn't believe this. Was everyone around her working for her dad?

"Now that I'm safe, can someone please tell me what is going on?" January asked, looking back and forth between both of the men in front of her.

Neither said a word. Didn't even let on that they'd heard her at all.

"I know you have your orders and all, but you can't just show up in someone's room in the middle of the night and—"

Before she could say another word, Nico turned around in his seat and shoved a phone in her face. Grabbing it slowly, she frowned and stared down at the screen, seeing a number she didn't recognize. She sucked in a breath before bringing it to her ear.

"Hello?"

"January."

It was her father. Tears came to her eyes at the sound of his voice. Though he'd only spoken one word, his tone concerned her. It was stern in a way that she recognized. Something was wrong. *Very* wrong. And whatever it was could possibly change her life forever.

"Yes, Daddy?" Her voice came out like a whine. Instantly, she hated that she felt so small and powerless, so young, in that moment.

"I asked Legend to get you tonight and take you somewhere safe. You'll have to stay there until I can get you back to New York."

"For how long?" she asked, in between biting down hard on her bottom lip. "When can I come home?"

There was a pause. A short one, but long enough to tell her everything she needed to know.

"I'm not sure when that will be," he replied with a sigh. "And I'm not sure when I'll be able to call again. Just know that as long as you're with Legend, you're safe. I know you haven't seen him in a while… but I know him to be someone I can trust. I love you, baby girl."

Closing her eyes tightly shut, January didn't fight away the tears that fell from her eyes.

"I love you too, Daddy."

A few seconds passed as she held the phone to her ear, listening to him breathing on the other end. And just when she was on the brink of collapsing into tears like the little girl that he still thought of her as, the line went dead. The sound of the void on the other end of the phone forced her back into her body, back into reality, and pushed her to steady her mind. Whatever was going on had her father stressed to the max, which meant that she needed to get herself and her mind together. The last thing he needed was to have to worry about whatever she was feeling and had happening on her end.

January loved her mother, and they had their own kind of bond, but the bond she had with her father was something magical. It was her mother who gave birth to her body, but Outlaw gave birth to her soul. Their connection was beyond physical. They connected on a soul level.

He always had a way of feeling what was happening with her. Whenever January was in distress, he knew it before she got the chance to tell him. If she was happy, he was calm and clear. Whoever wronged him that day had a good chance of having their sins forgiven. He'd freely give out second chances, against his nature.

But if she was frustrated, angry or sad, he was ready to wreck some shit. He became a different kind of reckless when she wasn't in a good mood. In many cases, how he absorbed her emotions determined whether someone he was punishing lived or died. January didn't know what was happening right now, but she did know that she needed his mind to be calm and clear.

Wiping the tears from her eyes, she held the phone out in front of her and Legend grabbed it without looking, tucking it into his pocket. Her eyes traced his jawline, picking up on the tension there. She watched him repetitiously bite down on his back teeth and then release. It was a micro-aggression that told her he was bothered. Something was weighing heavy on his mind.

Settling back into her seat, she looked out the window as the car pulled off, driving through the parking garage. Nico drove quickly but with precision, whipping through turns before diving into a long, dark tunnel. Squinting hard, January peered into the darkness, wondering how the hell he could see anything, especially with the large, dark shades on his eyes that nearly covered his face. They had to have some kind of infrared technology built into them because it was impossible to see outside only using human eyes. All of the lights on the car were turned off and there wasn't a single one lit in the tunnel. It was like they were driving through space on an invisible highway.

The highway to hell, January couldn't help but think.

They exited out the end of the tunnel and entered into another area where they intersected with yet another tunnel. There was a car parked outside of the entrance. Or so January thought until it suddenly pulled behind them. She turned in her seat to look at it, but she couldn't see inside. The tints were too dark, definitely past the standard for being legal. Nico drove up a ramp towards a dead-end wall. She wasn't at all surprised when the wall retracted up into the ceiling to reveal an exit from the underground roadway. The car jerked, alarming her, as they entered into the busy streets of Los Angeles and she nearly jumped out of her own skin. Another car fell into place ahead of them. It was a black sedan, and she knew instantly that it was definitely part of the security team just from the look of it.

Why won't anyone tell me what happened? What is going on?

Her nerves were on edge, clipping oxygen from entering her lungs. Her breath caught in her throat and she felt the prickly sensation of fear building at the base of her neck. She took another glance at the car behind her and then swiveled back around in her seat to look at Legend, only to realize that he was looking at her through the rearview mirror that had at some point been turned in his direction.

"Relax," he said, under bent brows over smoldering eyes. However, she picked up on a small amount of softness in them that hadn't been there before. In a tiny way, it provided her a little comfort.

January ran her hands over the top of her thighs and exhaled heavily, trying to inhale some bit of peace. The effort was futile.

"Relax," he repeated, this time with more tenor.

"How can you say that? How can you even *think* I can relax?"

He didn't answer. His eyes are on something else in the rearview mirror. Whatever peace January was trying to conjure up dissipated the second she recognized the renewed hardness in his eyes.

"You see it?" Legend asked Nico, who replied with a simple, "Mm hmm."

Without warning, Nico mashed the gas and the car bolted forward, racing at top speed as he swirled around the black sedan in front of them and started weaving in and out of traffic. Time began to move sideways, and January's body filled with anxiety that crippled her. Out of habit, she gripped the handle of the door, feeling like she was on the brink of insanity. Against her better judgment, she turned to look out the back window and picked up on a black Charger with dark tints, speeding along as it followed the trail that Nico made.

Someone was following them.

Before she could catch her next breath, shots were fired. January screamed, covering her ears with her hands, trying to block out the sound. In her subconscious, she knew that she was safe. She knew the car was bullet-proof. Legend wouldn't forget that type of simple detail. However, the sound of gunshots pointed in her direction took her back in time to a place she didn't want to be. The scar on her leg seemed to throb with its own recognizance of the events that had led to it being there. Her heart drummed in her chest and a sour taste settled in the back of her throat.

"Relax," she heard Legend say once more.

She didn't know if he was saying it for his own benefit or for hers because he was definitely wasting his breath if he were saying it for her.

Like a Nascar driver, Nico swerved in and out of lanes and turned corners on two wheels without even denting the calm, cool and collected expression on his face. Allowing her head to drop back on the seat behind her, January closed her eyes and started singing a song in her mind. It was the only thing she could think of to force herself out of focusing on the madness.

"Hang on," she heard Nico say, making her force her eyelids back open.

Hang on?

"You're a little late, don't you think?" was what she wanted to shout but before she could even think to, it became clear why he'd said it.

He hit a nozzle on the dash of the car, causing it to accelerate into some speed that was reserved for use by only God or Superman. January's whole, entire life flashed before her eyes. For some reason, she decided to open them to escape from her mental revival of all her dearest childhood moments, only to see that Nico was tearing down back alleys, racing away from whatever danger that was behind them, putting the entire fucking pedal to the metal. Feeling dizzy, January closed her eyes again.

After some unknown amount of time, she opened them once more, realizing that the car had decelerated, and they were back to normal speed. Her nerves slowly crept back into whatever could be considered normal for the moment and her heart evened out its beats. When she turned to check behind her, she noticed that they were alone and no longer being followed.

Finally.

"Where are we going?" she dared to ask, realizing that in spite of her calm down, her voice was trembling.

Legend peeked over, for the first time since getting in the car, turning fully to look at her. His eyes lowered to her hands which she then realized were still gripping the arm rest on the car door.

"Somewhere safe, for now," he replied.

January's widened gaze whipped over to him. "For *now*?"

He nodded. "Yep."

"W-w-w-well… well, what happens when it's not safe anymore?"

As if annoyed by her question, Nico squealed the tires around a hard-left turn, and her body slammed against the door. It was an unnecessary move. Even Legend cut his eyes at him, giving a silent warning.

"My bad. I almost missed the turn," he said with a shrug.

Yeah, right.

Ignoring the obvious lie, Legend returned his attention to January.

"It's safe for now. If it becomes unsafe at some point, we'll figure that out when that moment gets here."

That said, he turned around in his seat to face forward, signaling the end to their brief question and answer session. There was nothing left for January to do but relax her body and relax her mind. Obviously, they were both done with her questions and the comfort already provided was the only amount they would currently give. The only peace she would find in this moment would be to surrender and go with the flow.

Fat chance of that happening, January thought as she closed her eyes. She fought away the confusion of her thoughts and allowed the lyrics to make their way into her mind once again.

NIGGAS AIN'T SHIT.

Niggas really ain't shit.

Of all the things that had changed in Brooke's life, that's the one thing that had always stayed constant. She'd said it once, said it twice and said it again... and again. At some point, there was always some woke ass female who came along to peer at her through her rose-colored eyeglasses, looking at Brooke like she was some bitter and hurt chick, bruised by the experiences of her past, and told her that it's not true: there are some really good men out there. The fact was, if there were, they were definitely in hiding because Brooke had never come across one that hadn't fit that statement.

She had even tried to consider a few times that maybe *she* was the problem. Maybe it was the type of man she was choosing. She'd always had a thing for bad boys—Men who had a little edge to them just excited something inside of her, awakened her 'chakras', as January called them. Specifically, they awakened whichever one was connected to her vagina. Maybe *that* was the problem. Her pussy chakra was obviously broken because it only responded to men who really didn't give a damn.

She really couldn't understand it, to be honest. She knew her worth, knew that she was a good woman with a great heart and had a lot to offer the world and could be the total package for any man. And she wasn't the type of woman who had a list of specific and unchangeable criteria that he had to fit in. She wasn't expecting the perfect man. Brooke just wanted someone who could reflect and mirror the kind of love she gave him. Someone she could grow with who could be genuine and honest with her. Someone who could hand her his heart, fully and completely, and allow her to do the same without having to deal with a whole bunch of extra bullshit. Unfortunately, it seemed like every relationship she'd been in came with exactly that: a whole lot of bullshit.

I can't believe I keep doing this shit, Brooke thought, looking around at the empty hotel room she'd found herself in. The one Nico had left her in.

Something told her that nigga was no good the second she laid eyes on him at the club a few hours before. Supposedly, he was there to watch Onyx perform because Legend couldn't make it, but the second he walked through the doors, his eyes were on Brooke. And, she hated to admit it, as much as she tried her ass couldn't stop looking at him either. She couldn't resist, though in her heart, she knew he was nothing but bad news.

Pure sexy thug, flashy as hell with a smile that had obviously broken a lot of hearts, Nico was very obviously a demon hidden in tailored clothes and expensive shoes. God's curse to females, perfectly and irresistibly gift-wrapped by the devil to fool them all into opening their hearts when he only wanted their open legs.

Thankfully, she was able to push him away the first night they'd met. Mainly, because her boyfriend, the boyfriend she was too embarrassed to openly claim, had the half of her mind that was wrapped around Nico's finger involved in some bullshit. He *always* had her involved in his bullshit. But after coming back to watch Onyx a couple more nights and running into Nico who continued to persist,

Brooke eventually opened up to the idea of somewhat dealing with him.

Why the fuck not? was her thinking.

Though she loved Trevor, deep down she knew he wasn't the one. And she hadn't caught him yet, but she couldn't get over the feeling that he was cheating on her. Brooke wanted to feel wanted, cared for and touched. She didn't even really want sex, just some level of intimacy, and Nico seemed like the one willing to offer her that. So after pushing him away, she finally gave in and agreed to let him take her home after the club. They talked for a while and then one thing led to another which led to another which eventually led to Brooke being holed up waiting for him in this empty ass hotel room feeling dumb as hell.

The screen of her phone illuminated in the dark and Brooke sucked her teeth before grabbing it, knowing who it was before she even looked at the text.

I'll be back soon. Thanks for waiting for me, shorty.

"Whatever," Brooke said, rolling her eyes. She couldn't even force herself to respond, she was so aggravated. The read receipt was all he needed and all she was willing to give. She hadn't even given Nico any pussy and he was already fucking up. After finally being able to convince her to pay him some mind, they spoke for hours in the club until it closed and when he offered to grab a hotel so they could continue the conversation—code for talk a little and then fuck —she'd even agreed.

It was more for her than it was for him. She hadn't had sex in over a month since the semester started, and she was horny. But as soon as they stepped into the room, his phone rang, and he told her he needed to step in the hall to take it. About five minutes after that, he told her he had to leave to take care of some business and would be right back. That was *hours* ago. He wasn't taking care of no business. He probably had a girlfriend somewhere who had gotten suspicious about his whereabouts.

Brooke was fully convinced that he'd left her to go see another bitch.

Before Brooke could put down the phone, another text came rolling in. This one from Onyx. Crazy how they both texted her almost at the same time. There must've been some truth to that theory on twin telepathy.

Did you make it home?

With a sigh, Brooke threw herself back down across the bed and prepared herself to type out a lie.

Yeah, I only stayed for a few minutes after you left and then called a ride.

Good, was her reply.

Brooke didn't like not telling Onyx the truth but the last thing she wanted was to admit that she had fallen victim to her brother's mind games. Since the first time Brooke got the nerve to finally confide in Onyx about her situation with Trevor, she had been telling Brooke to leave his ass alone and focus on herself so the right man could come along but Brooke continued to tell her no because she knew Trevor was the one, he just needed her help to become the man she knew he could be. Every time Brooke said it, Onyx would look at her like she was crazy and drop the subject so that Brooke could hold on to whatever was left of her dignity. How could Brooke tell Onyx that she was being played once again, but by another man this time... her fuckin' twin?

After a few minutes of trying to force herself not to, Brooke gave in and went to Trevor's Instagram to see what he'd been up to since the last time she checked and started watching his stories. The first few were of him doing the same shit he was always doing, driving around in Brooke's car, playing music and showing out for all his female followers who loved looking at his sexy ass. The next couple stories were of him showing off his body, along with a few thirst trap pics. Brooke didn't feel no type of way about it because that was the kind of shit he felt he had to do in order to keep his page active and it seemed to work. Every one of his posts had hundreds of comments from women begging to perform all kinds of sexual favors to the point that she didn't even want to imagine what he had going on in his DMs. Rolling her eyes, Brooke nonchalantly passed through the videos of him showing off everything the good Lord had blessed him with until she landed on some videos of what looked like a party—a house party to be exact. Half-dressed and fully drunk women were everywhere, dancing and laughing while drinking from red cups along with a few men who Brooke recognized. Then the camera angle switched and there was Trevor, drinking Hennessy straight from the bottle while two white girls danced on him, one on each side, rubbing their stank ass coochies all over him.

The fuck?

Brooke felt her anger begin to rise but it wasn't until she looked a little closer that it rolled over to full-on rage.

Wait... is this nigga really doing this in my fuckin' apartment?

Pressing down on the clip to pause it from going to the next slide, Brooke took a good look at the furniture and decor, knowing damn well that what she was thinking couldn't possibly be right. But it was there, all the evidence she needed, right in front of her fuckin' face.

Closing the app, Brooke went straight to her call log and pressed on his number before putting the phone on speaker. Biting her bottom lip, Brooke squeezed her eyes closed, trying to catch her breath as the line began to ring. She couldn't believe this shit. Here she was, living in a fuckin' dorm that she was secretly paying for with her scholarship so her parents wouldn't know, while she allowed him to have her apartment until he got on his feet, and instead of doing what he needed to do, his ass was throwing parties and probably fuckin' other women in it. Brooke was *pissed!*

"Hello?" Trevor answered the phone sounding half sleep. It was an act. The Instagram video had only been posted an hour ago. His ass wasn't asleep that fast.

"Nigga, stop playing. You ain't sleep. What the fuck are you thinking throwing a party in my damn apartment?" Brooke nearly screamed. Obviously, all that mediation shit that January was teaching was lost on her.

"What?" he asked followed by a short pause. "Oh, you talkin' about that video. Choc, that video was from days ago."

Brooke rolled her eyes at him using the pet name he'd given her when they first started dating. Choc was short for Chocolate Baby, something that he came up with because of the color of her skin. He rarely used it now, but the times he did, was only when she'd caught him up in some shit and he was trying to calm her down. Now that Brooke thought about it, that was happening more and more since she left for school, so he was actually using the name quite frequently recently.

"Don't Choc me. I don't care when the video was taken. You're staying in my apartment for one reason and one reason only, and that's not to be throwing parties while letting nasty ass females rub all up on you. Why do you keep doing this shit?"

Brooke felt tears of frustration at the back of her eyes, but she tried to force them away. Truthfully, she wasn't even mad at Trevor, she was mad at herself. Mad because she knew that at the end of this conversation, she would still be pissed off and he wouldn't because they both knew that he was going to do what he wanted, and Brooke wasn't going to do a damn thing. She loved him more than he loved her, if even he did, and that was the silver lining that meant, in every battle, Brooke would always loose.

Trevor sighed heavily before speaking again.

"Choc, you know what I do to make money. The easiest way to do it is to throw parties. Every bitch you saw in that video was doped i and who you think they got the shit from? I could make moves on the street and risk being caught up in some shit that'll send me to jail or I can throw a party and make way more money while selling the shit safely. What would you rather me do?"

"I wouldn't rather you do either one," Brooke tearfully replied. "Trevor, you should be out here with me, taking classes towards your degree so we can—"

"Choc, I'm not as smart as you and you know that. My only chance at going to college and doing something with it went down the drain the second I tore my ACL."

Brooke's heart felt like it was bleeding, and she could no longer hold back her tears. Mainly because she knew he was right. Before Trevor started dealing, he was the star basketball player at their high school, the kid from the hood who everyone knew would be an all-star professional player one day. All of that came to an end during a homecoming game where one wrong move ended any dreams of a basketball career. He went through deep depression and became so angry that he pushed everyone away. Everyone but Brooke. She was the only one able to get through to him and with her help, he some-what got his life back together. His parents weren't shit and the friends he had weren't worth a damn either. When it came to the ones he could depend on, he only had Brooke. That was one of the main reasons she couldn't leave him.

"Choc, I'm only doing this for a year to save up enough money to get my license to be a barber. Once I get enough money together, I'll stop. I just don't wanna keep leaning on you. You think it feels good to be driving around in your car and living in your shit? I mean, I appreciate it, but it's not supposed to work this way. I'm supposed to take care of you, and it fucks me up that I can't. But I promise once I get on my feet, I got you."

Sniffing, Brooke hung her head and listened to Trevor tell her all the things he always said whenever she went off about anything. She couldn't argue because she knew what he was doing and, in that moment, how he explained the way he was doing it made sense. But it just didn't sit right with Brooke and she didn't know why. She felt like she should be holding him down because she loved him. Brooke didn't like what he was doing but she had to trust that he would find his own way eventually. Love didn't control, love was unconditional and allowed room for growth. That's what she was doing with Trevor—accepting the decisions he made for his life, supporting him in the ways that she could without compromising her values and praying that he would become the better man she needed him to be one day. So why did it feel like he was getting everything he needed, and Brooke always wound up with the short end of the stick? The only thing she wanted was him. She wanted to be loved and to feel appreciated. He was so focused on money that he didn't even see that she didn't want that. Brooke only wanted his time.

"I know, Trevor. I just—I haven't seen you much since I started school. It's been weeks and you're always working or sleeping and... I just feel so empty inside. I miss you."

What Brooke was saying sounded pitiful to her own ears. It was against her nature to be so vulnerable. Trevor was the only person in the world who she did that with. Mainly because it felt like he was the only one who could give her what she needed. The problem was, he always promised to but never did.

"Choc, you know that any time you want to see me, all you gotta do is call. I always make time for you as long as I don't have no other shit going on. It's just hard because... I can't afford to miss out on this money. I'm trying to get this shit together for us."

Brooke heard what he was saying but she was experienced enough to read between the lines. Trevor wasn't exactly lying; he did make time for her whenever he didn't have other shit going on. The problem was, he *always* had other shit going on. Brooke wanted a man who gave her the type of love where he would drop everything and anyone for her when she needed him. Brooke was an option when she wanted to be a priority. But how could she say that without sounding selfish? Of all people in the world, she knew first-hand what Trevor was dealing with and what he had gone through. Brooke knew it was hard for him to have to rely so heavily on her. At the same time, she was left wondering when he would realize the same things for her.

"Okay, Trevor," Brooke said, wiping the last tear from her eye. "I understand. Just... make sure nobody messes up my shit. If my parents come visit, I still have to pretend that I live in my apartment."

"You know I got you," he replied.

No, you really don't but I'll keep on pretending you do anyways.

Brooke's mind was constantly screaming the things she was too much of a coward to say.

"I know," was what she said instead.

"Go to sleep and let me hit you up in the morning. You got an early class?"

"No, all of my classes are late," she told him for the millionth time. He never remembered.

"Okay, good. I'll hit you up when I get up then. Just try to relax, Brooke. This shit ain't gone be like this forever. And I got love for you, for real. You're my best friend."

Brooke flinched at his words. That was another thing. Trevor didn't like labels for whatever reason. He'd never officially asked her to be his, somehow they just moved from friends to having sex which plunged them into a 'whatever ship' without a formalized commitment.

"Yeah, I know," Brooke said, knowing that he would either ignore or not pick up on the sarcasm in her tone.

"Love ya, Brooke. Now get some sleep."

"I love you back, Trevor."

They hung up and Brooke tossed the phone to the side before laying back on the bed, feeling confused, needy, half-stupid and used. How down was too much when it came to holding a nigga down? How long was a ride or die chick supposed to ride? Why did her cup feel half empty when she did everything to keep his full? Brooke couldn't figure out where to draw the line between loyalty and stupidity. To be totally honest, trying to figure it out was fucking with her. Brooke wanted to pull away, bury her feelings, so she could just focus on her, but she couldn't because whenever Trevor offered her whatever crumbs he had to give, she couldn't force herself not to push him away. Brooke felt alive in his presence and struggled in his absence, forcing herself to wear a mask that allowed her to focus on school in the daytime and then would spend the nights in the club dancing and drinking her pain and loneliness away. This was no way to live and she knew it. Brooke couldn't be half-loved anymore. She had to cut him off fully to save herself but if she took everything away from a man who had nothing and no one, what kind of person would that make her?

Rolling over onto her stomach, Brooke buried her face in the pillows. Her emotions took over once more as she began to cry uncontrollably. Out of the two of them, only one of them would be getting some sleep. It definitely wouldn't be Brooke.

TRIGGERED.

"AND THIS IS WHERE WE DIVERGE," NICO SAID TO LEGEND.

From the backseat, January watched as they both bumped fists and then exited out of their sides of the car. Since neither had spoken a word to her, she stayed cemented in the seat, wanting to hold on to this moment and not move, for some strange reason. She guessed it was because, for the moment, she felt safe. They were in a field out in the middle of nowhere with only a single car as the other object in sight outside of the presence of Mother Nature. Everything around them oozed of peace; much different from whatever situation had led them there.

Nico walked over to the car on the other end of the field as Legend stepped around to the driver's seat and got in. January didn't say a word as he shifted the gears forcing the car into reverse, and then drive, before taking off. Nico left in the opposite direction.

After about fifteen minutes of driving, he took a quick and sudden turn into an alley that dead-ended into a brick wall. Like before, the wall lifted after he keyed what she assumed was some sort of code into his phone and they drove down a ramp, descending into another underground tunnel.

"Where are we?" January asked when she could finally find her voice.

Not readily speaking, Legend drove on until they entered another parking garage, much like the one underneath her dorm. He drove into a parking space near a far wall and then killed the engine on the car.

"We're at my place. One of them, anyways. Get out and let's go inside."

She curled her nose at his demanding tone but didn't move another muscle. "You could at least say 'please.'"

He snorted at that but didn't make any attempts to show any bit of manners. She was starting to think that any sort of civility she'd seen in the weeks before now had been part of his disguise.

"So this is where you live when you're not pretending to stay in the dorms?"

It was her way of taking a shot at him—somewhat referring to the fact that he'd been living a lie, and lying to me, for a while now.

"Not really. It's more of a safehouse that I keep in case I need it. You'll be safe here."

"Are you staying with me?"

He glanced over his shoulder into her face, sending her a look that clearly said her question was ridiculous. "Of course. And if you knew what I knew, you would want me to. Now get out."

Indignant in her rebellion, January took her sweet time unbuckling her seatbelt and by the time she moved to open her door, he was already outside of it and did the job for her. For a moment, she wondered if he was opening her door out of a show of chivalry or just because he was tired of waiting for her to do it herself. Most likely, it was the latter.

Or at least, that's what she thought until he took her hand to help her out of the car. Her stomach filled with butterflies. Why it was reacting in that manner towards a man who had proven himself to be a liar was beyond her. Out of instinct, she snatched away but, of course, he didn't flinch.

They entered an elevator and she relaxed against the back wall of it, trying to keep a cool head. More than a few times January found herself glancing in his direction, trying to pick up on his thoughts or any visible emotions, but he seemed the same as he'd been the entire time—absolutely calm. She wondered if he was only playing it that way because he didn't want her to panic. On the inside, he had to be feeling *something*.

The elevator doors sounded off with a *ding*, and he held out his hand for hers once again. This time, she took it. She felt him give her a little squeeze, or maybe she imagined it. She wasn't sure but it put her at ease, nonetheless.

God, I hated to admit that I felt anything for this man.

In this moment, hating him seemed much more attractive to her.

Legend tugged her down a small hallway toward the only door on the floor. She closed her eyes, hoping and praying there wasn't anyone waiting for them on the other side. She couldn't help but think about how he said he was taking her somewhere that was safe… until it wasn't. What if that time was now?

She found herself absentmindedly moving closer to him, seeking some sort of protection that she innately felt like his presence could offer. Her nerves were getting to her. Though he seemed totally calm, her life had changed dramatically in the span of a couple hours and now she was in an unfamiliar place for a reason that she wasn't yet aware of. For the first time in a while, all she really longed for was to be back home.

"You're too close," Legend said in an even tone without even looking in her direction. "Stand back."

She did as he said but with a deep frown. With her muscles tense from fear, alarm and plain ole aggravation, she watched as he reached out to push his thumb against what looked like a finger scanner on the wall ahead. The device lit blue and then green once it registered his marks. Another gadget rose out from the top of it and he dropped his head, pushing his right eye to it. A thin red beam of light scanned his eye and then, once again, a green light glowed as it finished.

This was insane.

January was in absolute awe. Even with the life she'd lived, she never saw this kind of security. Never even thought there was a need for it. Dumbfounded, she continued to watch in silence.

Once Legend's eye had been scanned, another contraption popped out and he pressed his pointer finger against a small silver pin which pricked it for blood.

"You've got to be kidding me," she couldn't help but say and rolled her eyes. He was on some real James Bond shit.

If Legend heard her, he didn't respond. Beneath his feet, the large white square that he was standing on began to glow with white light and January suddenly realized why he said she was standing too close when a small screen the size of a keypad started to glow with red numbers, calculating what she assumed was his weight, along with another number that she wasn't sure of.

Once finished, the wall in front of them descended into the ground, just as the one in the garage did before, to reveal the inside of a hall that led to yet another closed door. Legend stepped forward and she started to follow until he put up a single finger in the air to tell her to stop. He continued to walk forward over a long panel that, like the square he'd been standing on before, glowed with white light. When he reached the end of it, the light dimmed, and she heard the click of the lock on the door in front of him.

She was absolutely stunned. She wasn't quite sure of all that she'd just seen but she knew for a fact that it was on another level from anything she'd ever witnessed before.

Legend walked through the door and disappeared, leaving her standing alone in a room that had technology that could probably rival what they had in the White House. Her ears picked up on a few beeps interrupting the silence, and then he reappeared. His eyes, stern and cloudy with some emotion she couldn't read, were focused in on her.

"You can come in now."

January stepped cautiously, as if there was some trap door under her feet that would open up and send her on a long drop to hell if she didn't tread lightly. When she finally reached where Legend stood waiting, she glanced up and picked up on the humor in his eyes.

"The security system is off. You can relax," he said, smirking for the first time that night.

"Why in the world does anyone need this much security? What do you have in there?"

He shrugged. "It's necessary," was all he said.

He had a way of doing that. Picking apart her questions to vaguely answer only the ones he felt like responding to while not even bothering to acknowledge the others. For someone who demanded so much information about her life, and even still knew so much about her that she'd never even told, he was a complete mystery to her.

"Wow," she whispered when they entered the living space. It was dimly lit by recessed lighting in the ceiling, but she saw enough to be fully impressed.

Then Legend flipped a switch, fully illuminating the rest of the... house? Condo? Penthouse? Mansion? She wasn't sure what it was just yet, but she did know that it was breathtaking.

"It's not as lavish as some of the places you've lived in, I'm sure, but I hope it'll do."

January lifted a brow at what she suspected was clear sarcasm, but he didn't crack a smile. Yeah, the homes her parents owned were over the top. Mainly because of her father's 'larger than life' sense of style. But they weren't anything like this. Legend's taste perfectly matched her own in so many ways. If January had to choose, she definitely preferred his space.

His style could be described as minimalistic with a splash of opulence. High ceilings, marble and hardwood floors and floor-to-ceiling windows made up most of the space, but Legend's décor was simple, modern and sentimental. Every piece of art and decoration mounted on the wall or placed on top of the custom-made furniture felt like it carried a special meaning. Nothing felt ordinary or out-of-place.

Legend watched as January walked into the middle of the living room, preceding carefully, as if with caution, while soaking it all in. The hardwood floors squeaked with her footsteps as he closed the door behind them. Locking it, he set what she assumed was the alarm system. The motion detectors inside the room beeped twice, indicating something only he knew. He walked around and pulled the curtains to the windows, even though they were tinted. Then, walking around the perimeter, he double-checked behind the security system, making sure every space was properly locked down before returning back to where she stood.

"This place is huge," January whispered, marveling at the luxury all around her.

"Take your pick of whatever room," he said, shrugging as if it were no big deal. And, for him, it wasn't. He liked nice things, but it was just his particular way of life. He didn't place his worth into the things he had.

"How long am I staying here, Legend?"

Another shrug came from him. "Until I get a call from Outlaw saying that it's safe to move you out of the state."

"Why wouldn't it be safe to leave now? What's going on?" January asked, placing her hands on her hips and steeling her feet into the floor. A stance that told him that she was prepared to stand there all night if she had to in order to get the answers she deserved.

I don't have time for this shit, Legend thought. He was getting annoyed. Not only was he working on less than two hours' worth of sleep in the last 48 hours, he didn't have the answers she demanded.

"Stop with the questions. Pick a room. Go to bed." His tone was hard, colder than he'd intended, but being nice wasn't getting him anywhere. Maybe being an asshole would.

His sudden shift in mood from cold to frozen solid, brought tears to January's eyes. Swallowing them back, she tried to force her bottom lip not to tremble.

"What am I to you, Legend? Was the entire thing just a job for you? Do I even matter to you at all?" she continued in a near rage, unable to give in to the silence that followed each time Legend refused to answer her questions.

She was a ball of uncontrollable emotions. Her passion showed like flashes of lightning rippling through her eyes. The intensity of the pain had the potential to ruin her in a way that nothing else could. She couldn't understand—would never understand—how he could be by her side, in her space, form actual intimate bonds with her nearly every day, and it all be fake. Somehow, she'd managed to convince herself that what they had was real and being presented with the evidence that it was only a job for him felt like it was ripping her apart. The only thing that could put her back together was the truth. She needed to know everything so that she could properly assess how she felt. She needed to know it all.

Looking at her waiting for his response, Legend blew out a breath and ran a hand over the top of his head in sheer and utter distress.

"January…"

"No," she interrupted, stopping him by raising a hand in the air. "I need you to answer my questions and I want the *entire* truth. You told me that you don't work for my father anymore… you said that wasn't a lie but obviously it was. I'm tired of all the secrets, the mind-games and I'm tired of being played for a fool like I'm someone's property and can't make my own decisions or be in charge of my own life. You need to tell me what's going on and how long you've been lying to me. And you need to tell me *now*."

Fuck, he thought, looking right into her teary eyes. *This is going to be one long, fuckin' night.*

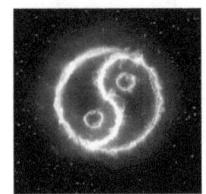

GENTLEMAN IN THUG'S CLOTHING.

SOMEHOW IN BETWEEN BEING MAD AND CONFUSED ABOUT TREVOR and totally pissed off about Nico who still hadn't returned to the room, Brooke fell asleep. It wasn't until she heard a key in the door followed by a heavy whine as it was opened that she stirred awake.

Then appeared Nico. Looking as fine as ever.

Before he returned, she had been mad as hell, but it was definitely hard to stay mad at someone so drop dead gorgeous. She rolled her eyes.

This shit really isn't fair.

"Aye, my bad for leaving you hanging like this," he explained as he walked into the room, shutting the door closed behind him. "Like I said, I had some unexpected business to take care of."

His brows furrowed as if he was in deep thought about something. Brooke snorted and crossed her arms in front of her chest, fully over the entire situation. Fully over men, in general.

"Unexpected business?" she asked, tone dripping with pure skepticism.

He nodded, not saying anything else verbally as he slipped his watch off his wrist. Then he started to kick off his shoes while she watched, trying to keep her jaw from hitting the floor.

I know damn well this nigga is not about to even try *to have sex with me. Not after how everything just went down.*

"Yes," he replied lifting his eyes to meet hers. "Nothing you need to be concerned with."

He pulled his Gucci belt, unfastening it like a pro to loosen up his jeans. She wanted to stop him there to set him straight. There was no way in hell that they would be fucking tonight.

But damn, if I don't want to at least get a glimpse of what this nigga is working with.

When he removed his jeans, letting them freefall to his feet with ease like a seasoned pro, a massive, delectable bulge showed prominently through his Calvin Klein boxers.

And Brooke was instantly struck stupid.

She took a deep breath and released it slowly, feeling like she had been waiting her whole life to let that one go. Like it was the first real inhale and exhale she'd taken in life.

Damn, she thought, feeling her willpower weaken. *What in the trap God heaven do we have here?*

It wasn't until the ambient glow of Nico's silenced cellphone pierced through her consciousness and brought her crashing back down to Earth, reuniting her with her senses, that she remembered the Golden Rule: Niggas ain't shit. *Especially* this one.

Whenever a weak moment came around, it was imperative that a woman spoke the truth to herself. It was most imperative when it came to men as sexy as Nico. The truth was: No matter how good it looks, or how fancy the packaging, he's just like the others.

Stay woke, sis, Brooke coached herself. *He's no different from the others.*

"Your 'unexpected business', I mean, your main bitch or maybe even your side bitch, is calling you," she said, crossing her arms in front of her chest.

She was being hella disrespectful. But in her mind, it was necessary because he was on some disrespectful shit.

She knew she wasn't Nico's girl and he barely knew her like that, but he'd been trying to get her attention for a while even though she was being a loyal girlfriend to Trevor and ignoring him. All the persistence and consistency only to finally have a chance and then leave her alone in a hotel room for hours. *Bullshit.*

"*Main* bitch?" Nico asked, squinting his eyes together really tight. He looked legitimately confused. Brooke had no doubts that he was. Niggas never understood that women were always many, many steps ahead of them. A woman's intuition always told them what was up, whether they listened to it or not. Women always knew the truth, even when men thought they were on some clever shit.

"Yes, your main bitch. Or your side," Brooke further clarified, jerking her neck as she spoke. "The one you left out of here to go deal with. Now that you tended to that, I guess you finally made your way back over here to pacify me with some dick, huh?" She waited for sheer dramatic effect for a response to her rhetorical question. Smart enough to know better than to respond to a woman who was on one, Nico didn't respond.

"Well, it looks like you got an issue. She's still blowing up your phone and I have no intentions of fucking you. Not today and not ever. So how about you do us all a favor and take me home?"

Nico's expression steeled and his eyes tightened into thin slits. Quite a feat for someone who already had very narrow, chinky eyes to begin with. Heat billowed off of his body in waves, and his stance, mixed with the way the tension in his body tightened his muscles had him looking like the Incredible Hulk. His eyes, normally a beautiful hue of chocolate brown, seemed to go completely black.

Sitting with her back against the headboard of the bed, Brooke crossed her arms in front of her chest and held onto her glare as well as her attitude. She wasn't weak and feared no man. She'd be damned if she folded to anyone without a fight.

"Shorty, what the fuck you mean? I don't have no main bitch or a side. Do I look like the type of nigga who gotta hide a bitch to fuck another one?"

"You say that as if it's not the way of the world. Ain't that how y'all niggas do it?"

Nico looked at her as if she'd lost her mind. "I don't know about other niggas, but that ain't how I do shit. If I'm fucking two chicks, they both know it because I'm fucking them at the same time. I ain't got time for that ducking and dodging bullshit."

He waved a hand as if to indicate that what she was suggesting was far beneath him.

What an egotistical asshole.

Brooke rolled her eyes, fully and completely over Nico and the 'denial through honesty' charade he was trying to convince her of.

"Yeah whatever, nigga," she scoffed, lifting her hand to wave him off. "That must work for the other girls you fuck with, but it won't with me. You seem like the type who is always saying that 'I don't do labels' shit so you can do whatever you want to do without a woman placing expectations on you."

"The *fuck* you talkin' ab—"

"So maybe you don't *call* her your girl, but I don't give a damn. Bottom line is, I'm not about to play the role of your side bitch!"

Brooke was so caught up in what she was saying that by the end her voice was elevated, and she was accompanying each word she spoke with a clap of her hands. She was so angry that she even had tears building up in the corner of her eyes. It was insane; she didn't even like Nico that much. Why the hell was she so mad?

Running his hand over his face, Nico sighed heavily before leaning over to the nightstand to grab his phone. He then stepped to the side of the bed, closest to where she sat, breathing heavily to calm herself down, and then stuck the phone nearly under her chin.

"Look," he said. "I want you to see something."

Defiant, Brooke turned her head sharply, feeling an unwanted sinking feeling that told her she was about to be put in her place.

"Nah, don't try to act like that now. You wasn't worried about a nigga's privacy five minutes ago when you was assumin' your way in circles around my shit. So, let me show you all the shit you think you know."

She tightened her jaw by clenching her teeth. Hard—to the point that she probably could've formed dust from her back cavities.

When she finally got enough out of her feelings to look down at the screen of his phone, he unlocked it and immediately scrolled to the call log. There were a couple missed calls from Legend. Some earlier in the night from Onyx and the rest from before they saw each other at the club. Then they went to the messages. The first unread message was from Legend asking if he'd made it home alright despite the 'bullshit they had to deal with earlier' and the other was from Onyx asking where he was. Not one was from an insecure female trying to check on the whereabouts of her man. Actually, in this scenario, *she* was the only insecure female in the room. Literally and figuratively.

Imagine that, she thought. She felt as if she were about to fall face-first onto the ground she was losing. *This is some bullshit.*

"I'm not the nigga you want to think I am, love," he said, dropping the phone in her lap. "Don't believe me? Take a look."

Peering at him under lifted brows, she watched him pull away and then turn his back to her as he adjusted his clothes—this time putting them on rather than taking them off. This was obviously a test; he wanted to see if she was going to check his phone. If she was the type who would do something like that.

Well, the answer is yes, the fuck I am!

Brooke checked phones, computers, wallets, medicine cabinets, seat cushions and all because, as she'd said plenty times already, she wholeheartedly believed that niggas weren't shit.

"They'll hide something right in plain sight," she told January one day, preaching with all the vigor and emotion of a minister in the church's pulpit as she supported her claim. *"And they were getting smarter with how they cover shit. Hiding the next bitch's name under things like 'Scam Likely' so their girl won't think a thing when he ignores the call."*

Her life experiences had made her a little bitter and a lot paranoid. But, in her opinion, it was better to be paranoid than to be taken for a damn fool.

"I'll be back," Nico suddenly said. Without another word, he turned around and walked straight into the bathroom. The door closed behind him and Brooke's stomach jumped. This was the perfect time to check his phone and he wouldn't even know. She could still pretend to be the confident and secure woman she should've been who didn't check anything because she knew any man she was dealing with better not *ever* think of fuckin' around.

That's the woman I want to be, she found herself thinking.

How different would it be to literally give no fucks about what a man had going on when he was on his own because her focus was on her and her alone? To be the kind of woman with eyes fully on her *own* business and, if a man couldn't keep himself in line as she basked in her light, she let his ass go at the first sign of betrayal and was on to the next. To be honest, it was tiring as hell tracking down Trevor's activities in the streets. A full-time fuckin' job that Brooke never even wanted to have. She didn't want to waste any more of her life trying to date *and* raise a man. She had no clue where things would end with Nico, but she knew how she didn't want them to start. She didn't want to begin anything based on suspicion and lies.

Nico had placed his phone in her hand, unlocked and ready for her eyes to pry into every hidden detail of his life. She felt special in a way that went beyond words. Regardless to if he knew how to hide things or not, niggas just didn't do shit like this. Niggas didn't give their phone to a woman, unlocked, and then walk out the room, leaving her to do with it what she wanted. He was different. Because Nico wasn't a nigga; he was a grown ass man.

The bathroom door opened, and Nico slowly walked out spreading Chapstick on his lips, nonchalant, as if he didn't have a care in the world. His eyes were focused on Brooke, a clear question inside them as to why she hadn't yet changed her position at all.

Taking a deep breath, she straightened her back and tried to ignore the nagging at the back of her mind, telling her she was dumb. Her motto was 'niggas ain't shit' for a reason; she truly believed it and would jump at the opportunity to prove it was true. But here she was acting a way she never had before. She eyed him curiously as he walked more into the room. From what Onyx told her, she and Nico were from Miami and they grew up around Haitians.

Did his sexy ass put roots on me?

"I'm not going to check it," Brooke said, holding his phone out in his direction. "I'll just hope that you'll respect me enough to be honest with me before you do something that might involve me in some bullshit."

She expected a joke, a chuckle or even a smirk accompanied by some slick ass response, but Nico didn't give her that. With his eyes piercing hers, his facial expression as serious as a heart attack, he looked her straight in the eyes and spoke to her with all the confidence, sincerity and appeal of a grown man.

"I'm not a square, Brooke, so don't think of me as one. Don't try to put me in that box because niggas like me never fit. I don't have time for bullshit. I don't even have time to be here right now but I'm ignoring some things just so I could lay in the bed next to you and get to know you. No sex, no nothing. Just talking."

The way he said it was almost as if it sounded incredulous to his own ears. As if he couldn't even believe what he was saying. He seemed to take a moment to wrap his mind around that thought before speaking again. Brooke simply watched him closely inspecting everything about him. Her mind was running marathons through the silence. Her entire body felt warm and at peace as he spoke, a confirmation that she truly believed everything he was saying. Not because he seemed to be telling the truth but because it resonated with what she already felt deep down about him.

"You don't really know me, so I'll forgive the fact that you seem to wanna think I'm like every other nigga. But I'm tellin' you right now... I'm *not like* every other nigga. Don't make that mistake of thinking I am again."

Damn.

Brooke really didn't know what to say to that. So… she didn't say a damn thing.

With her mouth glued shut, probably the best thing in the moment, she sat quietly and watched as he straightened up his clothes, placing his wallet and cellphone back in his pocket. His body was chiseled to perfection, something that could easily be seen through his clothes, but she wished like hell that she had kept her big ass mouth closed so she could have really seen what he was working with before she had caught an attitude and changed up the vibe. It was obvious that he no longer had the 'cuddle and chill' plans from when he'd first walked into the room.

"Get up. Get dressed."

He spoke with authority like he wasn't expecting to be questioned. And, by some miracle, she fell in line and did exactly as he commanded. Brooke wasn't about to question a damn thing. Sliding from under the sheets, she got up and began to get dressed as he watched her every move with a stare that silently spoke to his appreciation of everything he saw.

It was crazy the way that she easily surrendered to him in a way that she'd never done for any man she'd met before. She was proving what they said to be true—things just hit different when you were in the presence of a *real* man. He could tell you to do things that would have you mouthing off otherwise, but when he said it, it didn't quite end up that way.

"You're taking me home?" she asked, once she was dressed and had gathered her things.

"Nah," he replied, thumbing through his phone once again. "Tonight, you'll stay with Onyx. You can go back to your dorm when it's safe. I'll tell you when."

Brooke frowned, feeling a stirring feeling in the pit of her stomach that had her uneasy.

"Why isn't it safe now? And where is January?"

"She's good. No more questions," was his reply.

A crease formed in the center of her forehead. This ordering her around shit was quickly getting out of hand. It was cute at first, but Nico was *not* her man and she had to draw the line somewhere.

Not your man yet, a voice said in her head.

She frowned at the thought because the voice that had said it, definitely wasn't hers.

Couldn't be.

Nico was cute and all. Had the sexy thug thing going just like she liked it, but she wasn't trying to claim a man who didn't want to be claimed. She'd heard enough about him from his sister to know that all he could give her in the relationship department was hurt feelings and a broken heart. Like his cousin, he didn't do commitment.

"Not my man *ever*," Brooke replied back to the voice in a low whisper.

"Huh?" Nico asked, looking up at her.

She froze. *Shit… was I speaking aloud?*

"Nothing," she shrugged, feeling the heat of shame creeping up at the nape of her neck. "I wasn't talking to you."

Lifting his brows, Nico looked around the room before asking the obvious question.

"Well, who were you talkin' to?"

Hell, she didn't know.

"Myself?" Brooke shrugged again, saying it like a question.

With a smirk, he bent his head and looked at her under his thick, hooded brows.

"You do that often?"

A sheepish expression gave away the embarrassment she was trying to hide.

"Sometimes," she admitted.

Laughing, he grabbed he grabbed her gold clutch from a chair by the door and handed it to her.

"You know, there are things that can be said about people who talk to themselves," he continued with a smile that made her knees wobble in her stilettos. "Some call folks like that crazy. But I ain't judging because those same motherfuckas say the same about me."

Looking up at him, Brooke locked into his eyes, instantly relaxing in the humorous glimmer that she saw in them. His smile was so infectious and before she knew it, she was grinning from ear-to-ear.

"Let's go," he said before turning and walking towards the door.

When he held it open for her, she walked right through it, heading to some unknown destination with some man who she barely knew.

But somehow, she knew in her heart that, wherever it was that he was taking her, she was meant to be there.

TRUTH.

"I'M *WAITING*, LEGEND," JANUARY SAID, CROSSING HER ARMS IN front of her chest, she stomped one foot, angrily showing her impatience. "Speak. Tell me the truth. The *whole* truth."

Sighing heavily, he ran his hand over his face, feeling exasperated, winded and totally depleted of all energy.

He couldn't say anything because he couldn't lie to her. But he also couldn't tell her the truth... Which was that instead of one gangster thinking he was working with him, the reality was that he was working for *two*.

California was run by a black Mexican cartel leader named Fernando Rosario. As part of the *BBM* organization, the Rosarios swore their loyalty once they joined the fold, however, as long-time friends of the Dumas' family, Fernando made it clear that he would always keep his relationship with his Miami friends alive. With Fernando Rosario being a friend of both Outlaw and Legend, Sr., it made California a safe zone. However, all that changed a week ago when Legend received a call from Fernando's son, Capone, stating that his cousin had been killed in New York by one of Outlaw's men. Fernando demanded that Outlaw hand the boy who had killed him over to be punished but Outlaw refused. With January in California, making her an easy pawn in their game, Outlaw called Legend as soon as he'd learned of his presence there, and asked for his loyalty in protecting his daughter and keeping her safe.

But not only did Outlaw place a call, his father had reached out as well. Legend Sr. knew that Outlaw, having no one else he could trust, would reach out to Legend. And so, he hatched his plan to take over Outlaw's empire once and for all, by hitting him the most vulnerable spot of all when it came to a gangster: his heart.

"He's going to ask you to take her so that the Rosarios can't get her," Legend Sr. had said. "And I need you to do just that. But when the time is right, you'll deliver her to another location where Outlaw will be brought to make a choice: hand over his empire, all of his power, by publicly and legally handing over the control of his throne to me or save his daughter."

It was an impossible choice to some, but everyone who knew Outlaw knew what he would choose. He valued family over everything. His loved ones earned his undying loyalty by birthright. And real talk, Legend's personal code for life mirrored Outlaw's in every way. In so many ways, they were the same man. They thought the same way, acted the same way. They believed in the same things.

Family was *always* over everything.

And now, with the weight of the world on his shoulders, he stood in front of January, the woman he knew for a fact that he loved in however way a man like him could choose to love, he was presented with a choice of his own. A split decision: one that forced him to dive deeply into the very definition, his very core belief, of what family was. In the *BBM*, he'd formed bonds that went far beyond blood. He'd made brothers out of men who weren't family by birth but became family by loyalty, the latter more respected by Legend than the former. However, he couldn't denounce the loyalty he would always have for his father, the man who raised him, taught him, led him and molded him into the man he was today. Their differences with each other were a matter of principle, and nothing else. They saw the world in different ways. But that wasn't enough to toss away the ties that made family.

"January... it's deeper than that," he tried to express, feeling as if his back were pushed against the wall. This was the reason he shouldn't have let her too close. This was the situation he'd been fighting. If he'd never let her in, he wouldn't have these problems right now because he simply wouldn't have given a damn.

"It's *not* deeper than that, Legend," January battled, growing angrier by the second. "It's simple. Open your mouth and tell me what's going on. *All* of it. Tell. Me. The. Truth." She clapped her hands dramatically behind each word. "Are you working for my father? Can I trust you?"

Another sigh.

More delay.

Legend began to feel anxious.

When anxious, he began to feel angry.

This was the reason he didn't *do* love. Or commitment. Or women. Women were complicated. They complicated *everything.*

He was at an impasse. There was no way to answer her because he wasn't able to answer the question for himself.

On one end stood a man who was every bit of his father in the streets; a man who wasn't his father by blood but definitely his father by any other definition. And on the other end was Legend's father. Legend was a combination of two of the world's deadliest men. To choose between them would be to tear himself into two. He was the physical essence of his father but, metaphorically, he was the incarnation of everything Outlaw stood for, a walking embodiment of his principles and ideals. Family was over everything but both men fit the definition of family to him.

The only thing left to consider now was... which family would Legend choose?

ONLY A
BAD BOY
can love her

The Finale

Coming Soon

VISIT WWW.PORSCHASTERLING.COM
to join the mailing list

NOTE FROM PORSCHA STERLING

Thank you so much for reading! I hope you're enjoying January and Legend's story so far.

If you haven't already, join my reading group now. If you're not in there, you've been missing out on some LIVE interviews with me and... the REAL Outlaw.

Yep, I found him! It wasn't too hard being that he just happened to already be on the book covers—but yes, Outlaw *does* actually exist, and if you're in my Facebook reading group, you could speak with him. We'll be doing a few Live discussions before the release of the next book so join now!

Please make sure to leave a review! I love reading them!

I would love it if you reach out to me on Facebook, Instagram or Twitter! Also, join my reading group!

I love to interact with my readers because **I appreciate all of**

you. Hit me up anytime and tell me what you think about the book 😊

Peace, love & blessings to everyone.
I love you all. 👑

Porscha Sterling

ABOUT THE AUTHOR

Porscha Sterling is an African-American Romance author and publisher of Royalty Publishing House, Inc.

Join Porscha's Mailing List. Text PORSCHA to 25827
To find out more about her, visit her website

READ MORE ON THE LIT READING APP!

Read more books like this one **for less**! Check out some other new releases on the LiT Reading App. Go to www.litreadingapp.com to learn more!

www.ingramcontent.com/pod-product-compliance
Lightning Source LLC
Chambersburg PA
CBHW020423030726
47495CB00006B/1640